Hide

Hide

S.J. MORGAN

MidnightSun

First published 2019 by MidnightSun Publishing Pty Ltd
PO Box 3647, Rundle Mall, SA 5000, Australia.
www.midnightsunpublishing.com

Cover design by Kim Lock
Internal design by Zena Shapter

Typeset in American Typewriter and Garamond.

Printed and bound in Australia by Ovato. The papers used by MidnightSun in the manufacture of this book are natural, recyclable products made from wood grown in sustainable plantation forests.

NATIONAL LIBRARY OF AUSTRALIA

A catalogue record for this book is available from the National Library of Australia

For my precious butty-bachs: Robbi, Phoebe, Larne.

Chapter 1

December 1983 – Queensland/Northern Territory Border, Australia

The parched countryside shimmers as it stretches, purple-orange, into the distance. The track is only wide enough for a single vehicle but at this speed we won't be the ones giving way. Not that there are any signs of life: since we turned off the main road, gnarled trunks have been our only company. The place is tinder-dry, wrung-out. Looks like every blade of grass is ready to blow. My T-shirt is heavy with sweat and it clings to my chest as I breathe.

It's taken long enough but I finally spit it out: 'Shouldn't we get back on the highway?'

'No, Alec. Not yet.'

My knee's jiggling like a freaking jackhammer. 'So, where are we going?'

When I get no response, I look over to him. Nothing. Just a blue vein pulsating along his leathery temple.

The question hangs there, swelling. Perspiration forms above my top lip.

Finally, he smiles; he fucking smiles at me. 'Well, Alec,' he says. 'Let's just call it...a detour.'

If I was watching this particular movie, I'd be thinking: 'Why doesn't he just open the truck door and fling himself out?' or 'Why doesn't he put his hands around that asshole's scrawny neck and squeeze?' But no, I do nothing.

I'd barely got out my cardboard sign when he stopped to pick me up at first light.

'Alice Springs?' I'd said.

He gave a grunt and looked in his side mirror.

'Okay?'

This time, I didn't even get a grunt. He just leaned across, one bony-fingered hand on the steering wheel, the other pushing open the passenger door.

I put my bag in the footwell and buckled the seatbelt. 'Alec,' I said, holding out my hand.

He glanced down like I was offering him a fresh turd.

Checking his mirrors, he put on the indicator and took the main highway out of Mt Isa.

I put the turd back in my lap and focussed on the road signs. 'Alice, one thousand, one hundred and seventy-two kilometres,' I read aloud. 'Should be there in an hour.'

My chauffeur slid his eyes towards me and didn't crack a smile. 'Zip it,' he said. 'I picked you up for one reason and one reason only. And it weren't for your company.'

Chapter 2

Summer 1983 – Swansea, South Wales, UK

Bono was belting out 'New Year's Day' from my speakers, his voice on a collision course with Van Halen upstairs. I sang along at the top of my lungs to give Bono a fighting chance. Stobes and me had this unspoken battle: every time one of us put a record on the turntable, so did the other. It was expected, like curry sauce with chips or a belch after a pint of dark. I always lost the sound battle, of course: Stobes had a half-decent set of speakers in his armoury whereas my fifty-quid pair of tins from Splott Market was never going to make any eardrums bleed.

Bono did manage to block out the doorbell though. The first I knew of visitors was when my bedroom door flew open and Black stumbled in. 'You're wanted downstairs, butty-bach,' he yelled at me. 'So, turn that shite off.' He and his mop of black hair exited stage right while I turned off the hi-fi and went to the door.

I'd never exactly kept a welcome in the hillside for Mum and Dad, yet they seemed surprised by my expression when I met them on the doorstep.

'You could at least pretend to be pleased,' Mum said.

'I am pleased! I just…wasn't expecting you.'

'So, this is the latest abode, is it?' Mum's gaze scuttled past me as she squinted through the dark hallway.

Trouble was, last time they'd seen me, I'd been moving into one of those neat, airy houses in the Hendrefoilan Student Village. House nine; my lucky number. A half-year down the track and it'd dawned on me that nine never *had* been that lucky. Me and uni were not happy bed mates, it turned out. And along with the student status, my grant money dried up and my housing options became more modest.

'So, did you want to come in?' I asked. I kept the door half-shut, ever the optimist.

'We didn't drive an hour from Cardiff to go straight home again,' Mum said. And she wiped her feet, gave me a kiss and stepped inside.

Ours was one of the brooding, crumbling Victorian houses perched half-way up Constitution Hill, the steepest goddamn incline in the whole of Swansea. We could just about see The Vetch from my room and when City played at home, we got the full roar of the crowd.

None of us knew each other, not really. We'd all ended up there through friends of friends, I think. But for four guys who didn't know one another from Adam, we got on pretty well. Maybe even got to like each other in a careless, couldn't-give-a-shit kind of way.

The ground floor was out of bounds to us, so I shared the upstairs with a mouldy, sub-zero kitchen and Minto. He was a headcase was Minto, but he mostly kept himself to himself. If you managed the final, lung-sucking ascent to the top floor – which hardly anyone did – you'd find Stobes and Black: tucked away like a pair of grubs in their tiny attic rooms.

As for me, I'd managed to land myself the best room in the place – a huge space with two massive windows and crick-your-neck ceilings. There were no shelves, barely any sticks of furniture really, so all my abandoned college books were lined up, tight against the skirting board like soldiers on parade. The one rickety table I owned was dwarfed by the huge room, but it had just enough space for my twelve-inch telly.

As soon as I brought Mum and Dad through the hallway, I spotted the tell-tale flare of Mum's nostrils. If she found the smell on the ground floor unpleasant, I figured she'd need a gas mask by the time she got to my room. Dad trailed behind us in his golf club blazer which he kept pressed and ready for weekend outings. I'd never imagined my place being on his list of must-see destinations but at least he'd made the effort. There seemed to be less of Dad lately. Where once he used to puff out his chest and stand tall and proud, now his body had reduced; sunk back on itself like he had a slow puncture.

As we started up the stairs, there was an almighty thud. Minto's voice cut through the gloom above us: 'Don't you ever try that again, you little slut. Now piss off.' There was a slap, then the slam of a door.

The three of us hovered, gripping the dodgy banister. 'I'm sorry,' I heard Sindy say. 'I didn't mean to. Please. Can I come back in?'

I was becoming used to this kind of thing. Since Sindy'd become a household feature, there was more drama at our place than there was on *Dallas*.

Mum was suddenly in front of me, heading up the stairs, two at a time.

'Oh,' I heard her say. 'Oh, Lord. Are you all right, love?'

By the time I caught up, Mum was crouched in front of Minto's closed door. I couldn't see anything of Sindy beside the outstretched stick of her leg.

'Hurry up,' Mum said to me, turning around. 'Close your eyes! Go and get your duvet or something to put around her. Don't look!' She formed a makeshift barricade with her arms and stayed there, all lipstick and skirt suit, hunkered down on the threadbare carpet.

In my room, I was about to pick up my duvet but remembered Sindy's body odour problem. Instead, I grabbed an old throw from the chair and chucked it in Mum's direction.

'Now, put this around you. You're all right,' she said. 'No need to cry, love.'

Minto's door opened and, as I ventured back into the hall, I was just in time to see Minto shove past Sindy before he tore down the stairs.

There was a 'steady on' from Dad just before the front door slammed.

'Come on, love, let's get you up,' Mum said.

Sindy was in tears again. She looked like a Dickensian waif, all bundled up in that big old blanket, with her bare feet and her matted hair.

She was led into my room.

'Have you got some clothes you don't need, Alexander?' Mum said. She looked around, ignoring the kick-ass view from my window. 'Let's get your young friend here dressed so we can go out, shall we?' she said with a grimace. 'I reckon we could all use some fresh air.'

Sindy was on the seat opposite me. My belt was pulled to its tightest, but the jeans still hung off her. And the short sleeves of my old Psychedelic Furs T-shirt reached halfway down her arms. The best I'd managed to find for her in the footwear department was a pair of flip-flops, five sizes too big. She'd hardly been able to walk in them, but Sindy was terminally accommodating.

I kept a close eye on the entrance as we huddled around the gingham-clothed table at the Copper Grill. It wasn't at all how my day was meant to pan out and I knew if Minto found us with his loyal sidekick, I'd be looking for a new rental by nightfall.

Sindy had perked up like a pooch on pet pills. I'd never seen her looking as bright and attentive as she did right then, sitting there with a doughnut and a milkshake in front of her.

'So, you don't live at the house,' Mum said, resting her forearms across the table.

'No.' Sindy stopped to take a bite from the doughnut. 'But I spend most of my time there. Minto's usually nice: he just has a bad temper. Also, I can be a really annoying person.' She said this seriously, but when she saw our faces, she laughed and sprayed sugar crystals across her plate.

Mum glanced at me with a pinched look, as if all this was somehow my fault. Trouble is, Mum treats every kid like they're porcelain. She hates any hint of neglect or abuse. I guess I could understand it: my little sister, Gina, died when she was three. One minute we thought she just had a cold – the next, it was lights-out. Meningitis. And people still say there's a God.

'I think you should stick with your friends who haven't got such a bad temper, Sindy,' Mum said, pouring herself some tea.

'I haven't got any other friends.' Sindy wrapped her sugar-coated lips around the straw and swallowed.

'If a young man treated my daughter like that,' Dad piped up. 'I'd knock him from here to kingdom come.'

We all blinked back at him. It was pretty much the first thing he'd said all day, but at least he sounded like he meant it.

Chapter 3

While the truck jostles and bumps along the ruts on the track, I sense us getting further from the highway. I look down, secretly watching my companion, trying to commit each snapshot to memory. Brown boots, small feet; canvas pants with a rip on the right knee; shit-green crew-neck jumper, washed too many times; loose thread on the hem, thinning at the elbows.

As I watch, he hooks an index finger along the neck of his sweater as if it's suddenly too tight. A jumper in this heat: the guy must be roasting.

My eyes move down, to the hands on the steering wheel. Short nails, clean, well-managed; gold band on the fourth slender finger. Those hands look more suited to piano-playing than to truck driving. Or to kidnapping. There has to be a mistake.

'How far are we from the next town?' I ask. I watch his profile, waiting for some sign he's heard me.

He has a sad look about him. His eyes are turned down at the corners as if they're used to disappointment and those lips of his look like they'd need wrestling into a smile.

'No idea,' he says, turning to me at last. 'But we ain't there yet, that's for sure.'

He watches – no, studies me – as if testing for a reaction.

'You got no map then,' I say.

He explodes a laugh. 'No, Alec. No map.'

I glance down into my lap, then out the side window, trying to keep my voice light and steady. 'You could drop me off here if it's easier,' I say.

He smiles to himself.

'I can make my own way back to the main road.'

He looks me in the eye and keeps his gaze on me far longer than someone driving a truck should. 'Why, Alec?'

'I jus –'

'There's nothing wrong, is there?' He rests his watery grey eyes on me.

'No,' I tell him. 'I just...want to get there.'

He makes no reply and I sink back in my seat. My attention shifts to the wing mirror and I watch as we kick up a dust storm behind us and head for somewhere that I'm certain isn't Alice.

Chapter 4

Until that day, I'd barely spoken to Sindy. When I first met her, I thought Minto was having a laugh – as did the others, by the looks on their faces. Minto stood in the kitchen doorway, his solid, leather-clad arm around this pale twig of a girl.

'Sinds,' he said, looking down at her. 'Meet the gang. That's Black over there. Stobie on the sofa and the ugly one there's Alec.' He lifted a finger from his can of ale to point in my direction and the others enjoyed a cackle at my expense. 'And, before you ask, no, he's not very smart.' He was on a roll, was Minto. 'And this is Sindy,' he told us, squeezing her into a loose headlock.

Stobes was sprawled on the torn vinyl couch next to the cooker. He took his cigarette from his mouth, like he was doffing his cap for her. 'All right?' he said, in his cheery London accent. Then to the rest of us: 'My sister used to have a doll called Sindy. You know, arch rival of Barbie. Bathtime Sindy, I think it was. Or was it Surfboard Sindy?' He shifted his eyes back to Doorframe Sindy. 'Which one are you, darlin'?'

Minto kissed the top of her head and whispered something in her ear. She left the room and I heard light steps on the squeaky floorboards in the hall.

The smile left Minto's face as he looked back at Stobes. He jabbed a finger in his direction. 'You watch your mouth,' he said. 'She's mind-your-own-fucking-business Sindy as far as you're concerned. Don't you fucking forget it.' His eyes slowly swept the room. 'And that goes for the rest of you tossers.'

The door slammed and we all blinked at the empty spot Minto had left behind. There was a moment's silence before there was a creak from the bed in Minto's room.

'Blow Job Sindy,' Black said, sliding his eyes to Stobes.

They let out a triumphant whoop then nearly pissed themselves laughing.

She was certainly a change from Minto's usual sort. If anything, Minto went for the older woman; usually buxom, too much make-up, mouthy. Not my type but at least I could see the attraction: these were women who knew what they were doing; who liked a good time and made sure you had one too. Sindy, though, she was one out of the box. She looked like she'd snap if she tried bending and I could see why Mum had wanted to feed her up; put some colour in her cheeks. Everything about Sindy screamed vulnerability.

She was friendly enough though, when you got her by herself, but she didn't have a lot going on upstairs. Whenever she was around, I found myself speaking to her slowly, like she was a freaking dimwit. 'Half a bubble off plumb' as Black liked to say.

I found her in the kitchen one morning, a few days after my folks had met her. She had a vest and pants on – and not the tantalising sort, either – a scuzzy old top and a pair of washed-too-often knickers. A bit like you'd expect to see on a kid of five. Or on Bathtime Sindy.

'You all right?' I said, putting on the kettle. 'Not using this water, are you?'

'No. I'm making toast.' Bright, cheery voice she had, all whipped up with a singsong Swansea accent, but, Christ, she was nervous. She couldn't speak without twisting a strand of hair or touching her face with those uncertain, skinny fingers of hers.

'Did you and Minto go out last night?' I asked. She made me uncomfortable, standing there, balancing one bare foot on the other.

'No. We watched telly and then went to bed.' Sindy rested her anxious blue eyes on me and smiled.

There was a metallic 'ping' from the toaster and Sindy reached past me. I took a step back, but she still managed to tread on my toe.

As usual, our shit-toaster wasn't giving up the bread without a fight and Sindy took a knife from the drawer.

'Hey, careful,' I said, as she leaned over the toaster. 'You can't use metal.'

This is the result of my very practical upbringing. Such nuggets of useful information have been hot-wired into me from birth; like 'Never Touch a Socket with Wet Hands' or 'Don't put Damp Clothes on a Paraffin Heater.'

'Use a wooden spoon,' I said, going into the drawer.

As she stabbed it into the toaster, I turned off the switch at the wall. 'Belt and braces, son. Belt and braces.' Another gold nugget, right there.

Sindy placed the two slices of toast on the counter and smothered them in raspberry jam.

'Got enough on there?' I said.

She stood back, tilting her head this way and that like it was a Dali painting. 'I think so.'

I dropped the wet teabag in the sink and gave my drink a stir while Sindy scratched at a sliver of jam that had dripped on her vest.

'You and Minto off out today?' I asked.

'I don't know.' She looked down and continued with her stain removal.

I splashed some milk in my tea. As I turned to go, I froze. Sindy was standing in the middle of the room, sucking the stain from her vest, the whole thing pulled halfway up her chest. I was treated to nips, belly button; the lot.

'Fuck! What are you doing?' I reached towards her to cover her, but immediately thought better of it. 'Christ, Sindy, pull your top down!'

She stopped sucking and the vest slithered down her ribs. She stared at me like I'd just slapped her.

'Sindy,' I said more gently, 'you can't just –'

I didn't get chance to say anymore. She left her toast on the table and ran out of the room, yanking the door shut as she went.

I reached behind me and perched on the sofa, my legs feeling like they mightn't hold me up anymore. I sat there blotting her flesh from my mind, trying to unsee the seen. Trouble was, once those glimpses of skin had disappeared, all I was left to contemplate was the look of pain on her face.

Chapter 5

'So, what drives you from Mt Isa, Alec?'

I give him a sidelong glance. 'You mean, why am I going to Alice?'

He awards himself a private smile. 'If you like.'

'Just...bumming around,' I say. 'Seeing the sights.'

'You got family?'

'What?' At the very time I need some peace to work out what the hell I'm going to do, my sidekick has transformed from mute to talk-show host.

'Brothers or sisters?' He pauses, reaching under his seat for a packet of smokes. 'Or girlfriends?'

'No. Just my folks. In Britain.' I instantly regret the disclosure: stranger in a strange land – what the hell was I thinking?

He holds the cigarette packet in my direction.

'Very wise,' he says, when I shake my head. 'Silent killers, these little bastards.' He sticks the filter tip between his lips and uses the lighter from the dashboard.

I watch his twiglet fingers and briefly consider shoving the hot lighter in his face. But even as I imagine his sizzling flesh, I won't trust my instincts. I'm overreacting. Right?

'You don't know Australia well then,' he says. 'The terrain. The geography.'

I shrug. 'Got a guidebook, haven't I?'

He lets out another of those laughs; the ones devoid of humour. 'You'd need more than some shit travel guide if you got stranded out here,' he says. 'In these temperatures, you could be dead within hours.' He levels his eyes at me.

'Is that right?' I say.

Prick.

I look out of the side window as the air ripples in the blistering heat.

'You did bring water with you, didn't you, Alec?'

I keep my eyes on the view. ''Course.'

I can hardly admit that my survival kit consists of the warm dregs of lemonade and half a packet of chewy mints.

'Always need water,' he says, almost to himself. 'It's the dry heat that gets 'em, see. People who don't know this place, they just shrivel up in the sun, like raisins.'

My palms are wet, and I rub them down the legs of my jeans. His eyes follow the movement and I instantly want to cover my crotch.

I shift my gaze to the dashboard and scan for snippets of information: a licence number; a logo; anything. But even the windshield is missing its registration sticker. Other trucks, I imagine, have furry dice; pictures of pouting bikini clad models; smart-arse stickers bemoaning everyone else's driving habits. Not this one though. This one has a box of tissues nestled in a floral, lace trimmed cover, like it's wearing a frigging nightie or something. And the dashboard stickers demand that I have faith in God and let Him be my guide. Christ!

'You Catholic? Church of England?' I ask.

'Used to be Catholic,' he says, blowing smoke from the side of his mouth. He crushes the half-smoked cigarette into the ashtray. 'But my god deserted me, Alec. He left me out in the wilderness. To shrivel up and die.'

The backs of my thighs spring a leak and I have to readjust my position.

He glances into my lap again, his eyes lingering longer than is decent. 'Getting hot, are you, son?'

I thread my fingers through the handle of my rucksack. If this guy tries anything, I'll mash the whole thing in his face. My head bumps against the side window as I pretend to rest my eyes. Like I'm fooling anyone. I need to think; to put my brain into gear and work out a plan of action. Contingencies: isn't that what Dad used to drum into me? Always have a Plan B, he'd say. Except I don't even have a Plan A.

The last place I remember was Camooweal. Had we turned off there? I toy with the idea of getting out my guidebook. Would laughing-boy snatch it from me; toss it out the window? Or could it be the final act of defiance that would send him headlong into violence?

'I need a piss,' I say.

'Sure you do.'

I look away. I can't stand much more of this not-knowing. Is this guy weird, a killer or some sad, seedy fuck?

Outside, the vegetation clings to the ground in clumps like it's on its knees and all the while the sun throbs, its silent pulse forming the backbeat to my every thought.

Keeping my body turned away, I finger the window handle, then the door latch; easing it from the door to test it out.

There's a loud click and the lock mechanism shoots down. Everything inside me clenches.

Chapter 6

Until Sindy came along, I'd only seen the anything-for-a-mate side to Minto. I'd thought of him as a gentle giant, wrongly smeared for his tatts, his piercings and his confronting looks. But I came to realise I'd misjudged him. He was a nutter: a Class-A psycho. And yes, he would do anything for a mate, as long as that mate had sworn allegiance to his beloved Apaches. His bite was infinitely worse than his bark and had I realised that at the start, I'd never have moved into that house on Oakdale Terrace and I'd never have met Sindy. Things would've turned out very differently.

I blinked in the darkness as the front door woke me. '4:52' my clock-radio informed me. The throaty roar of Minto's bike revved up outside. It sped off then faded into the distance. Who knew what he got up to at that hour?

I turned over and pulled up the duvet but just as I got comfy, there was a knock on my bedroom door. A hesitant, uncertain one.

I stood at the door, buttoning up my jeans. 'What d'you want, Sindy?'

Her face buckled and she ground her hands into her eyes, making no attempt to explain.

'Sindy? What is it?' I tried to stay patient, calm, but I was tired as hell.

She took a big, wet sniff.

'You'd better come in,' I said, glancing up the hall.

She hesitated and kept her eyes down. Her voice shook. 'I can't.'

I followed her gaze. She stood with her legs apart; her knees just covered by the nightie, red liquid trickling down and pooling at the fold of her white ankle socks.

'Shit – what happened?' I said.

Minto made no secret of his knife collection; it wouldn't be the first time he'd used one.

'I don't know,' she said, looking down. 'It won't stop.' She did a little jig as she realised there were spots on the carpet. 'Oh, no. It's getting worse.'

'Just come in,' I said and pulled her through the door. Her skin was cold, clammy and my hand felt oversized around her arm.

I got down on my haunches to find out where the wound was. 'What did he do?'

'Nothing,' she said, in tears again. 'He didn't do anything. But I woke up and there was all this blood and it had soaked into the sheets. And Minto got angry about it. I don't know what to do. Is it something really bad, do you think?'

'So, there's no wound?'

'No.'

'You haven't cut yourself anywhere?'

She shook her head.

I looked up at her as she rubbed her eyes. It took a few moments before I could bring myself to ask. 'Sindy? Are you sure it's not just... your period?'

I felt a knob having to ask, but what else could it be?

'I haven't started having periods yet,' she said quietly. 'Minto says I'm probably too scrawny to get them.'

The rivulets continued to dribble down her legs, a disobedient spot occasionally splodging on the carpet.

I got to my feet, suddenly feeling like an intruder. 'Looks like you've started,' I said.

Her lips trembled and she crossed her arms in front of her, clutching her sleeves as if I'd found her naked. 'What do I do?'

'What?'

She broke down again. 'I don't know what to do.'

'Well...I don't know either.' I didn't mean to sound impatient but, frankly, I was embarrassed. I ruffled my hair, stealing a glance at her. She changed position and stood with her legs crossed, bent at the knees, as if she was about to wet herself.

'Don't you...have anything?' I asked. 'Pads, tampons, that sort of thing.'

'No.'

I looked around – though for what, I had no idea.

'Why don't you go and shower?' I said. 'I'll find you some...underwear. And you can borrow a shirt. I guess you'll have to manage with a sock or toilet paper till the shops open.'

She stood, nodding; her lank hair stuck to her cheeks.

I chucked a towel, a shirt and my oldest pair of undies at her.

'Thanks, Alec,' she said in that sweet Swansea voice of hers. 'I'm ever so sorry.'

While she was gone, I poured hot water from the kettle onto the carpet stains and dabbed at them with a wad of serviettes I'd swiped from the burger bar.

This whole situation was so messed up: she was younger than my kid sister, Gina would've been yet here she was, servicing the bodily needs of our local chief bikie and not even understanding the workings of her own body. If it was Gina, Mum would've had her going off to school with every sanitary item the local chemist had on offer; she'd've bought books, videos; taken pride in setting her up for womanhood. Sindy was so unprepared; she was so unready, in every sense.

There was a light knock on my door and Sindy stood there, scrunching the dirty nightie in her hands.

'Put it in here,' I said, passing her a carrier bag. 'You can go and put the sheets in there too.'

'I can't get into his room,' she said. 'He locked the door when he left. I'm sort of...stuck out here.'

She looked away when she saw my expression.

'Well you can't stay in here,' I said. 'Minto would go nuts.' I looked around for the throw but Sindy hadn't returned it from the last time. I handed over my duvet, resigning myself to a laundry-run later. 'You'd better use the couch in the kitchen.'

'It will stop, won't it?' she said.

'Will what stop?'

'The blood.'

I kept a tight hold of my expression. 'Sindy, didn't you ever learn about this stuff?'

'A bit,' she said, looking down. 'But I didn't really understand and…I didn't know who to ask.'

'Your mum, maybe?'

'My mum's in Australia,' she said. 'There's only me and Dad and he doesn't like me bothering him with…'

'I think it lasts about a week,' I told her. 'Then they come every month.'

She chewed her bottom lip and nodded, then turned to go.

'Sindy?' I said, stopping her. 'How old are you?'

We looked at each other as the question settled between us.

'I told you all before,' she said, reciting the usual. 'I was sixteen last March.'

'Yeah, but really.'

She blinked back at me, hesitating. 'Fourteen. But please don't tell him I told you.'

She wobbled an apologetic smile and quietly closed the door behind her.

Chapter 7

My jaw is clenched so tight my teeth hurt.

Neither me nor the driver has spoken in a while. The silence is starting to feel as oppressive as the relentless fucking heat.

Do I put my boot through the windshield? Or wrestle his hands from the wheel? What do I do? What the fuck do I do?

I sit here like a gimp, is what.

My pits are soaking as I sit, jammed in indecision. 'You got a fan in this thing?'

'Nope. No fan, no aircon.' He looks smug; like suffocation is the next big thing. 'Why?'

'It's hot.'

'You're used to the cold, I expect,' he says. 'The bleak British weather.'

'Yeah, well, I lived in Wales.'

He shoots me a look. 'Wales.'

A pause stutters between us as I try to figure his expression.

'That's why I'm not used to the heat,' I tell him.

'Wales,' he says again. And it brings the discussion to a close.

It's a pungent combination: vinyl, cigarette smoke and aftershave. Always made me car sick when I was a nipper. Mum never left home without barley sugars for me. Sometimes worked, too.

As the sunshine bleeds through the window, it burns my arm. My salivary glands start working overtime and a wave of heat flushes my face.

'I need to get out,' I say, swallowing.

I hear the air escape through his nostrils. 'We ain't stopping, Alec,' he says. 'If you're gonna hurl, you'd better use that bag of yours.'

My cheeks and tongue moisten, and I close my eyes.

'Put that guidebook in your lap,' the driver tells me. "Bout the only thing it's good for.'

I suck in a lungful of stale air and it makes me retch.

There's a click and a whirr from somewhere to my right. The driver's side window opens a fraction. It offers no relief, though. Hot air blows in, like bellows on a furnace.

All I can think about is Mum and her barley sugars.

Then just Mum.

The cab is locked; we're off the highway; the guy won't stop. There's no escaping the facts.

As he looks across at me, I see the sharp edge of his Adam's apple rise in his throat. A thin gold chain glistens against his skin and all I want to do is yank it so hard that his skinny neck snaps in two.

'Look, mate,' I say. 'I feel like shit. When are we getting back on the road?'

'When I say so.'

He won't look at me; just keeps on staring ahead, keeping his body midline as the truck rocks side to side on the ruts. I could overpower him, easy. He's thin, scrawny; got muscles like sparrows' legs.

He takes his eyes from the track and turns to me, like he can read my freaking mind.

What if he's got a gun?

'Can you let me out?' I say. 'I'd really prefer to get on my way now.'

'No, Alec; no can do.'

'Why can't you?' My fingers grip the handle of my bag again; so tight that my nails almost pop my palms. 'What's your fucking game?'

The question lingers and seems to suck the air from the cab. I've placed all my cards on the table. But his are still face down.

He narrows his eyes and as his lips part, I smell the tobacco on his breath.

'Game?' he says.

'I just want to go to Alice.' I feel my face flush as the words come out fast; weak; pleading. 'I don't want any funny business. Or any detours. I just wanna get there, okay? I just want to get there.'

Something unpleasant shoots through his eyes. He presses his foot on the gas pedal and the truck starts bumping and bouncing like a goddamn space hopper.

'Please,' I say.

'You think you can call the shots?' he says, his knuckles white against the steering wheel. 'You think you can overpower me? This is my truck, Mr Sureshot. Mr Alexander David Johnston. This is my story, y'hear?'

My nails dig further into my palms. 'What? How do you know me?' My throat is so tight I can hardly swallow.

The driver shakes his head and I have to strain to hear him. 'This day's been a long time coming.'

I shoot forward as his foot hits the brake and my palms slap against the dashboard. Branches buckle and snap in our path and the truck tips and tilts, drumming up orange dust in its wake, like a magician's final flourish.

We come to a halt and the engine hisses, clicks and sighs.

Outside, the magpies sing their madcap tune and it seems to underpin the silence in the cab.

I don't dare glance in his direction, but I can feel his eyes on me. Is he checking me out again?

'What the fuck is this about?' I say. My voice trembles so much, the words only dribble out. I'm almost pissing my pants by the time he speaks.

'I think you know what it's about,' he says.

He undoes his seatbelt and every fibre of my being contracts.

Then he draws his face so close to mine I can taste his sour breath.

I press myself into the seat, willing it to swallow me whole. 'I don't,' I say. 'I haven't got a fucking clue.'

His pale eyes rest on me; weighing me up, examining me. I hold my breath and stare back at him.

I see him for the first time. I mean, really see him.

And I finally get it.

It's like a slow, drawn-out punch in the guts. Those eyes of his: their shape, their colour, even their sadness. I've never seen them before, yet I know them.

I can't speak.

He seems to decode my expression and his reedy lips curl into a smile. 'That's right, Alec,' he says, with a slow nod. 'You know what this is about, don't you? It's all about Sindy.'

Chapter 8

Friday night was meant to have been a quiet night: just me and Stobes enjoying a bevvie down the local. I didn't socialise much with the bunch at the flat, but Stobes was all right. He was from London originally, but he seemed to know the entire population of Swansea. Normally that was a bonus for me, but not that night: he bumped into an old girlfriend called Carys and I quickly found myself surplus to requirements.

Never one for third wheeling, I decided to leave them to it. I grabbed my pint from the bar and nodded across the room. 'I'm going to shoot some pool, okay?' I told Stobes.

He took a long drag on his ciggie as he looked back at me. 'On your own?'

'Got more chance of winning.'

He eased himself away from Carys to whisper in my ear. 'If you ask nicely, Minto might lend Sindy to you,' he said, gesturing over my shoulder. 'I'm sure she'd help jiggle your balls out of their pockets.'

I followed his gaze to where Minto's mob was taking up half the seating area; Sindy squashed between Minto and some guy in a Led Zeppelin T-shirt. She looked away as I headed to the pool table.

While I chalked the end of the cue, I could hear the conversation behind me: Minto was spouting off about the killing he'd made selling poppers outside college. 'Small change for me,' he said, 'but it's all beer money, ain't it?'

I had to face them as I lined up the first ball and I could see Sindy's twitchy fingers holding onto her glass of something canary-yellow and frothy.

Perhaps Minto saw me looking. As I potted a ball, I heard him say to her: 'That stuff looks radioactive, gal.'

'It's nice,' she said, offering him the glass. 'You want to try?'

'Not like that, Sinds,' he told her. 'With your finger.'

Minto's comment caused a few guffaws and by the time I turned around, he had Sindy on his lap pushing her pinkie in and out of his mouth. It created a bit of a ruckus amongst the lads.

'Come on, Sindy – don't keep it all to yourself,' Zeppelin-guy said. 'I wouldn't say no to a little suck on it too.'

I bent to pot another ball. By the time I'd straightened up, Sindy had moved to sit on his knee.

'Alec, my man,' Minto called over. 'How's it going?'

'Yeah, I'm all right.' I kept my eye on the pool table.

'Wanna join us? We're tasting Sindy's sweet delights.'

She blushed as soon as I looked over.

'No, thanks.'

'Suit yourself.'

I figured I'd finish my game then take off. Minto's bunch was getting louder and, from what I could see of Stobes at the bar, he looked like he had his hands full with Carys.

Sindy was holding her yellow drink, still on Zeppelin-guy's lap. He kept making out he wanted to steal it from her, like she was a freaking three-year old.

I lined up the cue ball, about to strike when a shout went up and Sindy's new friend was on his feet.

'You spilt it, darlin',' he was saying. 'You're going to have to mop it up.' He was pink faced with anticipation, pointing down to the wet patch on his crotch. 'You could lap it up. Like a cat.'

They were all looking at her, straight backed with possibilities.

The smile had left Sindy's lips; I could see her uncertain expression, searching for clues in the faces around her. Her gaze landed on Minto.

'Go on,' he said. There was a sharp, mean edge to his voice.

'You've hurt the man's feelings, Sindy: you're gonna have to make amends.'

Around me, the hubbub of conversation continued; explosions of laughter; the clank of glasses; 'Bat out of Hell' through the speakers.

'Here?' I heard Sindy say.

My guts tightened as I looked on: was she really only quibbling about the location?

Minto answered her, monotone. 'Sindy. Get on your knees.'

I paused; my cue balanced above the ball. I couldn't swallow, didn't dare move. Then Sindy turned and met my gaze, looked me square in the eyes.

I moved around the table and cleared my throat. 'Wanna come with me?' I said to her. 'I'm going home now – if you need to get back…'

Every pore started leaking as I stood there, waiting for her answer.

I needed her to hurry up. Hurry the fuck up. Stand and turn so we could get out of there.

At last, she smiled. 'No, it's okay,' she said. 'I'm…' She stopped when she saw Minto was on his feet, heading my way.

He came so close to me that my arse was crushed against the pool table. 'You got a problem with me, Alec?' he said.

I braced myself, ready to feel the knee in my balls; his fist in my gut.

He eased himself closer. 'Well?'

I kept my eyes on his, but I took in the periphery of his features: the Apaches logo tattooed across his neck; the piercings in his ears; the battle scar beside his eye.

He took a slow sip from the dregs of his pint as his eyes drilled into me; the leather of his jacket creaking as he moved his arm. Then the glass was empty in that big hand of his.

'Hey, Alec. We're splitting now. You ready?' Stobes appeared beside me, stupid smirk on his face like he hadn't noticed a thing. His eyes slid to Minto. 'All right, mate?'

Minto's pelvis released me, but his eyes didn't shift. 'See you then,

Alexander,' he said. 'Back at the flat.' He eyeballed me, second upon second before taking a step backwards.

'Good,' Stobes said, wrapping a chummy arm around my shoulder. 'Let's go get that kebab, eh?'

And with that, he led me out the door and saved my freaking skin.

Despite my telly being turned up full whack, I could still hear Stobes and Carys giving the bedsprings a good old hammering. I couldn't settle – not just because of the thudding above me – but because Minto and his mob could be back any minute and I knew they'd be even more sauced-up after a few club visits. The way I saw it, I had two choices: I could lay low and pray he'd forget about our incident in the pub; or I could throw some clothes in a bag and make myself scarce. Cardiff was only an hour away, so I got myself a seat on the night bus.

Mum couldn't have been more pleased. Despite it being barely light outside, she ushered me in and went straight to the kitchen to whip up a full English breakfast for me.

'So, how's that girl from the flat?' she asked, once she had me safely settled at the kitchen table. She stood over me with folded arms as I tucked into a massive fry-up.

'She's fine,' I said, dipping some bacon into the egg yolk.

'What's her name again?'

'Sindy.'

'That's right. Fragile little thing, isn't she? Does she ev –'

'Got any ketchup?'

Mum went to the cupboard and put the bottle in front of me. 'And that Mintie's a vicious-looking sort, isn't he?'

'Minto.'

'I don't know what you're doing living with someone like that. And I mean, Sindy didn't seem any more than a child. How old is she? I wonder if somebody should –'

'I don't know how old she is, Mum. I don't have much to do with her. With either of them.'

She went to the sink and squirted some washing-up liquid into the frypan. I heard her take a breath and I knew she was revving up for further probes in the Sindy Inquisition.

'Dad not having breakfast?' I said.

'No.' She stuck her hands in the suds and started scrubbing.

'Not like him to be in bed after six on a Saturday morning.'

There was a loaded pause and I watched the back of Mum's neck stiffen. 'Yes, well. It's been a while since you were home.'

I looked over to her. Perhaps Dad's long-awaited retirement from the Navy hadn't added the sparkle to her life that she'd hoped.

'It's good of you to come down for the weekend, though,' she said. 'I wasn't sure you'd remember, what with –' She stopped as the kitchen door opened.

Dad shuffled in wearing a pair of stiff-looking trousers and a polo shirt, nothing on his feet. 'A visit from the prodigal son, eh?' he said as he went past.

'All right, Dad?' I watched him as he went to fill the kettle. It might've been my imagination, but he seemed shorter these days, stumpier, like he was sinking into his own foundations.

'So, Alexander,' he said, taking a cup from the hook. 'To what do we owe the honour of your company?'

'Just thought I'd come and see how you're both doing.'

'If you're short of cash, you're on your own. We're having to tighten our belts.'

Dad had been going on, for the past six months, about how he'd squandered his life for an ungrateful nation and had been cut loose with barely a brass razoo to show for it.

'I don't need money, Pop,' I said. 'But thanks for checking.'

He sat next to me and stared into his tea.

'Did you hear back from that job interview?' Mum said, putting a hand on my shoulder.

'Yeah. No luck.'

'Oh well. Never mind, love. Something'll turn up. Any employer would be lucky to have you.'

Dad snorted into his cup. There was nothing unusual about that, but there was about Mum's reaction.

'Oh, for God's sake, Jim, don't start!' she said, slamming the tea towel down. 'At least he came home. At least Alexander remembered, which is a damn sight more than you did.'

Dad's brow furrowed and the obvious bewilderment about exactly *what* he'd forgotten seemed to be the last straw for Mum. She wrestled a chair out the way, flung open the door and marched from the room.

The thing about being home when you don't live there anymore is that everything changes. And everything stays the same.

In my room the chest of drawers stood in its usual spot; the mirror askew like always. A grease mark remained on the corner of my Clash poster and there was the familiar rip on Joe Strummer's cheek from where I'd fallen against him after too many ciders. But this wasn't my room anymore, not really. It was a place I stayed; a throwback to a former time; mine because of the memories. But it couldn't ever be really mine again, because I was living a different life.

I hopped onto my bed and settled down on the duvet, hands behind my head, looking up at the ceiling. Near the Bluebirds lampshade, I could still pick out the spot where Gina used to keep a horse poster. I always teased her about it, just to annoy her: I hated having to share my room, so I'd do whatever I could to tick her off. She used to threaten to call Mum whenever I got out my darts: she knew I'd start aiming upwards for the horse's eye on her poster. 'Stop it, Lalec!' she'd yell at me. Lucky for her, I was such a shit shot: I never touched the picture, let alone land a dart in the horse's eye. Made a right mess of the ceiling though.

I thought back to that poster, wondering if Mum had kept it. She'd kept everything else, all boxed up in that same room she'd earmarked for Gina.

And that was when it hit me. The date. Tomorrow would be August 7th.

I couldn't say that I really remembered Gina. Not in a concrete, 3-D way. There were photos, of course: most of them in those boxes. But Mum kept one framed black and white picture of us on the mantelpiece. It was taken at some campsite near Rhossili a few months before Gina got sick: me and her were looking up at the camera, both of us smiling to order, spades poised above sand-laden buckets, Gina with her podgy legs straining to hold herself steady. She still had little dolphin teeth and a tiny ponytail on top of her head, slightly off-centre. And to be honest, that was all I remembered of her: three-year old Gina of the photo, not Gina herself. Not Gina on the other side of the bedroom, groaning that her head hurt. My memory of her was snapshot quick, impersonal, unreal. And she was forever grainy grey in my mind, never quite making it up there to full colour status.

Had I not gone to John Walsh's birthday party that particular day, it might have been different. I mightn't have been so tired; perhaps I'd have even got out of bed sooner to get Mum. But I didn't. So, Gina kept moaning and I kept right on telling her, in my seven-year old way, to shut the hell up. It was the middle of the night when I woke and heard her retching. Then there was the distinctive splat sound of vomit-on-carpet. Gina was very quiet about it though: I remember the almost-peaceful murmur she made. Then a gurgle; an odd, wet sound that didn't even seem human.

'All right, all right. I'll get Mum.' I remember the deliberate sigh – hefty as I could make it – so she'd know what a nuisance she was being. I trod on the sharp, unforgiving leg of one of her Sindy dolls as I got out of bed. That pissed me off too, so I kicked it under my bookshelf, glad she wouldn't be able to find it next time she went looking.

It was only when Mum turned on the light that I realised. Gina was purple, like a beetroot. It was a colour that haunted me forever afterwards: I hated seeing clothes that colour, cars, books, bags – anything. Maybe it was just as well I only thought of Gina as grainy grey after that. I remember Mum half-lifting her out of the bed and Gina was stiff and taut, like a stick. I'd expected her to be like a rag doll, but no. It was like every muscle had gone into spasm.

'Go down to the phone box,' Mum yelled at me. 'Dial nine, nine, nine. Tell them we need someone now. Now!'

I shot barefoot down the street in my pyjamas. I gave a brief and breathless account of what was going on and where the ambulance needed to go. As soon as I put the receiver down, I wet myself and I stood there for a few minutes not knowing what to do. I think I was glad for an excuse not to go home, not to have to face whatever mayhem might be waiting for me.

It went without saying that Dad wasn't there. Dad was never there. Anytime anything happened in our family, Dad always missed it. It was like he had a sixth sense. Son's first day at school? Absent. Moving house? Couldn't make it. Death of the youngest child? Late again. Yet choose a day when I'd been caught nicking tapes from Woolies – oh yeah, he'd somehow manage to be around for that.

So, it was left to Mum to deal with. The ambulance arrived, and the greasy, balding paramedic shouted to Mum over his shoulder as they were wheeling Gina into the vehicle, 'It's not looking good. You do realise that, don't you?' Even at seven, I got what he was saying and if I hadn't, I could have worked it out by the look on Mum's face. I remember watching her mouth slacken, like her puppeteer had cut the string. 'What are you saying?' she said.

The guy pretended not to hear; probably realised he might have been better keeping his fat, insensitive mouth shut. I heard Mum behind me whisper, 'Oh, dear God!'

When it was all over, we went home in a taxi, just me and Mum. I'd changed my pyjamas, but I still smelt of piss. I kept sniffing, breathing it in, wanting to suffocate in the smell of it, because at least it took my mind off the moment. Our family had just been cut by a quarter and all I could think about was the strange murmuring Gina had made and wondering how she could have been so fucking peaceful about dying.

Chapter 9

I couldn't face a Saturday night at Mum and Dad's with only *The Sweeney* to keep me entertained so I rang Jake Hoskins. I'd known him since primary. Now he was a sales assistant at some clothes store on Queen Street. Always said it was just a holiday job but after three and a half years, even he had to admit it was turning into one hell of a long vacation! He told me where he was meeting up with his mates, so I invited myself along for the ride.

Just before I went out, Mum knocked on my door. I was cross-legged on the floor, flipping through a pile of LPs. She came in and sat on the edge of my bed, smoothing out my pillow like it was her favourite pet.

'You all right for money?' she asked.

'Ah, yeah,' I said. 'I've signed on: I'm due for a Giro on Monday.'

She reached into her pinny pocket and took out a tenner. 'Have this,' she said, placing it under my alarm clock. 'At least it will help with your coach fare.'

'Cheers, Mum.' I looked up from my Pretenders album and gave her a smile.

It was unusual to see Mum wearing an apron when she wasn't mid-bake. She was one of those ironed women who always made sure they were dressed for visitors. Except that day. That day she looked like she'd had enough of the bullshit. Her mouth wasn't lipstick-coated like it normally was; there was no furry film of powder on her cheeks and, for once, her bunions weren't wrapped inside pink slippers. They were out there, bulbous and bony as if she was finally fed up with apologising for them.

'You okay, Mum?'

'Oh, you know.' She forced a smile. 'This weekend was always going to be...difficult.'

I flipped through more albums. 'Yeah, course.'

'Alexander?'

'Uh-huh?' I pulled out my *Regatta de Blanc* ten inch.

'It means a lot that you remembered.' Her voice wobbled. 'I...knew you would.'

I nodded, guilty, but figured that perhaps my subconscious had indeed remembered. Maybe it wasn't the prospect of Minto's revenge that had sent me scuttling east, but Gina.

'Could I ask you something?' Mum said.

'Sure.'

'Would you come with me to the cemetery tomorrow? We could take something for Gina.'

'You want to go to the cemetery?' I hadn't gone back there since the funeral. I used to tell Mum I called in sometimes on my walk home from school, but I never did, really: could never stomach the idea. It had all seemed so cruel, so inhumane. Gina hated the dark; hated being shut in anywhere. Yet that's what we'd done to her: placed her in a box, put her in the ground and left her there to rot. I'd never been able to forgive the treachery. 'Okay.'

Mum stood and smoothed down the frills of her apron, hands pausing as if it had suddenly dawned on her what she was wearing. 'Thanks, love.' She hesitated by my bed. 'Don't mention anything to your father, will you? No point in upsetting him.'

I looked up from my album, but Mum had already made a beeline for the door.

'Whatever you say,' I told her. Though the way that Dad was lately, the chances of him being upset by anything – even a dead daughter's sixteenth – were pretty much nil.

The Windsor in Cardiff's docklands was no Hammersmith Odeon but a few decent bands played there on a Saturday night. The place had that closed in, suffocating feel of too many paunches enjoying too many pints, but the jukebox was cheap and they had good beers on tap.

Jakesie was already there when I walked in. He'd put on a few pounds since I last saw him and, judging by his outfit, he had more of a discount at Griffin's Men's Outfitters than was good for him.

'So, what are you up to in Swansea these days?' he asked, as we stood at the bar. 'Are you still studying?'

'Nah, I jacked in the course. Decided teaching's not my thing.'

'Fair dos,' he said. 'So, you got any other irons in the fire?'

I took a swig of beer. 'Still weighing up my options,' I told him. 'I might ditch the study idea and get a job instead.'

He looked at me like I had a screw loose. 'You'll be lucky,' he said. 'It's all Youth Opportunity Programmes now; part-time government schemes. There aren't any real jobs. Why d'you think I'm still stuck at Griffin's?' He took a mouthful of beer and shook his head. 'Fucking Thatcher.'

'Yeah, I know. But she's there thanks to people like my dad!'

'Mine too!' he laughed. 'He thinks she's the dog's bollocks.'

We stop-started a few more conversations but it was hard to hear him over the loudspeakers, and the few snippets I heard were still about politics. I drained my glass, keen for a reprieve. 'Another?'

'Cheers.'

As I turned, my elbow jabbed some warm, soft flesh. I looked up and an otherwise pretty face scowled back at me.

'Sorry,' I yelled, as the girl flicked some liquid from her arm. 'I didn't see you. I'll get you a refill.'

She shook her head and said something as she began to move away.

'C'mon, I insist,' I said. 'What are you drinking? Yard of ale? Slipper of champagne?'

The frown left her face and she stopped looking for a way through the crowd. 'Okay. Half a cider, please.' Her voice was even more difficult to hear than Jakesie's but I watched her moist lips form the words.

'Half a cider, coming right up,' I said, and I put my free hand on her shoulder to lead her to the bar.

Ten minutes later we were still there, trapped in that awkward no-man's-land of new acquaintanceship. I was holding Jake's beer, ready to take over to him, while Daniella – my new companion – was sipping her original cider and nursing the one I'd just bought her. I couldn't risk a gap in the conversation in case she saw it as her cue to leave so I was tossing anything out to keep a discussion going. 'I haven't seen you in here before,' I said, all Mr Original.

'I try to get here if there's a band on.' She ran a long-nailed finger around the rim of her glass. 'You're a regular then, are you?'

Her eyes were a deep, almost violet blue and what with the surprisingly dark lashes and eyebrows, her natural features had created their own networks of attraction; little pockets of interest.

'God, no,' I said. 'Must be a couple of years since I was last in here.'

She slid her eyes to me: 'Hardly surprising you haven't seen me then.'

Jake came over to claim his drink. He said a brief hello to Daniella but was obviously keen to make his escape. 'The others are here,' he told me. 'We'll be down the front if you want us.'

I nodded but returned to Daniella as soon as he left. 'So where are your friends?' I said, looking around.

'I got a lift with my brother,' she told me, 'so, I was hoping to see some of my mates down here.' She gave a sheepish smile as her eyes swept the room. 'Probably should've checked first though.'

She looked particularly cute when she smiled.

'So, are they workmates or schoolmates, these imaginary friends of yours?' I said.

She laughed. 'They're real enough! And they're mainly old schoolmates. I'm a uni student now. In Bristol.'

'Defected to England, eh?'

'It's barely across the border,' she said, waving a dismissive hand. 'I'm studying food technology.'

'Food technology? What's that – poking your nose into other people's meal choices?'

She gave me a playful slap on the arm and nodded at my drink. 'I could give you a detailed breakdown of the crap that's in your beer if you like.'

'I'd rather you didn't,' I said, holding my pint up to the light. 'So, are you on summer break now?'

'Yeah, kind of,' she said. 'I've kept my room over the holidays, though: it means I can escape from my parents whenever they drive me crazy.'

I nodded. 'Most of the time then, presumably?'

'Exactly!'

As I took a drink, Daniella glanced past me. 'All right, Dani?' I heard someone say. I turned and caught a glimpse of a dark-skinned guy with a ponytail.

'It's Daniella,' she corrected him. 'I'm good, thanks.'

'Yep, you're sure looking good.'

There was a certain pointedness in the way Daniella quickly returned her attention to me and her tone hadn't been friendly. I checked behind me again and caught the guy's eye, immediately wishing I hadn't. I looked away.

'Friend of yours?' I asked Daniella as soon as he left.

'Phil? He's just a mate of my brother's.' She gave me a wry smile. 'And, unfortunately, most of Mike's mates are dickheads.'

We shared a laugh and even though a pause sneaked its way in, Daniella didn't take the opportunity to leave. Instead, she edged forward on her stool. 'And what do you do?' She looked me up and down with that cool gaze of hers. 'Are you a doctor? Lawyer? Rocket scientist?'

I smiled. 'Yeah, I can see why you'd think that. Actually, I live in Swansea,' I said, neatly sidestepping the question. 'I'm just here for the weekend visiting my folks.'

'Swansea?'

'Yeah, I was studying there but now I'm...not.'

'Well, I guess it's a good a place as any to...not study. You're about as far away from Cardiff as me then; just in the opposite direction.'

She had quite a low voice – calm but with a bit of assertion to it. It sounded like a voice you could trust. A voice that could tell you the sky was green, and you wouldn't even have to look up to check. What with that and the long legs and steady gaze, I figured she could land someone like me in deep shit.

'Shall we grab that one?' she asked, as a table freed up nearby.

I didn't need to be asked twice.

We were an unlikely looking pair: that was obvious even to an optimist like me. I was in my faded, stretched T-shirt and jeans and there was her all la-di-da in her lacy peach dress and high heels. She was what Mum would call 'well turned out'.

The brother and his mates, meanwhile, were knobheads in their crisp, puffy shirts and ankle boots, supping on spirits.

Daniella groaned when ponytail guy stood up and headed in our direction with his empty glass. There were plenty of free spots at the bar, but he chose to stand at the end nearest our table. He ordered a whisky and his eyes drifted to us as soon as the barman took his glass.

'I was trying to remember your name,' he said to me. 'We were in the same year at school, weren't we?'

'Were we?'

Daniella was having trouble stifling a smirk as she and I locked eyes.

'Yes, we were,' he said. 'Westchurch High. Your name was on the tip of my tongue. Then I finally got it. Xander Johnston. Local man of mystery – if your reputation is to be believed.'

I gave an unconcerned smile, willing him away.

''Course I was mates with Kev Mitchell,' he said, eyeballing me. 'Jill's brother. Always two sides, eh?'

'Right.'

I wiped the sweat from my top lip. It was a long time since I'd had to face anyone from school. Let alone someone in the know.

His butt nudged my chair as he reached over for his drink. 'Cheers,' he said to the barman. He squeezed past us, even though he could've gone the other way. 'Watch yourself with this one,' I heard him say into Daniella's ear.

There was a fleeting drop in her expression but next second, we both rolled our eyes and laughed.

Thankfully, Daniella was far too polite to even question what he'd meant.

Hers was a big, kick-ass house in one of the posh neighbourhoods just outside Cardiff; all wide archways and terracotta tiling. It wasn't far away from us in terms of miles, but it was a world away in every other sense. While her folks' view was of the water, and the English coastline, Mum and Dad's backyard nestled against the main trainline into Cardiff city.

I parked on their gravel driveway and turned off the engine, the awkward goodnight-moment upon us.

'Why don't I give you my address in Swansea?' I said, rifling Dad's glove box for a pen and paper. 'Just in case...y'know, you're ever passing.'

'You realise Bristol's the opposite direction?' she said, laughing.

I waved away her protest. 'Ah, you could drive to Swansea in no time.'

'We'll see,' she said. 'Anyway, give me your address – you never know.'

I continued to hunt in the glove box but all I uncovered was a couple of prescriptions, a Swiss army knife and a Woolies carrier-bag – which presumably constituted Dad's Plans B, C and D.

Instead, Daniella handed me a pad and a pen from her purse. 'Here you go,' she said.

I scribbled down my details and passed the pad back to her but instead of writing her own address, she looked at what I'd written then put everything away.

I was about to move in for the goodnight kiss but was put off my stride by headlights streaming through the rear window.

'They're back early,' Daniella said, glancing up.

The car door slammed and Mike and three of his mates marched across the front lawn, giving us a few rude gestures as they went.

'Funny that you and Mike's friend were at the same school, eh?' Daniella said.

'Not really. But, like I said, I don't remember him anyway.'

'You must have made a bigger impression on him than he did on you.'

'Naturally.'

Daniella's glossy pink lips stretched into a smile, giving me sneak peeks of those perfect white teeth. She leaned in and planted a long, slow kiss on my lips. She tasted of apples and lipstick and I could have stayed there, enjoying her mouth for a very long time. However, an additional security light turned on and a silhouette appeared at the front window.

'The curse of the vigilant father!' Daniella said, with a sigh. 'Sorry.'

She left me with a final kiss then unfolded her long legs to get out of the car.

'Want to meet me for a drink before I go back tomorrow?' she said, resting on my open window.

'Sure.' Nice and casual, I sounded.

'Come over at twelve? We could get some lunch.'

'Well, there goes my lie-in,' I said, sucking in a breath. 'But seeing as it's you...'

She blew me a kiss before heading for the house and closing the door behind her.

And as I shifted the car into reverse, I thanked my lucky stars for spilled drinks and soft flesh.

Chapter 10

The following day, I stood considering the limited contents of my wardrobe. I didn't know where Daniella wanted to go for our lunch date, but I figured I'd need to look decent, wherever it was. Unfortunately, my old wardrobe was full of all the clothes that hadn't made the grade for joining me in Swansea, so pickings were slim. I reached in for a black shirt and gave it a sniff under the pits: yes, it was musty, ancient and probably on the tight side, but I figured it'd have to do. I pulled on my black jeans, put a few quid in my wallet and opened the door to negotiate another car favour from Dad.

But it was Mum standing there, blocking my way.

'All right?' I said, waiting for her to move.

'Sorry, love,' she said, staying where she was. 'I've been on pins all morning. I couldn't sleep. I was drinking tea at four.' She looked me up and down and I spied a hint of approval somewhere in the wrung-out tension of her features.

'This look all right?' I said, gesturing at the shirt.

'It looks lovely,' she said. 'Nice that you've made an effort.'

The comment caught me off guard: I didn't remember telling her about Daniella.

'Cheers,' I said.

It was only when I saw Mum's ironed trousers and dry-clean only jacket that realisation whacked me in the face. 'Oh yes,' I said, 'the cemetery.'

Mum rubbed at a mark on my cheek. 'All set?' She turned to go downstairs.

'It won't take too long, will it?' I said. I tried my best to make it sound casual, like an afterthought, but Mum spun around to me.

'What do you mean?'

'It's just that I have some other things to do – before I go back later,' I said.

'Today?'

'Well...I warned you it was a flying visit.'

'You're going back to Swansea today? Today of all days!' Her voice became more shrill with each word and, as she took a deep breath, her features seemed to fold in on themselves. 'Why am I the only one who cares?'

'Mum. It's not that...'

'First him. Now you! Why doesn't anybody care anymore?' She put her hands up to her face, her body rippling.

I reached out, but she shrugged me off. 'No. I don't want to hear it, Alexander.'

She swivelled on those Sunday best heels of hers and barged past me into the spare room, slamming the door so hard that the phone in the downstairs hallway chirruped on its rocker.

It was obvious I should have insisted on getting Daniella's number. Belt and braces, and all that. But I hadn't and, with Dad busy with the car and Mum having a minor meltdown, it looked like this was one romance destined to fail before it was off the starting blocks.

I left it as long as I could, but it didn't seem like Mum was coming out of that room any time soon. I listened outside the door and gently tapped.

When there was no response, I turned the handle.

Something heavy stopped the door moving and, as I shoved it open, I heard the slide and rustle of paper. I stared across the floor. It felt like

I'd just stumbled into Santa's storeroom, except this was more of a down and dirty Christmas scene: Mum, the abandoned toy, sitting amongst the packages with her legs splayed.

Last time I'd been in that room, we'd just painted it. Two years ago, Mum and I had spent the weekend before college started rolling two tins of magnolia over Gina's unicorn wallpaper and covering the pink carousel border with sensible white. The whole room, when we'd finished, was the vision of order and restraint, an anal-retentive's kingdom of glory: a place for everything and everything in its place.

Now it had morphed into a Salvador Dali nightmare. There were clippings over every surface of the wall – pictures of kids in hospital beds; headlines of doom; warnings about every infant illness under the sun. The shelves, the carpet, the bed – they were riddled with sheets and papers. And peppering it all, plastic carrier bags stuffed to the gills with bright-coloured clothes, bursting out the top like they were gasping for air.

'What *is* all this?' I said.

'It's my...' Mum waved an arm impatiently as if she couldn't work up the strength to think about it. 'It's my life, I suppose.' Her hand dropped into her lap as the comment landed. She said it like the admission was of no consequence, as if it was somehow natural or expected, like getting old.

As I stepped over piles of magazines, bags and boxes, I found it hard to reconcile the scene with the mum I knew. The mum who was sitting beside me, smartly dressed, perfumed and powdered; straight backed, strait-laced.

I moved a few carrier bags to squat down on the floor beside her but, even with those shifted, my hip was still crushed against hers.

'I...don't understand,' I said.

'Well, that makes two of us.' She looked into her lap and from the corner of my eye, I saw one or two spots soak into her trousers as tears escaped.

The only sound, when it eventually came, was the sharp click of my elbow as I reached across to hold her hand. Maybe it was surprise – or just awkwardness – but the gesture seemed to bring her to life. She lifted her head and looked around the room, like she was seeing it for the first time.

'It's since your dad retired,' she said. The sinews in her neck bulged and a tissue was balled so tight in her other fist, her knucklebones shone. 'Not because of his retiring, just…since. And I know it looks morbid with all these pictures on the walls, but it isn't. It...it helps somehow.' She chewed her lip, sucking it between her teeth like she was grinding her thoughts.

I couldn't think of any way to answer. I sat, trying to get a crease out of my jeans. 'Does he know?'

Mum mirrored my hand movement, smoothing down her trousers. 'Dad? Not really.'

'What does that mean?'

'It means...' She shrugged and it took her a few moments to gather what she wanted to say. 'Your dad doesn't seem to know what to do with himself anymore,' she said, 'let alone what to do with me. He's a bit… lost, I think.'

It was like I'd accidentally peeled back the band-aid of their marriage. The scab was starting to come off and I needed to press it back down again.

'Well, whatever's going on with him,' I said, 'he needs to be here for you now.'

'He is, love.'

I gave her a sidelong glance. 'I mean really here, not just…in the house.'

'Oh, he's always been here for me,' she said. 'For all of us. Even when he was away.'

I took in the headlines splattered across the walls. The room hardly looked like the hideaway of someone with a sympathetic soulmate. 'C'mon, Mum, you know that's not true.'

The drone of a vacuum started up in the garage: Dad doing his weekend clean and declutter of the car.

'How can you say that, Alexander? He's always had our backs.'

'Actually, he hasn't always had mine.'

The discussion spluttered to a halt and Mum pressed her fingers against her eyes. 'Why must it always come back to that?' She turned to me, tears welling up: 'And why dredge it up, today of all days?'

I opened my mouth to tell her – but quickly shut it again. After all, none of this was her fault. 'Sorry, Mum,' I said. 'I know, this isn't the right time.'

I also knew, of course, it never would be.

She wobbled a sad smile and I put an arm around her.

We stayed there, side by side against the wall as the vacuum hummed from the garage and Dad carried on, oblivious, with his duties.

Chapter 11

It was still light when my coach left Cardiff station on Sunday evening. The pavements were chock-a-block with day trippers returning home from the beach, pushchairs, kids clutching sticks of rock. Everything had a kind of summery pinkness about it; that rose-coloured spec feeling. For some reason, it made me think of Gina: it was her sixteenth birthday and she wasn't seeing any of this.

I pushed the thought away and, instead, scoured the crowds near the train station, in the wild hope of spotting Daniella heading back to Bristol. Just my luck that the first girl to notice me in months was now disappearing in the opposite direction – heading east, while I rolled deeper into Wales.

Once we were through town and past the castle, I had to give up hope of seeing her. Fate had stuck its fickle finger up at me again. The only thing I had to look forward to was finding out what Stobes had meant when he'd left a garbled message on Mum's answerphone: something about Minto and a boot-sized hole in my door. Presumably a welcome back gift for our 'chat' in the pub.

It wasn't until I got back to the flat, I realised Stobes had been economical with the truth: the hole in my door was big enough for a frigging rhino to charge through. I slipped off my backpack and squatted in the hallway, examining the damage, trying to work out if Minto had done any more than kick the crap out of the panels. Could I be sure he hadn't also crawled through the hole and taken a grand tour of my home and contents?

'Good for a bit of airflow, eh, butty-boy.'

I turned around to find Black standing behind me, bowl in hand. He took a mouthful of cornflakes – his favourite meal at any time of the day – and said, between crunches: 'What did you do to piss Minto off then?'

I stood up and unlocked the door. 'Fuck knows.'

He followed me in and went over to perch on the windowsill. 'They were high as kites, the lot of them,' Black said, waving his bowl at the door. 'You're lucky you got away with just a broken panel, the state they were in.'

'Was Sindy with them?'

It was a stupid question and I watched as Black's spoon stopped halfway to his mouth. 'I dunno,' he said. 'Think I was standing there, watching? No, I kept well out of it.' He tipped the dregs of milk into his mouth and put the bowl on the ledge. 'You looking for wheels?' he said. 'There's a Capri just come in. Unless you'd rather two wheels now you're an expert?' He smirked at me: my first attempts at learning to ride his precious motorbike the other week had almost wiped us both out.

'I'm not looking for any wheels,' I said.

Black was a petrolhead and worked as a mechanic at the local garage. I figured it was how he'd met Minto: the Apaches got their bikes tuned up there. You'd rarely go past without seeing a bunch of them, beefy and menacing, minding their machines.

To be honest, Black looked like one of them when he was off duty; stocky and solid in his leather jacket and tight jeans. I was never sure if he was called Black because it was the only colour he wore or simply because Black was his surname. He never said, and I never asked.

'Pity. The Capri's a crackin' car,' he said.

'I'm skint,' I told him. 'D'you really think I'd be living in this shit-hole if I had any spare cash?'

'This place? It's not so bad,' he said, looking out of my window. He dragged his fingers through his scruffy mop of black curls. 'Least, not if you ignore the mould, the dry rot and the stench.'

I laughed. 'What's your excuse then? You could afford something better than this with your salary.'

'All my cash goes on the bike and the car. You know that.'

Actually, most of his money seemed to go on beer, fags and getting high, but I wasn't about to say so.

He ambled away from the window and picked up my *Melody Maker* from the table. 'So where were you hiding all weekend?'

'Hiding?'

He flicked through the pages, pausing every few moments to look more closely at something. 'From Minto and his mates.'

'I wasn't hiding. I'd promised to go and see my folks.'

'Aye, aye.' He didn't bother to mask the smile. 'Stobes said you didn't get back from the pub on Friday till nearly closing. Didn't sound like you were planning a trip away.'

'Yeah, it was late when I left.' I unzipped my backpack and pulled out my clothes and cassettes from home. 'Didn't have much choice though: it was my sister's sixteenth.'

I watched him filter the info before giving a nod. 'Cool.' He pulled open the door and a few splinters fell away from the hole and landed on the carpet. 'I never knew you had a little sister.'

'Didn't you?'

'Nope.'

I stuffed some dirty socks in a carrier bag, ready for the next laundry-run. Black was still watching me. 'So, is she hot, this sister of yours?'

I carried on emptying my bag. 'She's dead.'

'Eh?'

'I went home to take my mum to the cemetery.'

His mouth opened then snapped shut again.

'It would have been her sixteenth today,' I told him.

Black stayed with his hand on the doorknob, staring down at the carpet like he was waiting for it to magic him away. Finally, he cleared his throat. 'Shit. Well. Christ. Better get going.' He lifted a hand as he turned away, then ran up the stairs so fast I could almost smell the vapour trail he left behind him.

Chapter 12

The following day, the athletics had just started on the telly when I sensed I no longer had the room to myself. Sure enough, I looked towards the door and there was Sindy, her pointy elfin face sticking through the hole like she was posing for a seaside photo.

I went back to my programme, but she didn't move. 'What do you want, Sindy?'

'Nothing.'

I kept my eyes on the screen. 'Why's your face poking through my door then?'

'I just wanted to see if it would fit.' She giggled. 'And it does, easy.'

I looked over. 'Yeah, we've got your man Minto to thank for that, haven't we?' That soon wiped the smile off her face.

'I told you he had a bad temper.' She stood up and opened the door, edging in slowly like I wouldn't notice. She hovered near my chair, a rolled-up envelope in her hand. 'Watcha watching, Alec?'

'Championship athletics.' I nodded at the screen. 'From Helsinki.'

She stayed quiet as she stood next to me, leaning against my chair. There was no conversation – both of us letting the TV take care of the silence between us.

'Minto not in?' I said, at last.

'Think he gets back tomorrow. He's away on business at the moment.'

I grinned, but she remained serious. 'Business. I see.'

I tried to stay focussed on my programme, but it wasn't easy with Sindy looming beside me like the angel of death.

'So, what are you doing here then – if Minto's out?' I said.

She unfurled her hand. 'I came to get this.' A few ten quid notes were sticking out of the envelope.

'What's that?'

'Pocket money. He gives me a bit extra if I've...' She slapped her hand over her mouth.

'What?'

'I'm not allowed to say. Sorry.'

I went back to the screen and shook my head. 'Don't worry, Sinds. I think I'll live without knowing.'

Even when I switched channels, Sindy made no moves to leave. It was getting late and I still hadn't eaten. 'Well,' I said, stretching. 'I'd better get –'

'Do you have a spare key for Minto's room? Or would any of the others?'

'You think Minto would trust any of us with his key?'

'Maybe not.' She sighed and twisted a strand of hair around her finger, her bird-like features even more beady from my vantage point.

'Why? Have you left something in there?'

She paused and shook her head. 'I've lost my key for home: I thought maybe I could stay in his room.'

'Don't reckon he'd be too happy with that.'

'I wouldn't touch anything.'

'Well, I can't help you, I'm afraid. You'll have to find your house key. Where's home anyway?'

'Just past the Pontwyn roundabout.'

Pontwyn was miles away and, as far as I knew, had absolutely nothing to recommend it beside a big, ugly industrial estate. 'You come all that way every day to see Minto?' I said.

She shrugged but as she looked away, the colour rose in her cheeks. 'It's not so far.'

I went out to the kitchen and took a burger out of the freezer. Sindy followed behind watching my every move from the doorway.

I glanced over to her. 'I'd offer you something but –'

'That's okay.'

The burger slid out of its packet with a brick-like thud on the table. I got out a frypan and added a dollop of lard.

'Okay, well, have a nice dinner,' she said finally, turning away. 'I'll see you...tomorrow probably.'

'Yep,' I turned the gas up. 'See ya.'

The sizzle of the burger didn't quite mask the creak on the stairs as she left. Nor the heavy patter of summer rain on the roof.

I paused, spatula in hand before turning off the gas knob. 'How are you getting home?' I shouted from the top of the stairs.

She looked up at me. 'I've got plenty of bus money,' she said, shaking her envelope.

'But you haven't got a coat.' I took a few steps down. 'Which bus stop do you walk to?'

'The one at the station.'

'The train station?'

'I'm used to it and it's nice and warm out.'

I dithered on the stairs while Sindy rummaged in the coat rack and grabbed herself a brolly. It had been humid all week and there was a forecast for thunder. 'But you haven't got a key,' I said, 'how will you get in?'

'I'll climb in the kitchen window if I can find a way to reach it.'

I imagined her in her back garden, pipe cleaner legs straining to reach the ledge. 'Look, wait a minute,' I said. 'Stay there.'

I hot-footed it up to Black's room. I knew he'd lend me his old jalopy for half an hour if I bought him a pint. He didn't even ask why: just handed me the keys and mentioned it was low on petrol.

Sindy was sitting against the front door, opening and shutting the umbrella when I hurried down. 'You know that's bad luck,' I told her.

'It's not! I don't believe that.' Even so, she put it in her bag and got to her feet.

'Black's lent me his car,' I said, holding up the keys. 'I'll give you a ride.'

Her face lit up. 'Hurray! And, see? It wasn't bad luck at all!'

I didn't reply, but I had to smile as she skip-skip-skipped beside me all the way to Black's old rust bucket.

We turned into a narrow lane just off the main road. I hadn't been that way before – had never had to – but it felt familiar, reminding me of every other dirt-blown street I'd ever known. The terraced houses, each with its own set of concrete steps, looked out onto a row of tumbledown garages, plonked there like an afterthought. The street wasn't paved, as such. There was just a bitumen strip in the middle and the rest was uneven concrete, trying its best to suffocate the weeds escaping through the cracks. The place had an unloved feel about it, like everyone knew it was a shit-hole and had given up on hiding the fact yonks ago.

We'd figured out a plan to get into the house. Sindy said the back window was dodgy, so if I climbed onto a box or a bin, I'd be able to pull open the catch and crawl inside.

It took a while to pick our way through the junk in her yard. I manhandled one of the oil drums towards the windowsill and clambered onto the rim while Sindy made a big show of holding it steady.

'Just give it a tug,' she told me from below. 'It comes open dead easy.'

She wasn't wrong. Had they had anything worth nicking inside, I'd've suggested they get better security. As it was, I made my way through the dank kitchen and opened up the back door for Sindy.

'Come on through,' she said, all housewifey the minute she was inside. I followed her across the cracked lino into a room with a big-patterned carpet and a sofa that looked like it should have joined the junk in the backyard.

Sindy and I both came to an awkward stop in the middle of the room and I realised I should've left the minute I'd opened the door for her.

'Well, now you're safely in. I'll get going,' I told her. 'Stobes will swipe that burger of mine if I leave it out.'

Sindy giggled but she seemed unsure how to bring matters to a close. 'Okay. Thank you for –'

A door slammed upstairs and Sindy's hand shot up to her head, closing her fist around a clump of hair. Her eyes widened as she shouted: 'Dad?'

'Sind? What you doin' home? You said you was busy today.'

She shot a look to me and lowered her voice to a whisper. 'You have to go.'

I nodded, about to hurry off to the front door but she grabbed my wrist before I could make a move.

'I'll only be a minute, Dad. I just forgot something,' she shouted up the stairs.

She pushed me through the kitchen. 'Go the back way. Hurry up!' she said. 'If he finds you, he'll tell Minto.'

'Minto?' I half turned. 'He knows Minto?'

'Just go!' Her bony fingers sank into my arms as she pushed, but loud footsteps on the stairs had us both frozen. Sindy's gaze pinned itself to the doorway.

I'd never seen her look so rattled. There was a noise by the front door and, in the hall mirror, I caught a glimpse of a skinny guy carrying a canvas bag. The door slammed and we heard his footsteps hurry down the outside steps.

It wasn't until there was the clunk of a car door that Sindy let her arms drop. 'Sorry,' she said, turning away. Her voice was shaky.

'He doesn't like you having visitors, eh?'

'I'm never, ever allowed to bring strangers to the house.'

The fridge clicked into action; its motor whirring too loud.

'Well, I'd better leave you to it then,' I said again.

'Oh, you don't have to now. Dad won't be back tonight. He almost never sleeps here.' Sindy twirled on the spot.

'Where does he go?'

She lifted the lid on a clay jar on the sideboard and stuck her hand inside. She chucked a chocolate bar at me. 'He thinks I don't know where he keeps these things.' She opened her wrapper. 'He has lots of friends. I think he stays with them.' She bit into her chocolate and leaned towards me, speaking in a whisper. 'Lady friends.'

'Yeah?' I took a bite of my bar and had a wander around the room. 'He doesn't have your Swansea accent, does he?'

'No, he travels a lot. I don't even know where he was born! He's never said.'

Most of the pictures on the wall were the gaudy, mass-produced sort. Sultry looking women; stalking cheetahs; cheap knockoffs like you'd see in a Chinese takeaway. There was one framed photo though: some unshaven bloke wearing a baseball cap, his arm around a gangly young girl. 'That you and your dad?'

'Yes!' She clapped her hands at my impressive powers of deduction. 'It was taken at a caravan park when we went on holiday.'

I bent down and peered closer, trying to decipher Sindy's expression. She was smiling broadly but her body looked stiff, as if it had been placed under her head unwillingly.

'Here,' she said, handing me a can of shandy. 'There's only one but you can have it.'

'Cheers.' I opened it, took a few slugs and passed it back to her.

She was busy sorting through a pile of books and paperwork on the table. 'There are some more recent photos in here,' she said, easing open a fat photo album. 'Dad loves photography so he's always taking pictures.'

I needed more to eat than a few bites of chocolate, but I didn't have the heart to just ignore the album she'd pushed in my direction. After the first few pages of beach views, more photos of Sindy started appearing. There was one of her standing in her pyjamas, hair wrapped up in a towel, looking about four or five. Another one showed her outside school, waving at the camera as she turned towards the school gate. 'First day at school,' said the label in spidery handwriting. Despite her wearing exactly the same as the other kids in the background, you could tell that Sindy wasn't like them. Her shoes looked scuffed and her socks were rolled around her ankles as if the elastic had already gone. Her skirt was too big and even her hair had a neglected look about it. I remember Gina always had brightly coloured hair-ties and ribbons when Mum did it for her in pigtails. Whereas, even though I couldn't pick out the detail, I somehow knew that Sindy's ponytail was held in place with some tired old rubber band and a couple of rusty hairclips.

'I never actually went to school,' she said, nudging me with her very pointy elbow.

I looked at her. 'Eh?'

'The picture's just for show. I never had to go to school really,' she said, looking pleased with herself.

'How come? Didn't some education bod come and…chase you up?'

'Nope,' she laughed. 'Dad says school's for losers anyway.'

I flipped through some more pages, thinking. 'So, what about your mum? Where's she in all this?' I asked.

'I told you! She lives in Australia, but I don't know what she does there.'

'You don't keep in touch?'

'According to Dad, she's a sorry bloody excuse for a mother.'

A loud clap of thunder seemed to shake the house as if to provide a booming finale to the statement.

Sindy reached over and flipped some pages for me, clearly shutting the door on the discussion.

'There's a picture somewhere of me at the dry ski slope,' Sindy said. 'It's really good: I look about twenty. Like a model.'

She stopped at an odd set of photos: ones showing a steam-covered shower door. Through the glass on each photo, you could pick out an eye or a pair of lips where a patch of condensation had been wiped away.

'What are these?'

'I told you Dad likes photography,' she laughed.

I peered at the first few pictures. At the ones exposing an eye. 'That's... not you, is it?'

'You recognised me, just from an eye!'

My gaze drifted down the page but now with caution; with a dread that I might need to suddenly pull away.

The next pictures focussed lower on the face – a pair of pink lips barely visible in some photos, while others showed an open mouth pressed to the glass; steam filling the hollow in the centre.

'Your dad took these?'

'Yes, they're good, aren't they?'

Over the page, the palm of a hand was pressed against the shower screen. A small hand, pale and splayed.

'How old were you?'

'Eleven, maybe. Twelve. Not that long ago.'

'He...came into the bathroom, while you were showering?'

'To take the photos, silly.'

'Mm.' I couldn't look at her.

'It's okay, he is my dad, you know.' Sindy's eyes smiled back at me, cheery, unconcerned.

I returned the smile but closed the album. 'They're good,' I said. 'Interesting.'

'Don't you want to see the rest? Most people like the later ones.'

'No. Thanks.' I found myself backing away, easing myself free of the things I didn't want to know. 'I really have to get Black's car back to him now.'

'Okay.' She placed the photo album back on the teetering pile on the table. 'You can see them if you come around again. When Dad isn't here.'

'Great.'

'Remember not to tell Minto, though,' she said. 'About you being here.'

'Don't worry!'

She waved as I went down the concrete steps. I found myself stopping when I got to the bottom.

'So how did your dad get to know Minto if you can't invite people over?' I said.

'Oh, Minto's different.' She pushed her hair behind her ears, showing off a pair of big hoop earrings. 'It was Dad who introduced me to him. Minto's a family friend.'

'They already knew each other?'

'Business partners,' she said. 'Dad says they're business partners. It's good, isn't it?'

I managed a nod before walking away and turning my back on the whole sick mess.

Chapter 13

It wasn't like she needed encouragement. After giving her a ride to her house that day, Sindy was all over me like a rash; popping in whenever she knew Minto wasn't around; 'happening' to be passing whenever I set foot outside the flat; wandering out to the kitchen every time I put the kettle on. It wasn't that I wanted to avoid her, but there was no happy medium with Sindy; no middle ground. And I knew it wouldn't be long before Minto started smelling a rat – he might have been many things, but Minto certainly wasn't stupid.

It was Friday teatime when she knocked on my door. Had I not had the hole patched up, I'd've had some warning it was her, but as it was, I assumed Stobes was at a loose end and wanted to go for a pint.

'Yeah, come in,' I shouted.

Sindy's head appeared, her fingers squeaking as she held onto the door. 'Hi, Alec. Are you busy?'

I went back to the newspaper, hoping she'd take the hint, knowing she wouldn't. 'I am a bit.'

'Minto's gone down The Adam and Eve. I told him I'd see him later.'

'Nice.'

'You could come too.'

I looked up. 'Me? Why?'

'Not with me,' she said, quickly. 'I mean, you could just...go down there and play pool or whatever.'

'Yes, but...why?'

She shrugged and picked up my stapler. 'I just thought it'd be nice.'

'I don't think so, Sindy. I've got a lot on. Anyway, it's still hot – I don't want to go to some sweaty swill-hole in town.'

'Hottest day on record,' she told me.

'There you go then.'

She came out from behind my table. I hadn't seen what she was wearing when she first came in but now, I could see the black and white kilt with the fishnets and black ankle boots. Her top was white, stretchy and ribbed. She had nothing on underneath, so the outline of her nipples was clearly visible. It wasn't like she needed anything for support, but she definitely needed something for decency.

I was suddenly aware of her watching me as I took in her appearance.

'Do you like it?' she said. 'It's too hot to wear much.'

She perched on the corner of the table, taking a big lungful of air so that her T-shirt clung even more closely to her skin.

I looked away. 'Yeah, so like I said – I think I'll give town a miss, so maybe you'd better get on your way, eh?'

She looked crestfallen. 'I just thought...'

'Look, Sindy.' I folded the paper and got out of my chair. 'You look lovely. Don't take it the wrong way. But you're Minto's girlfriend. He wouldn't want you in here talking to me. And I think...'

'Oh, he might not mind, actually.'

'Trust me: he would.'

'Not if you paid him.'

For some reason, I laughed. 'What?'

'You could pay him. He wouldn't mind what we did then. Really. I know he wouldn't.' I could sense her enthusiasm rising. 'You could suggest it – if you came to the pub.'

'Sindy...'

A knock on the door silenced us and had it opened at that moment, we'd have looked like the guiltiest fucking pair this side of the Tawe.

'Who is it?' I shouted.

'Someone you don't deserve!' A girl's voice. One that I recognised but couldn't place.

Sindy let out a sigh. 'Guess I'll go then.' Her shoulders slumped as she made for the door: the T-shirt didn't look half as tight on her as it had before.

I reached past her for the door handle. 'Thanks for the invite though,' I said. 'To the pub, I mean. Another time.'

'Okay.'

I opened the door.

'Hi, stranger. Remember me?'

I was so busy gawping, I barely registered Sindy slipping past me and heading off down the stairs.

'So, are you going to invite me in?' Daniella said. She glanced behind her. 'Or did I catch you at a bad time?'

'Oh, no,' I said, quickly. 'That was just…she's with one of the guys in the flat.'

'Good.' A dimple appeared as Daniella smiled, like a cheeky 'x marks the spot'. I hadn't seen her in full light before and certainly not this sober, so I found myself studying her, hurriedly taking in all those vaguely remembered features: the shiny newness of her skin and those pink lips that had suddenly tilted up to me like a beckoning finger. I pressed my mouth against them a bit too hurriedly– smudging them with an embarrassingly slippery kiss, sexy as a wet haddock.

'Well, come on in,' I said, straightening up and making a grand sweeping gesture as if it would somehow make up for it. 'Jeez, I can't believe you're just suddenly...here!'

'Me neither,' she said, her eyes everywhere as she wandered in.

I kicked magazines under the bed and shoved bundles of clothes onto the table as she meandered over to inspect the view.

'You're lucky I kept your address given that you stood me up,' she said.

I pulled my crispy undies off the radiator while Daniella turned to look at me, her arms folded; long fingers tapping against her sleeve.

'I'm really sorry about that,' I said. I sat on the bed, my hands still awash with crumpled underwear.

'Some of my friends said I was mad to even come,' she told me. 'They said you probably had a girlfriend or wouldn't remember me or that you...'

'Nothing like that,' I said. 'I felt really bad about not turning up that day.'

'Really?'

I nodded. 'I swear. If I could've let you know, I would have. But I didn't know your phone number or anything.'

'No, I realised that,' she said, perching beside me. 'It's the only reason I gave you the benefit of the doubt.'

Her arm was warm against mine and she smelt clean and fresh, like she'd never been unwrapped.

'So, how...did you...get here? Swansea, I mean?' If the conversation took any more of a nosedive, I'd be asking one of Mum's 'how was the journey, love?' questions.

'I drove. Dad's kind of given me his old Marina. He says it's a loan but...y'know.'

She shrugged and laughed, and it was only then I realised she was every bit as nervous as me.

'Nice.'

'I'm staying with my mate, Kirsty,' she said. 'Remember I told you I had a friend here?'

I didn't but I nodded anyway. 'Oh, yeah.'

'I haven't been round there yet. Thought I'd get this over with first.' Another giggle. 'In case I really did find you here with a live-in lover.' Her throat moved as she swallowed. 'Who did you say that girl was?'

'Oh, just a friend of Minto's.' I nodded at the wall. 'Minto's got the room next door.'

'There's just the two of you?'

'No, there's Stobes and Black upstairs.'

She laughed again. 'Stobes and Black? Sound like a pair of undertakers. Stobes and Black.' She deepened her voice and put on a posh accent. 'Carefully disposing of family members since nineteen twenty-two.'

It caused momentary amusement, but the nervous silence edged back in.

'So, do you want to...do something?' I asked. 'Or are you in a hurry to get to your friend's place?'

'I'll see her later. Let's go out,' she said, jumping to her feet and putting a hand towards me. 'You can show me what this sad little backwater has to offer.'

With a set of wheels, we had the whole of Swansea at our disposal. We could've headed into town, but I suggested we take the short drive along the coast to one of my favourite spots.

'Mumbles!' Daniella chortled, as we headed out of the city. 'I'd forgotten there was a place called Mumbles.'

'Yeah! What's so freaking funny?' I said. 'It's got a pier, a beach...it's got a lighthouse, a castle nearby – what more could you want?'

She finally managed to stop laughing. 'I dunno. A decent pub, maybe?'

'Demanding, aren't you?' I said, shaking my head. 'But, as it happens, it's got a ton of decent drinking holes.'

'Sounds promising,' she said as we pulled up at the lights. She applied something glossy to her lips. 'And in light of this new information, I approve of your choice.'

I grinned across at her, taking in the enticing sheen of her smile. 'Good,' I said. 'You can give me a proper thank you later.'

I felt surprisingly proud to show off my adopted home as we weaved through Mumbles. It was like I was seeing it afresh, through *her* eyes – all those squished together cottages; the tiny lanes and blink-and-you'll-miss-them stairways. And then, on the other side of us, the expanse of golden coastline, sweeping in a perfect curve like a painter's flourish.

Of course, we were enjoying it at its best: the heatwave had continued through August, so everyone was out in their summer clothes, strolling the promenade or sipping beer as they sat looking out over the water. With the sun starting to dip behind the hill, it was like the place had decided to put on a show just for us – and to prove to my attractive out-of-towner what this 'sad little backwater' was really all about.

I decided we'd start off in my favourite pub. It was set back from the road, with cracking views of the sea, and of the hills across the bay, silhouetted against the sky. The place was normally awash with skinny-ribbed, turtlenecked-clad students, but most of them had buggered off for the summer, so now it was full of locals, enjoying the balmy evening and the student-free peace.

Daniella looked as summery-stunning as the surroundings. Her hair was loose and wavy, and she was wearing this off-the-shoulder dress that made me want to press my lips against all that exposed skin.

'So, you still haven't told me what was so important that you had to stand me up,' Daniella said as I slid onto the sofa beside her with our drinks. Although her tone was casual, it wasn't the first time she'd mentioned being ditched by me, so I figured she was still pissed off.

'Long story,' I told her. 'And boring as hell. Trust me: you don't wanna know.'

She took a long sip from her glass, her blue-painted fingernails dark against the dayglo orange of her juice. She looked me straight in the eye. 'Actually, I do.'

She clearly wasn't a woman to be brushed off with vague excuses. I liked that in her.

'It's very boring,' I said, stringing her along a bit further.

'Well, not knowing is very annoying. Boring would at least be a change.'

I put down my pint. 'Okay. If you insist. But prepare yourself for a sharp dose of tedium.' I cleared my throat, rubbed the frost off my glass and shifted in my seat. I guess I hadn't discussed the nitty-gritty of my home life with many people and I felt like I was suddenly being asked to strip off. 'Thing is,' I said. 'We have a few...issues in our house.'

'Mm, don't we all? Go on.'

I hardly knew what to tell her because the whole tale had a kind of domino effect: I couldn't tell her about Mum without explaining the cemetery visit. And if I told her about that, I'd be forced to go over the stuff about Gina. Then more about Mum. And maybe Dad too.

I gave her concrete details; the facts, like I was reading a news bulletin. First there was this, then that, then that. Dosh, dosh, dosh, job done.

'Your poor mum,' she said, shaking her head.

'Yeah.'

'And she didn't cotton on to the fact that you hadn't actually remembered the date?'

'Nah. I don't know how I forgot. It's always been etched on my brain: her birth day; her death day. This time, though, it just slipped my mind.'

'It's sad really, isn't it?' Daniella said. 'I mean, Gina was one of you; an intrinsic part of the family, and yet...none of you remembered something as important as her sixteenth birthday except your mum.'

'Time passes,' I said. 'You have to move on at some point.' I looked down, wishing I believed it.

Daniella kept her eyes on the table. 'I bet your mum hasn't – moved on, I mean.'

'She does a bit too much living in the past,' I said. 'That's the other reason I ran out of time to see you.' I took a breath, gearing up to serve the main course. 'Mum's developed a problem,' I said. 'She's turned Gina's room – well, the spare room – into a kind of mausoleum. It feels... sick, somehow. Like she's not letting Gina rest. Jeez, when I first saw it, it felt like Mum had gone down to that fucking graveyard and dug her up.'

All the time I talked, I didn't look at Daniella – I just kept right on going so I wouldn't have to suffer any reactions. As soon as I stopped though, I made the mistake of glancing across. She was looking at me, wide-eyed: horrified yet fascinated.

'And that's only the tip of the iceberg,' I found myself telling her. 'She's also got bags of outfits she's bought for Gina. Stuff from all the high street boutiques: you name it, she's probably got it in every size, colour and style option. No wonder Dad's skint. He's paying to keep his late daughter in the lap of luxury. And Mum knows it's crazy, but she can't seem to help herself.'

We stared at the table and both reached for our drinks at the same time.

'Sounds like other people need to help her,' Daniella said. 'You. And your dad.'

'Ah, Dad barely talks about Gina,' I said. 'It's like, because he was away when it all happened, he shouldn't have to –'

'Hey! Fancy running into you again.'

I looked up from my pint, swiftly recalibrating as Sindy stood there, smiling. She was still wearing the same little kilt and fishnet number I'd seen on her earlier, but it was now topped off with a triple layer of make-up. She rested her knee on the edge of my seat.

'All right, Sindy? Thought you lot were off down the Adam and Eve.'

'We were. I mean, we did. Then we came here.' She was clutching a black bike helmet so big it looked like her wrist might snap with the weight of it.

She looked across at Daniella and gave her a half-smile. 'I saw you earlier at the flat, didn't I?'

'This is Daniella,' I told her. 'Where's Minto?'

'They're parking the bikes outside.' The way her words smudged into one another hinted at why her knee needed to rest on the seat.

'Having a big night, are you?' I said. I kept a close eye on the door. 'Maybe you'd better go and save them a spot at the bar – it takes ages to get served in here.'

But Sindy was busy studying Daniella. 'So, are you Alec's girlfriend?'

'There's a gap over there,' I said, nodding towards the bar. 'If you're quick you can get in there.'

A blast of air from the doorway heralded the arrival of Minto and half a dozen of his cronies. He removed his gloves, looking around as he planted himself in the middle of the room, legs apart like he was rooted for the evening. Punters with drinks moved around him, instinctively avoiding eye contact. He'd have no problem getting alcohol for a clearly underaged drinker.

'You'd better go, Sindy,' I mumbled – and it was all I could do not to give her a shove. Too late, though.

'Alec. The local not good enough for you anymore, eh?' Minto said. His large hand landed on Sindy's shoulder.

'Always nice to have a change,' I mumbled.

I waited for him to go and in the meantime kept my eyes fixed to the pattern on the carpet.

'Over here, lads!' Minto said – and with that he gathered a few stray chairs and squeezed them around our table for two.

'You can have these seats in a minute,' I said quickly. 'We were just off anyway.'

Minto was paying no attention to me; he was busy gesturing to one of his mates at the bar. He pulled Sindy onto his lap as he sat down and refocussed his attention.

'Not going to introduce me to your new lady friend here?' he said, leaning forward with an outstretched hand to Daniella. 'I'm Minto. Like the breath fresheners.' He met her eye as she shook hands. 'The ones you suck.'

She slipped her hand from his. 'Daniella.' Then turning to me: 'Shall we head off, Alec?'

'Sure.'

'Not so fast,' said Minto. 'Alec here owes me a pint, don't you, Alec?'

'Do I?' I stood up and reached into my pocket while Daniella picked up her bag. I put a few quid on the table. Fuck knows why I handed anything over, given that he owed me a new door. 'Have the next one on me,' I said.

'Money? That's not very sociable of you,' he said. 'Not very sociable at all.'

Daniella was right behind me, her way blocked as we were both forced to engage with Minto at the table.

'What do you think, Sindy?' Minto said. 'Don't you think that's a bit rude of Alec? You want his company, not his money, don't you?'

Sindy smiled up at me from Minto's lap. 'Yes, that'd be good.'

'You think Alec's a nice boy, don't you?'

Sindy giggled. 'Yes, he is.'

'You think he's a nice, clean, attractive boy. Don't you?'

'Alec – let's go,' Daniella whispered into my ear. 'Just push past his chair and get out of here.'

'We're off,' I said. 'See you later, all right?' I tried to squeeze past the chairs, but no one was shifting.

'Why don't you go with 'em, Sinds?' Minto said. 'Be nice for you to have some different company. You don't mind, do you, Alec?'

'What?'

Minto laughed and pushed Sindy off his lap, giving her arse a pat for good measure. 'Go on. Go with them. Alec doesn't mind.' His focus shifted behind me. 'Nor does the lovely Daniella.'

I paused but reached behind me for Daniella's hand, figuring we needed to leave – and if that meant having Sindy along, so be it.

'Actually, the lovely Daniella does mind.' I felt my hand jerk as Daniella stopped. She was looking down at Minto. 'Alec and I are only seeing each other for one night so we've got a lot to catch up on. No offence to you, Sindy, but I think we'd like some time to ourselves.'

I felt my jaw slacken as I waited for Minto's reaction. My hand had become almost too slippery to keep hold of Daniella's. I sensed a universal breath-hold amongst the group. Even Sindy looked between us like she was ready to make a run for it.

Minto leaned back in his chair and looked Daniella up and down. 'You make a very compelling argument,' he said, with a wry smile. 'Sindy wants Alec's company; *you* want Alec's company. Lucky Alec, is all I can say. But you're the visitor so...' He pulled Sindy back on to his lap, smoothing her thigh. 'Never mind, Sinds. We'll keep you entertained. Won't we, lads?'

There were dirty laughs as Minto ran his big paws over Sindy's small body. The tattoo on his hand spelled 'loyal' and the sight of it against Sindy's flat chest made me want to hurl.

Sindy caught me looking and she smiled – but there was something else behind the expression; something cold and unexpected.

Daniella's lips tickled my ear. 'Let's go, Alec. Now.'

And we did. We flung open the pub door, both of us suddenly greedy for fresh air. Raucous laughter belched from the building behind us and, as we headed away, the wild echoes of it seemed to follow us all the way home.

Chapter 14

All I know is that I was in a deep sleep when it happened. Daniella was staying with me for the third weekend on the trot, so I'd been sleeping soundly, confident for once that I was doing pretty bloody well on the romance stakes.

A loud thwack woke me, and my bedroom door shot open like it had been hit by a wrecking ball. Daniella bolted upright as the light flicked on and three people raced into the room. There were thundering footsteps everywhere – above us, each side of us, below us – I could hear doors being kicked open and orders barked all around. My heart pogoed then seemed to shudder to a halt as one of the men ordered us up.

Daniella and I somehow synchronised our movements so that we managed to keep the duvet clutched around both of us. I could barely take my eyes off the guy barking instructions in our direction, but I was aware of the others rifling through my possessions, chucking stuff on the floor and tipping things out of bags and boxes.

Next door, Minto's voice sliced through the wall, yelling and cursing between thumps and bangs. Above our heads, the scrape of a bedframe; in the hall, more heavy footsteps on creaking stairs.

Daniella's bare leg touched mine as she edged closer behind the duvet. The guy in front of us didn't do anything – just stood there, 'minding' us while his sidekicks took apart my belongings. They were uniformed, smart looking. It started to dawn on me what was happening and why. The realisation brought me comfort.

'Fucking bastards!' I heard Minto yell from his room. 'I told you, I've got nothin'!'

One of our room-searchers gave a shake of the head to the guy in front of us. They both looked to the chunky one in the corner who was busy flipping through my dusty paperbacks and dropping them one by one into a pile on the floor.

'You won't find anything,' I found myself saying. 'I'm not into that shit.'

The cop ignored me and glanced instead towards Fat Lad who shook his head. 'Nothing.'

In the end they left as quickly as they came, skulking out the door like a bunch of partygoers at the wrong address.

I could feel Daniella's arm still shaking against mine as the house became silent again. I had the tremors myself, but mine were of the too-much-coffee kind: every nerve pumped, primed and ready for action.

'How about that?' I said, half-laughing. 'How about that!'

'Shit! I've never been so scared in my life.' Daniella wrapped her arms around me, and we stood in the middle of the mess, holding onto one another. 'I can't believe what just happened.'

'You don't get drug raids in Bristol then?' I said.

'No!' And once she'd had chance to get her breath back, she sounded almost rueful. 'It was a rush, though, wasn't it?'

'Well, kind of,' I said.

I could feel her starting to shiver. The summer's sticky temperatures had dropped away, and my cavernous room had returned to being chilly again. 'Listen, why don't you go back to bed?' I said. 'I'll go and make you a cuppa. Or do you need something stronger?'

'Have you got anything stronger?'

'Nope.'

She slid those slender legs of hers onto the mattress, pulling the duvet with her while I stood there in my undies.

'Tea it is then,' she said.

In the kitchen, Black and Stobes were having a smoke and I could hear low muttering as they stared out of the window. They spun around when I came in and I sensed their relief when they saw it was me.

'They pull your room apart too?' Stobes said. 'Fucking shit storm in mine.'

'Yeah, mine will take some putting back together,' I told him.

'What I don't get is how come they didn't find anything,' Black said, lowering his voice and nodding towards Minto's room. He looked both amused and amazed, as if Minto had performed some impressive sleight-of-hand trick.

I filled the kettle. 'How d'you know they didn't?'

'Cause he's still here, that's why,' Black said. 'They'd have taken him in otherwise.'

'Don't s'pose he was that bothered,' Stobes said to Black. 'What they'd have found here would have been nothing in the grand scheme of things.'

I looked at them, trying to read the subtext.

Black looked at me and shook his head. 'C'mon, Alec – you think Minto would have anything much here?'

'I dunno. Where else would he keep it? At Sindy's?'

Stobes and Black exchanged another glance. I felt like the kid in the playground not included in the game.

'Minto has his fingers in everything,' Stobes said. He waved a dismissive hand around us. 'But what's here – this is nothing. Fuck all.'

'Just as well Sindy wasn't here,' Black said.

'You sure she wasn't?' I said. 'She was with him earlier.'

Again, with the knowing glance: Black and Stobes swapped a dirty smile. 'She's probably otherwise engaged, butty-bach,' Black said.

There was a noise in the hall and each of us instinctively made ourselves busy.

Minto didn't look surprised to find us gathered in the kitchen. 'Fucking pigs!' he said. 'Did they ask you lot anything?'

Black stubbed out his fag in the sink. 'They were more action than words.'

Minto nodded. 'Pricks.'

'They didn't find anything?' Black said, folding his arms and looking at Minto. 'How was that then?'

Black was the only one who knew him well enough to dare going down this track. Though even he didn't get off scot-free. Minto tossed him a look. 'They didn't find anything 'cause the pricks don't know what the fuck they're doing.' He helped himself to the water I'd just boiled. 'What pisses me off is how come they knew I was here. At home – now, tonight.'

There was a shrugging of shoulders as we all exchanged glances, but Minto only slid his eyes in my direction. 'It was like the tossers were tipped off or something.'

The kitchen became mighty quiet as Black and Stobes followed his gaze.

'What?' I went over and refilled the jug. 'You think I tipped them off? Like I'd welcome having my room ransacked in the middle of the night. Yeah, sure!'

Minto raised his eyebrows at the others before looking back in my direction. 'Just sayin', Alec. Just sayin'. No need to get your jocks in a knot. If you did nothing, you have nothing to fear, do you?'

And he kept his eye on me a second longer than he needed.

By the following morning, the whole event had a whiff of unreality about it. Had it not been for the shambles in my room, I might have assumed I'd dreamt it all. But when I opened my eyes the scene was still there – my meagre possessions scattered around the room as if someone had picked up the flat in the night, given it a shake and plonked it back down again.

Daniella was sleeping messily, mouth slightly open and one pale arm crooked upwards so her knuckles rested against her lips like she was giving them a kiss.

There was a loud belch from the other side of the wall and along with it came the reminder of Minto. 'Just saying, Alec. Just saying.' The comment kept jabbing me, poking me to make sure I didn't relax, didn't get complacent. And careless.

I got out of bed and went over to the window, peering down to where Minto's motorbike was perched against the kerb, the curve of the petrol tank like a big, fat smile.

'What exactly's going on in that pea-sized brain of yours?'

I looked over to the bed where Daniella was grinning at me. She hadn't moved – her fingers were still bent in the same position near her mouth and the outlined sprawl of her legs was visible beneath the duvet; the tip of her big toe peeking out of the end of the cover like it was on surveillance. Same sleepy position, but she was awake now as if the power button was on and all her dials aglow.

'I'm contemplating stuff that's far too complex for you to understand,' I told her, going over there. I landed on top of her, the duvet forming the meat in our cosy little sandwich.

'Is that right?' She struggled to shift to a more comfortable position, and I figured that quick thrust of hers against my crotch was no accident. She nodded towards the window. 'What were you looking at?'

'The weather. The street,' I said. A brief pause. 'Checking if Minto's bike was there.'

'Of course it'd be there – it was his disgusting belch that woke me up!'

'*Some*one's belch.'

'You think it might have been sweet little Sindy, do you?'

'No!' I laughed, digging my fingers into her ribs so she'd wriggle underneath me. 'I just mean it could have been anyone. It's pretty much open house at Minto's.'

She took control of my wrists and rolled me over, so we were side by side. 'I wonder how he's feeling about the late-night visit,' she said. 'You reckon the police found anything?'

'Sadly not. As Black said, if they'd found anything, he wouldn't still be here. He'd've been busted.'

'Shame he wasn't then.'

'Damn shame,' I said. 'Mind you, he didn't look pleased to have been put in the drug squad spotlight.'

Daniella's blue eyes got bigger: 'You've already seen him today? When?'

'No, last night in the kitchen.'

'Last night? Why didn't you say?'

'Ah, I was tired and…' I shrugged: I didn't even know why I'd kept it from her. 'I think I was trying to put it out of my mind.'

'Why?'

'He was pissed off.'

'Well, of course he was. Everyone was.'

'No, I mean he was pissed off that somebody had grassed him up.'

'Oh.' A line formed between her eyebrows. 'Do you think someone did then?'

'Must've. Can't have been a lucky guess really, can it?'

Her gaze drifted towards the window as she mulled it over. 'I wonder who.'

'There must be plenty of possibilities.'

She looked off into the distance again and I probably should have left it.

'Maybe it was someone who got fed up of Minto playing the hard man,' I said. 'Someone who doesn't like the way Minto treats his girlfriend.'

'Mm.'

'Maybe someone who got pissed off at the way he treats his flatmate and his flatmate's property.'

Daniella looked back at me and then to the plywood screen still holding my door together. She passed me a smile.

I didn't need to say any more – obviously I didn't – but despite all that, I couldn't resist a smug little nod that proclaimed, 'Yeah. I did that!'

Chapter 15

Neither Daniella nor I said it out loud, but it was no co-incidence that we found ourselves, the following Friday, somewhere that Minto definitely wouldn't be. His bulk might have cast a shadow over half of Swansea, but I was pretty sure we'd be safe seventy ks away at my folks' place.

I decided against giving Mum and Dad advance warning of our plans. I figured if they found out I was not only going to pay them a visit but would arrive with a girl in tow Mum would have a conniption fit in all the excitement.

We parked the Marina outside the front gate, and I saw Daniella look all around as she undid her seatbelt, taking in the thirties terraces, the dishevelled gardens, the seen-better-days cars. Even though it was still late summer, there was a wintery gloom about the place, as if the sun's full warmth could never stretch quite as far as these rail-side streets.

'Isn't this nice?' Daniella said, a bit too cheerily.

I knew instantly she saw me as some sort of poor relation, and I didn't bother answering.

'Are you sure they won't mind me just calling in with you?' she said as we got out of the car. 'I feel I should have brought flowers or something.'

'Mum will be too busy gushing over you to worry about whether you've come bearing gifts.'

Daniella gave me a teasing smile. 'You mean I'm not just next in a long line of girlfriends turning up at your door?'

'Most of them only get as far as my country club. They rarely get parental visiting rights. You should feel honoured.'

'Better be on my best behaviour then,' Daniella said, closing the gate.

As I struggled to get my key in the lock, I turned to her. 'Now, remember they're not expecting me, so I've no idea what the situation will be in there. But can I just apologise in advance for absolutely everything they say or do? I hope you aren't expecting much.'

'Alec!' she laughed, thumping me on the arm. 'Don't be so mean – I'm sure they'll be lovely.'

'See? You've already built up your expectations to unattainable levels,' I said.

The front door flew open almost yanking my arm out of its socket.

Dad stood there, looking like he'd be caught with his pants down. 'Oh,' he said. 'I wondered what all the noise was.'

'Us, Dad.'

Daniella gave him a big smile and held out her hand. 'Hi, there. I'm Daniella, a friend of Alec's.'

Dad fumbled his hand from his pocket. 'Jim,' he muttered.

'Oh, look who's here!' Mum said, emerging from the kitchen. She hurried out to give me a kiss then stood smiling at Daniella while I made the introductions.

It was suddenly very cramped in our hall, but Dad soon disappeared upstairs.

The intensity of Mum's fluster would have probably registered on the Richter Scale, but I was at least relieved to see her looking her old self, rather than the ravaged person I'd left behind a few weeks earlier.

Mum clearly couldn't wait to get us sitting down with a mug of tea in our hands. I wondered how long she'd been hanging out for a cosy little scene like this again. Only Jill Mitchell had had this treatment before.

Once the potted life story had been wrung from Daniella, Mum homed in on present day and Daniella explained about her food technology course. I could see Mum taking in everything about her: the clean hair, the polished nails, the Osmond teeth – all that and career ambitions too. Mum's smile seemed to get wider with each snippet until she looked almost giddy with approval.

'And have you got a nice place to live?' Mum asked her.

I knew all too well where this was leading.

'Yeah, not bad,' Daniella said. 'But the kitchen's tiny. Barely space to boil an egg!'

'Oh, I'm sure it's nicer than Alec's,' Mum said, right on cue. 'His place is absolutely filthy. I honestly don't know what...ooh, that reminds me!' She turned to face me, finally. 'Someone from the flat phoned for you – about an hour ago.'

'Really?' I said. It was strange: I hadn't mentioned my plans to any of the others. 'Who was it? Stobes? Deep voice, London accent?'

'Was it him?' Mum said, pausing as she stood to clear the cups. 'No, I'm sure it was the other one, Mintie. Daniella? Can I get you more tea?'

'No, thanks. I'd better go see my parents.'

'It wouldn't have been Minto, Mum,' I said. 'It was probably Black. Thick valleys accent.'

'No, it was Minto. He's the nasty one, isn't he? It was definitely him.'

Something unpleasant shifted in my stomach. 'But how could he have got your number?'

'I don't know, love, he didn't say.'

'I never told any of them I was coming,' I said.

Daniella and I slid our eyes to one another.

'Well, anyway, he wouldn't leave a message,' Mum said, placing the cups in a stack. 'Just said he's really looking forward to seeing you when you get back.' She reached across for the teaspoons. 'So, that was nice of him, wasn't it? Maybe he's not so bad, after all.'

The sun was already over the yardarm by the time Dad emerged from the garage later. I was at the kitchen table, reading the sports section and sucking on a beer. I'd invited Daniella over for dinner, but Mum had put the kibosh on that by making the shock announcement that she had people coming over.

I watched the back of Dad's head while he stood at the sink, trying to get the engine oil off his hands. 'Trouble with the car?' I said.

'No. Just maintenance: that way, it won't give us any trouble.'

'Right.'

'Not seeing that new girlfriend of yours?' he said.

'Yeah, she's picking me up in a while. We're heading into town.'

He nodded and I watched him pick up his bits and pieces from the windowsill. He always put items on in the same order: first the wedding band, then his gold signet ring and finally his watch. I wouldn't have a clue what Dad's favourite colour was, or how old he was when he started driving, yet something as personal as putting on his jewellery and I could pick him out in any line-up.

'You're not staying to help entertain these friends of Mum's then?' I said.

'No. They're from church. I don't know them.'

I almost choked on my bottle. 'Since when has Mum been a God botherer?'

Dad was about to reply when Mum appeared in the doorway, wearing a stiff-looking black dress and jacket. What with the scraped back hair and the severe expression, she looked more professional mourner than party host.

'What are you two still doing here?' she said.

I nodded towards the clock. 'Daniella's not picking me up for another hour.'

'Well you can't stay here,' she said, 'I need you both out.'

Dad and I exchanged a glance in a rare moment of shared inconvenience.

'Can't I just stay out the way?' I said, getting up.

'No, Alexander, you can't!' She put a French stick onto a bread board then went and filled a jug with water. 'I told you I was having people over, so you'll just have to make yourself scarce.'

I looked over her shoulder at the food extravaganza. 'Is that all you're feeding them? Jeez, you'll be all done by seven!'

'Alexander! Just go, will you?' she said, manhandling me from the room. She looked past me at Dad. 'Jim, can you take him out with you? I want the pair of you out from under my feet. Now!'

And with that, we were ousted from the family home and forced to drown our sorrows at the local pub.

The number of times Dad and I had gone out for a pint together could be counted on one hand. And without Mum, almost never. So, the two of us in The Hollybush had us well out of our comfort zones. It felt like being on a first date.

Once we'd got our drinks, Dad chose a corner booth, as far away from the jukebox and slot machines as possible. As we slid into the seat together, I already had my chosen topic for the evening up my sleeve.

'When did Mum start showing an interest in the church then?' I asked, taking a sip from my pint.

We were a family of fierce atheists as far as I was aware: growing up, there hadn't been so much of a whiff of Sunday School for me, so I'd assumed our disbelief in higher powers was cast in stone – for all of us.

'Oh gosh, well it was a few months ago she started going to services,' Dad said, 'but it didn't last long. I mean, she doesn't go any more.'

'So, what about these church friends of hers?'

'They're some sort of breakaway group from what I can tell,' he said. 'I don't think any of them goes to regular services now.'

Dad didn't say any more; just kept staring down at his drink like he had a secret tucked under his beer mat. Turned out he did, too.

'It's séances,' he said.

I gave him a double take.

'That's what they do, back at the house.'

'No! You're kidding!'

'She says it's...communing with the other side.' He took a sip of beer. If he had an opinion about it, I didn't sense it from his tone. He just announced it, matter of fact, like he'd just said she enjoyed watching tennis.

'So, they're into Ouija boards and spirits and stuff like that?'

Dad sat back in his seat. He furrowed his brow and looked into the distance as if this was the first time he'd really thought about it. And perhaps it was. 'She says it's serious; not something they do for fun. It's...' He shook his head. 'I don't know what it is to be honest, but it's obviously important to her.'

'Christ!' I said.

It made me uneasy, thinking about what all these snippets might add up to. It was as if the old dependable mum was slipping away and was slowly being replaced by someone new. Someone weird.

'Presumably the séances are about Gina again,' I said.

Dad visibly flinched at the G-word. It always made him prickly. He swept up his drink. 'What do you mean 'again'?'

'Well, you know.'

He looked me in the eye, like he was daring me to continue; defying me to venture down this no-through road. 'No, Alexander, I don't.'

It was often like this with me and Dad: we didn't go in for long discussions yet sometimes we'd get locked into these ridiculous back-and-forth battles where neither of us would give an inch. We used to get on fine when I was little, according to Mum, but she reckons I've grown up too much like him. Actually, nothing could be further from the truth – Dad and I are light-years apart – and possibly in different galaxies too.

'C'mon, Dad,' I said. 'You know Mum's never really got over Gina.'

He shifted in his seat, smoothed down his trouser legs. I could almost hear the squeak of his discomfort.

'Well, I s'pose we've all had problems dealing with it.'

I let the comment go. 'D'you ever go into Gina's room?' I said. 'Have you set foot in there lately?'

'The spare room.'

'All right, the spare room. The one Gina was going to have. When was the last time you went in there?'

'I have no idea.'

'Well, maybe you should take a look.'

I watched him avoid eye-contact with me.

'It's probably time we painted over those pink unicorns, I know that much,' he said, risking a brief smile.

I looked away. 'There are no unicorns, Dad. We redecorated. Years ago.'

He paused. 'Oh. I hadn't realised.'

'No, well why would you?' I took a swig from my pint.

There was a silence – a kind of pivot in time where the conversation could have tipped either way.

'Meaning?' Dad said.

'Meaning, you were away when we did it. As usual.'

Amongst the amicable chatter of the pub, a swelling bubble of discontent had formed at our table. I could feel the throb of it, like a blister about to burst.

'I had to be away. I was earning money,' he said. 'For the family.'

I placed my glass on the table with more of a thump than intended. The conversation, together with the beer was giving me gut rot. The longer the silence stretched, the further I felt us getting from one another.

I leaned forward. 'Well, you're not away now, are you? You're supposed to be here for her. So, how come it's still me that Mum has to turn to and not you?'

I watched as Dad continued to avoid me. He shifted his empty glass to sit more centrally on the beer mat. Everything had to be just-so with him. Of all the things he could've cared about, he always chose things that didn't matter – the order you put on your rings; the space around a beer mat, the cleanliness of a barely used car. It was as if he'd got everything topsy-turvy: manners; neatness; order; routine, these were Dad's rules. But unity, trust, family, loyalty – he didn't seem to have the same need for them.

'Look, Dad,' I said. 'I'm not trying to…I just want to be honest with you.'

He still didn't answer. We were a mirror image of each other: hunched over our drinks, heads down. Nothing new for me, but it wasn't how Dad normally looked. It was like his internal frame had snapped along the way and now he seemed, suddenly, vulnerable.

'Dad,' I said, again. 'I didn't mean...it's just that Mum really needs…'

'Hey! Mr Johnston. Hi, Alec,' Daniella bent down, aiming a cheery kiss at me. 'Your mum said I'd find you here.'

It was shocking to be pulled from the moment. She stood there, hovering above us as I tried to mentally retrace my steps and figure out what I was meant to be doing.

'You ready?' she said when I looked at her. 'I'm parked on a loading zone so can we…' Her eyes swept to my glass and she made a gesture for me to hurry up.

Even with all her 'shift your arse' cues I couldn't snap into action; it was like my brain had frozen over. Dad hadn't moved either – he hadn't looked at Daniella, let alone acknowledged her.

'Alec?' she said, again.

I finally managed to stand up.

Daniella hesitated, looking between Dad and I, perhaps waiting for him to lift his head to say goodbye. But he sat there, not moving.

'See you later then…Mr Johnston,' she said.

I knew she'd get nothing, so I physically turned her around and guided her towards the door. I remembered to mutter a 'See ya, Dad,' as I walked away.

Daniella turned to me as we headed towards the exit. 'Everything all right?'

'Let's just go.'

'Okay,' she said. 'Hey, d'you want to try that new bar in…'

'Daniella, I just need to go and see Dad a minute.'

'But I'm parked on a loa...'

'Yes, a loading zone! I know! So, move the car – or don't – just do whatever you want. I need to go back and see Dad.'

She blinked back at me, open-mouthed like she didn't know who I was anymore. I watched a whole host of expressions flit across her face. It was another pivotal moment. I really didn't know which way it was going to go.

'You've got two minutes,' she said, looking me in the eye. 'Then I'm off.' She spun on her heels without waiting for a response and disappeared outside.

I had no idea what I was going to say to him – or if I was going to say anything at all – but as I headed back to the table, I felt this overwhelming sense of sadness.

'Dad?' I perched on the chair opposite him, addressing that now familiar spot on his head.

'You should go, Alexander.' It was hard to hear him over the loud chatter, but I could pick out enough in his tone to know he wasn't annoyed.

'Look, I get that it was hard for you too,' I said. 'I do. I understand.'

I don't know what I expected. Perhaps I'd watched too many soaps and was waiting for him to reach across and put his hand on my shoulder. But there was nothing. Just a continuation of the long-running silence.

'Does that girlfriend of yours know?' he said, finally, nodding towards the door.

'Does she know what?'

He slid his eyes to me. 'About her predecessor. About Jill: what with all this new-found, heartfelt honesty of yours.'

He might as well have just thumped me in the gut: the wind was sucked out of me.

I stood up so fast the chair tipped behind me. 'Christ, Dad!' I said, spitting the words at him. 'Christ! How could y…fuck you!'

I gave him one final look, one chance to redeem himself. But there was nothing in his expression that gave me even a sliver of hope.

Chapter 16

'Alec, my man! How's it hanging?'

I was barely awake: it seemed only a few minutes since I'd come back from the night out in the city with Daniella – the one preceded by the disastrous date with Dad.

Now I was in Mum's hallway, holding the receiver to my ear, trying to make sense of the voice.

'Minto?' I said. 'What do you want at this unearthly hour on a Saturday morning?'

There was a gruff laugh. 'It's early, is it?'

'It's still dark, man!'

'Is it?' he said, laughing again. 'I haven't been to bed yet. But if it's pre-dawn, it would explain why Sindy's flaked out buck-naked in my room.'

I faltered at the image, struggling to take up the reins of the conversation again. 'So, is something wrong?'

'Well, Alec,' he said, suddenly more serious. 'I didn't want to worry your very helpful mother with this, but there was no rent money for Mr Patel from you. It was odd: Stobes had left his, as had Black, but there was sweet F.A. from Mr Alec Johnston. And our poor Mr Patel has six unhealthy mouths to feed.'

I rubbed my eyes, trying to wake up and shift my brain into gear. 'I left it though,' I told him. 'I put it in the envelope with everyone else's before I left. Thirteen quid.'

'What can I say, mate? It wasn't there. But don't worry: I put it in for you again. So that's twenty-six you owe me.'

'What? It wasn't there last week?'

'Nah. Remember I told you?'

He was lying through his fucking teeth, but I knew I couldn't say it.

'We'd better talk about it when I get back,' I said.

'Yep. Can't afford to slip behind, Alec. Especially with the rent on the up from next week.'

'Eh? The rent's going up as well?'

'Cost of living, I guess. Profit margins. Perhaps Mr Patel has got himself a seventh mouth to feed.' There was a pause. 'So, when are you coming back?'

'Later.'

'I know that, Einstein, but when, exactly?'

'I dunno. Why?'

'Just wondering,' he said. 'I've got a bit of a gathering. Saturday night an' all that. People might spill out to the hall, the kitchen, that kind of thing. Just wanted to make sure you wouldn't be using your room – wouldn't want the noise to disturb you.'

There was a basic padlock on my door but given half the door was a temporary plywood screen, I didn't fancy my chances on the security front.

'I guess I'm likely to be there later,' I said, changing tack. I could hear in the pause he knew I was bullshitting. 'Don't worry about the noise, though,' I added. 'I'm fine with that.'

'That's the way, Alec,' he said. 'Live and let live.'

There was a click as he hung up the phone and I was left there, grasping in the dark, to work out the real purpose of the call.

The early-morning discussion meant my whole day was thrown out of whack. By the time I stumbled out of bed, Dad was already at the shops, and Mum was in the kitchen, splattered with flour and surrounded by baking tins.

'Good morning!' she said. 'Or, should I say: good afternoon?'

'Mm.'

'I was going to make something for you to take to Daniella's tonight,' she said. 'What time are you off?'

'I dunno.' I stretched and yawned. 'Hopefully not late – I want to head back to Swansea as soon as I can.'

'Why's that, love?'

'Just stuff to do.'

I wasn't about to tell Mum about the early morning call, even though it had been eating away at me. The rent was one thing, but why was Minto so interested in whether I'd be back for his party? He'd never alerted me to gatherings before and it definitely had nothing to do with him being neighbourly. If it hadn't been for the meal at Daniella's, I'd've dashed back to Swansea before any shenanigans got started.

I leaned over and dipped a finger into one of Mum's mixing bowls. 'So, how did your church friends enjoy their evening?' I said.

'Yes, thank you. It was very nice.'

I did another taste test, just to be sure. 'And what do you lot talk about? The state of the chapel roof? What the bishop's hiding under his cassocks?'

'Don't pretend you don't know,' she said, pouring mixture into the tins. 'Your dad told me that you talked about it.'

I put up my hands in surrender. 'Yeah, we did.' I continued poking and prodding in the mixing bowls. 'So, wouldn't seances be seen as the devil's work?' I said. 'All that chanting and hand-holding.'

'No, Alexander.' She wiped her hands on her apron. 'And if you're just going to mock, I'd rather not discuss it. It's not a board game with dice and plastic counters. It's serious. And very moving, actually.'

It was a knee-jerk reaction to tease her. Because, if I really thought about all these changes, it scared the pants off me. Scrape the surface, and it was as if nothing was enough for her anymore. She was filling gaps in her life, stuffing trinkets and mumbo-jumbo into the cracks of her existence. All this hoarding and gathering and communing: it was like she was trying to prop up her world with spirits and otherness because she'd suddenly realised her real world was threadbare.

'Gina was with us,' she said, putting a hand on my arm. 'She was here.'

I looked back at her.

'I think she's been restless. Maybe it's why I've been so restless too... Anyway, it felt wonderful to know that she's watching over us.'

'Right,' I said, looking away. 'And what does Dad say about all this?'

I sensed Mum watching me. 'Why d'you ask?' Her tone had changed. 'What happened with you two last night? I knew something was up as soon as he came back from the pub. He barely opened his mouth.'

'That's nothing new.'

She pursed her lips then went over to the sink. 'Seriously, love. What's up?'

I shrugged. 'I guess a few home truths were tossed around.'

'What sort of home truths? I wish you wouldn't drag up all your old complaints.'

'Oh, don't worry, there were things he didn't need to drag up too.'

'Such as?'

I looked down. 'It doesn't matter.'

Mum came over to me, lowered her voice. 'Don't be too hard on him,' she said. 'Dad's still finding his way.'

She went back to her tins and her mixtures, clattering trays, making herself busy. 'I mean, if Dad could talk about…but he can't. Never has. And now, I think…it's probably too late.' She swallowed, then looked up with a determined smile. 'And that's fine with me. It's fine.' She brushed away a loose hair and looked down at the bowls. 'What d'you reckon, love? Chocolate or vanilla?'

I went over and put an arm around her: she looked like she could really use one. 'Why don't you pick what *you* like?' I said. 'Try putting yourself first for once.'

She chuckled at the strange notion and reached for the cocoa tin. 'Your father's favourite,' she said. 'I'll make chocolate.'

Chapter 17

The atmosphere remained tense between me and Dad for the rest of the day, so rather than ask for a lift, I took the train to Daniella's house. It involved two changes, a long wait and a twenty-minute walk from the station, but such was the price of making my point.

Their place looked even more imposing in the late evening sun than it had when I'd taken her home that first night. I looked beyond the manicured front lawn to the huge windows on the first floor: those rooms would have big-ass views, not only of the distant coastline but of the hills beyond. I imagined an antique brass telescope in the window and Daniella's dad, all monocled and sailing-capped, keeping an eye on marine movements.

It struck me, as I wandered up the gravelled path, how gaping our differences were. This house was only one part of it, but in every aspect, we were at opposite ends of a vastly different spectrum. She had so much going for her. I had so little.

I licked my palms and quickly flattened my hair as I stood at the front porch.

'Hey, you!' Daniella said, as she threw open the door. She ran a hand over my black shirt as I walked into the hall. 'Nice!' she said. 'Very Jean-Jacques Burnel.'

I certainly hadn't picked her to be a Stranglers fan, but I took it as a compliment.

'Come through,' she said, leading me past a wide staircase. She whispered: 'Let's get the meeting-of-the-parents out the way first, shall we?'

There was a glance down at my empty hands and I realised they should've been filled with Mum's baking. I could see the tin still sitting on the hall table. I started to explain but Daniella clearly had other things on her mind. She lowered her voice again. 'Now, don't mention anything about the flat and who you live with,' she said. 'The last thing they need to know is that you're mixed up with a bunch of bikies.'

'I'm hardly mixed up with them, they're just –'

'Just keep them out of the conversation,' she hissed. 'I'll...explain later.' She took a breath and reverted to her normal voice. 'Anyway, come through,' she said.

The house reminded me of one of those grand old seaside bed and breakfasts, with rooms every which way and far-into-the-distance hallways. We went through a glass panelled door at the very back of the house which opened to a kitchen the size of Manhattan. A fair-haired woman in black looked up from her pastry making: I wasn't sure if this was the maid or the mother.

'Oh, you must be Alec,' she said, going over to the sink to wash her hands. She wiped them and stuck one out to me. 'I'm Liz,' she said. 'Daniella's mother. It's lovely to meet you.'

'Hi. Good to meet you too.'

She opened another door, off to the side. 'Larry,' she called. 'Larry! Come in here and say hello.'

No monocle or sailing hat, after all: Daniella's dad was dressed in a white polo shirt, dark trousers, neat deck shoes – tanned and toned and clearly making the most of his comfortable lifestyle.

'Nice to meet you, Alec,' he said, giving me the once-over. He did a good job of keeping the smile on his face, but I could almost taste his disapproval. I definitely wasn't what he'd had in mind for his little girl.

'I'll just put this in the oven then we can go through to the lounge,' Daniella's mum said. 'Can you sort out drinks, Larry?'

'Will do. Come in and take your jacket off, Alec. What's your tipple?'

They weren't a bad bunch, but the set up felt too plastic wrapped for my liking. And I was clearly something of a novelty as far as they were concerned. I got the impression my predecessors were good college boys who did well at rowing and wore blazers for dinner. The more information I was asked for, the more I felt like Exhibit A in Son-in-Laws-To-Avoid.

It was into this slowly collapsing scene that Daniella's brother Mike appeared.

'Oh, there you are,' his mum said, looking at her watch as he came through the door. 'I was afraid you were going to miss dinner.'

I had to smile: they were such a six-on-the-dot sort of family.

'Sorry, got held up,' Mike said, shuffling off his coat. He made an impressively determined effort not to see me.

'Mike – let me introduce Alec,' Larry said, getting up. 'Alec, this is our eldest, Mike.'

I went over with the obligatory outstretched hand.

'Yeah, we met,' Mike said, eyeballing me as we shook hands.

'Oh well, there we are then,' Larry said.

The parents headed off to the kitchen while Mike sprawled himself on the sofa. 'Dad give you that message from Simon?' he said to Daniella.

She immediately flushed so I assumed Mike's tidbit was especially for my benefit.

'Yes, thanks.' Daniella smiled across at me. 'Someone I was at school with.'

I nodded.

'He's going out with my friend, Lisa,' she added.

A silence hovered.

'So, I was talking about you earlier,' Mike said, turning to me. He picked at the seam of the sofa arm, like he was deep in thought.

'Yeah?'

'Yes, Phil Harcourt was telling us where he knew your name from. Remember? The guy with the ponytail who spoke to you at the pub?'

'Alec already said he didn't remember,' Daniella said.

'Ah yeah but then we remembered *why* Alexander's name was so familiar,' Mike said. His eyes drilled into mine. 'It's because you were the one involved with Jill...Jill...now, what was her surname?'

'Mitchell.'

'Jill Mitchell, that's right!' he said, slapping his palm on the arm rest. He tilted his head to one side, like he was suddenly overcome with sympathy. 'Terrible about all that, eh?'

'Yeah.'

Daniella looked from one to the other of us. 'What was?' she said, reeled right in just as intended. 'What happened?'

Mike looked at me, then furrowed his brow like he was struggling to recall. 'Didn't she...'

'I got you a lager,' Larry said, opening the door and presenting Mike with a chilled glass and a bottle. 'Hope that's okay.'

'Yes. Cheers, Dad.'

'Right – I've been charged with getting you lot to the dinner table,' Larry said, looking around at us. 'Shall we go on through?'

I stood up and followed the rest of the family but just before we went through the door, Mike put a hand on my shoulder to stop me. 'Xander,' he said.

'Mm?'

There was a pause as he waited for the others to disappear.

'We both know you're not being straight with my sister so let's cut the bullshit, shall we?'

I blinked at him, my heart thumping. 'I dunno what you're –'

His voice was low, his speech fast: he wanted to have his say before anyone came looking for us. 'Don't even try it,' he said. 'You've got history. And, as I'm sure you're well aware, the last thing our mother needs right now is the whiff of scandal.'

I wanted to put a hand up, ask what the hell he meant about his mother, but he kept powering on like a freaking army tank.

'So, here's the deal,' he said. 'You can either front up with Daniella or if you won't, I'll do it for you. Understood?'

'Come on, you two!' Larry shouted from the other room. 'The football discussion can wait till later.'

'Understood?' Mike said again, holding me back.

'I've got nothing to hide,' I told him. 'I'll talk to Daniella. In my own good time.'

He paused, clearly sizing up what his response should be. How we'd got into this ridiculous mental arm-wrestle I had no idea. 'Better make it soon,' he said. 'I'm sure you'd rather her get your version of events than mine.'

'What are you two doing?' Daniella said, appearing in the doorway. 'The food's on the table.'

We followed her without speaking.

'Everything all right?' she whispered to me.

'All fine,' I said.

And I put the whole discussion away with no particular plans to ever get it out again.

By the time grapes and a cheeseboard appeared on the table, we'd exhausted all conversation. I knew everything there was to know about Larry's orthodontic business, about liberal party politics (thanks, Liz), and why Mike was clearly destined to be something big in the city.

As soon as a silence descended, Mike leaned back in his seat and looked at me, a glass of port held close to his chest. I knew the little bastard had just been biding his time.

'I'm still trying to get it all clear in my mind, Alec,' he said. 'Sorry if I'm being dense but where did you say you took your A' levels: Westchurch or Bishops?'

'Bishops.'

'Right,' he said, drawing out the word like it was far too complex to grasp in one go.

'I came away with two Cs and a D,' I added. 'In case you need to get that clear too.' The sharp edge to my tone got the Hursts shifting in their seats.

'Not bad given you changed schools halfway through,' Mike said. 'Unusual step, swapping schools mid-course.'

'Not really.'

'Why did you change?' Daniella said. I could tell she was using everything in her power to sound casual, non-confrontational – just to balance out Magic Mike's more aggressive line of enquiry.

'I didn't like Westchurch, that's all. It was full of...' I glanced in Mike's direction. 'Well, you know the sort.'

'And of course, you were friends with that girl, weren't you?' Mike said. He was like a dog with a freaking bone. 'That would have made things quite tricky at Westchurch. I remember it was a big deal at the time.'

I held his gaze. 'So, how's the old place these days? You're having to do retakes, I hear.'

'He did wonderfully well with his A' levels,' Larry said. 'But he knows he can do even better with another year's study.' He paused to take a sip of port. 'Mike'll get the grades he wants this year: I've no doubt about that.'

The blip that followed was just enough for me to get to my feet and tell them I had to be up early. Mike looked gutted to have not managed to pull the stuffing out of my story, but I had no doubt he'd come at me from another angle next time. It was all in the planning. I just needed to stay one step ahead of him.

Chapter 18

After the meal at her folks' house, Daniella lent me her Marina to drive back to Swansea. The first term was still a week or so away, so she was in no hurry to return to Bristol, and she knew I was desperate to check the flat after Minto's odd message.

I'd called into Mum and Dad's to gather my things and it must have been the small hours when I finally turned into Oakdale Terrace. I could hear the thump-thump of Minto's music system the minute I switched off the engine. In front of the house, all I could pick out were silhouettes: people leaning against walls; the tiny glow of a cigarette moving between hand and lips; leather-clad bikies standing around the cluster of motorcycles near our steps.

I hoped Minto would be inside rather than out: a welcoming party from him and his mob the minute I got out of the car was not what I needed. I'd parked a way down the street, but I had to make my approach eventually and the moment I got within shouting distance, I heard Sindy: 'Alec! You're back!' She came running down the street like a kid in her mother's cast-offs, barely able to run in the high heels.

'Hey, Sindy. How you doin'?' I kept my voice low in the hope she'd follow suit.

'Minto!' She gave an exuberant wave and shouted to the group in the front yard. 'He did come after all! Look!' She wrapped her arms around me, like I'd been away for years.

'Well, well, well, Mr Johnston,' Minto said, coming slowly down the steps to meet me. He held out a hand. 'Glad you changed your mind.'

We smiled at one another while we shook hands, as if the conversation had no subtext.

'Got a new set of wheels, have you?'

I followed his gaze. 'Just a loan.'

'Shame,' he said. 'Thought you'd come into money. Hoped you were about to clear your debts.' He rubbed the stubble on his chin, sizing up my reaction.

'We'll go over that later, shall we?' I said, nodding at my rucksack. 'I just want to go up and dump my stuff for now.'

He inhaled deeply and shook his head. 'I'm not worried, Alec,' he said. 'I know you're good for the money.' And he slapped a hand on my back like an over-zealous uncle. 'Get your gear sorted then join in the fun, eh? There's plenty of home-brew in the kitchen.'

Getting to the kitchen meant negotiating an assault course of heavy-petters on the stairs and tanked up smokers on the landing. I decided to bypass the home-brew and head straight to my room. The door was wide open, my tinpot padlock bent and broken on the floor. I took a breath, certain I'd be faced with at least one copulating couple on my bed. But when I strode in, loudly clearing my throat as I went, I realised it was empty. The immediate relief was overtaken by something else; something more unnerving. The bed hadn't been touched; in fact, nothing looked like it'd been touched. I turned around in the middle of the room, trying to work out if anything at all looked different. The only thing I spotted was my clock radio – its digits flashing red like they always did after a power cut.

'Hey, Alec! All right, mate?' Stobes poked his head around the door.

'Stobes!' I said. 'You don't know how my lock got busted, do you?'

He looked between the door and the padlock on the floor. 'Sorry, mate,' he said. 'It was shut last time I went past.' He glanced behind him and into the hall. 'Could be anyone though – I'm not sure even Minto knows half the bunch that are here. It's fucking bedlam.'

On cue, there was a crash in the kitchen, followed by laughter.

'Yeah!' I said. 'I see what you mean.'

There was no chance of any shut-eye, what with the noise and the fact I couldn't lock my door, so I followed Stobes out to the kitchen and sampled the home-brew. It tasted every bit as bad as it smelled, but I kept hold of my glass just to seem sociable.

Thankfully, people started heading off once the sun came up. Motorbikes fired up and roared off into the distance and the thudding bassline from Minto's room fell silent. Once I'd secured my door, I clambered into bed still dressed, and closed my eyes, only the sound of Sindy's bright chatter through the wall to disturb my peace.

If I'd had any doubts about the need to get shot of that flat, the scene I woke up to halfway through Sunday laid them all to rest. I'd had to wedge my door shut using a pile of magazines that I'd rescued from the back yard, but it was outside my room the real horrors began. As well as the sea of beer bottles and crushed fag butts, there was the unwelcome addition of condom packets, needles, used tissues and a few discarded pieces of underwear. There were stains along the wall that I didn't dare get anywhere near and parts of the carpet were so wet that you could see the brown liquid ooze when you trod on it. To top it off, I was greeted in the kitchen by a cowpat of vomit, its edges uneven where someone had apparently trodden in it and spread it towards the bathroom. The place stank of beer, piss and sick and it was like the whole house had morphed into the men's bog at Cardiff Central.

'Fucking hell,' said Black, stumbling into the room in his jocks. 'Look at the state of this place.' He sniffed the air and dry-retched. 'Got any air-freshener? It's absolutely honkin' in here.'

'I know. I was going to fix myself something to eat but I think I'll go out and grab a burger.'

'There's half a sausage on the floor outside my room if you're interested,' Black said in his cheery Welsh way. He paused a moment. 'At least I fuckin' hope it's a sausage.'

'All right, gentlemen?' Minto strode into the room, all leathered up for a burn on his bike. He flexed his fingers and adjusted his gloves. 'Good night, eh, lads?'

'Yeah, tidy,' Black said. 'Bit of cleaning to do though.' He zipped up his jacket and headed towards the door with Minto.

'Sindy's a trooper,' Minto said. 'She'll soon have it sorted.'

With a car sitting outside, I figured I could go elsewhere to eat. I'd also bought the weekend paper so I could scour the property pages in privacy and peace. At least, I would have if I'd been able to find the frigging keys. I searched through every pocket in my wardrobe; turned out all my bags, checked every drawer. Nothing, nada. I mentally retraced my steps at the party. Surely, I wouldn't have been stupid enough to put them down in the kitchen or the hall? I took a deep breath and ventured out of my room and into the stinking cesspit that was the rest of the house.

Sindy was in the kitchen, cleaning the sink. She was wearing a huge pair of floral rubber gloves and one of those classy nudie-aprons. While she was scrubbing away at a small stain by the plughole, the rest of the kitchen behind her remained an unholy crapfest.

'You seen any keys?' I said.

She turned around. 'Hi, Alec. Um...no. What did they look like?'

'Metal with long jagged edges. Usually fit into keyholes.'

Her whole face shone as she let out a laugh. 'I know that, silly! But were they on a keyring or anything?'

I tried to remember details, but the home-brew had fried my brain. I knew Daniella only kept a single key for the car, but I was sure it was attached to something.

Sindy furrowed her brow. 'Was there a horse or something on the keyring?'

'No, I don't...' And then it flashed into my mind: a sports car keyring. I'd laughed at the irony.

'Yeah, a black horse on a yellow background,' I said. 'Have you seen it?'

She looked delighted and took off her rubber gloves, all secretarial efficiency. 'Come with me.'

I hesitated before following her into Minto's room. I'd never been invited to the Inner Sanctum and I was wary about venturing in during his absence.

It wasn't as I'd imagined. I'd assumed heavy metal posters, bike ads, porno calendars, general petrolhead paraphernalia. But the walls were relatively uncluttered, apart from one three-part poster high up on the wall facing the bed. It was of two dark-haired birds, each wearing a white mesh top. They were both sitting, facing the camera, skirts hitched up to their thighs, no underwear. The girl on the right was sucking on her fingers, smiling like she'd had the shag of her life. The other had a bead of blood on her bottom lip.

'Oh, that's Minto's,' Sindy said, following my gaze. 'It's a bit rude but he loves it.'

The rest of the room was unremarkable: an el-cheapo wardrobe, a pair of decent speakers on the wall and an expensive looking amp and tape deck on the chest of drawers. I wondered where he kept that knife collection he was always bragging about.

Next to the double bed was a toilet roll with a bin at the side, an ashtray full of butts and a candle stuffed in an empty beer bottle. It could have been any guy's room. What was strange, perhaps, was that there was hardly any evidence of Sindy. She pretty much lived there, at least half the time, yet there was no femininity in the room. Apart from a flash of raspberry-pink on a huge black suitcase on the wardrobe. I figured that had to be hers.

'Is this the one?' Sindy said, holding up Daniella's key.

I took it from her. 'Thank Christ for that. Where did you find it?'

'It was just here,' she said, pointing to the table. 'It was with Minto's wallet and bike keys. I remembered seeing it when I was getting dressed.'

'Really?'

'He probably just found it at the party and was going to give it back when he saw you.' She jumped onto the bed and sat cross-legged, making her skirt ride up her thighs.

'I should go,' I said. 'I've got things to do.'

The smile fell from her face. 'Oh. All right. What are you up to?'

'Just...stuff.'

'What stuff?'

'I dunno,' I said. 'I've got to go out and get something to eat. The kitchen's hardly attractive, is it?'

'Sorry. I need to clean up the mess,' she said. 'At least Minto's not back till tonight so I have plenty of time.'

I headed for the door. 'I'd offer to help but...'

'It's okay,' she said, putting those massive rubber gloves back on. 'You shouldn't have to: Minto said you never wanted to come to the party in the first place.'

I placed the banana shake in front of her and put down my own coffee. I hadn't thought the idea through before suggesting it. If I had, I'd have probably dismissed the notion before I'd put my mouth into gear. Still, Sindy was delighted. It was a greasy dive of a place, but it was moments from the flat and everything was dirt-cheap.

'So, how did Minto know I didn't want to come to the party?' I asked. I liked to think I didn't have an ulterior motive for bringing her out with me, but it seemed too good an opportunity to waste.

'He said he rang you and that you sounded...worried. He said you didn't want to come to the party, but he was pretty sure you'd show up.'

'I was surprised when he rang,' I said, all matter of fact. 'I can't remember giving him my folks' number.'

'No, he had to ask Stobes.'

'Stobes. Yeah, of course.'

'How d'you think they make banana milkshakes?' she said, licking the froth off her straw. 'Bananas don't have any juice.'

'Guess they just mash 'em up.' I looked at the dayglo yellow of her glass. 'Don't think a fresh banana's gone near that one though. Just chemicals.'

She nodded and held it up to the light as if she was expecting to see them.

'Did Minto mention any rent money missing?' I said. 'That was why he rang. The money I'd left wasn't in the envelope.'

'Not sure,' she said, shrugging. She sucked up the bubbles around the glass. 'He doesn't really tell me those things.'

'Mm. What about Mr Patel – have you ever met him or does Minto go to his house to take the rent?'

'Who's Mr Patel?'

'The landlord. He owns the house.'

Her attention wandered as a chocolate fudge sundae floated past our table.

'He's an Indian guy,' I told her. 'Short and skinny.'

Her eyes scoured the menu board and I knew I was losing her.

'Sindy! Have you met him, or seen him at the house?'

Her whole body seemed to shrink as she registered my impatience. 'I don't know, Alec. Sorry. I don't think so.'

I stopped the waitress as she was headed past our table. 'Could we have one of those chocolate sundaes, please?' I said, pointing to the dessert that had captivated Sindy.

Sindy whooped and gave me a toothy grin. 'Thanks, Alec!'

'How d'you know it's for you?' I said.

She looked into her glass with a shy smile. 'Just hoped.' She drained the rest of her milkshake in a noisy finale. 'I don't think I've met any Mr Patels,' she said. 'Anyway, you've got it wrong. He doesn't own the house.'

'He does.'

'No. He definitely doesn't.'

'How d'you know?'

'Because...my dad does.'

I felt my jaw slacken as I looked back at her. 'What?'

'I don't know how it happened, or when he got it, but Dad said to me the other day when I was coming over: 'Make sure that lot are all looking after it. It's my money invested in that place now, so they'd fucking better.' She looked up and grinned. 'Sorry for swearing.'

As soon as dessert arrived, I knew it would be the last I'd get out of Sindy. But there was one more thing that needed to be squared away.

'Hey, Sindy – don't tell Minto about any of this conversation, okay? Not about us coming here, or about what we talked about or anything. D'you understand? It's important.'

'What about the key? He'll know that's gone.'

'Just tell him I asked if you'd seen it, so you gave it to me.'

'Well, that's true, anyway,' she said, a bead of chocolate sauce on her bottom lip.

I looked away.

'Is it a car key?' she said.

'Yes, why?'

'A brown car? That big one at the end of the road?'

'Yes.'

'He borrowed it,' she said. 'I saw him go out in it after the party.'

'What? You sure?'

'Yes, and he was gone ages.'

I looked back at her, tucking into her ice-cream – it was probably the best value ninety-five pence I'd ever spent.

Chapter 19

Sindy was back in the kitchen in her floral gloves. I'd read the paper, made a few phone calls but after her revelation about Minto using the car, the prospect of driving it again brought a fresh level of menace. I had no choice though: I said I'd be at the house at four.

Everything seemed normal as I sat in the driver's seat, but why wouldn't it? It wasn't my car so I wouldn't know if anything was out of place. I checked the glove box, the visors, under the seats – for what I wasn't sure. All kinds of scenarios rattled round in my head: from a car bomb under the chassis to a used condom between the back seats. Did he want to kill me or just mess up my life? I searched the interior for stashed cash, for hidden drugs, for hard porn, anything Minto could try to pin on me. But there was nothing. Perhaps he'd just fiddled with the brakes and I wouldn't know till I got to the bottom of Constitution Hill.

I turned the key in the ignition, wincing all the while in case I was about to be incinerated in a tangle of Marina metal. But no. The comforting purr of the engine was just as it should be.

I briefly picked up the folded *Evening Post* on the passenger seat, reminding myself of the address. 50 Ashton Crescent, Uplands. It was out of my price range, but I figured I might be able to knock 'em down. The new uni year was about to get going so this place was clearly too rich for most students' blood.

I put the car into first and flicked on the indicator. I was about to pull out when I checked my mirror and spotted Sindy, tearing down the steps of the house, flapping her arms at me. 'Alec, wait!' She was too far away for me to hear, but it wasn't difficult to lip synch her battle cry. I quickly switched off the engine, in case she was trying to warn me Minto had booby-trapped the car.

I'd obviously watched too many action movies, because when Sindy opened the passenger door she was all smiles. 'Can I come for a drive?' she said. 'I've never been in one of these cars.'

I looked at her and paused. 'It's a Marina, Sindy.'

'I know. But Minto's not back till tomorrow now so I've got ages to clean up. Please? Can I?'

I couldn't help thinking of the pile of vomit that would infest the kitchen for a bit longer, but it hardly seemed like Sindy's place to scrape it up.

'All right,' I said. 'Just to the shops and back. Then I have to go somewhere by myself.'

She put on her belt while I pulled out of the street. 'Is this where you're going by yourself?' she said. 'Ashton Crescent?'

I snatched the paper from her and tossed it into the back. 'No. Now which shop did you want to go to?'

She shrugged and looked into her lap. 'Whichever one you want. There's nothing I need.'

'We'll go to Gateways then. That's the nearest.'

Her head remained bent and she said nothing.

'Maybe I can get you some sweets,' I said. 'Or a *Smash Hits*. We might as well get something now we're out.'

Still nothing.

'Or do you want gum or some crisps?'

I looked over again and there was the faintest shake of the head. Then a sniff.

'Aw c'mon, Sindy. I didn't mean to snap at you – I was just in a bit of a hurry.'

She sniffed again and brought a hand up to her face.

'What's the matter?' I said. 'I've told you I didn't mean it.'

'You're moving out!' she said, still crying. 'You're leaving.'

'What?' The question came out so quietly, I don't think she heard. 'Why d'you think that?'

'I'm not stupid, you know. You all think I'm stupid, but I'm not. I know what a flat-hunting page looks like. I know why people circle addresses and write down the phone numbers. I'm not an idiot.'

'Hey, I know, I know. I never said you were. It's just...my business rather than yours or anyone else's. The place is probably taken so I doubt I'll be moving out anyway.'

'But you're looking. You want to move out.' She was shouting at me as if we were in the middle of a full-scale row.

I pulled over and watched the traffic go by, trying to decide what to say to her. I wanted to be honest, but I knew anything I said could and would be used as evidence against me. And Christ knew what would happen if Minto got so much as a whiff of it.

'I'm just...not very happy at the flat, Sindy. That's all.' It was the first time I'd said it out loud or admitted it to anyone – myself included.

'Why, though? It's not so bad. I know the wallpaper's old and the kitchen's hardly big enough for...'

'I don't think Minto wants me there,' I said. 'And seeing as I don't like it there much myself, why wouldn't I go?'

She ground the pads of her palms into her eyes and suddenly pushed forward and whacked her head on the dashboard – once, twice, three times.

'Sindy, stop it!' I pretty much had to grab her by the hair to stop her doing it again. 'What d'you do that for?'

'I don't want you to go,' she said, sobbing. 'Please don't go, Alec. I'll do anything you want, anything.'

I stop-started a whole host of responses but each time, it seemed like the wrong one. In the end, I just put an arm around her and let her cry against my shoulder.

It seemed ages later that I felt her weight shift as she lifted her head. I could still see the flash of red where she'd whacked her forehead.

'You okay now?' I said. Her sobs had calmed to a few hiccoughs. The normally pale skin of her cheeks was blotchy, red and strands of hair stuck to her nose and lips. I pulled one or two bits of hair away. 'Jeez, you're a right old snot fest,' I said.

It made her laugh which worsened the mess, so I grabbed Daniella's tissue pack from the shelf and took one out for her.

'Sorry,' she said. But her chin was still trembling.

'You'll be all right.'

The reassurance started her off again and I had to reach for a second tissue.

'I hate the thought of you going,' she said.

'Why? You hardly ever see me.'

She swallowed loudly, struggling to get the words out. 'But I know you're there.' More gulps and hiccoughs. 'And I don't know what I'll do if you're not.'

I nodded, holding my tongue against my teeth to stop myself probing more. It was better not to know, to not understand. Trouble was, I'd forced myself to believe one of only two scenarios: the first that Sindy was stupid and didn't know that Minto was just using her; the second that she *did* know what was happening but didn't really mind.

'Thing is, Sindy,' I said. 'I mightn't have a choice about moving. Like I said, Minto doesn't want me there.'

'He does! He wouldn't have let you move in otherwise. You, or Stobes or Black.'

She made it sound like we were the chosen ones.

'But if he's putting up the rent, I can't afford it anyway.' I said.

Her face brightened as she clutched at the sliver of hope. 'I'll talk to my dad. He won't put up the rent if I tell him not to.'

I looked at her and her face fell.

'It's not the rent being too expensive though, is it?' she said. 'Otherwise you wouldn't be going to see a place like Ashton Crescent. That's where the posh houses are.'

'No, it's not just the money,' I admitted. 'There's no point me staying somewhere I'm not comfortable. Minto kicked my door in when I was away, didn't he? It was broken into again before the party. Now he's saying I haven't paid the rent when I know I fucking well have. He took my…well, Daniella's car without telling me. How much am I supposed to put up with?'

She nodded and sucked her top lip.

'It's not like anyone there is a real friend, in any case,' I said.

The comment popped out before I could stuff it back in my stupid mouth. 'I didn't mean you,' I said. 'I meant the other guys.'

'S'alright. I know I'm not one of your friends.' She looked at me and attempted a smile. 'I'd like to be a friend though.'

'You already are, Sinds. Honest.'

The statement seemed to buoy her. 'Can I just come with you for now?' she said. 'To the house. I'll just stay in the car, but can I come there with you?'

'Why?'

'I dunno.' She shrugged. 'I guess I don't like the flat much either.'

'Was it really nice?' Sindy asked, injecting the question with as much gloom as she could muster.

'Ah, it was okay,' I said, putting my wallet back in the glovie.

'Probably got lots of students going for it, have they?'

'Mm…not so much. Term starts soon, so most students are sorted by now.'

I was aware of her watching me, studying every part of my face for clues; for signs, perhaps, of betrayal.

'It looks really nice,' she said, peering past me. 'Must be expensive.'

'Yep. That's probably why it's still available. It costs more than the flat, that's for sure.' I put my seatbelt on and started the engine. 'Did you change your mind about wanting something from the shop?' I said as we drove away.

'No.'

'Sure? I'm buying. Could be a once-in-a-lifetime opportunity. I don't get my wallet out very often, you know.'

She didn't answer straight away but was staring out of her side window. 'You got your wallet out at Ashton Crescent,' she said.

'What?'

'You got it out at the house. It was in your pocket when you went up, but you had it in your hand by the time you came out.'

We looked at one another.

'Like you'd needed to pay a deposit or something,' she said. She turned to her own window again and I could just pick out the irregular rise and fall of her stomach as she tried to stifle her tears.

Never before had I felt like such a shit.

Chapter 20

Daniella was about to head back to Bristol to start the final year of her course, so I was duty-bound to deliver the car back to her in Cardiff. It wasn't until I'd taken it for numerous outings that I accepted it wasn't booby-trapped. Minto probably had a laugh, watching me sweat every time I turned on the ignition. Maybe it was the only reason he ever borrowed it.

At least it wouldn't be for much longer, I reminded myself. Soon, very soon, I'd be a Minto-free zone.

Daniella gave me a wave as soon as she spotted me. When I saw how cold she looked, I wished I'd suggested meeting in a café rather than in Sophia Gardens. She didn't have a coat with her either – just a black polo neck sweater, jeans and pixie boots: clearly no match for the icy wind that had whipped up.

She gave me such a delicious hello that it made me realise how much I was going to miss seeing her when she went back to uni. Although we were only an hour or two away from each other, our meetings wouldn't have the spontaneity we'd enjoyed over the summer.

Despite the cold, Daniella insisted we go for a walk rather than agree to my suggestion and head for the nearest pub. We followed the river up to the weir, keeping close to one another to get warm.

It struck me how much happier I felt in Cardiff than I did in Swansea. There was no checking over my shoulder, no wincing at the sound of every motorbike; no minding what I said to who. But it also made me worry that the new place in Ashton Crescent wasn't far enough away from Minto. It was within spitting distance. Perhaps there wasn't anywhere in Swansea that was far enough away.

'Was everything okay at the party?' Daniella asked, slipping her hand into my jeans pocket as we walked.

'Not really. The door to my room was open and the padlock was busted.'

'Shit!'

'It was all as it was meant to be but...'

'Yeah, I know – someone had been in there.'

I carried on thinking aloud. 'And with Minto, it's not just what he might have taken as what he could've left.'

Daniella looked at me. 'How d'you mean?'

'I dunno. I'm just...if he suspects me for the drugs bust, which I think he does, he could try and get even, somehow.'

'He doesn't know anything about that,' Daniella said. 'How could he?'

I shrugged. 'Just a feeling. Christ knows what I was thinking, grassing him up like that. If I'd realised what a nutjob he was, I'd've kept my trap shut. Freakin' Apaches.'

Daniella was quiet for a moment. 'Y'know, my mum would do her crunch if she knew I was dating someone flatting with a bunch of bikies.'

'Aww. Why? Would she worry about me?'

Daniella almost choked. 'Ha! No! Mum's only concern would be her own pristine reputation. Didn't she tell you? She's running in the local elections. It wouldn't do for her to have anyone in the family associating with gangs and criminals.'

'Oh, right.' I thought back to Mike's warning about scandals. No wonder he didn't see me as ideal boyfriend material.

'Still, I think you did the right thing tipping off the police,' she said.

'It was worth a shot. If it *had* worked, Minto would be out of your hair by now, wouldn't he?'

I gave her a grim smile. 'Whereas he's become a freaking nit infestation instead.'

Daniella pulled me into her. 'Ach, he's all bluster,' she said.

'But that's just it: he isn't!' I said. 'He hangs out with the biggest crooks in Swansea. These are not people you want to mess with. Trust me, it's serious. They mean business.'

When Daniella didn't answer, I glanced across at her. All that sparkle had gone from her eyes and now she just looked pinched.

'Look, it's fine,' I said. 'You don't need to worry.'

'Sure!'

'No, I mean I have some good news.'

I hadn't intended to tell her yet: I'd wanted to save my announcement for a more significant moment, like when we were in bed together, but seeing as I'd put the fear of God into her, it seemed only fair to tell her there was light at the end of this murky tunnel.

'It just so happens,' I said, 'that I've found a new place.'

Her eyes widened and her lips formed a silent 'what?'

'I move in three weeks.'

She stopped and flung her arms around me like I'd just won *Sale of the Century*. 'Oh my God, Alec! That's fantastic!'

'It's just a room in a share house,' I said. 'But it's decent. Clean.'

'I don't care! It's away from Minto!' She pulled me into another tight hug. 'Thank God!' she said. 'You'll finally be free of the lot of them!'

Daniella kept the engine ticking over as she pulled up outside Mum and Dad's house. I undid my seatbelt and reached into the back seat for my bag.

'Have you told your mum you're moving yet?' she asked. 'She'll be so relieved: I think she hated you living there more than I did.'

'No, I wanted you to be the first on that particular scoop.'

She kissed me on the cheek. 'I'm touched,' she said. 'Thank you.'

I was hoping to enjoy a bit more of her gratitude, but she moved the moment along. 'Now, what's the name of this Indian place you mentioned for tomorrow?' she said. 'I'll book a table. Is eight okay?'

'Yep. It's called The Shish Mahal and it's near the roundabout, next to that new wine bar.'

'I'll never remember the name,' she said, searching the glove box for a pen. 'And draw me a map as well: I have no idea which roundabout you're on about.'

I could have told her there was no pen in the glove box: I'd scoured every inch of that car for Minto's booby-traps so I knew every nook and cranny. But then Daniella slid her hand below the glove box, to a narrow shelf where she took out a pen and a folded piece of paper. It was a secret space; one I hadn't seen, and I wondered if there were other hidden compartments I didn't know about.

'So, what was the address?' she said.

I reached past her and shoved my hand in the shelf, giving it a quick once-over.

'What are you doing?'

'Nothing. Just seeing if there was another pen,' I told her. 'I was gonna draw you a map.'

Drugs. That's what I'd been expecting my fingers to find, I realised. A little plastic bag full of pills or powder or weed. Just enough to get someone busted.

The fact I hadn't found anything brought me no comfort: I figured Minto had just been one step ahead of me in finding hiding spots.

Daniella was watching me as she held out the pen and paper. 'Come on, then. Draw me a map,' she said.

I took them from her and drew a few lines and arrows on the folded sheet. I sensed she was still watching me.

'What were you expecting to find?' she said. 'You seem awfully twitchy.'

'Nothing. Why?'

'It was like you were checking for something. Like you might have left something in here you didn't want me to find.'

'Like what for Christ's sake?'

'I don't know. You sure you haven't had some other woman in here?'

She said it in a jokey way, but I sensed there was a genuine query wrapped in there.

I looked up from my drawing. 'I think I'd remember if I had.'

'You weren't looking for discarded underwear or empty condom packets then?'

She held my gaze as I looked back at her.

'No, Daniella. I wasn't searching for abandoned knickers. I make sure all my conquests leave fully dressed. All right?'

'Glad to hear it,' she said.

And I handed her the sheet, cocky and smug, pretending all was well.

Chapter 21

Daniella had picked a table by the window, so I could see her, looking groomed and gorgeous, as I approached The Shish Mahal. I knocked on the big glass window and pulled a face at her. She glanced up briefly and went back to whatever she was reading.

The heaters were on full blast when I walked in. Even on a Sunday, the place was busy. The waft of Indian spices had my digestive juices limbering up as I walked towards Daniella. I couldn't wait to sit and eat.

'Hey,' I said, kissing the top of her head and taking the seat opposite her. 'You're here before me! My map was obviously extremely accurate and easy to read then.'

She didn't look up. 'Yeah, it was fine.'

I sat upright, like a toddler waiting for attention, but the seconds ticked by and she still refused to look at me.

I exhaled and leaned across the table. 'Okay, let's have it,' I said with a sigh. 'My mind-reading skills are shot. What have I done?'

She sat back in her chair and folded her arms. 'I don't know. You tell me.'

'Fuck, what is it *now*?' I muttered, just loud enough that she'd hear.

Daniella treated me to one of her withering looks.

'Can we not do this?' I said, gesturing between us. 'If you've got something to say, just say it. I can't stand these pointless mental games.'

She picked up the piece of paper she'd been studying and dropped it in front of me.

I recognised the squiggles and arrows of my directions and my attempts at drawing junctions.

'What's up with it?' I said. 'Did I miss a set of lights or something?'

'Turn it over.'

'Why?'

'Just turn it over, Alec.'

I did as I was ordered and looked down at the sheet.

It looked like a bad quality photocopy – a snippet from some old newspaper article. There were a couple of dozen words or so on the copied shred of paper, but my eyes sprang to three of them: Alexander David Johnston.

I glanced up at Daniella, confused. 'What the hell is this?'

'I don't know. I was hoping you could tell me.'

I skim-read the lines, immediately recognising what a tantalising little trail this would have been for Daniella. The article began mid-sentence where the clipping had been torn, catching the juiciest snippet.

'...a student at Westchurch High School in Cardiff. Witnesses reported seeing her leave the Agastino Cafe at Central Station with fellow pupil, Alexander David Johnston, but police have yet to establish...'

'How did you even get this?' I said.

'It was in my car, remember? It was the scrap piece of paper you used to draw the map on.' She snatched it from me and shook it in my direction. 'Is this what you were looking for when you reached into the glove box? Is this what you didn't want me to find?'

'No! Of course not. I didn't know it was there, did I?'

'You seemed to be checking for something.'

'I wasn't! Nothing like that anyway...I still don't know how this could have been in there.'

'Well you're the only one who's borrowed my car,' she said. 'And seeing as it's an article about you...I'd imagine you put it there, even if it was by accident.' Her throat moved as she swallowed. 'I'm guessing you didn't mean me to see it. That's why you were suddenly so edgy and looking for pens in weird places!'

'Daniella, look. I haven't got a clue what it's about.'

'You went to that school though – it's your name. Your full name. It has to be about you.'

'Look at me,' I said, reaching across and grabbing her hands. I held her gaze and chose my words carefully. 'I do not know where this article is from or who put it there. Maybe it's a joke. Someone's typed it out and printed it to look like it's been torn from a newspaper. But it's nothing to do with me. At this moment I know as much about it as you do.'

Her eyes continued to bore into mine, clearly looking for signs of deceit and double-dealing. 'So, it's a complete mystery then, is it?'

'A complete mystery.'

The waiter arrived. 'Good evening sir, madam. Can I tell you what we have on our specials board ton –'

'No, can you just bring us some poppadums?'

The waiter beat a hasty retreat, but he was very closely followed by Daniella who shot from her seat, swiped up her bag and headed to the ladies.

The longer I sat looking at the sheet, the more shakily my heart rattled. It could only have been Minto. All that time I'd been looking for weed or for planted weapons; for dodgy brakes and faulty steering. But this was how he'd decided to play it. Sneaky. Personal.

It felt like someone had lit a furnace in my stomach. My hands were wet with perspiration as I screwed up his fake newscoop and dropped it in the ashtray.

I drained my water glass and poured another, trying to cool myself down.

Despite all the verbal dodging and weaving, there was a massive part of me that really wanted to tell Daniella. Explain it all to her and finally, finally get it out in the open. But no sooner did I imagine conjuring up the words than the rolling sickness in my stomach started. I couldn't make myself talk about it. This was a story I'd jammed so far down my gullet that it would take some magical hook to ever fish it out again.

I looked again at the ashtray and slid it to the other end of the table.

By the time Daniella came back I made sure I was absorbed solely in the choices on the menu. 'Fancy splitting some pakoras?' I said as she sat down. 'Or do you want to go straight to mains?'

'I don't care.'

We kept our eyes away from one another and still hadn't spoken by the time the waiter returned. Even as he was standing there, Daniella kept her head down, so I ordered a selection of dishes, handed the menu back and the waiter hurried away.

'You don't believe me then,' I said to Daniella, sitting back in my seat.

'I don't know what to believe.'

There was a long pause.

'Look,' I said. 'I'll be honest: I didn't want to tell you this, but I think Minto borrowed your car. I found the keys in his room.'

'Right.' Her response was monotone, and she didn't even bother to look at me.

'So, I reckon you were meant to find that fake article.'

She glanced at the ashtray and took out the crumpled ball.

'You're saying he made this up somehow?' she said. 'It's not real – it's just meant to look like a newspaper clipping.'

'Exactly.'

'C'mon Alec, why the hell would he do that?'

'I have no idea. But – look, you can see it's not a real newspaper cutting. And Minto's a fucking headcase: you know that as well as I do.'

She looked down, flattening the sheet with her hand. 'So, you've never been to this...Agastino Cafe?'

'Not as far as I know.'

'It exists though.'

'Does it?'

She nodded. 'I've heard of it. How would Minto know that though? He lives in Swansea. He wouldn't even have heard of some station-side café, an hour from where he lives.'

'Look, I don't know, Daniella! Maybe he looked it up in the fucking phone book. Who the hell knows? But if he's going to go to the trouble of making up a fake newspaper report, I'm sure he could easily find out the name of some local landmark, couldn't he?'

She shrugged. 'If you say so.'

'What does that mean?'

'It means I don't know what to think! I don't know what to believe!' She looked around, fidgeting in her chair as she tried to keep control. 'I mean, Mike keeps dropping hints about you and...when I think back, even on that first night I met you, his friend tried to warn me off.'

People on nearby tables were starting to glance in our direction, tune into our juicy conversation. I could sense them itching to drag their chairs closer, string words together, work out what the argument was about.

'So, you'd sooner believe them than me? Is that it?'

'No, of course not, Alec. But things don't seem to add up, do they?'

I got to my feet – more because I couldn't bear to sit there any longer than because I had a plan in mind. 'If you don't believe me, that's fine. We can just forget it.'

Daniella refused to look at me, but the rest of the diners made up for it. I picked up my wallet and eyeballed the woman on the next table till she looked away.

'You're playing right into his hands, Daniella,' I hissed, bending down to her ear. 'This is exactly what Minto wants. Well fucking done!'

'And Mike?' she said. 'And Mike's friend? It's not just Minto, it's all of them.'

'Well,' I said. 'Sounds like they've made your decision for you.'

I marched off and threw open the heavy glass door; power-walking out of there so fast my thoughts had no chance of catching up. But the further I hurried down the street, the more I sensed something at my heels, just half a step behind.

I looked back into the shadows, hoping to see Daniella hurrying to catch up with me, tell me it was okay.

But no one was there.

It was just the limp and hobble of my own past, desperate and determined to catch up with me.

Chapter 22

I slapped the cash directly into Minto's hand and I made sure that Stobes and Black were in the kitchen at the same time. I was glad to finally get it sorted. 'That's last week's rent plus the two that…disappeared, and the next fortnight's,' I said. 'Five weeks in total. Sixty-five quid.'

'All right, all right, calm down Alec,' Minto laughed, looking between me and the others. 'You'll be asking for a tax receipt next.'

Having a receipt last time would have saved me two weeks' rent, but I wasn't about to mention it. We both knew he'd shafted me out of twenty-six quid.

I was about to head off when he called me back. 'Alec? Don't forget it'll be the big two-zero after that. Twenty a week is still a bargain for that massive room of yours.'

I hung on to the doorframe and tried to avoid looking at him. 'Bit rich for my blood,' I said. 'I'll sort something else out.'

His eyes slid to the other two before returning to me. 'Beg your pardon, Alec?'

The bravado of my announcement dribbled away. 'Yeah – I'll have trouble finding that much dough. I'll get another place.'

Stobes sat at the table licking a ciggie paper while Black put his hands behind his head, settling in for the entertainment.

Minto strode towards me. 'Sindy?' he shouted over my shoulder. 'Get here.'

My heart sank: Sindy and her loose lips was all I needed.

'What about your room though?' Minto said, as Sindy came in.

I shrugged. 'Just get someone else –'

'Get someone else? I can go to the trouble of getting someone, can I, Mr Johnston? Me?' he said, jabbing a finger into his chest.

'Or...I could see if...'

'Did you hear about this?' Minto said to Sindy. 'Young Alec here is flying the coop.'

Sindy smiled at me. I could see she didn't have a clue what he meant.

'He's leaving home,' Minto whispered in her ear. 'Buggering off.'

'Oh. Yes,' said Sindy, letting out a giggle.

'Seems a bit rude to me,' Minto said. 'A bit impolite. I invite you here out of the goodness of my heart…' He paused and looked across at Stobes and Black. 'All three of you in fact, but only Alexander here is throwing it back in my face.'

It was news to me that Minto had made the decision about us all moving in.

He folded his thick arms and stood too close to me. 'Not moving in with that classy bird of yours, are you Mr Johnston?'

'No, I'm not.'

'Reckon she's pretty keen on you. For the moment, at least.' He gave me an unpleasant grin. 'I get the impression you're her bit of rough. Relatively speaking.'

The others snorted, quietly egging him on.

'Looks like her family have a bit of coin behind 'em too. Could be well-in there, Alec if you play your cards right.'

I tried a half-hearted smile, wishing he wasn't standing so fucking close.

He circled me slowly. 'Perhaps she's attracted to that unshaven look, the tight jeans, the spiky hair, eh, Alec?'

'Or my magnetic charm,' I said, all nice and cheery like we were just mates shooting the breeze.

Minto perched on the arm of the sofa, settling into his bit of foam-filled amateur psychology. 'Thing is,' he said. 'You're not too dirty or too risky for her,' he said. 'You're the safe-dangerous option. Soft porn rather than hardcore if you get my meaning.'

'Mm.' I didn't know or care what the fuck he was on about.

'I don't think she'd want anyone seriously troublesome though, do you? I mean, a bit of black hair-dye and a studded ear is one thing. A dodgy past on other hand...that might be a risk too far. Don't you think?'

I swallowed. 'I have no idea, mate.'

'No, you don't, do you?' he said, and the smile slipped from his face along with the friendly tone. 'Back to this little rental conundrum,' he said. 'Two weeks isn't much notice, is it?'

'Well I can't afford twenty a week so...'

'And what am I to tell Mr Patel?' Minto said.

I was careful with my reaction, making sure I gave nothing away.

'It's okay. Alec already knows about Dad,' Sindy said. 'He knows Mr Patel's not the owner now.'

Black and Stobes frowned at one another and I saw Minto shoot a glance in their direction. He took in a deep breath and grabbed Sindy by the top of her arm. 'Anything else you want to tell everyone?' he said. 'This stuff is none of your business, so keep your big idiot-mouth shut.' He led her out of the room so fast her bony little feet couldn't keep up. She stumbled, bleated and we heard Minto practically drag her the rest of the way.

Black nodded at the door. 'Sounds like she's going to be in a bit of strife,' he said, getting out of his seat.

Stobes laughed as he leaned over the bin, clearing his jeans of tobacco and ash before going back to the sofa. 'She'll have a sore arse tomorrow, that's for sure,' he said. 'Mind you, I hadn't realised we'd got ourselves a new landlord.'

'Makes no odds to me,' Black said. 'I couldn't give a toss who gets the rent money.' He looked at me. 'So, is our little butty-bach really shifting?'

'Reckon so.'

'You won't find anywhere cheaper – even with the rent-hike.'

'I know but...money's not everything.'

Stobes got to his feet again, his long legs unfolding like a crane fly. He took a deep drag on his rollie. 'No wonder Minto's disappointed. Reckon he saw you as potential comrade material.'

'Comrade?'

'Well, you know. Mates helping each other out. He makes a better friend than he does an enemy, that's for sure.'

'Aye. You'd do well to stay out of his bad books,' Black said, nodding. 'And, fair dos, there's a lot of advantages to getting in with his fraternity.'

'Can't say I'd noticed,' I said.

Stobes looked at me and paused, like he was still weighing up how much to say. 'You could have money in your pocket, mate; the security of knowing you've got people watching your back. S'all I'm sayin'. But if you want to flounce off over a bit of rent money, so be it. Your loss. He won't like it though.'

'And when Minto doesn't like something,' Black added, looking at Stobes. 'You fucking well know about it.'

I looked between the two of them. Was I being threatened? Advised? Warned? Without me realising, they'd become a double act, promoting the ways of the Minto Club.

'Ach, don't worry about it, Alec,' Black said, standing up. He slapped me on the shoulder. 'I'm sure that lovely ground floor front bedroom will work out just fine for you in Ashton Crescent.'

I stood watching his back as it disappeared out the door, wondering if there could have been anything else for Sindy to have given away.

Chapter 23

I hadn't been able to get in touch with Daniella since our row at the Indian restaurant. Whenever I tried phoning her student flat, the communal phone was out of order and when I called her parents, they said she hadn't been home. In my more optimistic moments, I persuaded myself that she just needed to calm down, and we'd get back to normal. At other times, though, I was scared she'd had enough of me, what with the dodgy acquaintances I had, the helpful hints from Mike and now this fake newspaper article.

I tried my best not to worry about it but whenever I thought of Daniella – of not seeing her anymore – I got this dull ache in my stomach. I wasn't about to run off and marry her, but I had to admit she'd brightened every dank little corner of my existence. The prospect of going back to the shitty life I'd had before I'd met Daniella was deeply depressing.

I hadn't figured exactly what I was going to say to her as I stood outside her student room, clutching a box of chocolates. I just knew it was my turn to front up and show some balls.

'Oh!' she said, blinking back at me. 'Alec!' I tried to tell myself her shock was the happy kind, but there was no spark in her eye, and the tremor in her voice was more of the panic-stricken than pleased variety. 'I wasn't expecting you,' she said.

I wanted to peek round the door, see if she had someone with her but I kept my cool and nodded down at the chocolates. 'A peace offering,' I said. 'I know you've had to put up with a lot of shit from me lately. I just thought...maybe we could...iron over the cracks a bit.'

She didn't smile as she looked back at me. 'It's iron over the creases. Or paint over the cracks.'

'What?'

'You can't iron over cracks.'

I thought about it for a moment. She was so much smarter than me.

'How about just smoothing things over – with an iron or a trowel? Maybe a paintbrush? Or even these,' I said, handing her the chocolates.

The fact she hadn't yet slammed the door in my face gave me hope.

'Please?' I said. 'They were the most expensive ones in the shop. That's a first for me. I'm normally very cheap. You know that.'

She sighed and pulled the door open. 'You'd better come in.'

On her bed, a dog-eared copy of *Practical Cell Biology* proved to be her only company and, thankfully, she was quick enough to give that the boot so I could sit down next to her.

'I didn't expect to see you again,' she said. 'When you walked out of the restaurant, I thought that was it.'

I nodded, almost afraid to answer: my track record for calming things down with a speech wasn't great. 'Did you want that to be it?'

She sat, hugging herself, tense. 'I think I did, actually, yeah.'

It wasn't the answer I'd been hoping for. 'Past tense?'

She met my gaze and shrugged.

'You really want to give Minto the satisfaction of breaking us up?'

She all but rolled her eyes. 'That's the only reason you're here, is it?'

'Course not.' I risked an arm around the shoulder, a slight nestling in. 'But it did give me the excuse I was looking for.'

She shook my arm off her. 'Why d'you need an excuse, Alec?' she said. 'Is it so hard to just admit you acted like a jerk and apologise?'

'Yeah, I know I was a jerk. That's why I'm here…'

'All I want to know is that I can trust you, for God's sake. Is that too much to ask? Just to trust you?'

I could see she was struggling. Her eyes had that glassy look about them that they always had when she was upset. It made me want to put my arms around her, make things better, but I also knew she wasn't a woman to be soothed too easily. I swear, she usually knew what I was thinking before I did.

'You can trust me!' I said.

She sat, watching me then studying for hints of lies and betrayal.

'I don't understand what's going on with you,' she said. 'That article... all the things Mike keeps saying. I want to believe you, I really do, but... you're so cagey; so shifty.'

'I'm not!'

She leaned back against the wall and looked up at the ceiling. 'You are, Alec. I don't think you even mean to be. It's just that you never expand on things – you always give away the bare minimum in terms of what you're thinking and feeling.'

'So? It doesn't mean there's anything sinister lurking in the background.'

She turned her gaze on me. 'You sure about that?'

'Look, I promise you!' I got to my feet, suddenly too wired to keep sitting next to her. 'Whatever Mike says or Minto or any of that lot from my old school – this is me, promising you I have nothing to feel guilty for and nothing to confess. This is my promise. I haven't done anything wrong.'

I chose my words very carefully. I wanted to be certain I wasn't lying to her. Yes, it was the bare minimum, just as she accused me, but what if I told her everything and she questioned my innocence? It was one thing to have her doubt me when she was swamped by uncertainty and hints, but how would I ever bear it if she felt that way after hearing the truth? I just needed her to trust me.

Daniella was still watching me; cool, detached, weighing things up.

'Y'know,' I said to her, 'just because I don't shout my every thought from the rooftops doesn't mean I'm hiding stuff. Or that I don't feel anything.'

That seemed to stump her. She shook her head, like she'd lost track of her own argument and leaned forward again. 'I know, I know. I guess you're just...different to the people I usually meet.'

I sat down, close to her and moved a few strands of hair from her face. 'So, what is the usual type you meet?'

'Conventional,' she said with a sigh. 'Safe.'

'Ah yes, boring.'

That finally earned me a smile. 'Yes, okay Alec. Boring, if that's what you want to hear.'

'Well there you are then,' I told her. 'You wouldn't want me to be like them, would you? But it doesn't mean I'm a bad person or a liar or a cheat.'

'I know.'

'I'm just a private person. I find it hard to open up.'

She turned those blue eyes on me, and I could see she liked my latest incarnation: Alec Johnston, Man of Mystery.

'I get that,' she said.

I leaned forward and gave her a slow kiss. It felt good to touch her lips again. 'It's not that I'm keeping any misdemeanours from you,' I told her. And technically, that was true. 'But I'm not ready to be an open book either. Maybe you wouldn't even want that.'

She looked kind of mesmerised by my little speech. 'I s'pose you're right,' she whispered.

I leaned in for a gruntier kiss and, as we eased back on the bed, I was finally given the welcome I'd been hoping for.

Chapter 24

I figured the worst was behind me: I'd fronted up to Minto that I was leaving, I was paid up with my rent and I'd found a new place to live. All I had to do was stay out of everyone's way for the next week or two. It meant I was basically killing time until I could piss off out of that rancid flat for good.

For very good.

The mistake I made was assuming that Minto was as happy to see as little of me as I was to see of him. But if there was one thing I should've learned about Minto, it was this: if you make assumptions, he'll go out on a limb to prove you wrong.

That's why I wasn't prepared for all four of them turning up at my door one evening, just when I was settling down for a night in with the box. They stood there like a bunch of cut-throat carol singers, telling me – not inviting me – that we were going out to celebrate my new place. Sindy looked so sodding pleased about it all, I wondered if this was her idea.

I was hauled out of the room, handed a helmet and, as soon as we were outside, directed to the back of Black's machine. Five of us on two bikes didn't divvy up too well of course, so Sindy had to perch on the front of Minto's machine with Stobes taking rear position.

I hadn't wanted to join them: I'd pretty much begged to be left alone, but the more I argued, the more I started to sense that a refusal, even a polite one, would be like gobbing in Minto's face. I had no choice.

I imagined us going to one of their favourite haunts in the city, but as we headed further from home, I started to worry less about which pub we were going to and more about whether I was about to end up in a ditch with a knife in my throat.

A regular house in a suburban street wouldn't normally seem menacing, but as we pulled into the concrete driveway of this particular residence, I knew a pub full of punters would have been preferable. Whose house were we being taken to? And more worryingly, why?

I'd expected a carpeted hallway beyond the front door. What I got was something very different. Inside, it wasn't a regular house at all. It was a huge open space and I presumed the house was extended out the back as it seemed to stretch for miles. There were big warehouse-style roll-up doors and Minto opened them to reveal a massive parking area out the back; its high walls protected with glass and barbed wire.

'Welcome to our world,' Minto said, turning to me. 'Hope you're impressed: it's by personal invitation only, you see.' He pointed to a sign on the wall that said 'Apache MC Morriston HQ. Fuck Off Unless Invited.'

'I'm honoured,' I said. And I was guided inside.

'You been in here before?' I asked Stobes.

We were both sitting on the red leather couch, near an old jukebox.

'Once or twice,' he said. 'I'm not a regular. I mean, I don't attend the meetings or anything.'

'Meetings? They have meetings?'

Stobes looked at me, crossing one skinny leg over the other like some cartoon giraffe. 'It's a bone fide club,' he said. 'They have stuff to agree on, tasks to do.'

'I hadn't realised.'

He leaned forward, rolling his beer can between his hands. 'I s'pose these groups have had a bad rap,' he said. 'The press would have you believe they're the new Mafia but in reality, it's just a bunch of guys getting together.'

'Quite the knitting circle,' I said, watching a couple of inked-up heavies play pool in the corner.

'I'm not saying they're all angels,' Stobes said. 'But they seem all right. To me, anyway, speaking as an outsider.'

'So, you're not one of them?'

'Nah, I'm more of...a casual acquaintance. Like, I know I could call on them for a bit of help if I needed it. And vice versa. I'm counted amongst their numbers if need be.'

'Right.'

'Like I told you Alec. They make much better mates than enemies.'

'You said.'

'There are worse people to hang out with, that's for sure.'

Stobes seemed to be winding up his Political Broadcast of Behalf of the Bikie Party speech.

I wondered if this was the message I'd been brought in for. Minto didn't do anything without a purpose, without a thought of how it would help him. I figured this was the reason behind my little leaving do. Perhaps there was a sense of urgency now I was quitting: a final shot at getting me on board before I cut myself loose.

There was a roar of laughter from the bar. As I looked over, Minto caught my eye. He put down his drink and headed over. Stobes seemed to take his cue: he got to his feet and left us.

Minto slid heftily along the leather seat. He looked around, saying nothing, like he was simply admiring his creation.

'I didn't realise this place existed,' I said, once the silence got too much for me.

'And why would you?'

'It's...good, though,' I said. 'Friendly. Well-equipped.'

'That's the point of it, I guess.' He edged closer to me, his thighs wide and meaty in their leather pants.

'Shame things didn't work out back at the flat,' he said. 'I thought we were doing all right, the four of us.'

'Mm.'

Having him so close was making me nervous. I was cornered – sitting on his turf with his bunch of buddies, no way of pissing off out of there without their say-so and their petrol.

'I always hoped we'd get along, you and me,' Minto said. 'I got the impression you were the sort I could do business with.'

'Business?'

'You've got it going on up here,' I said tapping his temple. 'You know what's what.'

This was certainly a new angle from him. 'Oh, I dunno,' I said. 'I'm just a regular –'

'We could use someone like you. And that's the real shame of it,' he said.

I didn't like the way this discussion was going. Last week, I was Public Enemy Number One as far as Minto was concerned. Why had I suddenly become the creamy froth on his pint of stout?

'Well you know how it is once you've made a decision' I said. 'Now I've got the new place sorted, I'm kind of ready to move on.'

'I get it,' he said. 'And it's not like the new place is a million miles away, is it?'

He looked me in the eye and smiled.

'I don't suppose I'll be around much,' I said. 'I've got a few irons in the fire, work-wise. That'll be the end of my free time.' I looked away, hoping it'd be the end of the conversation.

'What sort of work you looking for?'

'I'm not fussy. So long as it pays well.' I could have bitten off my tongue as soon as I said it.

'It seems to me, Alec, you have a few choices. You can go and work in some shit job in the council or wherever, toe-ing the line and pushing the corporate pen, making just about enough to live on.' He leaned forward again and lowered his voice. 'Or you could choose a better path; earn what you're really worth.'

'Yes, I suppose so but –'

'I've got contacts, see; I could get you some well-paid work just like that,' he said, clicking his fingers. 'We have...import, export opportunities, for instance. Not just here but all over the world. The sky's the fucking limit, Alec.'

'You seem to have plenty of people lending a hand though,' I said. 'Can't imagine you'd need someone like me.'

He gave a low laugh. 'I don't need you, Alec,' he said. 'But I could use you. I know we haven't had a great start but you're not stupid.' He paused, like he was deep in thought. 'You know you'd be better off working with me than against me, don't you?'

And there it was again – just like Stobes said – better to have Minto as a friend than an enemy.

In another life, maybe I'd have been tempted. After all, what chance would I have for making any decent dosh? But I couldn't live with the stuff I knew Minto was involved in.

'Is it Sindy?' he said, watching me.

'How do you mean?'

'I get the feeling you don't approve.'

I shrugged. 'I...don't know much about it. I mean...what do you want me to say?'

He nodded, almost respectfully. 'Sindy does all right. She knows how things would be if she didn't have me watching out for her.'

'Sure.'

'Let me ask you something, Alec,' he said, leaning back and pushing his hands into his armpits. 'Do you think the world out there is full of people doing the right thing? It isn't. It's full of people creaming off their share. It's full of vultures making a fast buck, getting what they can for as little as they can. All these high ideals of yours, these ideas you have to work hard with decent people. It's all bullshit. And I'll tell you why – it's because every place, every company is filled with people taking their own cut. It doesn't matter where you work there'll always be people lining their own pockets. And all the time, *you* won't be the one making the big bucks. The people making the megabucks will be the ones working with people like me. Being part of a brotherhood allows you to share the love, you see, Alec.' He stabbed a finger into my chest. 'I help you, you help me. And, I tell you what, I've got a lot more love to splash around than most people. You might not like the dirty world you see me inhabiting, Mr Clean-Cut Johnston, but it's the real world. It's the way things are. So, you can either snaffle about at the bottom of a flashy, shiny ladder, or you can hack your way up a rickety one where you can enjoy the spoils and make the most of being at the top. What you see here is nothing,' he said, easing back in his seat again. His arms rested on the back of the sofa – he looked very satisfied with his lot. 'What you see here is a small shard of a very big iceberg.'

'Yeah?' I said, reaching for my glass. 'I've always tried to avoid hitting icebergs.'

Minto chortled and slapped his leathery thigh. 'Very good, Alec,' he said. 'See what I mean? You're quick, sharp. But you know what? There's not a whole lot of point being squeaky-clean unless you're in a spotless world. The people I work with, you know, they come from that squeaky-clean world you seem to aspire to. And I can tell you this much: it's a screen. A smoke screen of respectability.'

He gestured to one of the meat heads near the door and was immediately supplied with a drink and a packet of fags.

'Know why the pigs didn't find anything that night we had the visit?' he said, sucking on his smokes.

I shook my head.

'Think about it.'

I was pretty sure he was bullshitting: was he seriously suggesting someone was in the know?

'Because, I have nothing to fear, Alec,' he said. 'I have plenty of friends in high places. But you: you're all adrift and alone, you have everything to fear.'

This was the longest single conversation I'd ever had with Minto and as far as I was concerned, it couldn't finish quickly enough.

He cracked his knuckles and straightened himself out, stretching those bulky, tattooed arms to the sides. 'Come over and have a drink,' he said. 'Meet the other lads.'

And next minute, he took me up to the bar, like we were the very best of mates.

I knew my guard was down after the first couple of shots. It was only then that I dared risk a good look around the room; I mean, really take in my surroundings. It was such a weird sort of set up: an ordinary corner block house that gave no hint as to what lay inside its fifties-built walls. There was a huge Apache sign painted onto the wall next to the breeze-block bar – a copy of the one I'd seen outside, next to the Fuck Off notice. Then there was a motorbike, hanging on a couple of hefty chains from one of the steel rafters like some sort of metallic centrepiece. Its number plate was hanging off and its petrol tank had a deep fist-sized dent in it.

'It's a kind of shrine really,' Black told me, coming over when he saw me looking up. 'Dougie Ace took a bend too fast and never came out of it.'

'Hm. Shit.'

As I looked up, my leg knocked a table. Right next to it, a half-open trunk had rifle butts poking out of it, like it was a kids' box stuffed with too many toys.

'Don't worry, they're all registered,' Black said, watching me. 'All above board, here man. We've got our own premises license, our own liquor license, gun license. You name it, we've probably got a certificate in triplicate for it.'

'Sounds like you've got it all sussed,' I said. Though I was pretty sure guns were meant to be secured in a locked space; not stuffed into trunk like a lounge-room ornament.

'There's always plenty of people who know someone, so there's never a drama getting permissions sorted. As they say, it's not what you know but who you know, eh?'

Sindy appeared behind the bar in front of us, acting as makeshift barmaid. 'What'll it be, lads?'

'Nothing else, thanks,' I said.

'Oh, but I insist.' Sindy leaned across and whispered to me, even though Black could obviously hear her. 'Minto said I had to make sure you had enough to drink.'

'Did he now?' I said, glancing over to him. 'I'll have a juice then.'

'We don't serve soft drinks.'

'Fine, a beer,' I said. It didn't mean I had to drink it.

Black wandered off once Sindy had topped up his whisky glass. I perched on the bar stool.

'So, are you going to join?' Sindy asked me. She looked around the place with a dramatic sweep of the arm. 'It's great, isn't it? I knew you'd like it if you saw it.'

'Did I *say* I liked it?'

She laughed. 'You do. I can tell you do. Will you join, if you're officially invited?'

'Officially? Do I get a letter in the mail or something?'

She looked at me and paused. 'I don't think so. But they have to discuss it at a meeting. Someone would propose you and someone else would...nominate or second you or something like that.'

I took a sip of the beer I didn't want. 'I doubt I'll be joining.'

'Why not? You could come here any time then. There's pool and a weights room. There are even some bedrooms upstairs where you can watch TV.'

'Quite the resort,' I said. 'But...it's not for me. Reckon the price of membership might be too high.'

'It doesn't cost much,' Sindy said. 'There are yearly...subs I think they're called, but they –'

'I wasn't referring to the financial cost,' I said. 'I'm not really one for commitment.'

'They wouldn't mind that.'

Now it was my turn to lower my voice. 'Actually, I think they would. And I reckon they'd mind very much if ever I wanted to leave.'

'You wouldn't want to leave once you were one of them,' Sindy assured me. 'But if you moved away, there are always other branches to go to. An Apache chapter would never be far away.'

'Yeah,' I said. 'That's my point.' But I could see it was lost on her.

She topped up my glass before I had the chance to stop her. 'I really think you should join, Alec,' she said. And her voice was suddenly louder – her attention half on Minto who was leaning against the other end of the bar. 'I think you'd get a lot out of it.' Clearly, she needed him to know she was giving it her best shot.

'You're very persuasive, Sindy,' I said, playing along. 'But my mind's already made up.'

Something in her expression changed, as if someone had crept inside and pressed her panic button.

'But you have to,' she said in a loud whisper, leaning right across the bar at me.

I half-laughed. 'Why?'

'Please, Alec. You have to.'

There was a subtext to all this. I looked between her and Minto who was still at the other end of the bar with his back to me. 'I don't understand.'

Suddenly, she grabbed my hand with both of hers. 'Please, Alec. Don't make me tell him you said no.'

'But –'

'I'll do anything. Anything,' she said. 'Just don't tell him no.'

Minto chose that moment to turn around, bringing his pint over to where Sindy was now quickly wiping the bar. 'So, you set us up with our new recruit, Sindy?' he said.

She looked at me and swallowed.

'I'm still thinking on it,' I said. 'Sindy did a fine job though. Made it sound irresistible.'

'If that's the case, how can you resist?' Minto said.

'Just want to give it some thought,' I told him. 'I'm not sure how much longer I'll actually be in Swansea for, so...'

'Seeking out pastures new, eh?' He put his beer on the bar, his fat fingers still cradling it. Everything was inked up: he had 'Loyal' across one hand, 'Apache' across the other.

He must've seen me looking. 'Know what they call these?' he said, not waiting for me to reply. 'They call 'em job stoppers. You can't get a job once your face and hands are inked up. But, hey, do I look like I'm in need of a monthly wage? I'm not playing the same fucking game as most of society.'

He swept the room with his eyes – clearly some sort of signal for a handful of his mates to come over. I felt myself shrinking back on my stool.

'The thing is, Alec,' Minto said quietly. 'There's a general feeling that when you've been granted the honour of an invitation, the polite response would be to accept.'

'Yeah, I get that and I'm not ungrateful or anyth –'

'And there's also a general feeling that if someone isn't with us – when they've been invited to be – they're sort of...' He edged closer, shooting me a look between the eyes. 'They're against us. D'you see how that works?'

'Really, I'm –'

'Would you say you're with us or against us, Alec?' His voice was low, menacing.

'I'm not against you,' I said. 'I swear I'm not. But...I just –'

Minto turned to the grizzlies behind him. 'I think what Alec is trying to say is that he hasn't got the stomach for it. Is that what you're saying?'

'Maybe.'

He nodded slowly. 'Reckon we could soon fix that,' he said. A murmur of laughter rumbled behind him.

'Let me think about it,' I said, all upbeat, like we were negotiating over a second-hand motor. 'I'm sure we can work something out.'

He gave me one of those hefty slaps on the arm. 'That's the way, Alec. Give and take. It's what we're all about, eh lads?'

The balding guy at the back let out a massive beery belch, making them all guffaw. It took the edge off the moment and I allowed myself a breath.

'Right, let's get this poor kid home,' Minto said. 'He looks like he's about to piss his fucking pull-up pants.'

Chapter 25

It was a mixed bag of feelings, knowing I was finally about to get shot of the flat, particularly after the visit to the clubhouse. Minto had said no more about the matter – none of them had – but I had the feeling it was all still a work in progress.

There should have been relief at leaving, but now there was a fear-filled uncertainty to it. A lot of it was to do with Sindy. There was a sense of me abandoning her; leaving her to her fate. My presence at the flat hardly made a practical difference to her life – she was still caught up in Minto's crazy world either way – but I suspect we both felt better knowing I was there.

I could hear her in the kitchen talking to Black, his gruff laugh echoing down the hallway. He wasn't much better than Minto when it came to Sindy. Any way he could find to ridicule and use her, he would.

I decided to grab some of my kitchen stuff to add to the packing boxes. It was still over a week till I moved but packing and sorting made escape feel closer. It was like the chokehold was loosening.

As I walked into the kitchen, Black quickly moved away from Sindy while she stood, readjusting her clothes.

'He wouldn't stop tickling me!' she told me. Her voice was husky from laughter.

'And you're really ticklish I'll bet,' I said, as I searched under the sink for my pots. 'Who'd have thought, eh?' I brought out my frypan and a few never-used lids.

'You're not packing, are you?' Sindy said.

'Just gathering bits and pieces.'

'If you go, Minto's going to knock the wall down between your rooms,' Sindy told me. 'Says it'll be his own luxury suite. I might be able to have a wardrobe to keep some of my clothes here.'

'Really?' I said. 'Let's hope he waits till I've moved out then.'

Sindy laughed. 'He's got a few business trips planned. Says he might get some mates to do it while he's away.'

It was a relief to know he'd accepted I was going. Perhaps his talk had been all bluster; a final shot at persuading me to stay.

'Hey, Sindy. Is this Minto's?' Black said, nodding to a leather jacket on the back of the chair.

'Yeah, must've put a different one on,' she said, heaving it off the chair and sliding her arms into it.

The jacket swamped her, and her bandy little legs looked like they might buckle under the weight.

She caught me looking and laughed. Then she turned this way and that, doing ridiculous model poses. As she strutted to the other side of the room, I read the 'Morriston' insignia along the top. On the bottom 'Apache MC' stood in large letters with a big '1%' sign between two fingers.

'Apache MC, eh?' I said.

Sindy turned around, looking disgruntled that I was paying more attention to the jacket than to her.

She continued her catwalk strut, pausing every now and then to turn and pout or let the jacket slip from her shoulder.

Black gave her a clap and a few wolf-whistles, egging her on. She pulled it down over both shoulders and did a little shimmy.

I wasn't sure I liked where this was going.

'What the fuck d'you think you're doing?' Minto appeared in the doorway, blocking the light from outside. His T-shirt had got wet in the rain and was tight against his chest, showing off the effects of all that weight-training. His pecs looked fit to burst as he took a deep breath, waiting for Sindy to answer him. 'I said, what the fuck d'you think you're doing!' he yelled at her.

He didn't seem quite himself. He had a manic look in his eye and his breathing was fast and shallow. He was sweating like a pig, too.

Black must have spotted it. He heaved himself out of his seat and tossed his empty beer can in the sink. 'I'm outta here,' he said. 'Coming, Alec?'

I stood up, but my legs didn't move.

Minto hadn't noticed either of us in any case: his focus was solely on Sindy. He reached forward and snatched the lapel of the leather jacket, yanking Sindy towards him. In the same movement, he pushed her away again and her head thudded against the wall, making the cups rattle in the cupboard.

'Hey! She didn't mean any harm,' I said. I went towards him, my arm outstretched.

But he wasn't watching me: I might as well have not been there.

He grabbed Sindy by the shoulders and started tugging and pulling the jacket, trying to get it off her. I was afraid he was going to break her arms.

'You don't touch this, you understand, you little cunt?' he growled at her. He could barely spit out the words. 'You don't touch any of my stuff. I'm fucking sick of you, you hear? Sick of you.'

He grabbed a fistful of hair with his one hand and pulled the jacket free with the other and tossed it behind him onto the floor.

Sindy was screaming and crying as she tried to make him let go of her. I was still doing sod all with the outstretched arm gesture, trying to get in the way and stay out the way all at the same time.

Next thing, Minto flung her, without warning, towards the kitchen table. There was a clatter of chairs and she fell forward, hitting them all out the way like she was a bowling ball.

'You're endless fucking trouble,' he shouted. 'You stink, you're stupid. You're a fucking waste of space, Sindy.' He grabbed the back of her hair again. 'Now get up!'

'C'mon, take it easy, man,' I found myself saying.

That was it. He knew I was there. Minto's face turned towards me and that sick, wretched hatred shifted to my direction. 'What has this got to do with you, golden boy?'

'You don't need to hurt her.'

'Don't I?' he said. 'Why not? She screws up my life, stinks out my home. Fuck me, she even brought those pigs sniffing around here, turning the place upside down. Scheming little bitch.'

'I didn't!' Sindy sniffed. 'Why would you say that?'

'Don't you lie to me, girl!' Minto grabbed her again but this time with more force, more fury. My eyes followed his gaze to the big window. He was lining her up for the big one.

'No! Minto! It was me. All right? It was me.' I put a hand on Sindy's arm, ready to ease her out of his grip.

Minto straightened up, slow and stiff. He looked at me as he finally let Sindy go. There was no surprise in his eyes, though. Nothing to suggest what I'd said was news to him. Instead, the slow upturn of a smile.

Yeah, he had me.

That bastard had known all along.

Chapter 26

There was no way I could stay in the flat once Minto had had his fun with me. I still had almost a week before the new place was ready but with a big target plastered to my back, I'd have slept in the gutter rather than go back to Oakdale Terrace. If I'd been able to, I would've legged it to Bristol to see Daniella, but as luck would have it, she was staying with her parents.

Mum was pleased to have an unexpected visit from me but on the downside, my presence in Cardiff meant I was obliged to join Daniella for some anniversary party she and her parents were going to. I had a bad feeling about it, a sense that something didn't bode well, but I was in damage-limitation mode as far as Daniella was concerned and I knew this was my penance. Perhaps I would've been better listening to my gut.

The McAllisters – Pamela and John – had an even more impressive place than Daniella's. They were entertaining their guests in the conservatory, but this was no lean-to, like we had stuck on the end of our house. No, this one was palatial, rounded, with soaring glass ceilings and fancy white ironwork.

At first glance, I reckoned the average age of the guests was sixty. There were a lot of pearl necklaces and golf club ties, and had I not promised Daniella I'd give the party a decent go, I'd've turned around and walked straight out.

'So, you're the young man Daniella's been telling us about,' Pamela said, as we arrived at the drinks table. She poured wine into a glass for me. 'It's so nice to meet you at last, Alec.'

'Yeah, thanks. You too.'

She smiled at Daniella. 'Neil and his friends are out in the garden if you want to get away from us wrinklies.' Her eyes shifted to me again. 'Neil's my son,' she explained. 'Actually, it's possible you might know him – he's around your age so, you never know, you might have been at school together. You should go and say hello.'

We took our drinks and headed to the buffet instead. If we had to endure an evening like this, we decided we could at least make the most of the food.

Daniella spent the next hour trying to save my sanity by plying me with drinks and vol au vents, but I could feel my will to live slipping away with each passing second.

'Isn't it time to go to that other...event?' I said to her, nodding in the direction of the front door.

'We can't go yet. There'll be a toast for their anniversary.'

'When will that be?'

'Not long,' she said, avoiding my eye.

'Hey, Daniella!' someone called from outside the door. 'What are you doing in there? The party's out here!'

She looked up and waved – and then, before I knew it, we were heading out to the garden where some younger guys were standing around a fire pit. Daniella leaned in for a kiss with a couple of them, then took a step back to let me through. 'Oh, and this is Alec,' she said. 'Alec – this is Neil and John and...I'm sorry, I don't think we've met?'

I shook hands with Neil and John but stopped when I got to Daniella's new acquaintance. I hadn't seen him since the funeral.

I steadied myself and took a breath. 'Kev,' I said, holding out my hand. 'How are you?'

The moment our eyes met, his expression twisted. He paused, as if to catch his breath, then turned his back on me. Everyone watched in silence as he marched over to Daniella's brother, who was chatting to some of his friends. 'You could've warned me!' Kev yelled, turning Mike by the shoulder and gesticulating in my direction. 'What the hell is he doing here?'

I watched this play out like I was following a movie. We all did.

Mike looked confused, then slid his eyes to me as Kev hurried inside.

'Kev!' Mike said, dashing after him. 'Kev!'

It made things very awkward for the group of us that was left. Daniella looked up at me, her eyes asking the question that her voice seemed unable to, while everyone else kept their gaze on the grass.

'We'd...better go and see if he's all right,' Neil said, nodding towards the house and leaving us. John took his cue and followed him inside.

'What the hell is going on?' Daniella said, pulling me away.

People were still rubbernecking, standing on tiptoe to see if the action was continuing inside, half an eye on us to gauge our response.

I was still fumbling for a reply when Mike appeared. 'If you had an ounce of decency in you, you'd piss off home,' he said to me. Then to Daniella: 'I hadn't realised he was included on the invite tonight.'

'Why wouldn't I invite him?'

Mike looked at her. 'Why? Because that's Kev Mitchell. Y'know? Brother of Jill Mitchell.'

'But...who is this Jill Mitchell?'

Mike snapped his head in my direction. 'Christ! You still haven't bloody told her, have you?'

Daniella's voice was quiet, like she already knew it was something she didn't want to hear. 'Told me what?'

The pair of them stared at me but it was only Mike who spoke. 'Well, Alec?' he said. 'Alexander? Xander? Whatever name you're going by these days. Aren't you going to tell her who Jill Mitchell is? Was?'

None of us moved. I couldn't swallow, couldn't speak.

'Maybe I'll have to do it for you,' Mike said, edging towards me. 'Seeing as you haven't got the balls to tell her yourself.'

He kept his eyes on me, but it was only Daniella's eyes I was worried about. Only her eyes I could think of as Mike cleared his throat.

I heard it outside myself. He was talking about me, yet it wasn't really me. This was a different reality. The same scenes; the same characters but now with an untrustworthy narrator.

'She was Alec's girlfriend,' he said. 'Or rather, Xander's. She didn't actually know you as Alec, did she?'

That bit was true, but I didn't respond.

'Anyway, they were going out together when they were in high school.' He paused and I could feel his eyes on me as he tried to drag out the drama. 'Correct me if I'm wrong, won't you, Alec?'

Daniella folded her arms. 'Just say what you've got to say, Mike.'

'So, they had a big fight when they were coming home from the bay one night. She admitted she'd been cheating on him.'

He waited, as if inviting me to deliver the punchline, but my voice was locked too far down. I wished I could speak. After all, Mike had never even met Jill yet here he was, recounting a night in her life, like he'd been granted some God-given right speak on her behalf.

'Anyway,' he said, 'the next morning, her body was found on the beach, just below the cliffs. She was pregnant too. But not, it turned out, by Alec.'

As he finished, I sensed eyes downcast around us.

Who knows what Mike expected: A gasp? Shocked silence? What he got was awkwardness. Those who'd been near enough to hear seemed trapped. They didn't want to know this or deal with the fallout. They'd come for a party, not a pantomime.

I felt Daniella look up at me, finally, when Mike moved away. 'Why couldn't you have just told me?' she whispered. 'Why couldn't you have...said?'

I wasn't surprised to see her eyes well up and her pale face flush.

And it was hardly unexpected when she turned and marched away.

The only shock was that she was dragging me with her.

An icy, windswept beachside breakup: I wondered what could be bleaker.

Daniella hadn't said a word since we'd left the party and I certainly wasn't going to risk one. I figured she'd have enough to say once she got going, so I was in no hurry to begin the showdown – nor its inevitable fallout. There was a part of me that wanted to just stop her before she began and say: 'Enough: let's just bid each other farewell' – because that was the only way this little scene could play out. Trust was already on a knife-edge between us as far as Daniella was concerned. The only thing that stopped me from putting the relationship out of its misery was knowing that Daniella needed to have her say. It seemed the least I could do to stand and hear it: I owed her that much.

It wasn't easy, walking towards the water when it was too dark to pick out a foot in front of us. I think we just followed the sound of the waves and tried to stay upright on the pebbles.

Before we reached the shoreline, Daniella sat down. No warning, nothing said – she just suddenly plonked herself down at my side. I stood beside her not sure what I was meant to do, then I sat next to her, the hard edges of the stones offering maximum discomfort.

'It wasn't like you needed to lie,' she said, as if we were already mid-conversation. Perhaps in her head, we were. 'You had the perfect opportunity to tell me,' she said. 'Several opportunities, in fact. You could have just told me, explained. That's all you needed to do.'

'I couldn't.'

'Why not? If you'd told me, I would have listened, made up my own mind. But no, you chose to lie through your teeth and have someone else inform me.'

I picked up a stone, running a finger along the icy smoothness of its edges. It was solid, weighty and it was about the only thing in this whole situation that felt real.

'I didn't lie,' I said. 'It was...more that...I couldn't talk about it.'

'Even to me?'

'To anyone.'

'Why not?'

I felt her look across to me in the darkness, waiting.

'Alec? Why not?'

I shrugged but I doubt she saw me.

The longer the silence continued, the more I knew she'd be filling in the gaps, putting all the pieces in the wrong places. It didn't matter. I'd barely said a word, but I was already too exhausted to put things right.

'Was it because of Mum?' she said. 'That warning I gave you about no scandals. No questionable pasts.'

She was offering me a way out; an easy fix. Something concrete.

'That didn't help,' I said. 'I mean, I was shit-scared of either of you finding out. But...that wasn't the reason. That's not why I kept quiet, not really.'

I picked up another stone and eased my fingers around its smoothness, waiting.

'Was it guilt?' she said at last.

I looked at her. 'Guilt?'

'I'm not saying you...did anything wrong but maybe you felt guilty that she...that your girlfriend died; that it was her and not you.'

Daniella wouldn't say the word, wouldn't allow Jill's name to fall from her lips – and I was glad about that.

'People always think I have something to hide,' I said. 'I don't talk about it because I can't, that's all. I can't.' I looked down at the pebble in my hand then tossed it into the distance. 'No one ever...' I shut my mouth and shook my head.

'No one ever what, Alec?'

My face began to sting from the chill in the air. I hadn't been cold when we'd left the party, but now I could hardly stop my teeth chattering. Our coats were still at the McAllisters'. And I just wanted to be home. Home in the warm, not thinking.

When I didn't answer her question, Daniella reached across and found my hand. Her fingers were warm, comforting as they squeezed mine. But it wasn't a gesture that bode well. I knew what it meant.

'It's only because it hurts,' I said. 'They all want to know what-happened-when, who said what to who, how it was said, the whys, the wherefores, all the fucking pointless practicalities. But...' My jaw clamped itself shut, like its joints had iced over.

Daniella watched me but didn't try to coax more from me. After that, she just sat there, looking out at the grey water, her thumb stroking the back of my hand. It was that one movement that drove me on, made me want to finish what I had to say.

'None of that stuff mattered to me,' I told her. 'She was gone, that was all. She was gone, and I knew I wouldn't see her again. But no one ever let me just...I never got to just...deal with it; deal with her not being there anymore. It was just a wall of questions and suspicions and finger-pointing. Even from my own dad!'

'He didn't believe you?'

I shrugged. 'Put it this way, it wasn't a foregone conclusion.'

She looked off into the distance and shook her head. It was probably hard for her to imagine; she was from a background where loyalty was written into the family crest. They had each other's backs, whatever the situation.

'Well, that's pretty shit,' she said.

I wiped the grit off my hands. 'Anyway, after that, there were just a whole bunch of enquiries and reports; findings and evidence but...you know what?' My voice began to quiver.

Daniella looked at me and shook her head. 'What?'

'No one ever simply said, 'Hey, Alec: I'm sorry your girlfriend... died.' I swallowed, struggling to finish. 'No one ever said that to me.'

I squeezed my eyes shut as I tried to take control of my breathing. What I'd said, what I'd just told her – that was one thought I'd never put into words before. Just saying it out loud was one of the hardest things I'd ever done.

Daniella kept her gaze fixed on the horizon. I didn't have a clue what she was thinking. 'So, what happened in the end?'

'What happened was, I fell apart. I closed down; hated everything and everyone. I felt I'd lost her twice – I mean, she'd obviously cheated, and...I didn't know how to deal with any of it. I was just an angry, confused mess.'

'But what happened, with the police?'

Back to the facts, the answers, the assurances, times, dates.

'I was cleared,' I said. 'Well, I mean, it never went to court. No case to answer. Death by misadventure; that's what the inquest found. But I was never cleared by her family. They didn't believe me, whatever anyone said.'

The amber lights shone higgledy-piggledy back at us, marking out the hills and troughs of the landscape, the English coastline on the other side of the water.

'So, you hadn't known...about the baby?' Daniella said, at last.

'No.'

She shook her head. 'I see.'

'She was pregnant, mate. But not by you.' That's how the wanker of a detective broke it to me. Even asked if I had any ideas who the father might be.'

I sat, biting my bottom lip, keeping my eyes on the ripples of water, on the expanse of it, waiting for my mind to settle, my thoughts to be pulled back into shape.

Daniella rested her head against my shoulder and the wind whipped up her hair so that it stroked my face.

'Alec?' Her tone was uncertain, wary and I felt a subtle shift in the atmosphere.

'Mm?'

She didn't reply.

The seconds ticked by without her speaking and in the silence, I sensed what was coming: the guillotine slice of goodbye that was all-but dripping from her tongue.

I put an arm around her and pulled her close, giving her the permission she seemed to need from me. Even so, it took a few moments before I could steady my voice enough to speak.

'It's okay, Daniella,' I told her. 'I know. You've had enough. You can say it.'

She looked up, her eyelashes still moist and she kissed me lightly on the lips. 'Alec?' she whispered.

'Mm?'

There was a long pause, and I knew she was struggling. I drew a strand of hair away from her cheek.

'I'm not going anywhere,' she said, finally. 'I love you. And I'm really sorry your girlfriend died.'

Chapter 27

It was still dark when something woke me. It took me a few minutes to figure where I was but then I picked out the silhouette of my old Cardiff City lampshade.

Being home, at Mum and Dad's, brought me an odd sort of comfort. It was raining softly outside, and I heard the clicks and whirrs of the radiator on the wall.

I'd never imagined being so relieved to find myself at home. Perhaps I hadn't appreciated what it meant before. The move in Swansea was still to come, but the joy I'd initially felt about the new place seemed to be slipping further from my grasp. Ashton Crescent was still within easy reach of Minto and I had no idea why I hadn't broadened my sights. Maybe Daniella had been right when she'd suggested the only thing keeping me trapped in Swansea was me.

My spirits faltered as soon as Daniella flashed into my mind. The showdown with her brother throbbed like a fresh bruise and although I'd explained it all to Daniella, there was still the problem of the rest of her family.

'Alexander? Alexander?' My door opened a fraction. 'Are you awake?' Mum's voice whispered into the darkness and a bobbly outline of her head peered around the door.

'What's up?'

'Are you decent? Can I come in?'

She switched on the main light, half-blinding me.

'It's that girl, that friend of yours,' she said.

'Eh?' I sat up, my eyes watering from the thousand-watt bulb. 'Daniella?'

'No, the one from the flat,' Mum said. 'The young one.' She glanced back out into the hall.

'Sindy?'

'Yes, Sindy!'

I shook my head, trying to piece together what she was on about. Why were we discussing Sindy in the middle of the night?

'She's downstairs.' Mum pulled an old dressing gown off the peg behind the door and chucked it at me. 'You'd better come, love.'

Just as I'd been enjoying some distance between me and Swansea, it had followed me down the motorway and ended up at my door. I went with Mum downstairs, tightening the belt on this musty tartan monstrosity she'd given me. 'What time is it?' I whispered.

Mum took a hand from the banister and looked at her watch. 'Just gone four-thirty.'

'I'm really sorry, Alec,' Sindy said, shooting out of her chair the minute I walked in. 'I'm sorry for getting everyone up.'

'Oh, now don't you worry about that,' Mum said behind me. 'I'll go and make you both some hot chocolate. Alexander, turn the heating up – you'll get cold in here.' She went out to the kitchen, leaving the door ajar.

I pushed it shut.

'What the hell's going on now, Sindy?' I didn't need to add the 'now' – I didn't need to make it sound like she was always bothering me with something – but as far as I was concerned, it was the middle of the sodding night.

She pulled up her sleeves and held out her skinny wrists. Scratches and cuts criss-crossed all the way up, like she'd been marking herself with a compass point. 'I got really upset and scared,' she said. 'I didn't know what to do.'

I wasn't sure if she was explaining how her arms had got into that state or how she came to be on our doorstep.

I went over to open the curtains, just for something to do. Sindy always seemed to come out with these announcements that I had no answer for; statements I was at a loss how to respond to. The shallow ridges on her wrists hardly looked like someone determined to do any serious bloodletting, but the pitch of her voice was pretty desperate.

'Have you done this before?' I asked her.

She wiped her face with the edge of her cardigan. 'Only when things have got really bad.'

I didn't want to ask so I returned to practicalities. 'How did you get here?'

'I...hitched. It was freezing and it took me ages. But some people are nice.'

There was the bump on the living room door. I opened it to find Mum there with a tray of three mugs. I took two of them, thanked her then waited by the door for her to leave so I could close it.

Hard as I tried to focus on Sindy's issues, there was something on my mind more pressing than her latest drama.

'How did you find me?' I said. 'I've never given you my address.'

'Minto had it, remember?'

'He had the phone number but...'

Sindy shrugged. 'You were in his address book. And Daniella. I was going to go there if you weren't home.'

'But how did he get my address?'

'Aren't you in the phone book?' she said.

The simple logic left me speechless.

'Would it be okay if I stay here?' she said. 'Just till you go back to the flat. Minto'll be okay once he calms down.'

I took her jacket from the sofa to put on the radiator.

'It's okay, it's not wet,' she said. 'The lady who drove gave me a lift all the way to the door.'

'Right,' I said, nodding. 'But why didn't you go to your dad's house? You didn't have to come all the way here.'

She had no argument for that: I figured it was simply that she didn't want to.

'Look, it's not a good idea for you to stay here,' I said. 'If Minto has my address, how do I know he won't come to find you? I think you should have some breakfast, freshen up then...go back.'

Her body seemed to flinch. 'Go back? Today?'

I passed her the hot chocolate from the table. 'Minto will have calmed down.'

'He won't. Please, let me stay tonight, that's all,' Sindy said. 'One night, then I'll be gone.'

I could feel my resolve weakening the closer she got to tears.

However, even if the prospect of Minto turning up wasn't enough to persuade me, the current state of the spare room was.

'Tell you what I'll do,' I said. 'I'll ring Daniella – see if she fancies taking a couple of stowaways on an outing with her. All right?'

She wouldn't look at me.

'Sindy?' I said.

She sighed and kept her eyes on the carpet. 'Okay, okay,' she said. 'If you need to be rid of me, you can ditch me today.'

Chapter 28

Sindy did us a favour, really. After the Kev Mitchell incident, things could've remained raw between me and Daniella for a while. But Sindy forced us back to normality again; she gave us a reason to move on and to get stuck into the practicalities of the present.

If I was honest, I was relieved that the Jill story had come out. Less publicly would have been nice, but I was glad Daniella knew. It had been like a festering wound that finally got some air. We'd been able to examine it; clean it out, leave it to heal naturally whereas my knee-jerk reaction had always been to tuck it away, like a guilty secret, because it was just too messy to unwrap. There was no short version of the story, that was the problem; no throwaway line that would explain it. And really, I only ever dealt in throwaway lines.

I think Daniella was glad too – she'd been granted exclusive rights to the dark and dusty corners of my mind, and not many people had ever got that far. It meant that, when I called her to ask for a favour with Sindy, she sounded warmer towards me than she had in a while.

Despite the wind and the driving rain, we'd given in to Sindy's request to make a quick stop in the motorway services on the way to Swansea. The injection of sherbet lemons and rainbow drops certainly perked up her mood and she became a lot more chatty on the backseat than when we'd first set out.

I'd been hoping to catch up on a bit of shut-eye while Daniella drove, but there was no chance of that with Sindy around.

'What does C H stand for?' she said. 'There isn't a country beginning with C H.' She'd started playing some sort of spot-the-car-sticker game since we'd left the services, and as with most things involving Sindy, she'd managed to rope us all in.

'It's Switzerland,' Daniella said. 'Can't remember why.'

'F – France! And look, AUS – Australia!' Sindy shrieked, drowning out Daniella.

'How d'you know it's not Austria?' I said, turning around to her.

'I don't.' She popped a sweet in her mouth and looked out the window again. 'I've got an uncle and a cousin who live in Australia,' she announced. 'As well as Mum. They live in Queenstown.'

'You mean Queensland, do you?' I said. 'Queenstown is in New Zealand.'

Sindy threw a few chocolates into her mouth. 'I dunno,' she said, chewing. 'It's somewhere hot.'

'That covers most of Australia then.' I spotted more stickers. 'F – France. M – Malta.'

After a few minutes of silence, I realised Sindy had stopped looking at car stickers and moved on.

'How much would it cost to go to Australia?' she said, leaning over my headrest.

'A ton. Thousand quid at least.'

'I could save up. Minto gives me about forty a week. How long would it take to save?'

Daniella looked at me sidelong.

'That'd be two hundred every five weeks,' I said to Sindy. 'So, six months, I reckon, as long as you didn't spend money on anything else.'

'They don't have snakes, do they?' she said. 'I wouldn't want to go if they have snakes.'

'Nah,' I lied. 'It's only the scorpions and spiders that'll get you.'

She had another chocolate. 'I could never save a whole thousand anyway. Half my money has to go on bus fares.'

'So, Minto gives you money, does he?' Daniella said, looking at Sindy in the mirror. 'What's that for?'

'Just to spend. Chocolate, bus fares, records, that sort of thing.'

'But...why?'

'Because he's nice, I suppose.'

Daniella didn't say anything else; just seemed to concentrate on the road. Part of me wanted her to leave it; just keep her nose out. The less we knew the better. But another part of me was itching to know, dying to get my face pressed against the window for a better view.

'The money must be as payment for something,' Daniella said, at last. 'I mean, people don't give money for nothing, do they?'

'Parents give pocket money to their kids,' Sindy said. 'That's for nothing.'

'Mine wasn't,' I told her. 'I had to do the washing up. If I didn't – I got no pocket money.'

'Same here,' said Daniella. She glanced again in the rear-view mirror. 'What do you think you've done to earn Minto's pocket money?'

She certainly had the bit between her teeth.

I glanced around. Sindy had poured all the sweets into her lap. She kept her head down as she answered. 'I know what you're doing,' she said. 'But you know I'm not allowed to say. I told Alec I wasn't allowed to say.'

'Is that because it's something wrong?' Daniella said.

'No!' A sliver of defensiveness had crept into Sindy's tone. I reckoned she was a breath away from folding those arms of hers and shutting down any more questions.

'Some people might think it's wrong,' she said, at last. 'But that doesn't mean it really is.'

'Sounds intriguing, doesn't it?' Daniella said to me. 'I reckon it's... handling stolen goods: that's what the money's for.'

'No, it isn't.'

Daniella pretended not to hear. 'Sindy probably finds out where people leave back doors open or have equipment in their cars, and she passes the info on and Minto nicks the goods.'

'Minto doesn't take anything,' Sindy said. 'He's a businessman.'

'Businessman, eh?' I said. 'Flashy.'

'He doesn't sell anything to anyone who doesn't ask him,' she said. 'It's a rule. All his business comes through people asking him. He just helps them out.'

'Helps them out with what?' Daniella said. 'Stolen goods? Camera equipment, sports gear, electricals.' She flashed a smile at me. If she was trying to wind Sindy up, she was doing a cracking job of it.

'I told you he doesn't deal with that stuff!'

'What is it then?' I said, joining in. 'Guns? Knives? Weapons?'

Her voice was quiet. 'Sometimes.' The sound of sweets sliding into their bags came from the back. 'But if people ask for pills or something like that, Minto tries to help them out.'

'Pills?' said Daniella.

'Mm.'

'So, these people just come up to him in the street, out of the blue, in case he happens to have something.'

Daniella was proving an ace at acting dumb – I didn't need to join in. Sindy was tutting and sighing in the back like she couldn't believe the stupidity of her travelling companions.

'No! People know where to find him. But Minto's got friends all over the place. And not just in Wales. I mean in lots of countries. They all help each other.'

'He's like his own personal global charity, eh?' I said.

Daniella looked out of her window and paused a few moments. 'I still don't see why *you* get any payment though, Sindy.'

'I know some local kids, teenagers. That helps.'

'Do you?'

'It doesn't look so odd if I talk to them,' she said. 'They might think Minto's some creepy guy if he started talking to them.'

'He wouldn't want to give them that impression, would he?' said Daniella.

Sindy mightn't have understood the point, but I could tell the tone had put her on her guard.

Daniella was quick to make amends though. 'I suppose you get a percentage of whatever's sold,' she said, like she was talking to herself. 'A bit like at those house parties where you get commission on cosmetics and stuff.'

'It's not that...organised,' Sindy said. 'Minto just gives me some money whenever he has some.' She shrugged. The novelty of being centre of attention seemed to be wearing thin.

To be honest, I was relieved. I didn't like Daniella trying to wheedle information from Sindy; twisting the emphasis here and there to catch her out. And I certainly didn't want Daniella delving into Sindy's night-time activities.

'CZ – Czechoslovakia!' I said. 'Who can spell Czechoslovakia?'

Sindy was kept so busy with that conundrum, I reckoned the whole conversation would be safely forgotten by the time she got back to Minto.

Once we arrived in Swansea. I warned Daniella to drop us at the end of the street rather than risk going up to the house, but as soon as we peeled around the corner, we realised our mistake.

With a steep set of steps up to the house, Minto and Black had the perfect view of us from where the two of them were sitting, beer bottles in hand.

My instinct was to throw Sindy out of the car and have Daniella drive off, but given it was a no-through road, negotiating a three-point turn would have hardly made for a quick getaway.

'He's there!' Sindy said, throwing open her door. It was like nothing had happened between them. 'Come and say hello,' she said to us both. 'He'll want to see you before you go.'

Daniella and I looked at one another, probably both formulating the same flimsy excuse, but I saw Daniella's gaze shift over my shoulder, and I knew Minto was already on the pavement, peering in at us.

'Not even going to get your young lady to turn off the engine?' he said as I wound down the window. 'Not being anti-social again, are you, Mr Johnston?'

'We're in a bit of a rush,' I said. 'We just wanted to quickly drop Sindy off.'

I heard his fat fingers drum against the roof as he remained stooped at the side of us. 'Sounds like you all had quite the awayday, Sinds,' he said. 'Down by the seaside, beside the sea.'

'It was quite a surprise,' Daniella said, leaning across me. 'Amazing how Sindy managed to get hold of Alec's address like that.'

The comment did nothing to break the deadlock. Minto looked back at her, unsmiling.

'That's the beauty of a phone book, I guess,' I said. Why I was tripping over myself to smooth things over for Minto, I had no idea.

'No phone book required,' he said. 'I've got both your home addresses safe in my possession. Just in case. You know how it is.' And he kept his eyes on us, waiting for a reaction that didn't come.

'They were both really nice to me,' Sindy said, nudging up against him. 'They let me buy some sweets and a *Smash Hits* on the way home.'

'All cashed-up and kindness, aren't they?' Minto said. 'Anyway, there'll be a few people glad to see you; what with us not knowing where you'd gone an' all. It doesn't do to just fuck off like that, Sindy.' He caught her arm as she was about to leave. 'I need to know where you are.' His eyes switched to me again. 'I was afraid I'd have to track you down and bother these good folks' families.'

'I know,' she murmured. 'Sorry. I just thought you might need some time to calm –'

'If I need some time to cool off, gal, you'll know about. All right?'

She nodded.

'Now go inside. See Gazza – he's been asking for you.'

Sindy looked at us and smiled. 'See you,' she said. And she ran up the road in that gawky way of hers and disappeared into the house.

Minto remained where he was. 'I think it's time you and I had a little chat, Alec,' he said. His eyes swept across to Daniella. 'Would you excuse us, darlin'?'

She kept her hands on the wheel. 'I'm sorry?' she said, leaning across me again as if she couldn't quite hear.

He went around to her side of the car and spoke slowly and loudly at her through the open window. 'I need to have a private word with y'man, here.' He looked at me. 'We'll go for a quick spin together.'

'Sorry,' Daniella said. 'I have to get back to Bristol.'

The mistake I made was looking across at her instead of keeping a check on Minto. In that split second, he'd reached in and snatched the keys out of the ignition. 'I really must insist,' he said.

Daniella's hand shot down to the handle, but Minto was already opening the door.

'It's okay,' I told her, quickly. 'We'll be ten minutes at the most. Walk down to the Tenby: I'll bring the car back to you there, okay?'

'That's the way, love,' Minto said, taking her place in the driver's seat as soon as Daniella stepped out.

She didn't look at him but came straight around to my side. 'If you're not back in ten,' she said, leaning in. 'I'm calling someone.'

Minto let out a guffaw as he sparked up the engine. 'Don't worry your pretty little head,' he said. 'Y'man is quite safe with me.' And he put his foot on the gas before Daniella had time to argue.

We pulled up not too far from the house and Minto eased back in his seat as soon as he switched off the engine. The squeak of the vinyl seemed to underline the threat of his weight and bulk.

'Things seem to have soured between us, Alec,' he said. 'And I don't know why that is. Do you?'

'No.'

'No?'

There was a silence, and as usual, I felt obliged to fill it. 'I still consider you a…friend,' I said.

'Trouble is, it was someone I considered a friend who, it turns out, set up the drugs-bust,' he said. 'And the sort of person who gets the wrong idea about my chemical dealings might also get the wrong idea about Sindy. And that wouldn't do, would it? I mean, we wouldn't want anyone messing things up for Sindy: she relies on me.'

He smelt of stale smoke and aftershave and, hearing him talk about Sindy made me want to whack his face against the dashboard.

'If you think I'm going to turn you in or something, I'm not,' I said. 'What you do is up to you. I'm moving out – we don't need to have any more to do with each other. That's it, as far as I'm concerned. But I don't want you contacting my family or my friends – and I won't go near you and yours.'

He watched me, like he was sizing up just how much shit he could squeeze out of me. His smirk morphed into a chortle. He slapped a hand against his leather-clad thigh like I was the latest in in-car entertainment. 'Quite the little speech for one so timid.'

'I mean it,' I said – and the way my voice shook, I couldn't have sounded less like I meant it if I'd tried.

He leaned an arm across the back of my chair. 'Here's the thing, Alec. We don't like each other, not really. I gave you the chance to be one of us but no, you seemed to think you were destined for better things.' He looked off to the side, as if he couldn't keep a straight face. 'Trouble is, as you know, in my book, if you're not with us you're against us. And I have to say, I like things to go my way; I don't cope well with... disappointment. I don't like people interfering with my happiness, my goals. You know what I'm saying? Keep on side with me, and I'll do everything I can to help you, yeah?' He smiled but leaned over and jabbed a finger in my chest. 'But, fuck me over, Alec and you'll regret it. You'll pay for it in whatever way I see fit, whether that's through your meek little band of loser friends or through that no-hope family of yours. But one way or another, you'll wish you'd kept me as a friend. Do we understand each other, Alec?'

I nodded. 'Stay away from me,' I said, 'and sure, I'll stay away from you.'

He offered a slow, considered nod. 'I think that's a fair summary of the situation.' He opened the door and when he got out, I felt the suspension lift. He leaned on the open door, looking back at me. 'And when we say we'll keep away from each other, that includes you keeping away from Sindy, comprendez?'

'She's always the one who comes looking for – '

'Comprendez, Alec?'

I nodded.

'Good,' he said. 'Because if I find you so much as looking at her again, I'll rip your fucking throat out.' He slammed the door so hard, the whole car rocked. By the time I dared risk a glance in the mirror, he'd already disappeared.

Chapter 29

I gave Minto a very wide berth after his little chat to me that day, divvying up my time between Daniella's and Mum and Dad's. But I couldn't really settle, wherever I was, and I started to wonder if that was ever going to change, even once I'd moved. After all, would Minto truly let me go, or would he keep tabs on me from afar; follow me with those beady eyes of his regardless of where I went?

I had no choice but to go back to the flat the night before I was shifting. The bits of packing I'd done were patchy and haphazard; I needed to make sure I took everything with me. There was no way I'd want to make a return trip and beg Minto for something vital I'd left behind.

Howling gales and lashing rain accompanied my last night and even that felt ominous. Minto and his crew rolled home around three a.m. and after that, it felt as wild inside as it sounded outside. I kept a table against my door and a pillow over my head, hoping to God they didn't realise I was home.

We'd managed to squeeze everything into Daniella's car. My belongings were so tightly packed, I didn't need to worry about breakages: there simply wasn't room for anything to shift in transit.

I left Daniella by the car while I went back in to give the room a final once over.

I got to the top of the stairs and found Minto standing outside my door, his big arms folded across his even bigger chest.

'Ready for the off, I see,' he said.

'Yup. I didn't want to disturb you all: I heard you get in pretty late.'

'That's thoughtful of you, Alec,' he said.

He was still standing there like a bouncer outside my room, blocking my way.

I stuck out my hand. 'Well, all the best, mate,' I said. 'It's been a blast, hasn't it? I'll see you around no doubt.'

'Oh, certainly no doubt about that,' he said, ignoring my outstretched hand.

There was a difficult pause. I waited. Then waited some more. 'Say cheerio to the others for me, won't you?' I said. I gave him a friendly smile and stuck my hands back in my pockets. 'Right,' I said, nodding at my door. 'I'd better check I've cleared everything out.'

Our eyes met when he made no attempt to move.

Next thing, he had me in a headlock and was squeezing hard. I couldn't speak, could barely stay on my feet. Spit was dribbling from the corner of my mouth and I couldn't swallow. His gripped tightened and, for a second, I thought my neck was about to snap. But as the thought hit me, I was wheeled around and flung against the far wall, whacking the side of my face as I dropped to the floor.

I covered my head: I'd seen Minto's favourite moves. And I wasn't wrong. A searing pain shot through my ear as his boot found a way through.

'Minto! No! Don't!' I heard.

I thought it was Daniella but as I opened an eye, I recognised Sindy's slippers hurrying through the hall.

I tried to get to my feet but realised he had a boot on my thigh, keeping me down.

'Get back in the bedroom, you little cunt.'

'But –'

'Do you want to make things worse?' he shouted, pressing his boot down. 'Do you?'

I saw her furry feet turn then heard the slam of a door.

I was forced upright and suddenly Minto's face was in mine. 'Just so you know,' he said. 'I'm watching you and I'll always be watching you.'

'I got it,' I said, trying to back away. 'I got it.'

'I hope you have, Alec.'

He drew back his head and my world went black. I was aware only of noises, of far-away sounds. Another door-slam and the whoosh-whoosh of blood through my ears. Daniella's voice.

'Alec? Oh my God, Alec!'

I tried to open my eyes, but the lids were wet and sticky

'What happened? Oh, God. Let's get you up. Shall I get an ambulance?'

'No.'

A key-turn and footsteps. I couldn't tell if it was right beside me or out in the street.

'Get him out of here,' Minto said.

'You...did this to him?'

I was aware that Daniella was getting to her feet. I could do no more than grip onto her ankle, silently pleading with her to shut her mouth.

'Get him out of here. Don't make me say it again.'

Daniella's ankle was suddenly wrenched from my hand and when I heard her yelp, I knew he had her by the throat. I scrabbled to my knees but collapsed again as Daniella fell against me.

'Remember,' Minto said to us. 'I've got eyes and ears everywhere. Everywhere. You understand?'

I nodded, praying Daniella was doing the same.

He turned back to his room and closed the door, the fond farewell finally at an end.

Chapter 30

Even though I had a new place to escape to, Daniella and I were too shaken up to contemplate being anywhere near Swansea for the weekend. As soon as we'd dumped my belongings in my empty room, Daniella drove us to her student digs in Bristol.

The next few days was an odd existence. I was an invited guest, but I didn't feel at home. I knew Daniella was glad I was free of Swansea, temporarily at least, but I don't think she felt secure having me around. Perhaps I shouldn't have admitted what had happened at the clubhouse; about the thumb squeeze to join them. She seemed weird about it; like it was somehow my fault. I guess she felt it should never have got to that stage and she was probably right but the whole Minto infiltration had been so insidious: it had got out of hand so quickly. When I'd first moved in, along with Stobes and Black, Minto had seemed rough and ready, all bark and no bite. It had never occurred to me that he was part of any underworld; that his bark and bite were just the precursors to a far more threatening form of attack. Now though, I had no illusions.

As the week wore on, I sensed my resolve to return to Swansea waning. The small-town nature of the place – which had previously made me feel safe, or at least part of something safe – now felt menacing, intimidating. Every bar was a potential fight site, the streets patrolled by enemies. Every incline, every corner was freshly tarred with suspicion and risk, as if it had become my own personal warzone.

I sensed Daniella's discomfort too and knew her worry increased with each passing day. By the following Sunday, I sensed I had to give her some space. I figured Mum and Dad's would form a neat airlock before gathering my courage and my strength to head back to Swansea.

The house was quiet when I walked in, no off-tune radio hissing at me from the kitchen, no canned laughter from the telly in the living room. I leaned over the banister and called up the stairs: 'Hello? Mum?'

When no one came to give me a welcome, I left my bag in the hall but kept my jacket on. I felt the radiator: there was no tick-tick of heated water and the metal was cold against my fingers. Strange – even if they were out, Mum always liked to have the house warm for when she got back. I shouted upstairs again but the same silence as before bounced back at me.

I pottered about for an hour, making a drink and fixing myself something to eat. The football scores in the paper kept me occupied for a while then I watched a bit of telly until it got dark. I'd expected them to be back by then, from wherever they'd disappeared. Once all the God-squad programmes came on, I decided I should check their bedroom, see if there was a clue to where they'd disappeared.

It looked the same as always: bedspread turned down, cupboards shut, surfaces dust-free, everything in its place. Yet the main light was on. And when I stepped further into the room, my shoe scraped against something on the floor. I bent down. The corner of a suitcase was sticking out from beneath the bed, like it had been hiding. I kicked it further under and went over to the window. Another odd thing: the curtains were drawn and when I checked, all the windows were shut even though Mum always insisted on keeping a few ajar to stop what she called 'the stale smell of indoors.'

I turned around, surveying the room. I couldn't figure where the hell they both were.

The spare room was the same shambles it had been the last time I was home. If anything, it looked fuller; even more crazed. As I stood there with my head poked around the door, I knew that if anything had changed or was out of place, I was never going to spot it in there, so I closed up and went along the landing.

That's when I saw a single line of light beneath the bathroom door.

I stood there, contemplating.

'Anyone in there?' I knocked on the door. 'Dad? Are you there?'

Nada. Not even the sound of a dripping tap.

I sucked in a breath and knocked again. 'Hello? I'm coming in. Okay?'

In my mind, I put my shoulder against the door and forced it open. But in reality, I stood listening to the silence, not knowing what to do.

'Here I come, all right?' I shouted, banging the palm of my hand against the door.

I turned the doorknob and shoved the door open.

My entrance was so forceful that I tripped on the bathmat and nearly put my face through the shower door. Yet even as I shot into the room, I felt I could breathe again at finding no one in there. Yes, the lights might well have been on, but no one was home.

By the time I'd finished searching the whole house and garage, I'd managed to piece together some scraps of information. There was a light on at the back of the house, courtesy of the bathroom and one at the front in their bedroom where the curtains were closed. The car had gone from the garage and there were a couple of unwashed cups in the sink. The curtains and lights suggested they'd gone away, at least overnight. The closed windows pointed to some forethought and organisation, but the unwashed cups? They made me rethink: Mum left nothing unwashed. No way would she ever leave dirty cups in the sink if an overnight trip was on the cards.

Still, given the lack of bodies and bloodstains in the house, I figured I could wait another day to find out. I put my empty beer bottles on the draining board and headed off to bed.

It was the creak of the kitchen door that woke me. I'd slept like a brick all night and it took me a few minutes to work out where I was. At least they were home, judging by the noises downstairs. I needed the bog, so I clambered out of bed, had a pee and went to let Mum know I was in residence.

What I expected to see was her standing at the sink. Instead, what I found was Bill from next door, putting on his glasses and peering at some envelopes in his hand. His head flicked up. 'Oh! Alexander!' He put a hand on his chest – then on the chair – to steady himself. 'Good lord, I didn't know anyone was here.'

'Likewise.'

He regarded my near nakedness. 'I take it you didn't tell your mum and dad you were coming?'

'It was a spur of the moment decision.'

Bill looked back at the letters and nodded. He was all right, Bill; a bit doddery and hard of hearing but who wouldn't be at a hundred and ninety?

'So, where are they?' I asked him.

'Oh, I'm not sure,' he said, placing the envelopes into three neat piles. Always been a stickler for order, had Bill. 'Your Mum popped round and said they needed to go up to...' His brow furrowed, and he looked up at the ceiling. 'Southsea?'

'Southsea?'

'Somewhere like that,' he said.

'Not Swansea?' I said, looking at him.

'Yes! Swansea, it was,' he said.

'Oh. Crap.'

'Nothing wrong, is there?'

'It's fine,' I told him. 'I'd better try and get hold of them.'

'They seemed to be in a tearing rush, so I just said I'd pop in, make sure everything was all right till they came back. Still, now you're here...'

'I won't be staying,' I said. 'I'd better head back.'

'Where are you living now?'

'Swansea.'

'Nice,' he said, nodding.

And as far as I know, the penny never did drop.

Chapter 31

Mumbles looked completely different in the rain: the wind swept in straight from the bay and all those shop fronts that had seemed so welcoming in the sunshine now looked grim, with their grey stone walls hunkered down against potential invaders.

The only bright spots on the strip were the pubs, but even their welcomes were half-hidden by the salt-smeared windows. There were so many choices along the main drag: The Pilot, The Mermaid, The Antelope and they were just precursors to lots more hostelry options – 'barely time for a belch between bars', as Minto liked to say.

The reminder of him gave me instant gut ache and I turned up a set of steep concrete steps that led to Seaview Terrace and all its bed and breakfast signs. The light was already fading, even though we were probably only halfway through the afternoon. It had been quite a trek. A train ride from Mum's; a coach to Swansea and a bus ride to my new abode. That's when I found the message that Mum and Dad were in Mumbles, so it was yet another bus ride from there.

There was no obvious sequence to the house numbers, and I found myself filtering out the numbers and just scouring the lanes for a place called Esther's. That's where they were staying according to the message they'd left on my door.

I stumbled upon it almost by accident and I threw open the door, anxious to find out what my folks were playing at. They never 'took off' on holiday. Anything involving suitcases and accommodation was definitely off the spontaneity-radar. The only reason I could imagine was that maybe they'd come for a stickybeak at my new digs; make sure I really was away from Minto.

A jingling bell announced my arrival and, even this late in the day, the smell of eggs and bacon hung over the reception area. I bumped a hand on the bell, and it sent a woman hurrying in my direction from upstairs. 'Hello,' she said. 'Can I help you?'

Even before I'd explained, I recognised Mum's slippered feet coming down the stairs. 'There you are!' she said, pulling me into a hug as she reached me. 'We couldn't think where to look for you!'

'What's going on?' I said. 'Why didn't you let me know you were coming?'

'Come on up,' Mum said, lowering her voice and glancing at the receptionist.

We'd only got as far as the landing before she started unloading. 'We didn't know what to do,' she said. 'We couldn't get much joy from your new place. No one seemed to know where you were. I mean, we realised you might be at Daniella's, but we had no way of getting in touch with her. In the end, we had no choice but to come in the car and…'

'What's up, though?' I said, as we reached the top of the stairs. 'What did you need me so urgently for?'

'We didn't know what the safest option would be. But when we couldn't get hold of you, we just had to take a chance and see what we could do.'

Only Mum could say so much while saying so very little.

'Take a chance on what?'

She pursed her lips and let out a deep sigh, like I was being incredibly thick. 'Come and see,' she said. And with that, she let us into room number five.

The curtains were closed, and the bedside lights were on. Dad stood up as we came in, but I could already see there was someone in the bed.

'What's going on?' I said.

Dad put a finger up to his lips. 'Shh, she's asleep.'

I took a few steps forward, craning my neck to see who was under the sheets. It was hard to recognise the face, but I knew that lank, blonde hair all too well.

I looked from Dad to Mum. 'What's she doing here?'

If they answered I didn't hear. I was too busy peering down, working out why those familiar features looked so odd, so suddenly unfamiliar.

'Jeez,' I said to myself. Her skin was so puffy, the well-defined cheekbones had all but disappeared. I could only imagine the colour on all that swelling – fortunately there wasn't enough light to see. She looked like only an approximation of herself. 'How did you find her?'

Mum put a hand on my shoulder, and I heard her take in a breath. 'Maybe we should go out for a bit: I can explain in private.'

As far as I could see, Sindy was out-for-the-count but she stirred when she heard Mum's voice.

'Anything we can get you, love?' Mum said, perching on the edge of the bed.

'No, ta,' Sindy mumbled.

'Alexander's here.'

Sindy nodded but she seemed barely awake.

'We might take him out for a bite to eat,' Mum said to the back of Sindy's head. 'You could get some more rest.'

Sindy blinked open her eye and shook her head. 'I don't want to be on my own.'

The rest of us exchanged glances. Dad came over. 'What if I was just in there?' Dad said, nodding at the nearby door. 'In our room. Would you be all right with that?'

The sleeping arrangements hadn't occurred to me, but I guess it was obvious they wouldn't be all cosied-up in a family room.

'See – this is a connecting door,' Dad told her.

Sindy's eyes followed him. 'Could you leave it open a bit?'

Dad gave her a smile. A warm, protective smile. 'Certainly.' He turned to Mum. 'Why don't you take the car?' he said. 'I'm not hungry anyway. I'll sit in there and read the papers.'

'That all right, love?' Mum said.

Sindy ignored the question and looked at me. 'You won't be long, will you?'

'Nah,' I said. 'You get some sleep. We'll have a chat later.'

She wrestled out something close to a smile. 'We can talk about what we're going to do then, can't we?' she said.

And her eyes surged with such hope, such certainty I could fix everything, that I couldn't wait to be out of there.

Chapter 32

Mum has always eased very gingerly into awkward conversations; like she's putting on new shoes that she knows are going to pinch. I could taste her tension the moment the two of us got in the car.

'It's all such a to-do, isn't it?' she said, as we headed out of the car park. 'I bet you didn't imagine finding Sindy here with us, did you?'

'Nope,' I said. 'How the hell did it all happen?'

'I suppose we could've taken her back home with us really,' Mum said, still on her own particular train of thought. 'In some ways it's been more difficult being here with her rather than at home. There's always the risk of...oh, not here, love,' she said as I was about to turn into CJ's car park. 'Sindy told us all the places to avoid: she said Minto often comes to these cafes. Isn't there somewhere away from the main town we could go? Somewhere with a few less pubs?'

It made me wonder why they'd chosen a hideout right in the midst of Minto-land, but I figured I'd get the whole story soon enough.

I put the windscreen wipers on and cranked up the heater.

We ended up at some swanky restaurant in one of the bays: 'Clinkers' it was called, presumably on account of the occasional passing yacht. One look at the fussy menu and I knew we'd be safe from Minto.

It was surprisingly busy given it was a Monday night and we were outside the main town, but when I saw the Hallowe'en decorations and the special deal on Bloody Marys, I realised the rest of the diners were just hiding from the Trick or Treaters.

'I think I'll have the whitebait,' Mum told me. 'And shall we order some wine?'

She picked something cheap from near the top of the list and it got me thinking how much this trip must have set them back. I hoped the B&B had an off-season deal.

'So, what's the story, Mum?' I said, once we'd placed our order and got a drink in our hands.

'It was a couple of days ago,' she said. 'And look at the state of Sindy, even now: this is after a bit of recovery. You can imagine what she looked like when we first saw her. I wanted to get her to a hospital, but she wouldn't hear of it. So stubborn, she is.'

It was frustrating trying to keep Mum on track. She never said things chronologically or in a logical sequence. All the details were interspersed with a whole raft of other random thoughts. 'Yes, but how did you find her?'

'Well, she rang looking for you. She was so upset. She'd been to your new place and no one knew where you were or how to get hold of you. She rang us in desperation.'

'So, this is Minto's handiwork, the damage to her face?'

'Yes. And he's thrown her out as well.'

That piece of news came as a shock. 'Really? You sure?'

'She did tell me why, but I didn't really understand,' Mum said. 'We tried everywhere we could think of to get hold of you.'

'I was at Daniella's.'

Mum topped up our glasses. 'We thought you might be – but you've never told us her surname or where her parents live, or anything.' Mum looked at me like I'd deliberately kept these things from her.

'So, Minto threw her out,' I said, trying to keep her focussed. 'Then what?'

'What d'you mean, 'then what?' She had no one to turn to and nowhere to live!'

'But Sindy doesn't live at the flat,' I said. 'She lives with her dad.'

Mum opened her mouth then shut it again. She leaned forward, then back as if the news had put her all out of kilter. 'I don't understand,' she said. 'She made it sound as though she had nowhere to go – literally nowhere. Surely, she wouldn't have made us come all this way if she had a home to go to? It's costing us a fortune to stay in that place.'

The arrival of our starters saved me from having to answer but as soon as Mum was tucking into her whitebait, she kept right on going. 'The poor kid seems so frightened, that's the thing. If she went to the police, they'd soon put a stop to him, but she won't even consider it.'

'Minto's got a lot of friends,' I said. 'Going to the cops mightn't be the smartest move.'

Mum shook her head. 'I didn't think this sort of thing went on.' She picked up the salt cellar and showered some over the fish and quite a lot over the tablecloth. 'Why would she turn to you instead of getting help from her own father?' she said. 'He must know this Minto's a bad sort.'

'Yeah, well it's an odd situation,' I said.

Mum leaned back in her chair. 'To me, it all seems wrong. It's not normal that she's so young when he must be, what, in his mid-thirties?'

'No, it's not right.'

'I was going to suggest a women's refuge,' Mum said, 'but Sindy doesn't seem old enough for that.'

'She wouldn't go in any case.' I poured some of my wine into Mum's glass. 'You didn't have to go to the flat to get her, did you?'

'No, we told her to meet us at that cafe we all went to the first time. Remember?'

'So, she just waited there?'

'She'd managed to pack a few things, at least. She's got one or two bits of clothing with her and some...'

'She packed?'

'Yes.' Mum put down her fork and laughed as she thought about it. 'She's got this huge suitcase but there's very little in it. A few comics, some underwear and a jumper from what I could see.'

I rolled my eyes. 'Yeah, that'd be Sindy.'

Even so, it seemed strange she'd had time to pack if this was such an emergency.

Mum polished off the last of her whitebait and pushed her plate away. She looked around and let out a chuckle. 'It's rather nice having a posh meal together like this, isn't it?'

'Yeah,' I said. 'It is.'

I meant it, too.

'Pity your dad couldn't come too though,' she said. 'It would have been nice to have us all here together.'

'How's he been? He looks a bit perkier.'

Mum stacked our empty plates and pushed them to the edge of the table. 'Well, you know how he is, stuck at home not doing very much. But this has helped.' There was a definite spark in her eye as she looked back at me. 'It's an enforced holiday, really. I think it's doing him the world of good: a change of scenery, a different view out of the window, a bit of sea air. And Sindy's a funny little thing.'

'Yeah.'

The smile slipped from her face. 'I suppose, if I think about, it's good for me too.' She was careful not to meet my eye as she made the admission. 'Sometimes, those four walls...'

The waiter took away our plates and our mains arrived seconds later: a slab of gammon for me; a hefty steak and ale pie for Mum.

'I thought you'd enjoy being at home more now Dad's retired,' I said. 'All those years he wasn't there and now you get him all to yourself, every day.'

'Mm.' She cut into her pie, all focus apparently on her meal.

'Or is it more difficult having someone else around?'

'I suppose it just takes some adjusting to,' she said. 'For both of us. His life has been full of order and routine and discipline...and now, well, there's nothing he has to do. Nowhere he has to be. He's a bit...at a loss. Nobody needs him. And as for me, well, I don't know. I just feel lonelier than ever.'

I looked up from my meal as her voice waivered.

'Pass me the salt, would you, love?' she said, quickly.

I gave it to her and was about to return to our conversation, but she snuck in with something else. Something safe. 'How's that lovely girlfriend of yours?' she said. 'Have you seen much of her lately?'

'She helped me shift from the flat last week,' I said.

'Yes, how is it? Are you settled in?'

'I've hardly been there. We moved my stuff in and then went to Daniella's for the week.'

Mum looked back at me, puzzled, but I wasn't about to fill her in on Minto's farewell fistfight which had sent us scuttling east. Just as well my bruises were well-hidden; Minto was probably expert in delivering carefully aimed wounds.

'It's nice to see you with a girlfriend again,' Mum said.

I nodded, hoping she'd leave it.

But of course, Mum was never one to leave things.

'It seems such a long time since...well, you know. You and Jill used to spend so much of your time at our place – and the...'

She put a hand onto mine, even though I was perfectly okay and holding a forkful of gammon. 'It's well overdue, that's all I'm saying,' she told me. 'I was so pleased when you finally brought someone home. And Daniella's just lovely.'

'Glad you approve,' I said.

I poured myself some water and shifted the discussion neatly from Daniella to dessert.

'If you want to stay with us,' Mum said as I helped her with her coat outside the restaurant, 'I could sleep in Sindy's room and you could share with Dad. It'd be no trouble: save you driving all the way home.'

'I should get back,' I said. 'I haven't been there all week: it'd be nice to finally sleep in my own bed. I'll bring the car in the morning.'

'Oh, don't worry about that. It's just...'

'What?'

She stopped us, halfway between the restaurant and the car park. 'Would you mind staying at the bed and breakfast tonight, love?' The wind blew the hood of her coat down as she stood waiting for me to say yes.

'Why?'

'I don't know,' she said, looking down.

'But I'm only ten minutes away from you.'

'I know, I know. But I don't like the thought of you going back there. Sindy said Minto and you don't get along these days and that flat is still so close to where he is. I just...' She put her hand on my arm. 'Please – to put my mind at rest?'

I shrugged. 'Okay, I guess.'

'Thanks, love.'

We hurried towards the car, bracing ourselves against the sharp wind slicing across the bay. Mum took hold of my arm. 'You know the way back to the B&B, don't you?'

''Course.'

'It's not too bad there,' she said. 'It costs a bit but it's clean and comfortable.'

I unlocked Mum's door before I went around and slid into the driver's seat. The car park was nearly empty and with the restaurant behind us, there was a sense of isolation as we sat facing the rocky outcrops and the sweep of the sea beyond.

I started the engine and cranked up the fan and the heater. We sat with the windscreen wipers on full blast and waiting for the windows to demist.

'Mum?' I said. 'What did you mean back there? About feeling lonelier than ever?'

'Oh, take no notice,' she said, with a wave of the hand. 'Just 'silly old woman' talk.'

I'd had a sinking feeling in my stomach ever since she'd said it. I knew it could be a long time before we'd get another moment like this one.

'Is that what all the shopping and the séances and the clippings are about?'

I could see her instinct was to dismiss the idea, but she stopped and allowed herself to think about it. It took a good few pulses of the wipers before she spoke.

'I always thought the loss would fade away,' she said. 'Of Gina, I mean. And I suppose for a little while it did – on a day to day basis, at least.' She swallowed loudly and her breath sounded ragged. She picked at imaginary marks on her fingernails. 'But now it's worse than ever. Now it's so close, I feel it with me all the time. I think it's...I see these lovely young girls – on the edge of becoming young women. And I just miss her all over again. I think: 'our Gina would look like that,' and then I imagine her doing her exams and going off to college. Of getting a boyfriend, of settling down and looking forward to a family of her own. We'd have grandchildren...'

That was the word that finally tripped her up. She put a hand up to her face and her body crumpled.

'I'm sorry,' she mumbled, as I pulled her against me. 'I know it's ridiculous after all this time. I'm a grown woman. And it's not like you won't ever have a family and I know I should be over it and be getting on with my life but...I don't know. Perhaps I'm being punished for something,' she said, sniffing. 'Perhaps it was my fault we lost Gina in the first place.'

'No, Mum,' I whispered. But, jeez, as she cried against my chest, I could even feel myself starting to get choked up.

'I never expected it to get worse rather than better,' she said. 'I don't know. Maybe it's the change and everything, but Gina seems to be on my mind all the time now...and I can't stop myself noticing those important landmarks.' She sucked in some air. 'I haven't done it deliberately, but I keep track of when she'd be taking O' levels, her A' levels, applying for college, going to her first formal. It's as if I've had this...mental running commentary of her life. And all that's missing from it is her. She's missed out on so much, Alexander. There was so much more *life* she should have had.'

Her grief had whipped up to a frenzy and I could only hold her as her body bumped and trembled against me.

I'd had no idea: no fucking idea for all those years, that any of it had been going on.

And I figured Dad didn't either.

Reckoned it might have been one of the few things we'd ever had in common.

Chapter 33

The place had twin beds rather than doubles and I was surely thankful for that. Sharing a room with Dad was one thing but sleeping under the same duvet would've stretched the bounds of any father-son relations way beyond my comfort zone.

The prospect of an overnighter with the old man didn't bother me nearly as much as I would've expected. I didn't know if it was to do with him being away from his own turf or if he was enjoying the novelty of being needed, but that evening after Mum and I got back, he'd been almost sociable. Perhaps it was my imagination, but he didn't seem so stiff and uptight as he did at home. Everything about him was more fluid, looser; even his facial expressions. He didn't seem to grind from one scowl to another – an odd calm had come over him.

That's not to say we'd turned into an updated version of the Brady Bunch, but Dad at least looked up from his paper occasionally, and once I'd got into bed, he asked if I wanted a loan of the sports section.

After I settled down, Dad put out the light and I heard the swish and rustle of him undressing. I could see it all in my head: the sharp slice as he took the hanger from the wardrobe and slid his shirt onto it. The sound of change clattering on the floor from his pockets as he held the turn-ups of his trousers under his chin, ready to fold along the creases and place on a hanger. How did I even know this stuff? I'd spent so long telling myself he was never there that I'd almost forgotten all the things I did remember about him being in the house; all the funny ways he had of doing things, the set routines, the specific order he carried out certain tasks. It was endearing and infuriating all at the same time.

I could hardly stop my teeth chattering and I reached down in the hope there might be an electric blanket control dangling from the side of the bed. My flailing arm was met only with cold air.

'It's hardly Buckingham Palace, this place, is it?' Dad said in the dark.

'It's not too bad, just a bit chilly.'

'It's better than that place we stayed in Exmouth – do you remember?' Dad said.

'Exmouth? No, when was that?'

'You were probably too young to remember. You could only have been five or six. Anyway, I'll never forget the cooked breakfasts we used to have there – looked like the woman had been keeping them warm for a week. Eggs like rubber; black pudding as tough as bullets. It was a shocker.'

For some reason, the idea of Dad trying to swallow a rubbery egg made me laugh and I started sniggering under the sheets. I even thought I heard a few titters from Dad before we both went quiet. After a while, he got out of bed and slid open a cupboard door. The weight of an extra blanket landed on me and I heard Dad pad back to bed.

As my eyes adjusted to the dark, I could pick out the silhouette of his shoulder, rising and falling as he lay on his side, facing the wall.

I heard him sigh and clear his throat. It brought me an odd kind of comfort, like when I used to hear him downstairs after I'd gone to bed sometimes. He wasn't around much, but I never felt quite as safe in the house as when he was.

The tick-tick of his old travel alarm clock tapped a rhythm in my head, and it struck me how much I'd've relished this little adventure as a nipper.

'Dad?' I said, after a bit.

'Eh?'

'Thanks for looking after Sindy.'

He turned to face me. 'That's all right,' he said. 'I wasn't hungry anyway: it was no trouble to stay here.'

'No. I didn't mean tonight. You and Mum coming up here,' I said. 'Sorting everything out until I got back. Putting Sindy somewhere safe. You didn't have to.'

Floorboards above us creaked as I waited for Dad to reply; to acknowledge what I'd said.

'I'd hope someone would do the same for our kids if they ever got into trouble,' he said.

Kids, not kid. They not you. I wasn't sure how, but he'd managed to sneak Gina into the picture. Not directly. Not so you'd notice. But I knew what he was saying – it had once been the pair of us and in his mind, as well as in Mum's, it still was.

'Alec! Alec!' The whisper was gentle but the shake of the shoulders that accompanied it was anything but.

I blinked my eyes open. 'What?'

Sindy's face continued to look unlike itself, but the hair that fell, matted, over her shoulders was all too familiar.

'What's up? What time is it?' I said. And I looked over to Dad's bed, where the sheets were now so tightly tucked and folded; you could've bounced a coin off them.

'They've gone out to get breakfast and to get some things from town,' Sindy said, following my gaze. 'They said you'd probably need the rest.'

I wondered why Sindy hadn't figured the same and left me to get some more shut-eye: the clock showed just before nine.

She shook me again. 'You're not falling asleep again, are you?'

I avoided the gape of her nightie as she leaned over me. 'Just give me a minute,' I said. 'Why don't you go back to bed – I'll come in and see you when I'm showered and dressed.'

'Promise? You're getting dressed now, not going back to sleep?'

'Yes!'

She went over to the door. I now recognised the pink monstrosity she had on as one of Mum's nighties. A pair of Dad's socks finished off the ensemble.

'You won't be long, will you?' she said, holding onto the handle. 'Sorry, Alec. I just…'

'I'll be there in a flash,' I told her. But she still made me leave the door ajar while I went in the shower.

She was sitting up in bed, hugging the blankets around her knees when I went to see her. Her face seemed to visibly relax as soon as I walked in. 'There you are!' she said.

'D'you want anything? There's a bakery down the road. You must be hungry.'

'No, I'm okay, thanks.'

I perched on the side of her bed. 'Mum said you haven't been eating.'

'I feel sick most of the time, that's why.'

I poked her in the side through the duvet. 'You'll waste away.'

She didn't laugh and squirm like she was meant to. 'I won't.'

'C'mon,' I said. 'I can't believe you wouldn't chow down a doughnut or a chocolate scone if I went and got one for you.'

'I couldn't eat anything,' she said. 'And I'd probably throw up if you left me alone.'

I sat watching her while she avoided my eyes. 'Mum said you wouldn't see a doctor.'

'No.'

'They'll just treat your symptoms if that's all you want. Mum would go with you.'

She shook her head. 'I don't think I'm allowed.'

I looked at her and laughed. 'What d'you mean, not allowed?'

She glanced up at me but quickly looked away again. 'I don't think I'm…listed.'

A gust of wind made the windows rattle and it seemed to highlight the quiet of the room. 'It doesn't matter if you're not registered with one. We can get you in to see someone as a visitor.'

I stood up and fingered the curtains apart. It was dismal and grey outside; people on the other side of the street were battling against the gusts coming in from the sea; grim determination set fast on their puckered features.

'I've never seen a doctor. I don't want to.'

I looked over to her. 'Never seen a doctor?'

'Never, ever.'

I went over and sat on the bed again. 'Well, not that you remember,' I said. 'But I'm sure a doctor will have been there when you were born, when you had to have injections, that sort of thing. But you're lucky you've been so health –'

'No, there was no doctor,' she said. 'Dad told me. There were just a few girlfriends of Dad's mates.'

There wasn't an answer to that. I could feel the cogs whirring in my head again; more connections being made. Never been to school, never seen a doctor. Did Sindy even officially exist?

'I think the swelling's going down now,' Sindy said, pulling me back to the present. 'So, I wouldn't need treatment anyway.'

I looked down, following the pattern on the bedcover with my finger. 'Mum didn't tell me much,' I said. 'What actually happened?' I edged up the bed so we were shoulder to shoulder. I gave her a nudge with my arm, sort of playful. 'C'mon Sindy, you can tell me. I know what Minto's like.'

She still didn't move and I figured she wasn't going to answer but after a few seconds she found her voice. It started off a bit shaky and weak. 'Minto wanted me to go with these men at the clubhouse and I didn't want to. I was frightened of them.'

Now I'd been inside their den, it was all too easy to imagine the scene: I decided to stick to the whys and wherefores. 'They were Minto's mates?'

'Yeah. I was meant to do whatever they wanted.' She rested her head on her knees, her face turned away from me. 'Sexy stuff.'

'And you refused?'

'Dad was there too. He told me I had to go with them. But I didn't want to and so, I tried to get away. I know I shouldn't have kicked up such a fuss but...'

'You've got nothing to be sorry for, Sinds,' I said. I wanted to put an arm around her; offer her some kind of physical comfort but I didn't dare touch her.

We sat in silence staring down at the gawdy duvet cover. There was more I could have asked her; more that she maybe needed to say, but I didn't want to hear it. I didn't want to know what happened when they caught her, and I certainly didn't want to imagine how they might have dished out their revenge.

'It's all right, Sindy. At least you're safe now,' was all I could think of to say.

It didn't seem much and, when I thought about it, I wasn't even sure it was true.

Chapter 34

Mum didn't seem able to relax until Swansea was a distant blur in our rear-view mirror and beyond the next hour I had no idea what I was going to do. I'm not sure any of us did.

The rain didn't let up as we drove back to Cardiff. Mum and Sindy were on the back seat – that massive suitcase with the pink splash I'd seen at Minto's jammed in the footwell between them. Mum was doing a crossword while Sindy was reading out horoscopes; something that had become a daily ritual for her. Dad was beside me, keeping an eye on the speedo but managing to keep his opinions of my driving to himself.

Mum was on pins again as soon as we were at the house, the answerphone flashing away. There were no messages, just a shitload of hang-ups which put us even more on edge.

Later, Sindy sat in Gina's room while I tried to stuff bags full of clothes and newspaper cuttings into the cupboards. Mum had offered to do it, but we both knew the dismantling of something so precious to her was probably a step too far. I was only too happy to take it all apart.

Normally, I'd have imagined Sindy poking and prodding in all those bags, pulling out jumpers and trying them up against her, but not that day. She just sat there, like her batteries were spent and she only had the last dregs of juice left in her.

'You should ask Mum about these,' I told her, holding up one of the boutique bags. 'Bet there's gear in here you'd really like.'

'Okay.'

'Once I've found you some bedclothes, you can have a bath if you want.'

'All right.'

She jolted when the doorbell rang downstairs.

'Probably the window cleaner wanting his money,' I told her. 'Wait here a minute – I'll go and check.'

She followed me as far as the door and clung to the door frame as I peered over the banister.

As Mum reached the front door, she looked up as if she knew I'd be standing there. 'Stay there,' I said to her in a loud whisper. 'I'll answer it.'

I came down the stairs while Dad peeped through a gap in the living room curtains. I couldn't believe our family had been reduced to this cloak and dagger farce.

'It's Bill,' Dad said, straightening up.

Mum put on her smile and threw open the door. 'I was just going to pop in and see you,' she said. 'Thought I'd let you know the wanderers had returned.'

'I beat you to it,' he said. 'Happened to see your car was there. Nice trip?'

'Lovely, thanks.'

Dad returned to the living room while I hovered nearby, pretending to sort through the mail on the telephone table.

'All been quiet here?' Mum said.

'Yes, yes. I called in every day to take the mail off the mat. Plus, I paid the window cleaner for you.'

'Thanks, Bill,' Mum said. She turned to me. 'Go and get my purse would you, love? It's on the kitchen table.'

'Oh, and someone called to see you, Alexander,' he shouted as I got halfway down the hall. 'Yesterday afternoon it was.'

I stopped and turned around.

'Said he was a friend of yours.'

'Who was it? Did he leave a message?' I said, coming back to the door.

Bill shook his head. "Fraid not, son.'

'Was it a burly guy with leathers and tattoos?'

'He was a fairly chunky sort of a fella, yes.'

Mum and I looked at one another.

'Anyway, I explained you'd gone up to Swansea,' Bill continued. 'To see your mum and dad.'

I heard Mum suck in a breath. 'Bill! What did you say that for? It was none of his business – he could have been anyone.'

'C'mon, Mum,' I said, trying to hook her stress levels down from the ceiling. 'Bill wasn't to know.'

'Who tells complete strangers that a house is standing empty?' Mum said. 'Who tells potential burglars a whole family has gone away?'

'I'm sorry, Annie. I didn't think he was a stranger. He said he was a friend.'

'Anyone could say that, couldn't they? No one's going to stand there announcing they're a burglar!'

I could see she was close to a meltdown. Her face was flushed, and her eyelids were blinking nineteen to the dozen.

'Don't worry about it, Bill,' I said, opening the front door for him in the hope he'd take the hint. 'Bit of a rough trip home so things have been fraught. Thanks for letting us know though – and for looking after things. I'll drop the window money off later.'

'All right. Hope you're feeling better soon, Annie,' he said, looking at Mum with a wary eye.

'Sorry,' Mum managed. But as soon as the door clicked shut, she burst into tears.

It was like we were living a vague half-life, holding out for something extraordinary to happen yet we didn't know what. The phone went at least three times a day – we'd let the machine pick up any messages, but the calls always ended with a hang-up. I could almost smell Minto on the end of the line.

Sindy had barely got out of bed, let alone ventured from the house. I offered to take her out in the car, but she didn't seem to want to do anything, indoors or out. Mum took to buying her teen-magazines most days. I wondered if it was just an alternative to Mum filling the spare room with clothes, but she said it might do Sindy good to find out what real teenagers were like. I began to see her point. Up until then, I reckon Sindy thought she was a normal teenager: I'm not sure it ever occurred to her that other girls probably worried more about teenage spots and puppy fat.

It wasn't easy being back home full-time. I reminded myself it was only temporary, but it was suffocating having the folks there whenever I went into the kitchen in the morning; joining them for dinner every night; having to shove up on the sofa every time I wanted to watch TV. I couldn't see an end to it, that was the problem. Sindy wasn't perking up in the way she normally did after difficult episodes and Mum and Dad seemed in no hurry to get the situation resolved. I reckoned they enjoyed having the pair of us there, slouching on the sofas and leaving dirty plates on the coffee table.

We'd just finished dinner on Thursday when the phone went again. It had almost stopped being an event. Almost but not quite. Each of us still tensed as the first ring trilled in the hallway. We waited for the machine to read out the message, and for the usual click of a hang-up, but this time there was a voice.

'Oh, hi. It's Daniella here.' She paused, as if she was trying to find her place on the cue-card. 'I'm trying to get hold of Alec: he left me a message but –'

I dashed into the hall and picked up the receiver. 'Hey, it's me.'

'Oh, there you are!' The statement was more an accusatory than relieved. 'I tried ringing you back at your new place, but they said you'd barely been there.'

'Yeah, sorry. We've had a bit of a…crisis,' I said, lowering my voice. 'Sindy's here.'

There was a pause. A tapping-of-the-foot, folded arms kind of pause. 'Again,' she said, whacking me with a rolled-up copy of her sarcasm. 'Don't tell me: she wants me to give her a lift back again and stop at the services for sweets and magazines!'

I had to take the phone under the stairs so Sindy wouldn't have to come ear-to-ear with the sad details of her own circumstances.

'Jesus!' Daniella said, once I'd given her an update. 'Now you're free of the flat, you should get the police involved, Alec. She shouldn't have to keep dealing with Minto's crap.'

'C'mon, Daniella.' I lowered my voice again. 'You were there: you heard what he said when we left. And anyway, Sindy wouldn't say a word against him, or against her dad. She's been too well-trained for that.'

'So, what's the answer then?' Daniella said. 'If you do nothing, you're all going to end up in permanent hiding.'

I rolled my eyes, scoffed, like she was being ridiculous. But even as I stood there donning my fake bravado, I couldn't shake off the feeling that she might be right.

Chapter 35

After the call from Daniella, the phone didn't ring for a few days. I guess that's why we got careless. The fear and suspicion started to feel unreal, unwarranted, as if we'd wildly over-reacted to the whole thing.

I picked up the receiver with barely a pause when the phone rang after dinner.

'Alec, amigo! You're a hard chap to track down. I was starting to think you'd gone into hiding.'

'No.' My voice was surprisingly calm, given my heart was thumping the crap out of my chest.

'What a good lad you are, taking care of your old folks down there in Cardiff. How are they both, Annie and Jim?'

I could hardly bear to have him say their names. 'Fine.'

'And Bill from next door – he seemed a decent sort.'

'What do you want, Minto?'

He chuckled down the line. 'Well now, Alec-Xander, don't take offence but it wasn't actually you I rang to speak to. Can you put me on to the delicious Sindy?'

Should I deny she was there; that I'd even seen her? Should I pretend she'd gone? I stayed on the line saying nothing at all.

'Cat got your tongue, Alec?'

'No.'

'Right.' And his tone had an edge to it now. 'Put her on then.'

I didn't bother to ask how he was so certain she was with me.

'She's sleeping,' I said. I knew it sounded like I was reading from a script – I was embarrassed to even try and make excuses.

'Mate,' he said with a sigh. 'Just go and get her.'

I put the receiver on the table but stayed where I was, wondering what the fuck I was going to do.

I went into the living room where the others were oblivious to the call; glued to one of the soaps. 'Dad? Can I have a word?'

Mum snapped her head up, her worry-antenna sparking into action.

Dad followed me out into the kitchen.

'Minto's on the phone,' I whispered. 'If I don't let him speak to Sindy, I'm afraid he might just...turn up.'

'Maybe I should speak to him.' Dad raised his chin like he was suddenly one of life's movers and shakers.

'No,' I hissed. 'You'll only make it worse.'

I heard the living room door open. 'Alec?' Sindy came out. 'The football's starting if you want to see it.'

Minto would have heard it, of course. I imagined his barrel of a chest shaking with laughter as he listened.

'Minto's on the phone,' I said, my voice now at normal volume. I pointed to my dramatic shake of the head as I looked at Sindy. 'Do you want to speak to him?'

She looked between me and Dad. 'Yes, okay,' she said. And she scooted past me and over to the phone. 'Hey!' I heard her say. 'This is a surprise.'

She didn't look happy when she came back in the room a few minutes later. Her eyes had lost the spark that had only just started to seep back into them.

'All okay?' Mum said.

Sindy sat beside me on the sofa. She managed a vague nod, then sighed. 'My horoscope said there was a change coming.'

'A change?' Mum said.

Sindy nodded but didn't elaborate.

'How did Minto even know you were here?' I asked.

She shrugged and still wouldn't look at me. 'Don't know.'

I kept my eyes on the TV but even the excitement of Cardiff sneaking one past the Cambridge goalie didn't hold my attention. 'So, what did he want?'

Sindy sat with her body half-turned from me. The heating was on full pelt, but I could see she had goose bumps up her arm. 'He wants me to go back,' she said.

Over on the TV, the crowd was going wild and the noise seemed at odds with the stilted quiet of our front room. Mum stood up and pressed the 'off' button. 'What do you mean, go back?'

Sindy looked up. 'Minto said I have to.'

'Not on my watch,' Dad said.

Mum went over and crouched in front of Sindy. 'You don't have to do anything, love,' she said. 'We'll take care of it.' She looked at me and smiled, as if she really thought we could.

'I have to pack,' Sindy said, getting up. 'He's not sure when he's coming but he said to be ready any time.'

Dad looked over to me. 'You can't let this happen, Alexander.'

'What do you mean? What am I meant to do?'

'Maybe we'll talk about it afterwards,' Mum said, looking between us.

Sindy opened the door but stayed where she was, holding onto the handle. 'I know you're all trying to be kind,' she said. 'But there isn't a choice. There's nowhere else I can go. That's all there is to it.'

'It's a pity the rest of your family lives so far away,' Dad said.

I shot him a look: since when did Dad know about Sindy's far flung relatives?

'She hasn't seen them for so long though,' Mum said to him. 'They mightn't even recognise her.'

Clearly, Sindy had been doing a lot of blabbing to both of them about her Antipodean connections.

'Let's not worry about all that,' Dad said, looking at Mum. 'Sindy knows she's safe with us here.'

There was a silent 'for now' which seemed to hang in the air, but Sindy passed him a smile anyway, like she really believed it.

Chapter 36

A sense of despondency descended on the house and it made me realise how the last week had been strangely charged. It was as if we'd all been having an unexpected break from routine and there was a mad excitement to the not-knowing of it all. I wasn't sure if it had felt like that to Sindy, of course: I certainly hadn't expected her to sound so chipper when Minto phoned. I was disappointed: her reaction reminded me of one of those faithful mutts that goes back to its master, no matter how much it's been kicked and mistreated. I'd hoped that experiencing a bit of kindness might have made her re-evaluate. But, no. She was still the same ditzy Sindy who assumed she deserved no better.

Minto had put the whole family on borrowed time. That chirpy optimism that had become part of the household had slunk out again and we were left with nothing but a looming threat. Mum's shoulders had regained their slump and Dad's footsteps lost their newly discovered jaunt. Only Sindy seemed unchanged, even though she was the one with the sharpest blade hanging over her.

I found Mum in Gina's room later, folding clean clothes for Sindy and putting them on her bed, as if the exciting interlude was over. It felt like the costumes being packed up after a stage production – and when I thought about it, it did seem as if the last few weeks had been more 'performance' than it had been 'real life'.

'You okay?' I asked Mum.

'Yes, just sorting out Sindy's washing,' she said. 'And she might as well take some of those other clothes if she decides to go. They're doing no good gathering dust in here.'

'There's no 'if', Mum. I think the decision's been made for her.'

Mum tidied up the already-neat pile of clothes. 'Where is she, anyway?'

'Helping Dad with the car,' I said. 'He's teaching her about oil levels and tyre pressures. She actually seems to be enjoying it.'

Mum swept her gaze around the room. She didn't look like she'd taken in what I'd said. 'I suppose we might as well get everything out of here now the walls are clear again. Redecorate with some bolder colours.'

'Yes, good idea,' I said. 'So, you're feeling...better now?'

She didn't look at me but busied herself with the clean laundry.

'All this happened so quickly with Sindy,' she said. 'I didn't have time for anything else.'

'Yeah.'

She gazed around at the empty walls. 'I don't want to go back to how things were.' She suddenly levelled her eyes at me. 'Oh, love. Do you think she'll be all right?'

I knew what she wanted me to say but I'd already hesitated. 'She's survived up to now, hasn't she?'

'Barely.'

'She's tougher than we think. And really, we can only advise her: we can't force her to steer clear of Minto. You heard how pleased she was to hear from him.'

'I know. But have you told her – have you made sure she understands – that she's welcome to stay here just as long as she likes? Indefinitely if she wants. I've told her and so's your dad, but maybe she needs to hear it from you.'

'If she wanted to stay, she would. That's how she is.'

'Even so, can you spell it out to her? Let her know this is her home for however long she wants it.'

There was a neediness in her voice; an expectation. She didn't so much want me to ask Sindy as to convince her.

'I'll make sure she knows,' I said. 'Promise.'

When I went downstairs, Sindy was just coming through the back door. She had black fingers and an oily smudge on her cheek.

'Have fun in the mechanics workshop?' I said.

'Oh, no – I was just in the garage with your dad,' Sindy told me. 'He was showing me how bits of the engine work.'

'Cool.'

'He said he could teach me to drive if I wanted.'

I looked at her. 'Did he?'

Me – I'd had to make do with Red Rover Driving School. 'You'd better check the rules,' I said. 'You have to be seventeen before you can start learning.'

'That's all right,' she said. 'Minto says I easily pass for eighteen when I make the effort.'

'It doesn't matter how old you look, you have to be able to prove it.'

She blinked back at me, looking confused.

'You won't be around to have lessons anyway,' I said. 'Not if you're going back to Swansea.'

'I'm sure I'll be here for a few days yet,' she said. 'I could learn then.'

I shook my head. 'It takes months, Sindy.'

'So why did your dad say he'd teach me?'

I sat on the kitchen stool, watching her fragile wrists as she scrubbed her hands at the sink. 'I think what he meant was, he'd teach you if you decided to stick around,' I said.

'But I have to go with Minto, you know that.'

'No. Actually, you don't.' I used my foot to push a stool out so she'd sit down. 'Mum and Dad would both love you to stay. They like having you here – they're happy to look after you. You wouldn't need to have any more to do with Minto or any of the others. Not ever.'

'But...there's my dad, too.'

'You might have a more comfortable life here,' I said.

She looked down, picking the skin around her nails. 'Minto wouldn't like it.'

'You reckon he'd actually come and drag you back?'

She looked up at me like I was stupid. 'Yes.'

'He threw you out though, didn't he?' I said. 'If you kept refusing, wouldn't he just wash his hands of you?'

'No.'

'No?'

She looked down. 'All kinds of things would happen if they didn't look after me.'

'Sindy,' I said, leaning forward, 'you know things won't get better if you go back there. This is your chance to leave all that behind. Maybe your only chance.'

She was quiet. 'Minto knows I'm here now,' she said with a sigh. 'So, there's nothing I can do. Where else am I supposed to go?'

Her tone was one of defeat yet the look she gave me, when I met her eye, was full of hope – or perhaps something stronger. Expectation? Yes, that was it: it was as if she had ultimate confidence that I not only could but *would* find a way.

Chapter 37

My announcement, that I needed to return to my new digs in Swansea, seemed to catch everyone off-guard. I had no idea why: where did they imagine my dole cheques were being sent? How long did they think I could remain wearing the same couple of T-shirts? It appeared that neither Sindy, nor my folks, could cope with the idea of an Alec-free household, even on a short-term basis.

'Couldn't you do everything in a day then come back here?' Mum said.

'I could but what's the big deal? I'll still be close-by. Swansea's not that far away: you could practically hear me fart.'

She winced. 'All the more reason to do it in a day then. What do you need? We can get you some clothes if that's all you're going back for.'

'Mum! I moved in there three weeks ago and I haven't even unpacked yet. I need to check my mail, pay in my last Giro, sign on for the next one, pay my rent – you can't just put your feet up when you're on the dole, y'know.'

'Well, go on your signing-on day, then you can do everything else. Dad'll take you up, won't you, Jim?'

Dad nodded. 'Yes.'

'Good,' Mum said. 'I'd feel happier knowing Dad was with you.'

It wasn't quite the break from home I'd wanted, but if supervised day release was the only alternative to total incarceration, I figured I'd better take it.

We left early to get ahead of any commuters. I guessed that, if I pulled my finger out, I could have us home by three. The main thing was to sign on at the dole office – after that, we could take our time.

Dad handed me the car keys as we closed the front door and he sat with his arms folded for the first half-hour, drifting in and out of sleep. Every so often, his head would tilt then hit the side window and he'd snap back into consciousness.

I glanced at Dad's outfit while he was mid-snooze. He was hardly dressed for the downpours that were forecast: under his gold-buttoned blazer, he was wearing his white short-sleeved shirt. On the bottom half, dark trousers with a crease sharp enough to cut glass. He always put the creases in himself, not Mum. Old Navy habit, he said.

His hands were rested together in his lap, fingers intertwined, the gold of his wedding band and his signet ring just visible – the only two adornments he ever wore. For someone who'd joined up as a teenager, he hadn't fallen into any of the Naval clichés – he was a non-smoker, he never fell victim to too much grog and his skin was free of naked lady tattoos. He didn't even have so much as a Saint Christopher around his neck. I wondered what his ship mates must have made of him.

'What are you looking at?' he said in that tone he always had. He stretched himself out and yawned.

'Just admiring your creases,' I said. 'You could have an eye out with those.'

His eyes slid across to my jeans. 'You've got a lot more creases in yours,' he said.

'Touché, Dad.'

He looked pleased. One nil to the old man.

'What's the point in ironing creases anyway?' I said. 'It's not going to help you in battle, is it?'

'It's about the discipline; being the best you can be,' he said.

'It just seems pointless. Shining up your buttons, cleaning shoes, ironing creases – none of it matters.'

'You do it because it's the routine. Part of the order of things. A way of showing your loyalty and your respect for the rules.'

Loyalty. It made me think of Minto and his leather uniform; his clubhouse rules; those big meaty hands of his with the word pummelled into the skin.

'But if they're pointless rules...' I said.

'Obedience isn't pointless. It's its own reward. In the Forces, you can't have people acting irresponsibly, playing about with weapons, endangerin…'

'Weapons?' I said. 'You were in the Navy. I thought you played with rafts, not rifles.'

Dad looked at me sternly; he really was a pleasure to wind-up.

'We all have weapons training,' he said. 'I thought the term 'armed forces' might've spelled it out for you, but…'

Ding-ding. Another point to the old man.

'The crux of it is,' he said, 'you learn not to question rules. You obey orders. That's it: that's how you're trained. There's no other way it can work.'

Everyone blindly following orders: it had certainly worked for Minto.

I looked in my mirror as I indicated towards Swansea. 'You're a better man than me, Dad,' I said. 'No way could I do that.'

'Might do you good.'

I glanced across at him. Why I instinctively wanted to pick a fight with him whenever he gave me advice, I had no idea – but it might have had something to do with those trouser-creases. 'Guess I must be a disappointment to you,' I said. 'Couple of mediocre A' levels, dropped out of college, no job or any clue where I'm going with my life.'

He shrugged. 'I left school with nothing,' he said. 'But for me, the Navy was a safety net. I didn't know what else to do, so I did that. I was too afraid, I suppose. Too...' He looked away, like he was searching for the right word, 'too fearful to just drift along, hoping life would throw something at me.'

'Fearful?'

'I look at you sometimes,' he said, 'and I can't believe we're from the same stock. You just don't worry. You go here, you go there; you try this, you try that. I'm not saying I like it or that I approve – but I suppose I do...envy it.'

Envy was never a word I'd heard Dad mention in the same sentence as me. Was he paying me a compliment in that awkward, half-arsed way of his?

'Trust,' he said, after a few moments. 'That's what you have. Trust that disasters won't befall you.'

'Actually, I don't,' I said. 'I have hope, that's all. Hope that something will come along.'

He smiled to himself – not in a snide way either – but like he actually understood. 'For you, it usually does,' he said.

And perhaps he didn't mind that, after all.

Once I'd signed on, we drove to the new flat for me to grab some gear from my room. Everyone else was at work by the looks of it and the kitchen was awash with evidence of hurried breakfasts. Over on the worktop was a scattering of unopened envelopes, most belonging to me. I gathered them up and Dad followed as I hurried on through to my room.

I stopped the minute I reached the hall. In the lobby, beside my door, were bin bags and boxes. On top of the pile, an A4 sheet had 'Alec' scribbled on it.

'What the...' I picked up the sheet in case there was a note written on the back, but there was nothing. Even as I tried my key in the lock, I could see the metal was shiny and brand new. When the key wouldn't fit, I hammered on the door.

'Steady on, now,' I heard Dad say behind me. 'I'm sure there's an explanation.'

'I've been turfed out of my own room,' I said to him, slapping a hand down on the bin bag. 'I think it calls for some sort of reaction, don't you?'

'Was there anything in that pile of mail?' he said. 'A letter from the landlord, or something?'

I took out the bundle from my pocket and unfolded the envelopes. There was a Giro, a bank statement, a letter from Swansea City Council and one that had my name handwritten on the front. No stamp, no address. I tore it open. I recognised the landlord's details at the top.

'Dear Mr Johnston,' it began. 'It is with regret I must inform you that due to a number of financial irregularities, I am obliged to terminate your tenancy at 50 Ashton Crescent, Uplands with immediate effect. Despite repeated attempts to contact you, I have been unable to notify you in person of the current situation.

We have been made aware of rent arrears at your previous address and therefore our rental agreement is now...'

I didn't bother to read on; just handed the letter to Dad without speaking. There was no point in arguing the toss.

'How come you've got rent arrears in the last place?' Dad said.

'I didn't...I don't. The money I left for rent went missing,' I said, drawing quotation marks in the air. 'Just another of Minto's rackets.'

'Well, we should try and get it –'

'Don't even bother, Dad,' I said. 'The last thing I'm going to do is turn up at Minto's and ask for my rent money back. I value my kneecaps.'

'It doesn't seem right to me.'

'Of course it's not right. But Minto's a crook, a villain. And frankly, with all the other shit we've got going on with him, the rent money is the least of our worries.'

Dad nodded before grabbing one of the many bin bags of belongings. 'Come on then,' he said. 'Looks like Swansea really wants to be rid of you.'

Dad and I had already had a bite to eat by the time we heard the key in the door and the tell-tale rustle of bags. 'You two home already?' Mum shouted.

Dad folded up the paper. 'There goes the peace,' he said, getting to his feet.

I stayed where I was, in no hurry to pass on the latest accommodation news to Mum.

'Well, look at you two!' Dad said.

Mum, Dad, Sindy: they were all so comfortable with each other; such a natural fit.

'Alexander!' Mum shouted. 'Come out here: I've got something to show you.'

She sounded like the overly cheerful parent of my school years and as I gritted my teeth, I realised I'd reverted to my adolescence. Back then, Mum only had to open her mouth to piss me off and I could feel that irritation rushing in again like shots through a syringe. 'Yeah, in a minute,' I shouted.

The living room door opened and Sindy walked in, Mum and Dad shadowing her with smiles on their faces.

'What d'you think?' Mum said.

Sindy hardly looked like the same girl. I could see it was her, of course, but she looked so breathtakingly altered that I couldn't stop staring at her, as if she was some spot-the-difference cartoon.

'Jeez, look at you!' I said.

Sindy's cheeks flushed, reminding me once again that this unfamiliar looking visitor was still just Sindy.

But instead of the lank mousey hair she'd left the house with that morning, she'd come back sporting a bouncy, auburn mane that seemed to light up her whole face. The centre-parting that had once revealed a pimply forehead was replaced with a flicked fringe.

'Hm. I like it,' I said, going full circle around her, and peering into her hair like I was carrying out a nit inspection.

Sindy gave one of her messy snorts: the sort that couldn't be trimmed and tamed at any hairdresser's. 'I got my ears pierced too,' she said, showing me a pair of tiny studs. 'I've only ever had clip-on earrings before, and they hurt.'

'Wow,' I said, peering at her red lobes. 'These look like they hurt too.'

'And I got mine done too,' Mum said, coming towards me with her head a-tilt. 'See?'

'My God!' I heard Dad say, and I don't think he meant it in a good way.

'We had such a fantastic time,' Sindy said. 'We went shopping, had a huge three-course lunch in this really posh restaurant, got our ears pierced, had my hair done and I got my nails painted too.' She wiggled a set of glossy pink fingernails at me as she smiled. 'I think it's probably been the best day of my life.'

As she registered the comment, Mum's features took a kind of inward gasp. She put a hand on her chest and looked so choked up, I wondered if it had just become the best day of her life as well.

'And I got some great clothes too,' Sindy said, holding up bags from each of those decorated fingers.

I waited for Dad's cash radar to start beeping as the cost of this best-of-days started to mount up. But no, he stayed there nodding, all indulgence and generosity.

'Haven't you got enough clothes in that spare room to give to Sindy?' I said to Mum.

She waved away the idea: 'Oh, they're no good,' she said. 'If you're going to have new outfits you might as well have outfits that are in fashion, that's what I always say.'

I figured I must have missed her previous pronouncements about such things.

'It's good to see you both looking so happy,' Dad said. 'And I'm glad your appetite is coming back, Sindy. I was afraid you'd waste away.'

She looked down at her flat stomach and gave it a few sharp prods. 'I don't think so!'

She rummaged amongst the bags on the chair. 'I can't wait to try these on again,' she said, turning around. All her movements were more considered now; the flick of that bouncy hair; a painted nail to a lip – she was in makeover heaven. 'Hey, can I go and phone Daniella?' she said. 'She'll want to hear all about this!'

'Sure,' said Mum, tossing a smile towards me.

We'd come to realise Sindy loved any excuse to use Mum and Dad's phone; it was one of the new push-button ones and Sindy was obsessed with it. While she was in the hall, speaking to Daniella, Mum stood by the mirror, fiddling with her earring. I saw her gaze drift to my sports bag, still on the chair. 'Everything okay in Swansea?'

Dad and I exchanged a glance.

'Not really,' I said.

Mum's eyes met mine in the reflection and I gave her the bad tidings. I expected to see that pinched, worried look cross her face but she didn't even seem surprised.

'Something else will turn up,' is all she said.

'Yeah, I'll have to have a think about what to do.'

'There's no hurry, is there?' Dad said, getting out of his seat. 'I reckon you're better off staying here for now. It'll be Christmas before we know it so you can find something in the new year.' He headed for the door. 'Right, I'm going to make us all a hot drink.'

'Or a cold one,' Mum said, turning away from the mirror at last. 'It's turned out to be such a nice day, I fancy celebrating.'

She beamed at me, and I couldn't help feeling that my new-found homelessness had just become the cherry on her perfect day cake.

Chapter 38

I didn't know what had woken me. I hadn't heard anything but as I opened my eyes in the darkness, something felt different. I could hear Dad snoring away on the other side of the wall; the cistern above the bog drip-dripping like it always did; and somewhere in the distance I could hear the low hum of the motorway. It was the smell that reached me first. It wasn't a burning or smoky smell but the almost-comforting smell of something being warmed.

I sat up in bed, taking in a deep breath and straining my ears for clues but I could hear nothing. I got out of bed to go for a pee. In the hall, Dad's snoring sounded even louder, and I was surprised to see their bedroom door open. Dad's always been a stickler for making sure doors are shut, lights off. The bathroom door was wide open too.

I went in, peed in the darkness and was about to go back to my room when something made me hesitate. I stood on the landing, listening; willing Dad to stop his snoring, just for a moment, so I could hear properly.

I tiptoed downstairs and flicked the switch by the telephone table to turn on the hall light. Nothing. But I could see the lamppost outside, bathing the porch in a yellow glow.

Now I could tune in to the sounds of the house. Or rather the lack of them. The usual hum of the fridge had been silenced, and it seemed to turn up the volume on the muffled roar from the motorway; the throaty grind of a lorry in low gear. I stood in the darkness, just listening. There was another sound, barely detectable; a very quiet hiss. For some reason the sound made me think of Minto; I imagined him the other side of the kitchen door, sucking hard on one of his rollies.

As I remained there, paralysed, I forced myself to drop my shoulders, pull myself together. This was home in Cardiff, not some spooky dive in a Stephen King novel.

I followed the noise through to the kitchen, making as little sound as I could. Every door was open as I went past – the living room, the dining room, even the one to the cupboard under the stairs.

There was a glow in the kitchen; I spotted it between the hinges as the door stood ajar. And warmth – I felt the heat before I'd even crossed the threshold. I peeped round the door, just a head and shoulder, ready to retreat as soon as I came face to face with whatever was there. I jerked back before I'd even registered what I'd seen. Back in the darkness I realised all the gas rings were alight on the hob.

I took another breath and forced myself to straighten up, march into the kitchen like it was broad daylight and I had a job to do. All four gas rings were on and the oven door was open, gas on full blast. It meant it was hot in the room, even with the doors to the outside open. I strode through the kitchen and pulled the doors shut. I was about to lock them as well, but a thought stopped me: what if someone was still in the house? I turned off the gas rings and tugged the oven knob back to zero, plunging myself into total darkness again. I tried the kitchen light switch, already knowing it would do me no good.

I didn't want to be quiet; I wanted to make as much noise as possible. I bound up the stairs, two at a time, even in the pitch black. I knew Dad would have battery torches in every room, but I had no idea where to find one. I knocked loudly on their open door and shook Dad by the shoulder. 'Dad? Can you come downstairs?' I whispered.

There was no gradual transitioning from deep sleep to wakefulness; no snaffling to consciousness. Instead, his eyes opened wide, like he was one of those ventriloquist puppets, and he sat up. 'What's the matter?'

‘Are there any torches?’ I whispered. ‘There’s a power cut or something.’

He nodded and reached for a lantern torch from the table beside him. Plan A, as ever.

‘Sure it’s not just a fuse?’ he said, turning around to me as we headed down the stairs.

‘I dunno.’ I grabbed his arm to stop him going any further. ‘Dad. Someone was here – or might still be here. All the doors were open, and the gas rings and oven were on.’

His shadowed expressions turned this way and that as he took in the implications of what I was saying. But all he said was, ‘Okay,’ before going down the last few stairs.

He hurried through the hall and swept the torch beam around the kitchen.

‘Both back doors were wide open,’ I said. ‘Kitchen and conservatory.’

‘I see.’ He shone the torch out of the window into the garden. ‘I’d better go and check,’ he said.

‘The streetlights are on.’

‘Just us then.’ He opened the back door. ‘I’ll have a look at the fuse box.’

‘Dad – give me the torch: I think I should go,’ I said. ‘I know where the box is. You stay here – get on the phone if...you hear anything.’

He hesitated a second before handing over the torch. I could tell he was using all his willpower to not insist on going instead of me.

The fuse box was on the outside wall between the garage and the house, in its own little alleyway. The perfect spot for someone to get you by yourself, force you against the wall and overpower you.

I gave the area a thorough sweep with the torch before I went anywhere near: I checked behind me, in front of me; even above in case someone was lurking on the garage roof.

The metal door to the fuse box opened with a creak. The main switch was pointed to the ‘off’ position and none of the fuses tripped when I switched it back on. I was about to shut the door when I saw a piece of paper attached to the inside, held there by a blob of fresh chewing gum. 'Alec,' it said. 'Called in to fetch Sindy but no one was ready. Will call again soon. Very soon.'

I slammed the door shut as if to convince myself I hadn't seen it.

How the fuck had he got in? There were no windows open, thanks to Dad – and none broken as far as I'd been able to tell.

'Anything?' Dad said, hanging onto the back door.

'Nah, I just put the main switch back on.' I paused, weighing up how much to confess.

'Has he gone?'

Dad and I both spun around as Sindy stood in the doorway. She looked so unlike herself in that clean and prim white dressing gown; her hair wavy and styled as if she hadn't been to bed at all.

I looked at Dad then back at Sindy. 'Has who gone?'

She swallowed, and her voice was back to being as timid as it used to be. 'Minto,' she said. 'He was here.'

'How d'you know?'

'He came into my room and put his hand over my mouth. He said he'd come back for me.' She was close to tears but, for once, she managed to force them down.

'How the devil did he get in?' Dad said. 'I've checked all around and...'

'He's got a key,' Sindy said, lowering her voice.

I took a step towards her. 'What?'

'That day he had the keys to Daniella's car. You know, the ones on the horse keyring? He borrowed yours too. He gave the whole bunch to his friend, Tay. Tay gets keys cut for him all the time. Minto has a whole drawerful for other peoples' cars and flats and things. And he's always had the one to your room.'

'Why didn't you tell us?' I said.

'All right,' Dad hissed. 'This isn't Sindy's fault. We can get the locks changed. I just don't understand why...' He scratched his head and looked around, gesturing at the stove. 'Why would he leave all the gas rings on like that? Why light the oven? Why not make Sindy go with him now?'

I looked at Sindy and I could see she already knew.

'It's a threat,' I said to Dad. 'A calling card. Showing us what he could do if he wanted. This time, he lit the gas. Next time...'

Dad's features faltered, and I saw his hand reach out to the kitchen worktop. 'I'll ring a locksmith as soon as they're open,' he said. He shook a warning finger at me and at Sindy. 'Not a word about this to your mother, understand? I'll talk to her.'

Sindy did a 'cross my heart' gesture then opened the kitchen door, Dad following close behind. He kept his finger on the light switch, waiting for me.

'I'll be right up,' I said.

He hesitated but finally backed out the door.

I knew I wouldn't sleep, wouldn't relax a single muscle, till I'd made certain, one last time, that Minto was nowhere in the house.

Chapter 39

Given I no longer had a flat in Swansea, I had no choice but to sign on for my dole money in Cardiff. It wasn't a decision I took lightly. As I walked into the job centre in Westgate Street, I had the sensation I'd taken fifty steps back with my life. Yes, I explained to the prim woman on the counter, I had been a student; I had had a grant and I had jacked in the course. It *was* a shame, wasn't it? And yes, I was now living in the family home again. Temporarily, absolutely. She spun a form around to me and pointed to where I had to sign. And that was that – the death knell had sounded. My official residence was confirmed as 'at home with parents.'

My new status was underlined the moment I walked in the house later. I was about to escape, unseen, up the stairs when the lounge door opened.

'Alexander? Can you come in here a minute?' Mum said.

I paused, holding onto the banister. 'Can't it wait? I've just got in.'

'Quick,' she said, 'while Sindy's in the bath.'

I turned around and followed Mum into the room. Dad was already in there, papers and documents scattered at his feet.

'What's going on?'

'We want to talk to you,' Mum said.

I knew something was up because the telly wasn't on and Dad's briefcase was on the chair: the leather one they'd always told me was kept on top of the wardrobe 'for when the time comes'.

Mum looked at Dad as if waiting for her cue. 'Your father and I have been talking,' she said. 'About Sindy.' She left an overly dramatic pause.

'I can't bear to think of her going back to that...life she had. She's not safe.'

'I know,' I said. 'We've been through this a hundred times. But it has to be her deci –'

'She's got family in Australia,' Dad said. 'Did you realise that?'

The swerve in conversation took me by surprise. 'Yeah, 'course. Why?'

They exchanged a conspiratorial look. 'We were wondering if you could persuade her to go out there and see them,' Dad said. 'She'd be much safer: away from Minto plus she'd be with her family.'

'But she might not want to. I don't suppose she's ever met them: they'd be complete strangers. And they might not be interested in meeting her, let alone welcoming her into the fold.'

'You could ask Sindy though. Find out a bit more.'

'And she's got no money,' I said.

'We could pay,' Mum said. And again, she looked across at Dad who picked up a bank book and waved it in my direction.

'It's not much, given all the years I spent in the Navy,' he said, 'but I did get a lump sum. Plus, your mum and I had a few shares which we cashed in last year and put into a high interest account.'

'So, it'd be no problem financially. We could pay for you both,' Mum said, clutching her skirt as she leaned forward. 'You and Sindy.'

There was a pause, like all the air had left the room.

'Me?'

Mum nodded. 'I don't think she'd manage alone, do you?'

'And it's not like there's much going for you here,' Dad added. 'This could be the making of you.'

'Jeez,' I said. 'You've got this all worked out, haven't you?' And I sat back in my seat, watching them both. It sounded so far-fetched, melodramatic even.

'What do you think, love?' Mum said.

'I don't know. I'm still...taking it all in.'

The prospect of a free trip to Australia certainly sounded appealing, but only when I imagined me and Daniella in the picture, not me and Sindy. I didn't want to leave Daniella behind: we mightn't have seen so much of each other lately with her back at uni, but just knowing she was there, on the end of the phone, with her sensible head and her teasing laugh – that had kept me sane. Did I really want to risk her finding someone else while I swanned off with Sindy looking for some far-flung relatives who might not even want to see her? 'A sorry bloody excuse for a mother' – isn't that how Sindy had described her? But then, all she had in Wales was the even sorrier excuse for a father.

'Well don't take too long thinking about it,' Dad said, banging papers into piles. He was clearly director of operations in all this and was enjoying his new-found sense of purpose. 'You might have a very small window of opportunity; barely a chink of light if that boyfriend of hers is coming back.'

And he gave me that look over his reading glasses that said: 'Son, this time I mean business.'

Chapter 40

Organising a last-minute dash to the southern hemisphere seemed like an easy task compared to the one I was faced with next.

Daniella was finally back for a weekend and I was meeting her at her favourite Chinese restaurant near the rugby ground. I figured she could at least enjoy the food, even if the conversation wasn't going to be to her liking. We hadn't seen much of each other the past few weeks, partly because of all that had been going on with Sindy but mainly because it was term time: Daniella had assignments to do and lab work, even on weekends. Plus, she was the naturally studious sort: exams weren't till after Christmas, but I knew, even now with weeks to go, she'd be squirrelling away facts and figures, storing them up for when she'd need them to get her suite of A-grades.

Between Sindy's phone calls and mine, though, she'd been kept informed of the dramas at home. But not this latest development; this one was still fresh and ready to be put in front of her. And I had a feeling it wasn't going to be to her taste.

Daniella looked particularly lovely, all wrapped up in her winter-wondergarb. A lipstick-red coat, tight black jeans and red beret: the whole outfit matching perfectly with the rosiness of her cheeks. I stood up and gave her a hug as she came to the table. Her cheek was every bit as icy as the outfit suggested.

'God, it seems ages since we saw each other,' she said, slipping off her gloves and sliding into the seat opposite me. 'I'll be so glad when it's the holidays and I can forget about pathogens, toxins and cell structures.'

I fiddled with the pepper pot on the table. 'Mm.'

'Still, only a few more weeks of it,' she said. 'And there's lots going on at the end of term. You should come and stay. China Crisis are playing. Fancy seeing them?'

I shifted in my seat, my mental calendar floating past with its days filled up.

'Not sure China Crisis can compete with my own Welsh crisis,' I said.

She laughed and rolled her eyes. I could tell she wasn't really listening. 'There's a trip to London in a couple of weeks too. We could nab some seats, maybe go to Oxford Street and do some Christmas shopping.' She smiled at me hopefully, that cute dimple of hers putting in a welcome appearance. 'Shall I put our names down?'

I hadn't expected to have to bring up the subject so soon, but I was backed into a corner by her enthusiastic plans. 'I dunno, Daniella. There's a lot going on right now.'

She pouted. 'Sindy will be okay with your mum and dad. She's not your responsibility.'

'Or theirs,' I pointed out.

The waitress arrived, handed us menus and poured us both some water.

'God, it's so nice doing this,' Daniella said, looking up from the menu. 'I feel like I've been trapped in my room the last few weeks – I've had so many prac reports to do, it's crazy. I haven't been able to go to any parties or gigs. The bonfire night barbecue was my only night out.' She reached across for my hand. 'And even that wasn't much fun without you.'

I stroked her fingers. 'I know. It's been tough without you too.'

She looked down. 'So how is it, at home with Sindy and your folks?'

I groaned. 'I've been going stir crazy too, to be honest.'

'At least it's temporary. When you will you go back to Swansea?'

We paused to order our food then handed back the menus.

It let me off the hook for a bit and we chatted more about Bristol and what had been going on with her. But soon enough, she asked again when I'd be going back to Swansea.

'Well, it seems I've been evicted from my new place,' I said, unfolding the announcement as carefully as I could. 'Dad and I went to collect some things and I found all my stuff in the hall with the locks changed.'

'No! Oh, shit! Why didn't you tell me?'

'I assumed Sindy would've actually.'

'Nope. So, what happens now?'

'Well, I guess it makes me, officially, no longer a resident of Swansea, doesn't it?' I sat back and clasped my hands behind my head.

'Right!' she said, beaming at me. 'Congratulations.'

'Yep, the world is my lobster.'

The discussion wasn't calculated as such, but I knew where I was directing it: tossing out little snippets here and there that would, at some point, all be gathered together and presented to her in a palatable package.

'It was so depressing having to sign on in my old benefit office,' I told her. 'It was like I'd stepped into a big cowpat of my former life.'

That gave her a titter. 'You'll cope,' she said. 'It'll be easier to find work here. And then you can get back on your feet again, get your own place.'

'Mm.'

We put the conversation on hold as our food arrived; the sweet and sour providing just enough time for me to line up the rest of my news.

'Well, actually, Mum and Dad have come up with an alternative plan,' I began. I spooned rice onto my plate, careful to concentrate on the food rather than on Daniella. 'It'll get me out of that rut you always say I'm in.'

'Oh, yeah?'

'They're sending me to Australia. I'll be shipped off like a convict.'

She stopped chewing and looked at me. 'Australia?'

More rice. More sauce. I still didn't look up from the dishes.

'Sindy has relatives there, remember? Mum and Dad want me to help her find them.'

I risked a glance. She was prodding the meal with her fork like she was searching amongst the rice for a sliver of hope.

'They realise she's not safe, even with them,' I told her. 'And really, the only way she'll ever get a go at a normal life is by getting away. A long way away.'

Daniella still said nothing.

'I don't suppose I'll have to be out there for long,' I said. 'Go with her on the plane, get her sorted. Then home.'

'I see.'

Her tone had turned as wintery as her outfit.

'She can hardly go on her own, can she?' I said. 'So, the folks have offered to pay for us both, so I can kind of...deliver her.'

Daniella met my eyes at last. 'What, in the Biblical sense?'

'Eh?'

'Deliver her. From evi...oh, never mind. When's all this happening then?'

'Soon. Really soon,' I said, pouring us both some more water. I managed to spill it and made myself busy mopping it up with my napkin. 'I guess Minto's put us on borrowed time. We can't risk still being there when he shows up to take her back to –'

Daniella's fork clattered into her bowl. 'And exactly how long have you known about all this, Alec?'

I stopped dabbing. 'Not long.'

She started doing all that things she does whenever she's wound up: chewing her cheek, sighing, looking away, blinking a lot.

'It's not definite,' I said.

She gave me her 'yeah, right,' look.

'It's not!'

'Just be honest, Alec.' She sighed and pushed her food away. 'Be upfront for once in your life!'

'Okay. It's almost definite.'

She nodded and stood up. Her rosy glow had been whipped away and replaced with a less attractive blotchiness. She rushed off in the direction of the restrooms.

The food was well and truly cold by the time she came back. She sat in her seat, not eating, her head bent.

'You kept saying I should do something,' I said, leaning across to her. I put my hand on hers. 'I thought you'd be pleased.'

Her eyelashes were moist and dark. 'You really thought I'd be glad for you to disappear to the other side of the world?'

'C'mon,' I said, squeezing her fingers. 'It won't be forever.'

She looked around the room, her chin wobbling.

My cheery announcement felt wildly misplaced. I'd known she wouldn't like it: I could've guessed she'd be upset. Why hadn't I been a bit more sensitive?

'It seems...the only way out,' I said to her. 'Make sure Sindy's okay and then...well, then I can come back, can't I?'

A tear dripped into Daniella's lap. She didn't wipe it away and it took a few seconds before she could respond. 'You won't come straight back though. You'll find work, travel, meet people.' She kept a tight hold on her expression. 'Just as I should want you to.'

I got as close to her as I could across the table. 'Hey, this is still me,' I said. 'I'll be just as much of a slacker over there as I am here, so I doubt I'll do any of those things.'

She managed a laugh, but her features were still in danger of collapse.

'We will see each other some more before you head off, won't we?' she said, carefully wiping tears from her cheeks. 'I've missed you and now you're...'

'Yeah, course. I'll make sure of it.'

'And if you need any help,' she added, that good girl courtesy of hers coming out of the woodwork, 'just let me know.'

I leaned forward and touched her cheek. 'D'you know,' I said with a smile, 'I was really hoping you'd say that.'

'We have to go up to London,' I told Mum.

'London? What for?'

'If you're serious about this, we'll need documentation. Have you thought how we're going to manage that with Sindy?'

Mum looked horrified that her easy fix was already imploding. Her hand flew up to her throat. 'She'll have no passport.'

'That's right.'

'And presumably she won't know where her birth certificate is.'

It was fascinating watching Mum go through exactly the same flowchart of worry that I'd been through the previous night. However, it was at this point, that I'd paused in my thinking.

'I don't reckon she has one,' I said.

'No birth certificate? What d'you mean? Of course she does! Everyone does.'

I perched on the arm of the sofa. 'I don't think she's registered anywhere, for anything. She said she never went to school, has never seen a doctor, a dentist.'

Mum's brow knotted into a deep furrow. 'But, how...'

'I think they've made sure she doesn't exist,' I said. 'The Apaches, I mean. She wasn't born in a hospital, no one knew she'd arrived. And after that...' I shrugged, leaving Mum to figure the rest.

I could see her processing the information, just like I had. Her heart telling her it couldn't be true and logic telling her it most definitely was.

'That's awful,' she said, quietly. 'She's like a...non-person.'

'That's right. If she doesn't exist, there's no one who can protect her. She's completely at their mercy.'

Mum's knees seemed to buckle, and she sort of collapsed onto the chair she'd been resting against.

She shook her head. 'That's criminal,' she said. I knew she wasn't talking about the law; she was just talking right and wrong.

'As far as they're concerned, it's the perfect solution,' I said, and now I was thinking aloud, my gaze fixed on the carpet. 'She's reliant on them for everything. For always. How can she ever get a job if she doesn't exist? A benefit? How could she ever go to college? How could she get married? She can never have a life!'

It was only when I snapped my gaze back to Mum that I realised her eyes had welled up. Her face was pale, her expression horrified. And it made me think about Gina again, and how Mum had been trying so desperately to make her exist again, even though she was gone. And yet, here was Sindy, flesh and blood and full of life; but someone whose existence we could never prove.

It was quite a moment for Dad to walk in. He only popped in to get the TV guide and he suddenly found himself with Mum clinging to him, sniffing and blubbering into his neck.

'We need to get Sindy away more than ever,' she explained, her words muffled against Dad. 'But now we can't because there's no birth certificate so no passport and no way out of this…situation.' Tears took over again, and as the words filtered through to Dad, he put a hand gently on the back of Mum's hair as she cried.

I felt bad it had got to this pitch, but I'd had no idea Mum would have found my discovery so upsetting.

I went over to her, stood behind her and put a hand on her back.

'It's okay, Mum,' I said, gently. 'I might've found a way.'

She half-turned to me, and I spotted the surge of hope in Dad's eyes too. 'It can still be done?'

'Maybe,' I said, 'but there is a slight problem with the plan.'

'I don't care,' she said, taking a shaky breath. 'If it's possible, we should give it a go. What's the problem with it, love?'

'Well,' I said, looking between her and Dad. 'I think it's a good plan, but it's just not legal.'

The fact they hadn't instantly dismissed it gave me hope.

Sindy was upstairs reading her magazines, but I knew she never spent long on her own, so I had to be quick and economical with explaining my idea.

'It's just bureaucracy,' I said. 'Sindy hasn't got a birth certificate, but perhaps she wouldn't need that...if she had an expired passport. Say, from someone who'd now be Sindy's sort of age.'

'I see.' Mum's furrowed brow indicated that she didn't.

I waited, then looked at her sidelong. 'Like Gina, for instance.'

'Gina?'

'We went to Spain when we were little, didn't we?'

'But...we can't use hers,' Mum said. 'There'll be a record of her... they'll know that she can't get another one.'

'Only if the two departments match the records,' I said. 'Usually, they don't. Remember how we got that letter telling us Gramps was due for a new pension card? He'd been dead for three years.'

'But – what if they found out? If they *did* have a record of Gina – we'd be guilty of fraud, wouldn't we?'

I took a breath: I already knew the next bit was likely to be the trickiest. 'Mum, you know you had all that stuff in the spare room...all that information about childhood illnesses?'

She glanced at Dad. 'So? What about it?'

'I think you should see a doctor. Tell them you're still doing it.'

'Eh? Why would I do that?'

'It would give you a defence if it all went wrong,' I said. 'The doctor would have it on record.'

'Have what on record?' Dad said, looking as confused as Mum. 'I don't see what you're getting at.'

'Well...it's a kind of medical issue. And if you sent for a new passport for Gina and got found out, it would just be put down to another example of your...medical problem. A 'Get Out of Jail Free' card.'

I smiled, like it was no big deal.

Mum pursed her lips and traced a pattern on the carpet with her foot. Dad, thankfully, kept his mouth shut. The silence stretched.

'You want them to mark me down as doolally,' she said, looking at me finally.

I shrugged. 'Safer that than being marked down as a criminal.'

She looked down again and I could see her slowly start to nod as the idea took hold. 'I suppose...if you think it would help then yes. I'll make an appointment.'

Once I had the nod, I felt myself go into overdrive, like the idea had stayed coiled inside me too long. Now it was out, free and I wanted to speed it into action. 'We need to get through this fast,' I said. 'No delays. Me and Sindy will need to go to London to get same-day passports.'

'Can you do that? And...have you even told Sindy your idea?' Mum said. 'Are we sure she'll do this? Will she even agree to go to Australia?'

"Course she will,' Dad said. 'How many times has she said she'd love to save up and go?'

'We'd better make sure. You know how she can be: she changes her mind from one minute to the next. Oh, and we'll take Gina's birth certificate to London, just in case,' I told Mum. 'You know where it is?'

Stupid question: Mum was already on her feet.

She opened the door but stopped in the doorway. 'Oh! Sindy!' she said. 'What are you up to there?'

We all heard the click of the phone's handset being placed on the cradle. 'Just checking the time.'

Mum rolled her eyes and gave a good-natured tut. 'Why don't you come in here for a minute, love?' she said. 'Jim and Alexander need to talk to you. And it's about something a lot more exciting than the Speaking Clock!'

Chapter 41

Puzzle pieces fell into place far more smoothly than they had any business doing. Mum had armed herself with a diagnosis of anxiety and depression; I'd got the passport forms from the post office and both Sindy and I had the pre-requisite set of hideous photos courtesy of Cardiff bus station's photo booth. Passports and tickets were all that were left on the shopping list.

'Is this going to be a problem?' Mum said, waving something under my nose as she came into my room. 'Gina was named on my passport – she didn't have her own. Neither of you did.'

'No, that's okay,' I said. 'We just have to show that the new photos have been certified as Gina.'

Mum blinked back at me. 'But...we can't ask anyone we know to say it's Gina.'

'Ah, but I can,' I told her. 'Daniella said she's happy to do it.'

'Oh! Well, that's good then.'

While I sifted through the forms, I realised Mum was watching me.

'I can't believe it,' she said. 'You've got it all moving so quickly.'

'Yeah, well Minto's quite the motivator. I've still got to buy plane tickets, though,' I said. 'We're going nowhere otherwise.'

'Ah, that's the easy part,' Mum said, heading for the door. 'Don't worry about that.'

'Mum?'

She came back in and looked at me.

'You sure you can afford this? I feel...this is your retirement fund.'

Mum folded her arms and her features softened. 'Seeing Sindy sorted out would be the best retirement gift we could give ourselves. Dad says the same.'

'Even so, you two have been saving all this time and then…bang, it'll be all gone.'

'Not all of it,' Mum said, lowering her voice. 'When we went through the accounts, it made me realise how much we actually have. I don't know why your father has been complaining so much. There'll be more than enough left for us to enjoy.'

'You realise we have to leave soon, don't you?' I said. 'Me and Sindy. If we're going to do this, we have to go as soon as we can to get the paperwork sorted. We can't risk Minto turning up.'

I watched Mum internally brace herself. 'Oh yes,' she said. 'We'll be more than ready.'

The more we got done, the more impatient I was to leave. It was like revving the engine and waiting for that flag to fall. It set my nerves on edge and I sensed I was difficult to be with. The others had to creep around me; fearful of a mistimed comment or an ill-considered look.

I figured we could leave the next day to get the passports. Mum had gone to the bank to transfer savings into their current account; Dad had filled the car with petrol and Sindy had spread all she owned into that one huge suitcase.

I was zipping up the front section of my bag – the bit with the forms and Home Office leaflets – when I found an old photo Mum had put in of Gina, as if to prove to the good folk in immigration the same girl was asking for her own passport.

It was a black and white picture, taken in the garden before we built the conservatory. Gina was peering to the side, worried look on her face. She was holding her white stuffed unicorn – the one she nuzzled each night that always smelled of dribble.

'It's quite a clear picture of her face,' Mum said, giving me a start. She came further into the room, a pile of clean laundry in her arms. 'That's why I thought it'd be a good one to show the passport office.'

'They're not interested what she looked like fifteen years ago, Mum.'

'These are the ones Sindy had done, are they?' she said, putting down the clothes and reaching across for the photo strip. She held Gina's picture and Sindy's at arm's length, side by side. 'She could be the same person, you know. They're not dissimilar, are they? The shape of the eyes, the colouring.'

'Immigration are barely going to look. They just want the signatures, not a trip down memory lane.'

'I know, I know,' Mum said. She put a hand on my shoulder. 'I just thought –'

Our eyes met as the quiet of the room was upturned by the deep, resonant roar of an engine. I shot to my feet and kicked the bag under the bed. 'Get Sindy,' I told Mum. 'Make sure she doesn't go to the door. Hurry up. And warn Dad.'

Mum scuttled away.

I heard the creak of the gate outside and my stomach went into lockdown.

A loud rap at the front door.

I stayed where I was, listening to the silence in the house. Another knock, barely ten seconds after the first, had me easing the curtains apart, careful to keep myself out of view. A black motorbike stood like a beefy minder against the kerb.

Downstairs, I heard movement in the kitchen, and I realised Dad must have come in from the garden. I tore down the stairs in time to see him at the kitchen door. 'Go back,' I mouthed, gesturing him away. 'Back!'

The letterbox opened and the next knock was even louder. 'Alec, open the fucking door, will you? I can see you're in there, you twat!'

There was a murmur of voices that warned me Stobes wasn't alone.

I opened the door.

He and Black stood grinning at me, helmets under their arms like they were a pair of astronauts.

'About fucking time,' Stobes said, stepping inside.

Black ruffled my hair as he went past. 'Long time, no see, butty-bach. Missed us?'

I followed them through the hall where they waited to be shown where to go. I eased past them and opened the kitchen door.

Dad spun around like a startled ballerina.

'Stobes and Black have stopped by to see me,' I told him. 'Don't mind if we use the kitchen, do you?'

I could see him filtering my tone for clues.

'It's okay,' I told him. 'I'm just gonna grab a couple of cold ones from the fridge.'

'Right. I'll leave you to it then,' he said. And he gave the others a brief nod before he disappeared.

'So, what brings you two all this way?' I said, passing them each a lager.

'There's a club-meet down this way,' Black said. 'Thought I'd bring Stobes here for an outing.'

I looked between them. 'A club-meet?'

'Apaches,' Black said, and he turned to show me the patch on the back of his jacket. 'I'm in.'

'I'm just a hangaround: there for the weed and the women,' Stobes said, helping himself to a chair. 'So, Mr Johnston, how've things been?'

'Fine. Busy, you know.'

Black ran a leather wrapped finger along the gas hob then wandered over to the window, looking out into the garden. He was making me uneasy.

'What about you two?' I said. 'Everything good at the flat?'

'All quiet on the western front,' Stobes said. 'Well, even quieter these days with you gone and our little house-mouse gone AWOL.'

'Sindy's not there?' I said.

Black still had his back to us. 'Minto's moved her along, it seems.'

'How d'you mean?'

Stobes sat hunched at the table. He glanced over to Black before he replied. 'Someone else is taking care of her,' he said. He took a swig from his beer and flicked his bottle top across the table. 'Surprised you didn't know. Thought you'd've been her first port of call.'

'I haven't been in Swansea for a while,' I said. 'If she'd turned up at my place, she'd have been disappointed.'

Black moved from the window and perched, a bit too close to me, against the worktop. The silence stretched.

'Is that what you two are doing here?' I said, finally. 'Are you looking for Sindy?'

Black ran a hand through his mop of dark curls. He smiled at Stobes. 'Looking for her?' he said. 'Why? Is she missing? Did you say she was actually missing, Mr Stobes?'

'Nah. I never said she was. I think we said she'd been moved along. Unless you know different, of course.'

They both looked at me.

'Well, like I said, I haven't seen her.'

'Aye, aye. Then you've got nothing to fret about, have you?' Black said.

Stobes drained his beer and stood up. 'You should come over to the meet with us,' he said, giving me a slap on the arm. 'It's gonna be wild. Last one of the year always is.' He reached past me and put his empty bottle on the counter. 'Minto'll be joining us before he heads off on his business trip. He'd want to see you, I reckon.' He eyeballed me and it was all I could do to stop myself flinching.

'If you change your mind, we'll be hanging out at the caravan park in Sully,' Black said. And he passed me his empty bottle; his gloved hand keeping hold of it a second longer than necessary. 'You can't miss us – we're taking over the whole fucking place.'

'I'll see. Thanks.'

Black took his helmet from the table and Stobes handed him the keys. I shuffled down the hall with them and opened the door. 'Good seeing you, Alec, butty,' Black said. 'Cheers for the beer.'

I nodded.

Stobes stuck out his hand. 'Alec,' he said, by way of a farewell.

Outside, Black flicked up the bike stand and ground the engine into life. 'Hey, where's your lid, man?' he shouted at Stobes.

Stobes dashed past me and into the kitchen. He came hurrying out with his helmet as I stood, minding the door. He awarded me another whack on the arm as he went past.

'You've got one week,' he said, quietly. 'Minto'll get here in one week.'

And before I'd had time to register the favour, he'd gone.

Chapter 42

We'd been sitting in the waiting room for over two hours, clutching our number tag. There'd been a notice on the door, warning of delays. Seemed half the country was after an urgent passport and when I looked outside at the filthy weather, I could understand why. Still, it was hard to imagine sunshine, even on the other side of the world. I wondered if I'd make it back in time for Christmas. It was still a few weeks away, but I knew Daniella was looking to me for some kind of assurance. An assurance that I really couldn't give her.

I'd been over everything with Sindy – reminded her to let me do the talking but had gone over the details with her just in case. I'd told Mum it would be fine, easy, but in reality, I was shitting bricks. Sindy was the notorious loose cannon. We'd all offered her private bribes for good behaviour: I was locked into buying her a big box of chocolates if she got her passport and Christ knows what Mum and Dad had got roped into.

We sat stiff and upright in our chairs. Mum had been Sindy's personal groom that morning and with the curled hair and the funky get-up, she could definitely have passed for sixteen.

The passport officer was a jowly middle-aged guy with damp patches under the arms of his shirt. I figured the dampness was a good thing: a man who didn't respond well to stress would presumably try to avoid it.

'I've checked over everything,' I told him. 'I think the forms are filled in okay.'

The guy said nothing but flipped through the sheets, turning them over one by one. He looked at the photos, then at each of us.

I saw Sindy chew her lip and she was gently rocking her knee from side to side. 'I had to have loads taken,' she said. 'I kept giggling.'

I shot her a look to shut her up.

But Passport Man didn't seem to mind; he might've even warmed a little. He turned the photos over and looked back at the applications. 'And Daniella Hurst has known you for more than two years?' he said.

'Four,' I told him, reciting what I knew was on the form.

He scooped up the forms and wrote something on a slip of paper, signed it and stamped it. 'These will be checked by our Chief Immigration Officer,' he said. 'When are you travelling?'

I looked at Sindy the same time she looked at me: we hadn't predicted that question.

'Next week,' she piped up. 'We're going to see my family in Australia. They live in Mount Isiah. I mean Isa. Sorry.'

The officer looked at me rather than Sindy and I wondered if he was considering why she'd said 'my family' rather than ours.

'Collection service is open until four,' he said. 'You'll be able to pick up the documents from there once they've been approved.'

By three, the number of people in the passport office had ballooned. It was as if the whole of humanity had been barfed out into that space. Most had brought their extended family, and kids were crawling between chairs, wriggling about on the carpets and making the place look untidy.

'Number eighty-seven.'

I grabbed Sindy and took her up to the counter with me.

A reedy looking woman glanced at us briefly. She gestured to us to sit down while she unfolded a wad of typed papers. There were no passports in the pile, that much I could see and if I'd followed my instincts, we'd have hot-footed out of there and never looked back. I took a packet of mints out of my pocket, offered one to Sindy and to the woman, then sat back in my seat as if this whole process was no big deal.

'Alexander Johnston and,' she looked down at the form then peered at Sindy. 'Georgina Johnston.'

'That's right,' I said.

'These are your first adult passports, are they?'

'Yep. We haven't been overseas for years, so we were on Mum's before.'

The woman shuffled through the papers and compared two sheets, looking from one to the other. I watched the top of her head, trying to interpret every movement, every angle. When I swallowed, I was sure it was the loudest fucking gulp in history. I didn't dare look at Sindy; couldn't risk a move. I figured there were probably cameras everywhere, studying people's body language for signs of nervousness, guilt. I swallowed again.

'Do you have the stamped receipt?' the woman said, resting those eagle eyes on me.

'Yes.' And I was so keen to get it out of my pocket, I pulled the mints with it and the packet rolled across the floor. If the cameras hadn't been watching me before, they'd certainly have swivelled my way after that.

The woman got to her feet and, without offering an explanation, took the papers and receipt away.

'Where's she gone?' whispered Sindy.

I didn't look at her. 'Shh.'

'Has she gone to get the police?' Sindy sounded like she was about to cry.

'Just shut up!'

I saw Miss Marple returning to us and she wasn't flanked by police officers. I couldn't tell a thing from her expression: I guessed these people must have been trained by the Ministry of Blank Looks.

She sat down and before I could see what she was doing, two blue books appeared in front of us. 'You'll need to sign those as soon as possible,' she said. 'And I'd advise you to fill out the contact details in case of emergency before you use your passports for travel.'

'Right,' I said. And I had to swallow the wobble out of my voice. 'Thanks. So, is that it?'

'All done,' she said. And we finally got a smile out of her.

'Thank you,' Sindy said, getting up. She stuck out her hand to the woman.

'Not at all,' the officer said, shaking hands.

'Come on, Gina,' I said, pulling Sindy by the arm. She was at her most dangerous when she was relieved or excited.

I had to run down the stairs to keep up with her. In fact, I had to race after her as she sprinted down the street.

I saw Mum's face drop as she spotted us hurtling towards her. She said something to Dad and they both peered past us, waiting to see who we were running from.

No one looked more shocked than Dad when Sindy raced into his arms.

'We did it,' she told him, pulling him into a bear hug. 'We did it! So, guess what? You owe me an instant camera.'

Chapter 43

None of it felt real until we were at the airport. Then it was all far too real. Given we'd only got our tickets the day before, I'd barely had time to adjust. I don't think I'd ever really believed we'd get away with it, but there was no sigh of relief; no sinking back into my own smugness. It was simply a drip-feed of dread. I knew that every time we passed a border control, each time we were asked for documentation, I'd expect our number to be up. Every official at the airport injected me with a fresh rush of nausea. In my mind, it wasn't a case of *if* we'd be caught; it was simply when. Sindy was travelling on a dead girl's passport: we couldn't possibly be allowed to get away with it.

I'd had the briefest of conversations with Daniella. She knew the whole thing was imminent when she got a call from the passport office, and she'd had no choice but to sit tight till I let her know what was happening. When I did, I told her I didn't want a farewell.

I knew it was hard for her to accept but, frankly, I was too stressed, too hollowed-out to deal with anymore. If I didn't see Daniella, it was easier to hold onto the story in my head: the one where we'd fly to Sydney, onto Mt Isa, find Sindy's mum and I'd be home in time for Christmas. That was the only newsreel allowed to feature in my mind. It was for just a few weeks, then I'd be back and Sindy, Minto, the flat would all seem like a dream.

'She's like a bottle of pop, isn't she?' Mum said, as soon as Sindy went to the bathroom in the departure hall.

'I don't suppose she's travelled before,' Dad said.

'She's so excited,' Mum continued, looking at me. 'She's promised to get a photo of you both every day; then she's going to post them to us, so we get a sort of running commentary. Isn't that a lovely idea?'

I said yes, but I knew Sindy's enthusiasm for that camera wouldn't last the week.

Mum put a hand on my arm. 'We've put money into your account,' she said. 'We'll keep an eye on things: make sure there's always some in there. Travel will be expensive – the distances are so big. Has Sindy managed to get in touch with any family yet?'

'I told her not to,' I said. 'Better we check things out once we're there.'

Mum nodded. 'I hope it'll be a… nice surprise for her mother. I pray to God she's different from Sindy's father.'

'Yeah, me too. I just hope we can find her. Sindy's got some information but…who really knows till we get there?'

There was still no sign of her emerging from the bathroom and I could see Mum getting twitchy, turning around every few seconds, searching through the crowds. 'I should have gone too,' she muttered.

'There's plenty of time,' Dad said. He looked at me. 'Got your boarding passes safe?'

'Yeah, got everything.' I patted my pockets. 'I can't settle till we're on our way, though.'

Mum wasn't helping my nerves, wringing her hands and craning her neck as she waited.

'Alec, Alec!' I turned and spotted Sindy waving at me. But now she had company with her.

I hurried over and when I got there, I practically fell into Daniella's arms. Until that moment, I hadn't realised how badly I'd needed to see her, but of course, Daniella always had a better handle on such things than I did.

Mum, Dad and Sindy went over to the seating area, pretending not to watch us.

'I'm sorry, Alec. Do you mind?' Daniella said, as she hugged me. 'It just didn't feel right. I needed a proper goodbye.' She stood back and looked at me. 'I won't believe you're gone unless I see it for myself.'

'Yeah, same here!'

It was a relief to have her there; the warmth and comfort of that hand in mine. Yet, at the same time, her presence nearly crippled me. While I was dealing with practicalities, I could convince myself I was in control, knew what I needed to do. But having Daniella there was like putting a finger on the pause button, and that's when I started to question what the hell I was thinking. I could be arrested; we could *all* be arrested. And if Minto knew about any of it, he could orchestrate our downfall for himself; get his sweet revenge in one easy swoop.

Daniella reached forward and undid my scarf. I watched her as she took it off and wrapped it around her own neck. It looked good against the stark whiteness of her sweater and the colour was a perfect match for those violet-blue eyes of hers.

'You're hardly going to need a scarf over there,' she told me. 'It's the middle of summer.' She grinned at me and rolled her eyes. 'What an idiot.' We both laughed, but I saw her smile begin to collapse. She grabbed me and pulled me towards her.

'It's okay,' I said, as I held her. I began to recite my own assurances back at her: 'I'll be home in a couple of weeks. I'll find Sindy's family, make sure she's okay, then be back in time for Christmas.'

Daniella forced a smile and nodded a little too vigorously. Neither of us tried to say any more. She wanted to linger there, I could tell; just the two of us, in the midst of the airport mayhem. But my nerves were firing, and it felt like my insides were about to combust. I had to keep moving. I felt her resistance as I guided us through the crowd towards the others.

Sindy was in tears when we got there, the excitement replaced by something messier. She had one of Mum's tartan hankies pressed to her face.

'Just nerves,' Mum explained to me.

Dad ruffled Sindy's hair. 'It's certainly been a fraught few weeks, hasn't it?'

It felt hot, stifling as we all stood there, and I knew I was going to throw up if we didn't get moving.

'Time for the off, I think,' Dad said, watching me.

Sindy let out a sob, clutching more tightly onto Mum. I hadn't expected her to be upset; I'd imagined her excitement carrying her through, keeping her buoyed and bubbly, but now she finally seemed to realise the significance of what we were doing.

Even as I watched her hug everyone, though, it struck me that none of us ever knew what was going on in her head. Perhaps it was Minto she was crying for; or her dad. Nothing about Sindy could ever truly surprise me.

'Come on, love,' Mum said, pushing a strand of hair from Sindy's face. 'We all have to be brave.' She squeezed her shoulder and kissed the top of her head.

'Take care, Alec,' Dad said, pumping my hand up and down. 'Look after her, won't you?'

'Yeah, I will, Dad.'

In a different life, we'd've hugged and slapped one another on the back, but this was me and Dad at Heathrow not Pop and Junior in Hollywood.

Mum, on the other hand, almost strangled me with her farewell. 'Come back soon, love,' she whispered. 'Come back safe.'

Over Mum's shoulder, I could see Daniella looking more uncertain than I'd ever seen her. Something about her dazed expression summed up all the craziness of the last few months.

When we'd met, I'd been living a half-baked existence, nothing on the horizon to either dread or look forward to. And now, here I was, running from a savage mob with a strange girl in tow, heading for a far bigger unknown. It wasn't what I'd had in mind for my future, but at least it was living. It was movement.

Daniella wrapped her arms around my neck. 'I'm going to miss you,' she said into my ear. 'I love you.'

My throat seemed to have an invisible hand around it, squeezing all the air from it. I couldn't reply, could barely look at her. All I could do was nod and turn away.

I guided Sindy to the glass doors and all the while, she kept that snot-ridden hankie pressed to her face. We joined the snaking queue.

'I don't know if we should go,' Sindy said, looking behind her. 'My horoscope said I was heading for trouble.'

I tugged her arm to keep her moving. 'Well, you can prove those stupid things wrong then, can't you?'

'And I saw on telly they do have snakes there,' she said. 'Loads of them, all deadly.'

I kept pulling her arm. 'It's okay,' I said. 'You won't see any.'

'Promise?'

'Sure.' We were almost at the first counter. 'All right, Gina?' I said. 'Show your passport, say nothing.'

From the corner of my eye, I sensed the others waving, watching – a little trio of tears and trepidation.

Sindy stepped forward, gave in her passport, kept right on sobbing and sniffing. And she looked so deathly miserable that the officers hardly even paused.

Chapter 44

December 1983 – Queensland/Northern Territory Border, Australia

'That's right. It's all about Sindy.'

As we sit there, unmoving, the truckie's pointed features stretch to a smile. This is what he's been waiting for – the moment he gets to whip away the black cloth and uncover the sawn-in-half lady. Or whatever else he's got hiding.

I'm determined to give nothing away. 'What about Sindy?'

He looks at me long and hard, like he's taking a deep drag on one of those smokes of his. Except this time, it's me he's inhaling: my fear, my nerve, my resolve. The longer he stares, the more depleted I feel, as if he really is filling his lungs with my last remnants.

'Does a clever college boy like you seriously think Minto'd just let you and Sindy...' he looks skywards and flutters his fingers, 'disappear over the rainbow?'

'She didn't want to go with Minto,' I say.

'What's it got to do with you, what Sindy wants?'

'I...'

'I'm her father,' he barks. 'She's my kid; my responsibility. Capiche?'

When I hear the sharp intake of breath, I know I shouldn't have picked that moment to look away.

He yanks my T-shirt and yells in my face. 'Got something to say, pretty boy?' His knuckles dig into my breastbone as he tightens his fist.

'No...no. I was just...I didn't mean anything.' I hold up my hands in surrender, shrinking as far from him as he'll let me.

He eases off, a satisfied smile softening those sharp-angle features. He got what he wanted – terror, a begging tone, a companion shitting himself. Pretty much the same as Minto seems to look for in a mate.

He sits, gazing out the windscreen like he's only here for the view; all the time in the world. I know we're both aware of the heaving of my chest as I breathe, the spring tight tension of every joint. He'll wring every bit of fear he can out of me; get me so scared I can't even think straight. He mightn't have dirt under those neat fingernails, but it won't be the first time he's done something like this. I can sense it: it's just another day at the office for him.

Neither of us is willing to blink first. I remain as quiet and still as he does. Outwardly, at least. Much longer and I'll be a pool of sweat on the floor. The backs of my jeans are almost welded to my skin. I risk a glance in his direction – eyes only, of course. My head stays rock solid, facing front. He's got one arm on his leg, the other furthest from me lies along the ledge of the door, pressed against that tight-shut window.

I glance again and this time I see his profile turned away from me. He barely blinks. I follow the curve of his eyeball and get a sense he's watching something, attention no longer solely on me. Maybe it's my moment: the lapse I'm meant to be waiting for. My eyes slide left, checking the lock's still down. And that's when I spot it – a sandy trail moving across the length of my side mirror, getting bigger as it approaches. No wonder he's so quiet. Maybe, finally, he's the one shitting himself.

This new development has an instant effect on my breathing and my sphincter. When I swallow it's so loud it's as if my tonsils have hit the pan. He looks over to me and our eyes meet. I tilt my head deliberately to the wing mirror, just so he knows that, yeah, I've seen it too.

What I don't expect is for him to undo his seatbelt and clamber down from the cab. The lock clunks back into position as soon as the door slams.

I stay bolt upright; home in on the vehicle approaching.

I pray for a car but all I see is chrome. Chrome and two wheels. Chrome and two wheels. Chrome and two wheels. The throaty engine confirms what I already know. Story of my fucking life. There'll be no rescue mission; no tourists in a campervan haplessly blundering into the fray. It's just another weapon in laughing-boy's armoury; a nice bit of back-up so the odds are kept firmly in his favour.

The realisation makes my insides collapse: I'm nauseous with letdown. The blistering heat of the cab seems to intensify and all at once I'm the ant beneath the magnifier. Dashed hopes have ripped my nerves and my whole body gets the shakes. I swallow, breathe, swallow, breathe.

It's hard to ignore that distinctive movement as Minto gets off the bike. Half a world away yet here he is, right on my doorstep. He pulls off his helmet, steps forward in front of the truck to shake hands with my chauffeur. No smiles are exchanged. It occurs to me that I should be scrabbling around, grasping under the seats for heavy objects to fill my pockets with but instead the windscreen becomes my personal TV and I sit glued to these two soap-opera villains. It's like it's not really happening. And certainly not to me: I'm just a guy in a truck, waiting to be taken the rest of the way to Alice. Aren't I?

Sindy's dad strides off with a new-found sense of purpose. In the wing mirror, I follow his progress towards the back of the van until he returns with something in his hand. He's weedy compared to Minto's solid bulk: the shit-green sweater hangs on his body as much as Minto's black leather encases his. They're an unlikely pair, these two. As Minto turns, I read the insignia on his back – 'Apache MC Morriston. It seems so laughingly small town in this vast, baking, other-side-of-the-globe landscape.

Minto's giving instruction, pointing to something behind, nodding his fat skull. Sindy's dad listens, unmoving. He's got a sheet of paper in his hand like he's a real truckie, delivering goods.

My nerves judder the minute they look up at me. Minto removes the cigarette from his mouth and chucks it into the dirt as he strolls over. He jangles the key in the lock on my side and eases the door open a fraction, like he's waiting for me to spring out at him. When I don't, he throws open the door and grabs the front of my T-shirt. In one movement, he hauls me out of my seat, and I struggle to get my footing. He grabs me by the chest again and hurls me against the cab, keeping a firm hand on me the whole time. The back of my head ricochets against the door, bringing tears to my eyes. It all happens so quickly, it's like the stuffing's fallen out of me and I'm left with arms swinging this way and that as I'm tossed around.

His black eyes lock onto mine and a ball of fear punches me. It's hard to reconcile that this is the old Minto from the flat; Minto I've shared the odd pint with; Minto I've seen getting in from the supermarket. Now he's that other Minto: the Minto on the other side of the wall giving Sindy what-for; the Minto of the knives; Minto of the clubhouse.

'What the fuck's your game, you little cunt?' he yells at me. He crushes me hard in the chest with the flat of his hand. 'Who the fuck d'you think you're playing with?'

I shake my head, stuttering words: whatever words he wants me to say. The ones that'll make him back off and get his face out of mine. 'I don't know what...I haven't done anything.'

His features mash into a crazy, dark madness and I know they're not the right words. I trip over my tongue flailing for different ones. 'I just wanted to get away,' I said. 'And Sindy…'

His nostrils flare at the mention of her name and he pushes harder on my chest so I can't breathe, can't say any more. The metal of the truck is white-hot, I sense it sizzling my skin through the T-shirt

'Sindy's not your problem,' he says. 'Sindy was never your problem.'

'I know, but...'

'Sindy was only ever my problem.' His voice has sunk to a whisper. There's a long pause as he stays there, eyeing me. 'But now Sindy's not anyone's problem. She'll never be anyone's problem again.'

He keeps those pebbly eyes drilled into me, checking reactions, gauging responses. His lips ease into a smile. He moves closer, his breath suddenly close to my ear. 'Isn't that good, Alec? Isn't it good that she's...no longer a burden?' And he kind of croaks it, like he's warming me up for more of his sweet nothings. 'You, my friend, sealed her fate.'

I know he wants me to flail at the notion; to whimper; to curse. But I don't. I just swallow and nod as if I'd expected it all along. I can't even take in what he's saying.

'Do you want to know what happened to her?'

I shake my head. Whatever he wants to tell me, I know I won't want to know.

'Too painful for you, eh?' he says. 'You always did have a soft spot for her, didn't you, Alec?'

'I just –'

'She fell,' he says. 'Straight down. From a great height.'

When his gaze lands on me again, I make sure my own gaze isn't there to greet him. I feel my lips part as I struggle to take in more air. My breath is as shaky as the story he's spinning me.

The sun's cooking the top of my head and sweat trickles into my eyes. I can hardly keep them open but I daren't close them, even for a second.

He forces me to stand up straight then strolls around me, like a pissed off sergeant major. All I can do is brace myself for the jab of his fist which I'm certain will come any second.

When he's behind me, he comes close to my ear again. His breath is warm, and I feel the sweat run down my back as the sun's rays scorch my neck. 'Better hope they never find her eh, Alec? To lose one girlfriend like that could be seen as unfortunate. But to lose two, well, what are the odds?'

I still can't speak. Daren't. I know that, whatever I say will be used against me.

Behind me, I hear him unfold papers. It's not what I'd expected.

A crumpled white sheet slides in front of my face. 'Touching,' he says.

My writing stares back at me and I recognise the torn paper I placed on Sindy's bed before I left. 'Sorry, Sindy,' it says. 'I know you understand. Love Alec.'

I close my eyes at the absurdity; at the innocent-guilt of the words.

Minto will have laughed his socks off when he found it: really, it couldn't have been more perfect. As far as he's concerned – as far as anyone's concerned – this is my own confession. A pen and paper admission of guilt.

Chapter 45

By the time Sindy and I touched down on Mt Isa's little airstrip, we'd become almost used to handing over our passports, and having them handed back to us with a smile. I could've become fooled into thinking we were doing nothing wrong or that we were perfectly safe.

Sindy looked edgy and wired, though: she'd not slept the entire journey. Her eyes seemed to be everywhere as we made our way through the tiny building that served as a terminal. This was the Australia I'd come for; not the modern, bright lights of Sydney's airport where we'd had to transfer. There, it was all glass frontage and massive ceilings and it could've been anywhere in the world. The fake snow and Christmas baubles had looked laughably out of place in that sunny space.

By contrast, Mt Isa airport had only managed a few bits of tinsel. But as we stepped outside into the blistering heat and the blinding sun, I knew this was the red-dusted country I'd always imagined.

Sindy's massive suitcase – the one with the raspberry-pink splash – was proving to be a nuisance. The handle was dodgy, and the wheels had come loose so it was just as well the bus left from directly outside the terminal.

Sindy had barely said a word since Sydney, and all the exuberance I'd expected from her seemed to have dripped away. I found myself having to be the cheerleader as our bus trundled towards the township.

'Mt Isa, established in 1923, is located in the state of Queensland, Australia,' I read to her from my travel guide. 'The mine which dominates the town, produces lead, copper, zinc and silver. Locals know Mt. Isa as

The Isa.' I gave her another cheer-up smile; one of the many I'd had to offer over the past few hours. 'Sounds cool, eh?'

She shrugged and looked out into the nothingness.

It was hardly a tourist town; when we checked into the backpackers, there was apparently only one other group of travellers staying there. The rest were miners, working at the big plant we'd passed on our way in. At least it meant there was enough space for me and Sindy to have a bunkroom to ourselves.

I was itching to get started. My body-clock was all over the place, so I was wide awake at five the next morning. Sindy clearly had no such problems, and even by the time I left the backpackers at nine, she was still dead to the world on that top bunk. I wrote a note to tell her where I'd gone then headed for the post office.

Even at that time of the morning, the air had that 'baked' quality about it, and I had to smile as I passed a spray-on Santa in one of the office windows, and caught the strains of 'White Christmas' belting out from the tyre shop on the corner.

I took my time, and as I paused to read menus in café windows and to glance into grocery stores, it struck me that I felt relaxed. Safe. I hadn't felt that in a while: even Cardiff – normally my safe haven from the flat – had taken on a new and menacing air the last few weeks. Here, on the other side of the world, I could hardly have been further from Minto's reach. I could breathe again, long, deep, greedy breaths and now they wouldn't be cut short. I could look over my shoulder and not fear what I'd find there.

There were rows of phone books on the shelves in the post office. They were sorted by state and I was surprised by how thin a lot of them were compared to the ones back home. It made me realise that, despite the vastness of the land, it was still an empty and isolated place.

The surname Sindy had given to me for her mum was Haiden – not that unusual a name, but an unusual spelling. Perhaps if she'd been called Smith or Jones, we wouldn't have even given this a shot. But in a small town in the middle of nowhere, it seemed not only possible that we'd find her, but maybe even probable.

I felt my shoulders slump as soon as I saw there were no Haidens in the phone book. I'd built myself up to imagine this would be straightforward, even though common sense and past experience should've told me that, when it came to Sindy, nothing was straightforward.

I sat down with the other Queensland directories and tried looking up the name in the bigger cities. Perhaps she'd shifted to Cairns or Brisbane. When I came out empty-handed, I looked again at Sindy's scribbled notes. The other name she'd given me was Aaron Colbeck. I looked at it, wondering where this uncle fitted into the family tree. After all, Sindy seemed to think the mother wasn't married, so how could she have a brother called Colbeck? Different father, perhaps? Brother-in-law?

I closed the directories and put them back, deciding I needed to get some clarification from Sindy before I was sent further on this wild-goose chase. It put a dampener on my mood to be honest: I realised I'd been one of those stupid tourists who assumes everyone in Australia knows everyone else.

When I got back to our room at the backpackers, Sindy wasn't there. I hoped she wasn't far away, given she'd left the door wide open with all our stuff on show. I glanced down the empty corridor and just as I was going back into the room, I saw her coming up the stairs.

'Oh, Alec! You're back,' she said.

I nodded at the purse in her hand. 'Where've you been?'

'I rang the weather line.'

'What?'

'There's a telephone downstairs,' she said, speaking slowly like I was thick. 'I used it to find out what today's weather was going to be.'

'Sind…Gina!' I said, waving an arm at the window. 'It's hot and sunny. This is tropical Australia! It's always fucking hot and sunny.'

I probably wouldn't have been so bad-tempered if I'd had more luck at the post office.

'For your information, they have storms,' she said. 'It rains sometimes.'

'Well, not at the moment. So, stop wasting our money just so you can go downstairs and play with the frigging phone.'

I caught someone's eye as he was going past our room. 'Oh, hi,' he said, pausing. He backed up a step and looked at Sindy. 'You okay, Gina?'

I looked between them, confused: first, because who butts in on a stranger's argument; and second, because how the hell did he know Sindy?

'Oh, hi. Yes, I'm fine,' Sindy said, all smiles. 'Oh, this is my brother, Alec. Alec, this is Stu.'

We shook hands, but I was still recovering from Sindy's sensible introduction. She acted like a dumb kid most of the time, and then, suddenly, she could switch to normal-human mode.

'Stu's Canadian,' she told me.

'Well, good to meet you,' Stu said. He switched his attention back to Sindy. 'We'll be in the bar later if you wanna come say hi, okay?'

'Yep. We'll be there.' She looked across at me with a smile. 'Won't we, Alec?'

And, before I'd had chance to open my mouth, she'd set up our very first social engagement.

Chapter 46

Minto pushes me in front of him, adding little jabs in the back so I stumble to wherever he wants to lead me. Flies buzz around my mouth, in my ears and up my nose as if my decay has already begun. The little bastards look for any way in and their company makes me nervous; like they're the vultures blackening the skies overhead.

I'm pushed towards a massive corrugated building, its man-made presence startling amid the vast dry nothingness. We pass a generator by the back wall. It might be running, but with the blare of Black Sabbath, screaming from the massive speakers on the outside walls, you can forget about any soothing background hum. The roller doors are up, and I'm led to an inner door which Minto opens. The clubroom looks just like the one in Swansea but bigger. Way, way bigger. No residential corner block for them out here – no, they have room to spread themselves out as wide and loud and as in-your-face as they want.

Minto's lapping up my terror. His movements are slow, easy and he barely looks at me. He doesn't speak, doesn't need to: he has all the time in the world, every option at his disposal. This world is his oyster.

'What we have here, Alec, is part of an import-export venture,' he says, still wandering around, all bonhomie like he has no subverted agenda. 'It's a manufacturing hub, so the stuff we import gets made into something new, something more desirable, and the finished magic is exported.' He looks at me. 'Supply and demand. That's what it's all about. They demand – they keep demanding – and so, we supply. Everybody's happy. See how it works?'

He levels his gaze at me: the direct question clearly waiting for a direct answer. 'I guess.'

'It provides an income for a lot of people,' he says, as if he's giving me the executive's tour of the plant. 'There are hundreds involved in this. And all over the globe.'

'Yeah?'

'That's why I always hoped you'd find a place with us. Your own little Alec niche. Well,' he says, letting out a low chuckle. 'I suppose you have found a place with us, whether by accident or design.'

My gaze doesn't leave him for a second: I can't trust taking my eyes off him. He's like one of those desert snakes, upright and watchful, striking without warning – a head-flick and it's over. That's how it feels with Minto and his harmless chat. He's just waiting for his moment, waiting till my guard is down.

Black Sabbath has left us, but Motorhead's 'Ace of Spades' is now on repeat, adding an excruciating heavy metal torture to the proceedings. It's louder too and Minto doesn't adjust the volume of his speech, so I have to strain to hear what he says. Every sense is struggling to keep up and I'm afraid to so much as blink or swallow for fear of missing something vital.

Suddenly, Minto strides over to the door, throws it open and walks out. No explanations, no warning; just ups and leaves.

I'm left to nurse my panic.

I don't move far but once 'Ace of Spades' comes on for the third time, I risk a visual inspection of the room.

Someone's guarding the door outside, that much I can see from the shadowed strip of sunlight that occasionally moves. But if there are any hidden cameras and mics, I can't pick them out. The only things on the walls are speakers, Apache motifs and nudie posters.

I wander past the pool table and roll a ball into the pocket. Even that feels like a dangerous move, but the longer Minto stays away, the more uneasy I become. I need to walk, to have something to do with my hands and my feet. Stillness is aching.

I look over briefly to the bar – all those bottles and glasses and potential weapons – what's Minto doing leaving me alone with them? Behind the sofa, I spot another of those overfull boxes with gun butts sticking out. Has he really left me in here with an arsenal at my disposal? It has to be a trick.

I walk past them, swallowing and trying to put them from my mind but I keep coming back to them. I draw near, craning my neck to see just what's in the box and I see pistols in there too. Harmless looking things, next to their big, gruntier brothers. They won't be loaded. Of course, they wouldn't be loaded.

But what if they are? Perhaps they're for a quick getaway in an emergency – maybe a police raid would have them running in here grabbing their weapons. I glance out of the dusty window and before I've made the decision, I've pushed one of those little pistols into my pocket and moved away from the box.

I meander to the other side of the room, all innocence, and give the nudie posters a once-over. Someone in the past has chucked a dart and got a bullseye right in the nip. It reminds me of the dart holes in my ceiling at home and I have to close my eyes to stop the floor tilting as I think of my room.

There's a noise at the door and it flies open again. 'Bit of clearing up to do in here first,' Minto tells someone. I see the bouncer exit before the door closes again.

Minto parks his bulk on a stool, his arm crooked onto the bar and looks at me. 'What to do with you,' he says. 'That's the question. You know you're very inconvenient.'

'Maybe I should crawl back to where I came from,' I say. 'It's not like I'm going to grass you up.'

'Really?' he says. 'Your track record isn't too good on that score, Mr Johnston.'

Even over the vocal thrashing coming from the speakers, I hear a roar of motorbikes outside, belching into life. The sound grows then fades and I wonder where they're all off to and why Minto's left behind. Am I the bit of clearing up he has to do before he can join them?

My hand's in my pocket, tracing the contours of the trigger, getting acquainted with my unfamiliar friend. It won't be loaded. He'll know it won't be loaded – these phrases form a mantra in my head. It won't be loaded. He'll know it won't be loaded.

'Here's the thing, Alec,' he says. 'To kill you now would bring the inconvenience of your folks. James and Annie wouldn't let it rest, would they? There'd be police and investigations and pigs sniffing around.'

'So, let me go then.'

'Well, Alec. You can imagine why I'm not keen on that idea.'

'Look, you've won,' I tell him. My voice is weak, dry, no substance to it – it doesn't even sound like me. The yellow-bellied words do, though. 'Sindy's gone. There's nothing left for me to...' I shrug and look down. I think this is the first time it's hit me that Sindy has gone; that I won't see her again. I briefly wonder how I'm ever going to break it to Dad.

'It was Sindy I tried to help, that's all. I don't care what else you've got going on. Really, I couldn't give a shit about...all this other stuff.'

Minto seems to like my speech. He nods approvingly.

But something makes me uneasy again; something in his body language. He's not pondering, he's just waiting. Biding his time. Stalking and waiting for the moment to pounce.

The fact all the others have left is freshly sinister: a wave of nausea floods into my belly and sits there, festering.

The moment he stands, I yank the gun from my pocket and point it at him. It's a base, instinctive movement and one I hadn't known was going to happen. The decision hadn't reached my brain – survival, it seems, isn't a thought process.

'Don't move,' I say, as he puts up calming hands and makes to approach me.

He smiles. 'Alec, you know that thing's not loaded.'

'Sure? You want to risk it?' I spot a flicker of hesitation, a sliver of doubt. And a sliver is all I need.

He rolls his eyes and sits back on the stool, like he's annoyed at having to play my game.

There's a mirror over the bar. It means I can keep an eye behind me at the big dusty windows and the tree line outside. But something catches my attention: something inside, close by. It's a flash of pink. A deep red-raspberry pink that I instantly recognise. Why would Sindy's case be here, lurking behind the couch?

Minto's watching me, careful to show no emotion.

My voice rattles through my throat. 'She's not dead, is she?'

'What?' He runs a hand over his tattooed head and the gesture's enough to confirm it.

'Why would you kill her? She's a cash cow for you. You wouldn't toss all that income over a cliff. Certainly not to get me off your back.'

'Sure? You wanna risk it?' he says, throwing my words back in my face.

I swallow and his eyes trace the movement of my Adam's apple. He'll see the sweat on my top lip, the pulse in my neck.

He's about to say something else when there's a noise at the side of the room beyond the pool table. I turn my head but keep my gun pointed straight at him.

'Put it down, Alec.' Sindy emerges from the dimness and I see her holding a shotgun, tiptoeing forward like she's stalking a deer. The weapon looks hellish heavy in her small hands.

She shuffles forward, pointing the barrel at me.

Sweat prickles on my forehead, the back of my neck. Half a breath later and I've sprung fifty leaks.

'I feel like the odd one out, here,' Minto says, spluttering a laugh as he holds up empty hands. He sounds a lot chirpier all of a sudden, and I tighten my hold on the pistol.

'How much do you make from her?' I say, keeping my focus on him. 'You must earn a fortune. All those men paying big bucks to get their hands on her. And even bigger bucks for special treatments. Eh, Sindy?' I slide my eyes to her, hoping whatever I say will be enough to make her ease the barrel across; point the thing his way instead of mine. 'Do you realise how much he gets every time you service his friends? You could be rich by now, have anything you ever wanted.'

'It's not true.' I can see her arms are getting tired. If I was closer, I could whip that gun away in a heartbeat.

'Is that why she's been brought here?' I say to Minto. 'Do they pay more for young bodies?'

'It's not like that!' Sindy says. 'You've got it wrong, Alec.'

I look at her, realising I'm winding up the wrong person: she's the one with her finger on the trigger. 'You don't deserve to be treated like this, Sindy,' I say.

'It's you he's been using, not me,' she tells me.

Minto explodes a laugh. 'Children, children!' he says. 'Let's not squabble about who's my favourite. You've both been wonderfully...'

As he speaks, he suddenly lunges towards me. My finger jerks against the trigger and I pull, once, twice.

There's an almighty bang and Sindy lands on the floor, the clatter of a shotgun falling at her side.

I don't understand what's happened – there's dust and ringing in my ears.

The haze and smell clears, and 'Ace of Spades' comes to the fore again.

Sindy clambers to her feet and it's only then I spot the blood beside me. It's pooling on the concrete floor and it has Minto attached.

Chapter 47

We might've only just arrived in Mt Isa, but it already seemed to me that Sindy had lost interest in finding those relatives of hers. I could tell by the sour look on her face whenever I mentioned it.

We were in the bar at the backpackers that evening, waiting for the Canadians, when I next tackled Sindy about it. 'So, who's Aaron Colbeck?' I said, unfolding the piece of paper I'd taken to the post office. 'He's got a different surname, so presumably not your mum's brother. Maybe her brother-in-law or something?'

Sindy was sitting next to me on a bar stool. She leaned into me to look at the list of names again. 'I don't know.'

The strains of Slade's 'Merry Xmas, Everybody' thumped from the speakers as Sindy sipped her piña colada. 'Dad said he's my uncle. That's all I know.' She dipped a finger in her drink and held her pinkie out to me. 'Want a taste?' she said.

I kept my head down. 'No.'

I continued my study of the list, gradually easing away from her. Ever since we'd arrived, she'd seemed determined to be as physically close to me as possible. It would've been unwelcome enough at the best of times, but in this sticky heat, her proximity was almost unbearable.

She huffed a grumpy sigh and twisted around in her seat for the fiftieth time, to see if Stu was coming.

I tapped my finger at the piece of paper again. 'Look, how are we supposed to approach these people if we don't even know what relation they are to you?'

She shrugged as if to say this was my problem rather than hers. It was frustrating: I'd tried to pin her down for details countless times since we'd left Britain and, on each occasion, she'd been evasive to the point of being no bloody use whatsoever.

'Look, Sindy, do you…'

'Gina.'

'Gina,' I said, tutting. 'Do you want to find this family of yours, or not?'

'Of course I do,' she said, spearing a piece of pineapple with her umbrella stick. 'But there's no hurry, is there?'

'Oh, isn't there?' My beer spilled as I thumped it down on the mat. 'Well, maybe not for you, but I'd actually like to see my folks at Christmas, get together with Daniella, see the rest of my family. I don't actually want to spend my Christmas stuck here, in the middle of fucking nowhere, with you!'

Sindy took her lips from her straw and blinked back at me. Her cheeks flushed. I knew tears were almost certainly on the cards, but her gaze suddenly flicked to the side. A beaming smile appeared on her face. 'Hey, Stu!'

'Hey! It's our fellow travellers!' Stu said, shaking our hands as they joined us at the table. 'Boy, are we glad to meet some house mates who aren't miners!'

They were good company as it turned out and they took the edge off things between me and Sindy. Stu was a stocky, solid guy around my age and there were two girls, Lexi and Jules, a year or so younger. They were all from Edmonton and they'd been travelling around in an old station wagon, headed for another part of Queensland to pick up work.

'What about you two?' Stu asked. 'In Isa for a while?'

Sindy was about to answer. 'Not sure yet,' I said, quickly. 'We're hoping to visit some family but other than that, we'll see how we go.'

Jules sat rolling a ciggie. 'So – you two are, like brother and sister, or…'

'Yes,' said Sindy, a bit too proudly. 'Alec's my big brother.'

'Yah, you look a bit alike,' Jules said. 'Similar bone structure. I can see the resemblance.'

Sindy looked up and grinned at me, like it was actually true.

I couldn't figure out if Stu was 'with' either of the girls, but it turned out Lexi and Jules were just old mates of his from school. Lexi was the quieter of the two: ruddy cheeked and well-padded, looked like she'd easily survive the Canadian winters, whereas Jules was more your long, lithe sort, probably into yoga or running. She exploded into laughter a lot and tended to collapse against whoever was beside her whenever she had a fit of the giggles.

It was a much-needed airlock having company. Over a few beers, we heard a bit more about their plans. They were going to some place called Normanton, a few hours north, on the promise of work in a new hostel which was due to open there.

For me, it was a new experience seeing Sindy talk about regular things with regular people, and I could almost imagine myself her proud big brother as I watched her telling them all about her favourite TV shows and which films she wanted to see at the movies.

The coolest thing about the Canadians was they all seemed to like Sindy. Genuinely. Warmly. Jules found Sindy hilarious and I could see Sindy lapping up the attention.

After such a decent evening, it put a dampener on things when they reminded us that they were leaving in a few days for their work adventures. It would have been good to have had their company for longer.

Once they'd left Mt Isa, I knew all I had to look forward to was helping Sindy search for her family: a family that she seemed totally indifferent to finding.

Chapter 48

'I didn't mean it, I didn't mean it,' Sindy's shrieking as she paws at Minto. 'I'm sorry, I didn't mean it.' She's getting blood everywhere and I'm on the verge of puking.

I take her hand and pull her away. 'C'mon. We need to get out of here.'

She's still struggling to get back to him, so I yank her hard and her shoes slap against the concrete. We get to the door, but I look back and see her shotgun on the floor. 'Wait,' I tell her. And she does.

I run over and pick up the gun – it's still warm and I want to carry it at arm's length, as far away from me as possible.

'He's not really dead, is he? Alec?' Sindy whispers as I join her. 'I haven't...killed him?' She starts making this weird mewing sound and tugs at her hair. 'What will they do to me?'

I spin around, trying to gauge the situation, get my mental bearings. 'Where's everyone gone?' I say. 'Sindy! Where did the others go?'

She can barely form words. 'I don't know, I don't know. I can't remember.'

I grab her by the arm. 'Think for fuck's sake!' I'm shouting in her face. 'Could they come back?'

She rubs her cheek, not realising she's smudging Minto's blood all over her. 'They've gone to Alice Springs,' she says, gulping out the words. 'They're having a big meet. Till tomorrow at least. Minto's meant to...'

'We need to get out. Now.' I dash over and throw open the door. The sunlight is blinding.

I pull Sindy outside and we run towards the one bike left by the tree.

It's hotter than it's ever been in my life: I'm melting from the inside.

'It wasn't meant to go off,' Sindy says, sobbing. 'I thought it wasn't loaded.'

'Where are the bike keys?' I yell at her.

'What?'

'The keys to the bike, Sindy. Where are they?'

She shakes her head, her body convulsing as she cries. 'I don't kn... in his pocket.'

I glance back at the clubhouse. 'Shit.'

'I can get them,' she says. She's about to run back inside but as she reaches the doorway, she turns and stops. 'I don't want to see him,' she splutters.

There's no time to try and cajole her: I'm forced to hurry past.

Raw fear grips me the moment I step over the threshold. I can't believe he'll still be dead. It's like those horror scenes where you think the monster's been slain, then suddenly the body's gone and a shadow on the wall reveals a dagger, poised and ready.

But a shaft of sunlight shows Minto is just where we left him, his bulky form splattered across the concrete floor like a spilt pint. I'm about to put a wary hand on his jacket but I spot my bag, upturned in the corner. It gives me a moment to delay and I go and grab it before returning to kneel beside Minto. I still daren't touch him and I know this is all taking far too long. We need to get out. We need to get away.

I take a breath and look towards the door: somehow, I know Sindy will be watching me, taking in my every move. It crosses my mind I don't trust her.

'Come in here,' I say. 'Give me a hand.'

She takes a few steps forward but shakes her head at coming closer.

I return my attention to finding the keys and I keep my eyes on Minto's clothing – the collar of his jacket; the stitching on his jeans – anything other than the humanness of him.

He's the great ogre felled from the beanstalk. I won't look at his face but all the time I'm digging in his pocket, I smell and taste the metallic ooze of his blood and I have to hold my breath to stop myself retching.

Sindy's sniffing and sobbing. Did she really not know it was loaded? Or had that bullet been meant for me?

My fingers connect with the jagged edge of metal and I pull out a small bunch of keys. I yank my hand from his pocket and suddenly can't get away quick enough. Even as I stand, I'm half expecting to feel his hand around my ankle. Instead, I feel a dampness on my jeans and realise I've been kneeling in Minto's blood.

I touch Sindy's shoulder as I reach her. 'C'mon. Let's go.'

'We can't leave him here.'

'What?' I'm right on the edge, percolated. 'We can. We have to get out.'

'But...'

'He's dead. Okay? There's nothing to be done.'

'He's...' She still can't get it through that thick skull of hers. 'Are you sure?'

I blink back at her. 'Yes, Sindy. He's dead.'

Her mouth moves but no sound comes out.

'C'mon. We have to move. Now.' I drag her outside by the elbow and manhandle her onto the bike. My backpack has to be strapped to my front and the guns are a fucking nuisance. I get on the saddle and put the pistol in my pocket, the shotgun under my thighs. If that thing goes off, God help any driver overtaking me.

The bike weighs a ton, but I manage to get it into gear without dropping it. Just as well Black taught me the basics or I'd have had no clue. We skid and slide across the dirt, almost overturning the fucking thing, until I finally find my balance.

'Ace of Spades' jabs at my brain as we zig-zag through the tree line. White trunks, hot dust, endless sky, 'Ace of Spades'.

Chapter 49

The next day, Sindy was already with the Canadians, having breakfast, when I joined them in the communal kitchen. She was busy showing off the photo in that passport of hers, passing it around to each of them in turn. The cover was starting to look battered already, I noticed: mainly because whenever Sindy wasn't flashing the thing around, she'd have it wedged in her back pocket like it was her personal lucky charm.

The fans were spinning, full tilt, but everyone looked flushed and sweaty. Sindy was right in amongst them: flanked by Stu, and Lexi and opposite Jules, looking like she was really part of their world.

'Hey, have you guys done the mine tour yet?' Stu asked, passing Sindy's passport back to her.

'What mine tour?' Sindy reached past him for the jam and spread it inch-thick onto her toast. She looked puzzled. 'We haven't done the mine tour, have we, Alec?'

I took the spot beside Jules and grabbed a piece of toast.

'I think you'd remember if you'd donned a hard hat and descended fifty-feet under the ground, Gina,' Jules said to her.

'Actually,' Sindy said. 'If I was going underground, I'd keep my eyes shut the whole time, so I probably wouldn't remember. Though I would remember a hard hat.' She took a bite of toast and added: 'Or even a soft, floppy one.'

That set Jules off again and she sat there leaning into me as Sindy crunched her toast.

It was still early but already hot. We'd got used to having a crap night's sleep because the miners at the hostel were all on different shifts, and there was a lot of toing and froing in the small hours.

Lexi picked Sindy's camera up from the table. 'These are cool, aren't they?' she said. 'Are the films expensive?'

'Not sure,' Sindy said. 'I haven't bought one yet. Alec said we should wait till we're in a city: they might be cheaper.'

Lexi passed the camera to Jules to look at. 'But that means you can only take a few photos while you're in the outback,' she said. 'We've taken loads. We've got pictures of kangaroos, lizards, snakes, a koala.'

'I don't wanna see snakes,' Sindy said. 'Alec promised we wouldn't.'

'Is that right?' Jules said, giving me a look.

Stu was laughing. 'That's a brave promise to make.'

He glanced at Sindy as he bent down under the table. Just as she was reaching for the jam, she let out a scream and fell backwards off her seat. She scrabbled to her feet and was still hyperventilating when she came and clung to my back.

Stu held up the rolled-up magazine he'd tickled her leg with. 'You *are* twitchy about snakes!' he said.

It took a few moments for Sindy to see the funny side, but eventually she sat back down and enjoyed the afterglow of being the Canadians' centre of attention.

'So, when do you head off?' I asked, once everyone had quietened down.

'Day or two,' Stu said. 'The place isn't opening till next month, but they have to get the rooms and the grounds ready. We'll be general labourers for a while.'

'What sort of work after that, d'you reckon?'

'Cleaning mainly,' he said. 'Maybe do some pickups from the station; pool maintenance, that sort of thing.'

'Cool.'

'Yah. We get free board and meals, so we'll have money left for the rest of our trip.'

'Lucky ducks!' Sindy said.

He smiled at her and shrugged, like it was no big deal. 'Why don't you come?' he said. 'They need all the help they can get.'

Sindy's eyes almost popped out of their sockets. 'Ooh, we could, couldn't we?' she said, looking at me. 'I could answer the phones.'

Stu laughed: 'This'll be more your hauling and lumbering. Not sure it'll be as glamorous as reception duties.'

'It'd be so cool if you came,' Jules said, looking between us. 'We've got room in the car if you wanted to.'

'Can we, Alec?' Sindy said. Her pink cheeks were even pinker now. 'I'd love that. And these guys are our friends now. It'd be fun!'

I slid my eyes to her. 'We can't, Gina. We're still trying to find...y'know...'

'Oh, we can do that any time.' She folded her arms and sat looking sulky. 'Maybe I'll go with them then. By myself.' She turned back to the others. 'When would we go?'

'Day after tomorrow,' Jules said. She shifted her gaze to me and looked me up and down. I had the feeling she was keen for us to come as a package. 'You can't abandon your kid sister!' she said. 'So, how about it, Alec? You up for a little fun?'

I'd grown to have serious doubts about the names Sindy had given me. The surnames were not ones I could find in the whole of the Queensland area. There was no Plan B, that was the problem: I couldn't believe Dad had sent me away without a long list of contingencies. The trip had been made in such a hurry that the focus had been on getting Sindy *away*. And now that had happened, I was left with the problematic fallout. What was I to do with Sindy if we couldn't find her family?

It was stifling in our room with only a ceiling fan to cool us. But, for once, it wasn't the heat that woke me: it was the jab between my ribs. And something which seemed to stick to my back as I breathed. I reached down to my stomach and found a hand.

Sindy stirred as soon as I touched her, and she drew her knees against the back of my legs but didn't wake. I blinked in the darkness as her arm tightened around me.

'Sindy! What are you doing?' I hissed.

Her voice was small, delicate. 'What?'

I threw back the covers and got out of bed.

'I'm sorry,' she whispered in the darkness. 'I was cold.'

'In this furnace? Put some fucking clothes on then.'

'I didn't mean anything.'

'You can't just clamber into bed with me. You're meant to be...my sister.'

A car's headlights lit the room briefly and I saw the silhouette of Sindy's head, barely visible above the sheets.

'Look,' I sighed, trying to gather my thoughts. 'I'm sorry but…jeez, maybe you've been around people like Minto for too long.'

I heard her swallow, and guessed she was in tears.

'You just need to learn to be friends with people instead of…anything more, okay?'

She didn't reply.

'Sind…Gina? The only way this trip can work is if you accept that we're friends,' I said. 'Nothing more. No hidden agendas. Just mates... brother and sister. D'you get it?'

She sounded sullen when she answered. 'Yes! Okay!'

'Good,' I said, 'because, if you can't accept that, well –'

She seemed suddenly interested. 'Well, what?'

I flailed for a suitable threat. 'Then, I might as well go home.'

She pulled the sheets and sat up against her pillows. 'All right then.' She sounded deadly serious.

'What?'

'I'll stay with the others. I said I would. You go home.'

I knew she was only saying it out of defiance, a bit of bravado. She'd think differently in the morning, when it really came to it.

'Yeah, right,' I said, climbing up to the top bunk. 'That's exactly what you wanna do. 'Night, Gina.'

"Night, Alec.'

As her breathing steadied, though, the strange notion began to roll around like a loose marble in my consciousness.

Perhaps she would be better off without me. I couldn't see any way we were going to find this elusive family of hers, and the longer it took, the more resentful I was likely to get. Maybe she'd be happier with a bunch of people who accepted her for who she was. People who didn't know where she'd come from; what she'd been through. People who had no concept of Minto's Sindy.

I tried to push the idea away. Of course I couldn't just leave her.

It wouldn't be right.

As my eyelids began to droop, though, I was already planning a route. I could hitch to Alice Springs, see Ayers Rock then get a flight to Sydney. A spot of Christmas shopping; a cuddly koala for Daniella. Then home.

The whirr of the fan was making it hard to keep my eyes open. I imagined myself writing Sindy a note; making an 'Alice Springs' sign to hold up. I wondered where the best place would be on the highway to stick out a thumb.

'Sindy? I whispered into the darkness. 'D'you really mean it?'

The rhythmic sound of her breathing told me nothing, but it didn't matter. I already knew the answer.

Chapter 50

I've had to ease off the throttle and pull over as we return to the outskirts of Mt Isa. We're back in civilisation; potentially as big a danger as I faced from Minto. Can I be sure Sindy hasn't lied about where the bikies have gone and led me, instead, to another ambush?

I get off the bike and Sindy remains where she is, deathly pale, clearly still in shock. Minto's blood has dried on her face. More of it has soaked into the knee of my jeans and it feels like the bastard has come along for the ride.

The relentless heat is weighing me down, smothering my thoughts but I know thinking is exactly what I need to do. Calm down, clean up.

'We need to get changed,' I say to Sindy. 'And washed. We can't go anywhere like this.'

She looks down at my bloodstained jeans, swallows and nods. Her hair is stiff and clumped and I realise there's blood in there too.

'I need to put the bike somewhere,' I say, thinking out loud. 'We can't leave it where it'll get noticed.'

'What will we do after that?' she says.

'Leave.'

'Alec? Will we go back to Swansea?' Her voice wobbles, and I sense she's having as much trouble keeping herself together as I am.

The question ricochets in my head. It sounds so ludicrous, I almost laugh. 'No, Sindy,' I tell her. 'Not Swansea. It'll never be Swansea.'

I leave the bike in one of the residential streets near the main town, parked between a van and late-model saloon. I hope it will sit there, unnoticed and unremarkable, for a few days at least.

Sindy and I have to eke out the dregs of that warm lemonade I've had in my bag: my survival rations have turned out to be just that and, even though it's sticky and disgusting, there's enough moisture for us to get the blood off our faces and hands.

Once I've rolled up my jeans, we look unbloodied enough to walk into a store and buy ourselves new clothes. We take our new T-shirts and shorts, along with our bottles of shampoo, to the nearest public toilet.

It's the shotgun that's, literally, the biggest nuisance. If I could snap it in two, confident it won't go off, that's exactly what I'd do. Instead, I'm stuck with it, like a tourist with a freaking didgeridoo, until I can work out where to lose it.

I look around in the toilets. There's a gap where the breezeblock wall ends, and the rafters of the roof begin. It's shadowed, hidden, for the time-being at least, so I stand on the toilet lid, reach up and place both guns up there, pushing them back as far as I can.

'Alec?' Sindy appears by the urinals, shampoo bottle in her hand, hair stuck to her scalp like she hasn't rinsed it for long enough.

'Where are your clothes? The...dirty ones?'

'In the bin.'

I dash past her, into the ladies. She's left them in the wire basket, a blood-stained sleeve sitting there, loud and proud, like a fucking confession. Is that deliberate too? I yank all her clothes out of there, stuff them into my bag and join Sindy outside.

I have no idea what time it is, where we are in our day. When did I even hitch a ride? Have I slept since then? Time has become meaningless.

There are cars on the street, people around, but it isn't busy. I have the feeling it's afternoon; teatime, maybe. Everyday life is being lived around us but isn't touching us.

I give Sindy the once-over, making certain she doesn't look like a girl who's just shot a bikie. Then I look down at my own clothes and check my hands and arms for splatters and stains. My hands are still shaking and there isn't a nerve in my body that feels still.

'We'll get a cab,' I tell Sindy. 'Make our way to the airport.'

'And then?'

I shrug, trying to dredge something from my brain. 'Then...I guess...a plane.'

By nightfall, we've made it to an airport motel in Sydney and it's left to Sindy to do the honours with checking in. I can't even speak.

'Could we have a twin room, please,' she says.

I grab her by the shoulder and shake my head – I have to be alone. It's as vital as the need for air. I'm almost frothing at the notion.

She seems to understand and does as she's told. She hands over my bank card and puts my hand in the place I need to sign.

I snatch the keys from Sindy the minute we leave the reception desk and I almost run down the corridor. Sindy's shouting after me to wait. I chuck her key to her as soon as I stop outside my room, then I ram the key in the lock, turn it and throw open the door.

I kick it shut the moment I'm through and my legs buckle as I reach the mattress. I land face-first in the sheets and pull a pillow tight across the back of my head, stretching the material across each ear until I've blocked out all sight and sound. Then I wait. Wait for the tears, the shaking, the retching. I know they're all in there. But the longer I wait, the further they slip from my grasp.

I want to reach down my throat and hook the poison out. But it stays inside, swelling, congealing like a hard, black cancer.

The let-down is unbearable. To have these intruders inside when I need to spew them out is agony.

I force myself to gather the images I've tried so hard to shut out. Those censored scenes; the ones I forced my eyes from. Now I have to evoke them; call them up like the spirits at one of Mum's seances. But there are no spirits, no auras here or if there are, I can't summon them. There's just me in a hotel room, a lamp, a desk and the real world outside. Suddenly, I'm as emotionally parched as the landscape we've left.

I sit up, rock back and forth, back and forth waiting to feel something, anything. I wait and keep waiting; close my eyes.

Lie down again; crush my face into the pillow.

'You can manage more than that, Alec m'lad,' Minto says.

'What are you doing here?'

'Now that's not very welcoming.' He stretches a huge hand towards me: it's full of jellybeans, so many they're spilling over the floor. His hand covers my face and he crushes those beans into my full mouth, pressing them against my teeth, my tongue. A few drop down my throat and some wedge at the very back of my gums, where the dentist likes to probe and make me gag. I feel liquid rise onto my tongue.

'Look out lads, it's a technicolour yawn,' Minto chuckles.

When I open my eyes, I'm already leaning over the side of the bed, my last supper soaking into the hotel carpet.

Perhaps it's the shock, the surprise of being transported back to the present, but I'm suddenly sobbing as all those images in the clubhouse bombard me – as brutal as if Minto's thumping them into me with his own fat fist.

I'm back there, standing in the doorway and I cast my eyes on the scene we've left behind. Zoom in on Minto's head, his skull split open above his eyebrow, glistening blood pooling beneath his ear. I imagine myself lifting that head and finding the perfect impression of his ear like the potato prints we used to make at school. But Minto's head is heavy: hard to lift without cradling it; touching the tough skin of his face. A puddle of nausea ripples inside me and I welcome it. I have to grab hold of the hideousness of that moment and keep going.

I'm clutching the sheets, foetus-curled and rocking. The memory has me by the throat now, and I suffer the scenes again and again; hear the gunshot; wait for the life to drop from me. Because it was me who'd been shot: I was certain of it. I'd seen the gun, noted the roundness if its tip like its own bullseye, watched the jerk as it fired, still pointing my way.

Yet I'm still here. I'm still here. And Minto's not.

Chapter 51

For the first day or two in the airport hotel, I was barely aware of anything. My body and my brain were stuck on a go-slow and it was Sindy who rallied. A push-button phone in her room meant she ordered meals for me; kept the cleaners away and most importantly, she called home; told them everything, so that I had to tell them nothing.

And now they're here; ordered, like room service, from Sindy's bed.

Mum and Dad look after me and Daniella stays in the background, waiting until I'm ready to be properly with her. They're all quiet around me like I've taken on a new fragility. Suddenly, I'm not knockabout Alec anymore. I'm breakable. Broken.

I've been stuck inside for days. The biggest event since the folks and Daniella arrived has been moving from the shabby airport hotel to this one near the harbour. Now the coffers have been unlocked, there's no stopping Mum and Dad.

The others must be working on some sort of roster system to make sure I'm never alone. Daniella takes the biggest chunk of shifts. She's sharing a room with Sindy, but she spends most of her time in here with me. There's nothing I can say to her, though – and nothing she can say to me – to make all this better. Everything else seems like fluff.

I can tell that, each morning when she comes in, she hopes she'll find the old Alec back in the room. She puts on her brightest voice and her widest smile to test me out but each time so far, she's been left disappointed. As she comes in again today, I sense I'm going to leave the same sour taste in her mouth.

'Wow! Look at that!' she says, pulling open the curtains. 'I still can't quite believe it: Sydney, Australia.' She comes over, smiling, and kneels on the end of my bed. 'You know, you really should take a look. Perhaps even…go outside.'

I rub my eyes, trying to shield them from the bright sun. 'Why don't you go with the folks?' I say. 'Sindy too. You should soak it all up. I'll be okay by myself. I don't need a babysitter.'

'No one's babysitting you. We're just...concerned.'

She moves to sit on the bed beside me – not sprawled like she used to be, with her thighs warming mine. Now her feet are placed firmly on the floor.

'Look, maybe in a day or two,' I say. 'I need to build myself up to it.'

'Okay.' She remains as determinedly bright and sunny as the view. 'Come and have some breakfast instead then.' She stands and holds out a hand to me. 'Have it downstairs with us instead of in your room.'

'No, you go.'

'Alec, everything's okay,' she says, gently, sitting back down again. 'All that...other stuff is over with. You're safe now.'

'Mm. I'll join you later, maybe.'

'Alec –'

'Just let me be, will you?'

A harsh tone's guaranteed to send her packing. Before all this, she'd have stood her ground, read me the riot act. Not now, though. It's kid gloves all the way.

I don't join them for breakfast, but they've obviously discussed me over their omelettes. By mid-morning each one of them has been in my room at carefully spaced intervals. Sindy's the latest – she comes bearing pastries and pamphlets.

'I saved you this,' she says, unwrapping a serviette. Inside is some sort of turnover. That's the effect it has on my stomach, anyway.

'You have it,' I say.

'You sure? I had a few downstairs.'

She's already got her teeth round it before I can insist.

'What are the leaflets about?' I say, more so I don't have to listen to her chewing than because I want to know.

She puts the crumb-laden serviette on my bed. 'They're just about trails and walks,' she says. 'We thought it might be good for you.'

'Did we?'

'They're all worried about you,' she says, licking her fingers. 'They think you're getting morbid. Whatever that means.'

'It means thinking about depressing things.'

She looks at me as if she's hoping for a full morbidity closeup. 'So, do you only think about bad things?'

'I try not to think at all.'

She nods, still watching me. 'Me too. It's better if you don't think.'

I find myself studying her; taking note of her expression. We were both there, in that clubroom. We both suffered the same shock. We were both at the same crisis point, trying to get away. How come I'm still falling apart, and she's already found her reset button? And what about everything she felt for Minto? I'm almost outraged on his behalf: where's her fucking loyalty?

'So, will you do this walk or not?' she says. 'Because if you do, your dad says he'll take me on the cable car. I think it's a good idea for you to go. It looks nice.'

'And that way you can go on the cable car.'

She gives me a wide grin: the sort no one's risked on me for a while. It makes me feel better; momentarily me.

'So, will you?'

'Maybe.'

'Yesssss!' she says with a celebratory fist pump. 'That always means you will.'

Chapter 52

The next day, Mum and Dad persuade me to venture as far as the hotel lobby. They seem determined for me to witness life going on around me, even if I refuse to take part in it myself.

The lobby's a cavernous space with lipstick-red couches and low, black lacquer tables. There's tinsel draped around the walls – silver and red – so as not to clash with the furniture. It looks understated compared to the whopping great Christmas tree in the corner, dripping with multi-coloured decorations. Thankfully the piped music is Culture Club rather than Christmas carols, but down here, there's no escaping what time of year it is.

Mum and Dad have ordered mulled wine and mince pies while we wait for Daniella and Sindy to get back from their shopping date. Strong coffee's all I can manage.

It wasn't until Mum and Dad cornered me into this little meeting that I realised how carefully I'd been avoiding conversation with them. Yes, we've talked about home, about food, about everything that's immediate – but serious discussions have been steered clear of, like cracks in the pavement.

Our old lives seem unreal when I think of them now. It makes me wonder what would have happened to us had Sindy not come along. Perhaps, in a strange way, she was exactly what each of us had needed at the time.

'You still look tired, love,' Mum says, sighing over her mulled wine. 'It would do you good to really open up to someone. I'm not saying it has to be us or even Daniella. But somebody.'

I keep my eye on the door, willing it to swing open and deliver Daniella. Instead, it brings in other guests, all flushed and hot from their shopping trips; rolls of shiny gift-wrap tucked under sunburnt arms.

'What d'you think?' Mum says, when I don't answer. 'Would you see someone?'

'Maybe.'

Dad puts down his glass and sits back in his seat, like he always does when he's building up to an announcement. 'Post-traumatic stress disorder,' he says.

The phrase hangs there, as odd and misplaced as the Christmas baubles above us.

'A psychologist perhaps,' Mum says.

I look back at her and nod, though actually, I'd take a security guard over a psychologist any day.

'Whatever you need,' she says. 'You've been through so much.'

Her comment makes me wonder what Sindy's told them. Did any details come directly from her – or was it all filtered through Daniella? Which bits were embellished? What was left out? After all, I'm the only one who saw the specific movie that still plays in my head.

'What you need to remember is it's in the past now,' Dad says. 'It's behind you. And things that are past need to stay in the past.'

He meets my eye and perhaps he's not talking solely about my situation.

'It'll be a relief to move on,' I say, stretching. 'Get away from…here.'

'That's what you want, is it?' Mum's hesitant and I notice her exchange a glance with Dad. They've probably debated when to risk the 'future plans' discussion.

'I don't want to be in Sydney anymore,' I tell them, looking outside at the crowds. 'Or even, Australia.'

'No,' says Mum and there's a sprinkling of relief in her voice.

I look at them, perched on the edge of their seats, treating me with such fragility. My emotions are so splintered: every time I open my mouth, I hardly know what's going to come out.

'Y'know, I wouldn't be able to contemplate the future if it wasn't for you two coming here,' I tell them. 'Reckon I'd've just curled up in that room and...gone slowly insane.'

It would be like peeling a nail from its bed, admitting this stuff normally. But these are not normal times.

'I wish we'd never sent you away,' Mum says.

They seem on the brink of collapse, the pair of them. I want to buoy them up, tell them, hey, it's okay: I'm still here. But everything's on such a precipice that I'm not even sure I am.

The big doors swing open again and our space becomes swamped by shopping bags and chatter. The moment's shifted along like tins on a conveyor belt.

'We had a great time,' Sindy says, dumping bags in nearby seats. She's got herself a new pink plastic watch. The big round face takes up most of her wrist.

'Ooh, that's pretty,' Mum says. 'Where did that come from?'

'Oh, this?' she says, like she's amazed anyone would have noticed. 'Daniella bought it for me at the market.' She pushes her arm in Mum's direction so she can appreciate the up-close bulk of it. 'Ace, isn't it? And you never have to wind it.'

It takes a lot more than a stray bullet to throw Sindy's world out of whack.

'Looks lovely on you,' Mum says.

Dad nods. 'And it'll save you ringing up the Speaking Clock every five minutes, won't it?'

'Anyway, why don't you two go up and have a rest?' Mum says to me and Daniella. 'Dad and I can stay down here and see what else Sindy's bought.'

Having been forced out in public for the past hour, I'm almost too exhausted to stand, but the prospect of a quiet room and a bed are enough to make me move. I sense I'm the baton that's being passed: now it's Daniella's turn for an audience with Alec. We go up to my room. I'm almost asleep before we get there.

It isn't until I emerge from the shower later that Daniella unpacks her bag of enquiries. As I gather my clothes from around the room, I feel her watching me. I sense her studying my face, working out the precise moment she can risk sliding a question my way.

'I've been thinking, it's kind of strange, isn't it?' she says. 'How Sindy's dad picked you up as soon as you decided to go it alone and hitch.'

I unfold a T-shirt and give the pits a sniff.

'And when I say strange, I mean it was a chance in a million. He had to know.'

I realise she's been building up to this since she got here: little hints here and there, the odd quizzical comment. She obviously feels I'm strong enough now to field questions, join in the debate, maybe even provide her with some answers.

'Well, obviously he knew,' I say. 'He was sent to pick me up, wasn't he?'

'But how could he have known?'

'I guess they must've been trailing us the whole way.'

'Seems an awful lot of trouble to be tracking you halfway across Australia. How could they have known your route? And how come Sindy was already at the clubhouse? She must have been picked up almost the same time as you.'

'Look, I don't know. I guess they were lying in wait for us both. But…what's the point of going over it all now? It's finished.'

Daniella looks like she's about to tell me what the point is, but she bites her lip. Momentarily, at least.

'What if it was all Sindy?' she says, following me as I go between the bathroom and the wardrobe.

'What if what was all Sindy?'

'What if this whole...' she searches for the right word. 'Situation was Sindy's doing?'

'You think she masterminded all this, do you? For what? So, she could get a free trip to Australia? C'mon Daniella.'

'Alec! You know that's not what I'm saying. I'm saying, what if this whole thing has been a setup? From the time your mum and dad had to...rescue her in Mumbles. Wasn't most of this stuff of Sindy's making? The mention of these Australian relatives; the running away from Minto. He had a base here; what if this was all about Minto getting you over here? Or getting Sindy to Australia?'

'He could have got her on a plane just as easily as I could. He wouldn't need all this.'

'Really?' she said. 'Really? With his record? And with Sindy's non-existent paperwork? You think it wouldn't have caused a few problems at immigration? Same goes for her dad.'

I have to mentally bat her questions away like ping-pong balls. The thoughts aren't new, of course. I've been dodging them ever since it happened, but I can ignore my own questions far easier than I can shut out Daniella's.

Those words that Sindy spoke just before the gun went off: 'it's you he's been using not me'. I haven't told anyone. I've wrapped those words in tissue, placed them in a locked trunk and thrown away the key.

'Sindy's dad and Minto don't have criminal records,' I remind Daniella. 'Not for offences that matter, otherwise they wouldn't have got into the country themselves.'

That shuts her up. She sits on my bed, watching me as I find a million different ways to avoid her.

'So maybe they used you to get Sindy out here,' she says.

I feel my eyelid twitch as she continues to watch me. It's a habit that plagues me when I'm dog-tired. My eye develops its own little pulse and I feel it beating away like there's a moth caught under the lid.

I pick up clothes and stuff them back into drawers just for something to do; something to help me get rid of this excess energy I can feel building up in my body.

I slam another drawer and manage to knock over my roll-on deodorant.

Daniella comes up to me and holds me gently by the arms, forcing me to be still.

'I'm just wary of Sindy,' she says, pulling me into a hug. 'I'm suspicious of her part in all this.'

I won't tell her what Sindy said to me before that shot was fired. It doesn't matter. It's done. She'll have said whatever Minto wanted to hear. It doesn't make it true.

After all, if there's one thing I've learnt about Sindy it's that you can't trust a thing she says: and that even extends to her lies.

Chapter 53

The others seem to be coaxing me out of my room little by little, as if they hope I won't notice. Yesterday it was the hotel lobby; today it's early evening at the rooftop bar.

'It would be a shame not to see this before we go,' Mum says, as we stand on the balcony, taking in the full Sydney panorama. 'Though maybe you and Daniella should go to Circular Quay: see the Opera House up close before we leave.'

There have been a lot of 'before we leave' comments since yesterday. It's as if they need to keep prodding me with it; reminding me that, yes, it's decided, we're moving on soon. What they don't realise is that, much as I don't want to be here, I don't want to be anywhere else either.

I turn away from the view and focus on the beers behind the bar. 'I'm not really up for the whole tourist thing, Mum,' I say.

'No, of course not.'

She glances at Dad, who in turn glances at Daniella. We're almost the full set but Sindy has chosen the ensuite spa bath over a cocktail with us.

'Why don't we go and sit down?' Dad says. 'There's a table over there.'

We squeeze past the after-work drinkers at the bar and sit at the black vinyl corner booth, nursing our drinks. I spot another look pass between them.

'Have you listened to the news today?' Mum says.

I shake my head. I can't even remember when I last heard what was happening in the rest of the world.

'They've found the motorbike,' Dad says quietly, leaning across the table.

I look between them all, trying to work out what they want from me. It's obvious it would be found, and I'm just grateful for the delay we've had.

Daniella also talks in whispers: 'And the guns. They've found those too.'

Dad centres his glass on his beermat. 'They've reported nothing about a shooting, though. We don't even know if the police have found the bo...'

'They won't have,' I say. 'Minto's lot will have cleaned up the clubhouse. The last thing they'd want is him baking in the sun and sending the law sniffing round. It's not like the gang's interested in justice, is it? Only revenge.'

These are the topics that form our family discussions now.

'Well, we think we should leave,' Mum says. 'If you're well enough to travel, that is. We should get a flight home. Go before there are any –'

'Home?' The word nearly strangles me, and the mad flickering starts in my eye again. 'I can't go home.'

'But...'

'None of us can go home.'

They swap looks, incredulous, yet I can't believe we're even having this debate.

'You think we can just go back to our old lives?' I say. 'The gang, the clubhouse: it's all still there, exactly where Minto left it. The only thing that's changed is he isn't coming back. And their drums are going to be beating loud and pretty furious about that.'

Mum and Dad are floored by the news. Daniella though, she's keeping her eyes from me, chewing that bottom lip of hers. Her cogs have been turning, I can tell. She knows.

Mum's voice is shaky. 'Where would we go, love? I don't understand. We can't just up and leave our home.'

She looks around at each of us in turn, trying to gauge something from our expressions. Dad looks at me, then at Daniella. He slides closer to Mum and puts an arm around her. 'We've already up and left,' he says. 'Alexander's right. They've been to the house before; they'd come again. How would we ever feel safe?'

The truth sits there, festering, between us all.

'But where would we stay?' Mum furrows her brow. 'Perhaps Sheila and Roy down the road would…'

'Mum!' I speak more sharply than I mean to, but the discussion is shredding my insides. 'We can't go back to Cardiff. Maybe not even to Wales. We need to go somewhere else altogether. Somewhere that... somewhere we don't even know yet.'

'And soon,' Dad says. 'Now they've found the bike, we can't risk staying here either.'

We pick up our drinks as we sit thinking about it; each of us, no doubt, trying to reimagine our lives.

'Perhaps Dad and I should go and see the travel agent first thing,' Mum says, 'book a departure for as soon as we can. Could you be ready straight away?'

On a practical level, I know I could be ready in ten minutes. On an emotional one, maybe never.

'Sure,' I say. 'Why not?'

I sense relief from Mum and Dad at a decision having been made but I can feel Daniella looking at me, like I've forgotten something. 'And Sindy?' she says, finally.

I know what she's asking, but I plead ignorance. 'What about her?'

'Do we include her or not?'

'What do you mean?' Mum says, staring at Daniella. 'Of course we include her. What, you think we should just leave her here?'

'It's just…if she stays here,' Daniella says, 'she could have a fresh start, find some work, be independent.'

'But she doesn't know anyone,' Dad says. 'She'd be on her own.'

Daniella keeps her tone casual. 'She could easily find work. That's what she'd decided to do in Queensland, wasn't it, Alec? She could start again. Whereas, if she stays with us...'she shrugs and looks away. 'Who knows how things would end up for her.'

They look at me and I know they're all waiting for me to make the decision, the final judgement. They've left it till now, though: now, when we're about to confirm flights. The very last minute.

I'm at a loss. I don't trust Sindy. But then, I trust my instincts less. It's a mental coin-toss. Eeny meeny miney mo. Mum watches me with hope; Daniella is shaking her head.

My brain says one thing, my mouth says another: 'She'll come with us.'

Chapter 54

On Daniella's insistence, we haven't told Sindy of our revised plans. As far as she's concerned, we're still headed for Cardiff; back in time for Christmas then 'Top of the Pops' on the telly after a turkey dinner. Mum feels bad about it, but I persuade her that Sindy'll be twice as excited when she finds out that we're going somewhere totally new.

We meet in the corridor just before two a.m. Dad and I lug cases to the lift while Mum, Sindy and Daniella follow behind. Sindy's quiet, unhappy and I wonder, yet again, if I've made the right decision about her coming with us. She keeps checking that stupid pink watch of hers, and I don't realise why until Mum notices too. 'You booked the taxi for the right time, I hope,' she says.

I slow down and stare at Mum. 'She booked the cab?'

Ever since we got here, Sindy's put herself in charge of all phone communications: room service, laundry requests, extra towel orders – but when so much rests on this particular call, surely someone else should've made it.

'I'm quite capable,' Sindy huffs, snatching her shiny new suitcase off me. 'I'm not an idiot, Alec.'

'No one thinks that, love.' Mum purses her lips at me but Sindy's already off down the corridor, trying to be first to the lift.

'Don't worry,' Daniella says into my ear. 'I heard Sindy make the call. She said all that she needed to. Even remembered to tell them there are five of us.'

And, sure enough, when we get outside, the white minicab van is there waiting; its doors open, ready for us and our luggage. The driver's behind the wheel, filling in a log sheet: he's smartly dressed in a suit and a chauffeur's hat. He says good morning and helps the others in, while I put the cases on the long seat at the back.

Sindy's bagged herself the comfiest spot at the front, while the rest of us are left to buckle into the seats behind.

'Sydney Airport, please, driver,' she says. 'International terminal.'

The chauffeur plays along: he touches his cap and puts on his indicator.

As we drive through the city, it occurs to me that, despite having been here for nearly two weeks, I never really got to see Sydney. Each glimpse I had was fleeting and from a distance. And I know I won't be coming back again.

I rest my head against the window and look out at the city streets. The shops are aglow with festive displays and Christmas countdown calendars. Ten days till Christmas, nine, eight. They drum home the fact that time has moved on in everyone's lives except mine.

I have to crouch to see past the driver and take in the view up ahead. A sign says we're about to enter the harbour tunnel. Seems I'm never going to get a close-up of the Opera House. I really have given Sydney the cold shoulder.

Daniella's on the double seat with me. She's dozing: her arms folded, eyes closed, her head lolling this way and that. On her lap is her black handbag; the long shoulder strap snaking down and beating a rhythm against her leg.

Mum and Dad are behind us on the other side of the van. I look around to see if they've nodded off too, but Dad's using a torch to study a printed sheet. He hands the page to Mum and when I see the pained look on her face, I guess it must be the hotel bill. No doubt Sindy's been calling that pricy weather line number again, and who knows what else. Mum gives the torch back to Dad then puts the bill with the Sydney map on her lap.

When we emerge from the tunnel, it seems even darker than before. It's hard to see where we are but I haven't spotted any airport signs. As my eyes adjust, I realise we're in a quieter area now, more residential. There's space and fancy gardens either side of us, trees and parklands.

I rest my eyes, but my jaw stays tense: that's its default setting these days. Makes me realise how desperate I am to leave Australia. Red dust, red blood; that's the only holiday snap that I'll be taking with me in my head. Home, away: there's nowhere I want to be, and I wonder if there's any corner of this whole fucking earth left for me to feel safe again.

I sit forward, rest my elbows on my knees. We stop at traffic lights and a car waits behind us. Its headlights illuminate the cab so I can see under the driver's seat in front of me. There's a crushed sugar packet sitting on an oil-stained blanket and, next to them, an ancient-looking canvas tool bag. The van could do with a decent clean; there are crumbs on the carpet and scuff marks on the vinyl seats.

When we turn onto a narrower road, it's not what I'm expecting. My neck stiffens and my gaze darts into the darkness. I want to see planes in the sky; a control tower, long-stay car parks, something to soothe my sparking nerves.

I hear Mum snore gently. As she shifts position, the papers slide from her lap and I reach under Daniella's leg to retrieve them.

'Have a look to see how much further it is,' Dad whispers, passing me his torch.

I unfold the map, but I can't ignore the hotel bill that's on top of it. It shows an eye-popping total. Phone calls from Sindy's room make up most of the 'extras' list. Those pre-recorded info lines feature strongly but when I look more closely, I see there's a single local number that appears again and again.

'How far d'you reckon?' Dad says to me, leaning over my shoulder. 'We need to be there at least three hours before take-off. Should be fine. We allowed plenty of time.'

I stare down as the digits blur and marble on the sheet. 'Not sure yet, Dad.'

It's the same phone number all the way through. Calls made to it once a day, at least. Sometimes twice, three times. And the last one was yesterday at seven –which was the time Sindy was meant to be calling City Airport Cabs for this taxi we're all sitting in.

A wave of nausea sloshes through my stomach.

I look up from the sheet to try and catch my breath.

'Let me have a look at that map,' Dad says, removing the torch and sheets from me.

There's a long pause and I feel my heartrate ramp up. When Dad speaks quietly into my ear, I can pretty well lip-synch his words: 'I think we might be going the wrong way.'

My breath comes out in shallow wisps. I hear Dad turn the map this way and that.

As I face forward, I sense a pair of eyes watching me in the rear-view mirror.

I choose not to see them.

Instead, I fix my eyes on the back of the driver's head. He's taken off his cap now, and I study the grey-brown strands of hair, the sprinkling of dandruff, the chafing behind the ears. But then, without meaning to, I let my eyes trail down. Down, down, to a thin gold chain around a scrawny sunburnt neck.

Chapter 55

There's no safe passage. He has us all in one convenient package; sourced, processed and ready-to-be-delivered. We couldn't have made it easier for him if we'd tried. He's the child-catcher with the lollipops and we've just climbed into his cage.

My breathing's out of whack; I feel sick. We turn corner after corner and the streets become narrower. I don't even care what happens to me, but this is my family. They don't deserve this.

Daniella's awake now, staring drowsily out of the window. I slide my hand over to hers. She'll feel its heat, its tremor, but I hope she says nothing.

In the mirror, our driver is keeping his beady eyes on me. On all of us. He'll be studying every blink, every gesture, waiting for that exquisite jolt of realisation.

I keep my gaze on the road while I trace a finger along the back of Daniella's hand. I spell out each letter slowly, deliberately: I L Y. I never tell her that; she knows I never tell her.

She watches the movement of my finger and becomes very still.

The minute she looks at me, he'll see it.

'Alec?' she whispers. Her eyes stay down, she barely moves her lips. 'What's wrong?'

I take her hand again and draw an arrow pointing forward.

Her eyes widen and she snaps up her head. In that same moment, I launch myself forward. With one arm around his neck, I grab the gold chain and wrench it around my fist, pulling it as hard as I can bear. It grinds and crunches into my flesh and I hope it's eating deep into his.

The van's swerving and squealing; we brake, accelerate as his feet stab wildly at the pedals.

There's screaming, shouting as we bump and jostle close to the trees. Daniella's doing her best to help me; she's grabbing fistfuls of hair, fighting to keep his head back. Sindy is trying to steady the wheel but she's battling with me too. 'We're gonna crash, Alec!' she shrieks. 'Get off him!' She's clawing at me with her free hand, at my eyes, my face, my mouth. Behind us, Dad's shielding Mum from the suitcases and bags slamming around in the back. There's a jolting thump as we leave the road and the van rocks and tilts. I see Sindy's dad stamp on the pedals and, as soon as he finds the brake, we're all thrown forward. He's wrenched from my grasp. The engine stalls and in that split second, he's shoved open his door. 'Under your seat!' he yells back at Sindy.

I throw my door open and already have a foot on the ground when his hand catches my hair. He yanks me backwards.

'Stay there, ya little fucker!' There's no avoiding those eyes now. The headlights pick them out; they're gun-metal grey, addled with rage. There's a trickle of blood on his neck and an angry wheal where the gold chain has torn into his skin.

He holds a knife to my face and I hear the others stumbling from the far side of the van. Mum's making a strange sobbing sound and that's when I spot Sindy bringing up the rear. She has a handgun and it's pressed to the back of Dad's head.

We're jabbed forward, so we're in amongst the trees; it feels like we're miles from anywhere.

Sindy's dad barks at us to turn towards him. It means we're facing the glare of the headlights. We're placed in a neat row, lined up for Sindy's firing squad of one. I stand squinting, blinking; desperate not to lose that final sliver of vision.

Suddenly, I'm pulled away from the others, just a foot or two, but enough to let me know I'm in for special treatment. Sindy doesn't move; she remains on guard, pointing her gun towards the harmless huddle of people who represent everything I have in the world. I can't bear for them to feel what I'm feeling right now.

My wrist is wrenched, hard, up to my shoulder blade and I let out a yell. Dad yells too; a raw, ugly sound that tells me my pain is his too.

A blade presses under my chin and Sindy's dad brings his lips close to my ear, just as Minto liked to do. 'You've been a thorn in my side for too fucking long.'

It's like he's flicked a switch in me: I start speaking quickly, spewing out words, offers, deals, anything to stop him doing what he wants to do. 'Take Sindy with you,' I tell him. 'I'm not a threat. None of us is a threat.'

'I never said you were.' He eases round to the front of me, the sharp point of his blade digging into the soft flesh beneath my chin. 'I said you were a fucking thorn in my side.'

I watch the words fall from his lips. His jaw's tight and he's speaking through gritted teeth. With Minto, violence was entertainment, sport. For Sindy's dad, though, it's all emotion: it's about revenge and hatred and white-hot fury.

Mum's crying, and Daniella is quaking beside her. Dad is standing tall though, focussed on me, like he's trying to send telepathic messages. But if he is, I can't hear them.

The headlights pick out escaped belongings from the van – they're scattered around us all, half-hidden: the hotel bill; barley sugars; a packet of tissues; Daniella's bag.

'Please. Just take Sindy back with you,' I say, breathless. 'This can all be finished.'

He chuckles to himself. 'I'll decide when it's finished, pretty boy. And as for Sindy, there's no taking her back: she's been with me all along.' He breathes out another laugh. 'Did you actually think you were running the show?'

I shake my head: it's true, I never did.

'You were this close,' he says, like he's crushing an ant between his fingers. 'You imported the goods, sorted out the paperwork – made a decent job of it too. Sindy got to the motherland: our angel, given wings. But then…'

I hold my breath as he pauses. I take in the greying stubble on his chin, the dried saliva at the corners of his mouth, those jabbing, sharp cheekbones, so much like Sindy's. He's small, weedy yet he's looming over me like he's a fucking giant.

'You had to take out one of our own, didn't you? Be a goddamn hero.'

'I didn't!'

He twists my arm further. 'Fuck off. You sayin' Minto died of natural causes?'

'I didn't pull the trigger.'

I can hear Mum sobbing and it makes me doubt my own sanity. She's terrified and I'm standing here, arguing the toss with a violent psycho.

'See? You just can't seem to tell the truth, can you, Alec? Even though your life depends on it. And theirs.' He sweeps a hand towards them. They're close enough for me to see their faces; watch their fingers clutch onto one another's.

'I didn't shoot Minto!' I'm almost crying the words into his face. 'It wasn't me.'

His eyes trace mine. 'We have surveillance up there at the clubhouse. Didn't know that, did ya?' He eases the sharp point of the blade upwards, so it just grazes my skin; enough for me to feel the sharp pain and the wetness as blood leaks out.

He stands on tiptoe so he can get even closer – it's like he wants to crawl inside my face and eat me alive. 'Didn't pull the trigger? Are you sure, sunshine?'

'I didn't!'

'Yes, you fucking did,' he whispers, 'I saw it with my own eyes.' He stands still, studying me long and hard. 'Bang! Bang!' he yells in my face.

I jump, just as I'm meant to, and a bead of his spit lands on my skin.

'There was no mercy on your part,' he says. 'You pulled the trigger, you wanted him dead. There were just no bullets.'

He takes a step back, easing the knife away from my chin; enough to allow me to swallow. He glances over to the others and raises his voice. 'And the rest of you. You got this boy's trigger-happy finger to thank for what's about to happen to you.'

'No,' I plead. 'No. This is just between you and me; they won't say anything, I promise.'

He looks at me and laughs. 'You just don't get it, do you, son? This, right here, is what loyalty means. Sticking together – through the good times and the bad.' He looks over to Dad. 'You appreciate it, don't ya, Jimmy-boy, you old seadog. All for one and one for all.'

Dad keeps his eyes away.

Sindy's dad leans into me: 'Loyalty forever; *what*ever. Get it? That's the truth we live by. That's the truth our Sindy lives by.'

We're moments away now, I can feel it. My legs can barely keep me up. He'll give the nod and Sindy will pop us all from where she's standing.

Bile rises in my throat. I hear Daniella make a weird, high-pitched sound and I'm afraid if she doesn't shut her mouth, she's going to be first to go. I slide my eyes to her but she's breathing hard and staring at something on the ground near Sindy's leg. Our scattered junk is there, but I see nothing else.

'Ready for your close-up, lad?' I hear his fingers squeak as he tightens his grip on the knife handle.

I twist and squirm as he grabs me and while he struggles to keep hold, I push and pull while he squeezes my body.

There's a strangled yelp from Daniella, and we freeze as she leaps back. I don't understand what's happening. There's terror on her face and she's still staring at the ground near Sindy. For a second, I actually believe her.

Sindy screeches the moment she spots it: a long, dark shape half-hidden in the leaves beside her. Her body contorts and she's wailing, crying, almost frothing at the mouth. We're mesmerised, all of us staring, horrified, until Daniella body-slams her.

Something seems to jolt inside me and before those two even hit the ground, I've twisted away from the knife and grabbed the skinny hand that's holding it.

I force my leg around his then scrape, jab and kick at his calf with the heel of my boot until I throw him off-balance. He's not giving an inch, though: as he goes over, he pulls me right down with him.

I hear Daniella scream my name as fingers grab at my face, pinch my skin. Sinewy arms squeeze me, and nails scrape, hard, down my cheek, slicing it open like a peach. I'm holding up my hands, trying to protect my face when I'm scooped up then slammed onto my back.

I gasp for breath but a hand lands on my throat. He could finish me now: he has the knife and I'm helpless. But this – this moment – is what he's been waiting for: bare hands, face to face combat. He's got no appetite for an easy kill. He wants to watch me suffer; eke out every sliver of pain. This is his white-hot hatred – the rage that keeps on raging. He pushes, pushes; every ounce of his weight bearing down on me, all his fury and focus directed at snuffing out this weakening pulse. I can't swallow, can't move. My windpipe is a hairbreadth from snapping. I'm gasping for air, desperate to breathe. It feels like my insides are imploding. I sense movement, hear voices; separate, together, and I wonder if it's all in my head because this is it; I'm done. It's over.

A single shot. The echoes of it seem to punch through my body and, for a second, I'm back in the outback, at that clubhouse. I'm looking down at Minto, at the blood pooling under his head. My insides have turned to mush, and I hear crying but don't realise it's me till I feel big fat tears running down my cheeks. I wipe them away and slide my eyes to the pair of feet standing right beside me. And that's when I know: I finally see who's holding the gun.

Chapter 56

Late January 1984 – Gosport, England

There's been a sprinkling of snow. Nothing to compare with the heavy falls we had in Wales last year, but it's started to settle and it gives this little place a kind of wintry appeal. A sharp wind follows us as we walk from the boat ramp and head towards the main town.

There's not much here, any guidebook will tell you that. We're only a four-minute ferry ride from Portsmouth, but it feels unmistakeably quieter this side; safer. There are no dockyard police and no landmarks; historic ships and hovercrafts are on the other side of the water. There's barely any reason for strangers to come here.

High Street snakes towards the harbour like a pointing finger and we're at the very tip. As we walk to the town, we're hunkered down in our coats, with scarves around our faces and hats pulled down. We must be barely visible in the late afternoon gloom. Or so we hope.

We haven't been brave enough to venture far yet, but we stayed out for hours today. It's a relief to return here, to 'our' side, though. There's a fish and chip restaurant over the road and without discussion, we head towards it.

It looks warm, inviting and, positioned where it is on a sharp curve in the road, it allows a full view of the surroundings, like our very own sweep of surveillance.

We're ruddy-cheeked as we peel off our coats in the lobby. We're shown to a table, bang-slap in the middle of a huge bay window. It's feels like a goldfish bowl but who's to say which side of it we're on.

This part of the world is Dad's old stomping ground. The dockyard is where he spent much of his time when he was on shore, and it's where he did his training, years ago. According to Mum, we almost came here to live. In an alternative reality, this is where I grew up: I'd have had a life where I never met Daniella, and where I was untouched by Minto and Sindy.

Daniella reaches across and touches my cheek, like she can read my mind. It's taken a while, but she and I are finding our even-keel again. I don't quietly shut her out these days, and she's learnt how to handle the more fragile version of me.

The waitress brings us menus and points out the specials board. She has a lilting voice and I'm sure I can pick out the subtle strains of a Welsh accent in the rhythm of her speech. It makes me wish we'd gone somewhere else.

'They do scampi here, love,' Mum says, leaning across to me.

'I need a drink first.'

Mum says nothing at first and concentrates on her food choices. 'It'd do you good to eat something before you start on the beer,' she says finally, unable to resist. And none of the others disagree with her. It's like a silent intervention.

Dad's next to me, facing the big window; his hands on the table, one on top of the other, like he's hiding an ace. Mum's opposite him, a thick cardigan around her shoulders.

I look outside and watch the squat green ferry by the pontoon across the road. Further round are the lights of the main harbour entrance with the open sea beyond. Gateway to Europe; another big tick for our temporary home.

It's starting to rain now; icy droplets blow into the faces of the late shoppers as they dash across the road. Inside, it gets busier as a few of them come in to escape the weather.

I'm more than ready with my drink order, but the waitress seems rushed, weaving between tables. Finally, she comes over to us, but my desperate thirst doesn't seem to bother her. 'Are either of you Mr Colbeck?' she says, looking between me and Dad. 'There's an urgent call.'

I stare back at her, my guts giving a squeeze at hearing that name again.

'No, sorry,' Mum says, brightly.

The waitress continues her search, but she's already ruined my appetite. Every time those memories start to lose their sharpness, something happens to bring them right back into focus again.

'You all right?' Daniella says to me.

'Just that name,' I mumble. 'It's...nothing.'

I twist in my seat, looking for a different server. I'm even more desperate for that drink now: I haven't heard the Colbeck name since Mt Isa.

I've seen the psychologist twice and he's confirmed that Dad's tinpot diagnosis of PTSD is probably correct. Having a label – understanding what it is – does nothing to help, though. I want there to be pills; something I can slip under my tongue to melt away the pain and the visions. But there's nothing, it seems, beyond talk and time.

A waiter arrives at last and we put in an order: tea for three, beer for one.

'Did anyone remember to check the timer on the central heating?' Mum says, looking outside. 'I don't want to go back to a freezing cold home.'

Home is exactly what it isn't, but it is our safe haven for now; our port in a storm. It's out of the main town, near some old abandoned fort. It's a bog-standard house on a bog-standard street – a turn of the century mid-terrace; tiny from the outside, big on the inside. It doesn't even have a front garden for us to tend and it's reassuringly unnoticeable. We blend into that place as seamlessly as the cladding on the walls.

Today's the first time we've been out together, the four of us. We all-but barricaded our front door when we first moved in, but necessities dictate – and now, Daniella and I have ventured out for appointments; and Mum and Dad have made it as far as the post restante in town.

I don't know how Daniella has coped with any of this. While I've had Mum and Dad to share the load, Daniella's had none of the same treatment from her folks. She's had to volley excuses; pretend all's well when nothing is; toss them lies about exiting her course. They don't understand why her life has veered so far off-piste, but what they do know is, it's down to me. If I was the antithesis of a decent boyfriend before, I must be the devil incarnate by now.

I find Daniella's hand beneath the table. It's smooth, warm, familiar and I stroke her soft skin with my thumb. I never stop being glad she's here and thankful I found her.

Had it not been for Daniella – for that pico-second of audacity; those moments of mettle and distraction – none of us would be sitting here like this, tossing up between scampi and saveloys. Without her, Dad couldn't have grabbed the gun and the four of us would be in shallow graves, rotting in bushland, somewhere north of Sydney.

December 1983 – Sydney, Australia

Something tugged, hard, on my arm and there was a slip and slither as a weight slid from my chest. There were voices around me, movement in the darkness. I blinked, turned my head and saw that rage-addled face again, but the eyes were shut now, the rage gone. My own eyelids felt heavy, as if they were being weighed down. I tried to keep them open, but they seemed to close of their own accord.

'Alexander?' Dad's voice came from just above me. 'Alexander? Come on. We have to hurry.' The words had barely registered before I felt his big hands slide under my shoulders, forcing me upright.

I put my fingers to my throat, certain I'd find a knife there.

'You're okay,' Dad said.

I sure as hell didn't feel it.

Mum and Daniella were crouched beside me. 'Alec? Are you awake?' Daniella said. 'You're drifting in and out.' I could barely see their faces as they stroked my hair, rubbed my arms, planted kisses.

Dad was in a different mental space. His eyes blinked into the blackness. 'We need to hurry. We can't risk anyone finding us.'

'Where's the van?' I whispered, looking around.

'Over there,' Daniella said. 'I turned off the lights so we wouldn't be spotted from the road.'

I had to push through the pain in my throat to get answers. 'And Sindy?'

'She's locked in the van,' Mum told me. There was a pause as she straightened up and craned her neck. I heard her suck in a panicked breath. 'Oh my God! No! The door's open.'

Daniella shot to her feet and raced over. 'She's gone!' she shouted back at us. 'And so's her purse!'

Mum clutched her throat. 'Oh, lord!'

Daniella ran back to us, resting her hands above her knees as she tried to catch her breath. 'That means she has money, passport. We'll have to go after her: she can't be f –.'

'No,' Dad said, quietly. 'Just leave her.'

'Leave her?'

'We have the gun and the knife. We have the van keys.' He gave a shrug. 'What harm can she do now?'

I winced as the words spilled from his mouth.

'But she's out there,' Daniella persisted. 'We might be close to where they were taking us.' She lowered her voice, as if she was afraid someone might already be listening. 'What if we were being driven to a meeting point? With others from the gang.' She looked around at us. 'Sindy could lead them back to us.'

I felt the ground tilt as she said it, and everything seemed to collapse inside me. Was I ever going to wake up from this nightmare?

'All the more reason to hurry,' Dad said, helping me to my feet.

'According to the map, there's a river close by. We can be quick. We'll dispose of the weapons and the body there. And any bloodied clothes. Agreed?'

I felt my eyes blink slowly back at him. Did he really just say that?

'And we need to get rid of Sindy's suitcase.'

He was thinking, thinking the whole time, always one step ahead, while my brain and my body had turned to jelly.

'Alexander, come on,' Dad said, giving me a shake. 'We have to keep moving. Take your T-shirt off. Get fresh clothes out of your case. Clean trousers; clean everything. You'll have to wash yourself in the river too. Come on.'

Direct orders were exactly what I needed. The rat-tat-tat of bullet points; the certainty of straplines.

He was right, too: the river was down a slope, just beyond the van. It was wide, dark, quiet but, in amongst the trees, I could pick out lights, hints at civilisation. I didn't know if they were a comfort or a menace.

The water felt icy as I scooped it over my head and body. I gave a quick rub of my face and hands but every noise, every tree rustle had my heart thumping and I just wanted to get out of there. I used the sleeve of my old shirt to dry myself then tugged on the new one.

I scrambled back up the slope and could pick out the silhouette of Dad with his torch. Looked like he'd put all the things for the river together, and now he was with Mum and Daniella, checking the ground for our lost belongings. He was fast, smooth, efficient, on a kind of autopilot setting. This was his forte, I realised; dealing with complex, dirty, messy life. Who would've ever guessed?

It was left to me and Dad to cover the body. We used the oil-stained blanket from the van, and, as we covered him, I was careful to avoid looking at that face. The blanket made it bearable: disposing of an anonymous package was one thing but seeing a face disappear beneath the water was another.

Mum and Daniella came over to us, dragging Sindy's suitcase along for its first and final outing.

'We need to get this done efficiently,' Dad announced, nodding down. 'When we get to the water, just do exactly what I tell you, all right? Let's make this as quick and painless as we can.'

Quick and painless.

A slurry of guilt shifted as he said it. I could barely remember the sound of the gunshot that had dispatched Sindy's dad but the gut-wrenching cry that accompanied it still echoed in my mind. Sindy's scream had seemed to come from another place; it was a banshee wail that had an eerie, unearthly quality about it. It was a noise that somehow captured the fierce, instinctive loyalty between them – that base, illogical, primal connection that could never be broken.

I could see Mum's shoulders heaving as we prepared ourselves for the final task.

'This isn't right!' she said, turning to us. 'Whatever he's done, this is a person, a human being.'

'We didn't choose this, Annie,' Dad said. 'He did.' He put a hand on her shoulder. 'You go and wait by the van, keep a lookout. Make sure the map's there.'

She nodded and turned away. That sight of her, hunched and alone, walking into the pitch black was all the hurry-up I needed.

I took the top of the body with Dad; Daniella had the feet. For a skinny guy, Sindy's old man was far heavier than I'd have expected, and it took us a few moments to secure our grip. Once we had, we followed the track down to the river. None of us spoke. We picked our way carefully to the water, struggling to keep our footing as we grappled with our load. We placed him beside the water's edge, gathering ourselves.

'I'll get Sindy's case,' Daniella said. 'We can use it to weigh him down. I hope it's heavy enough.'

I looked at her. 'Bodies sink, don't they?'

'Depends,' she said, turning to go back up the slope, 'on relative density.'

Even when it came to dead bodies, turned out Daniella was way smarter than me.

She reappeared a few moments later, heaving the case to the water's edge. 'I brought the tool bag from the van as well,' she said. 'It's got a tow strap we can use.'

She unzipped the suitcase and flung open the lid. Sindy's comics, her plastic hairbrush and that instant camera were on top. Apart from a few bits of clothing, there wasn't much else in it. The sight of her belongings gave me a jolt, and I saw Dad pause too as he looked down at what was left of her. I could sense something in his hesitation: the realisation that although it was Sindy's dad we were disposing of, it was Sindy herself who we'd lost.

Dad tossed the knife, the gun and the stained clothing inside. He added the bag of tools and slammed the lid. He zipped it most of the way, keeping just enough open to let the water in, then Daniella handed him the tow strap.

With Sindy's case tied to the body, it was a heavy, awkward operation, getting everything into the water. The final entry was a three-way hefty shove rather than a gentle placement. There was none of the clean efficiency that we'd aimed for – this was as makeshift, rough and dirty as it could get.

No sooner had we shunted him from the edge than his body tipped briefly – almost majestically – before sinking below the surface. He was swallowed in one greedy gulp, destined for a murky descent to his very own patch of underworld.

I'm still holding Daniella's fingers beneath the table as she sits opposite me, studying the menu. When she's finished, she takes over stroking duties and she traces the scar on top of my hand from that thin gold chain. The skin is still raw and painful – as is the gash on my cheek – but I won't have treatment: all wounds heal eventually, or so they tell me.

It isn't until the food is on the table, and I've had a couple of beers that I begin to unclench. Apparently, my body's hard wired to look for danger signs now; it's my own internal security system. I just need to learn how to switch it off – or at least put it on pause – because I'm overloaded with fear. I see a police uniform and I'm filled with as much panic as if it was an Apaches insignia. Enemies are everywhere.

At least being hidden away has given us breathing space; time to think. Our lives feel temporary, and they're probably always going to feel temporary because we'll have to keep moving. We can never get complacent. Apaches are spread around the world like a pandemic, and they'll bide their time for as long as they need to. Which means we have to keep one step ahead: our life-plan should be that we never plan. Our movements will have to be as surprising to us as they would be to them. Predictability would be our undoing.

For now, though, we sit with a view to the outside world and we discuss how Bill will be looking after the house. We talk about football, about food, about all the things that don't matter.

Then the phone rings, shrill, on the counter and, thanks to Minto, it sets my Pavlovian nerves a-jangle.

I unconsciously tune into the waiter's conversation. 'For nine o' clock, Mr Haiden? Four people? Certainly.'

The back of my neck begins to prickle; it's suddenly moist with sweat and the heat reaches around my throat.

'Did you hear that?' I say, halting the conversation between Daniella and Mum. They both look at me as I lean towards them. 'They booked a table for someone called Haiden!'

Mum and Daniella stare back blankly and it's all I can do not to grab one of them by the throat.

'Hai-den. That was the other name in Mt Isa,' I say, tripping over my words. I stab at the table as I speak, trying to drum into them the significance. 'The other one was Colbeck, right? And now this: the exact two names I was trying to find.'

There's still no eureka in their eyes and Dad joins them in their little trifecta of confusion.

I speak to them slowly. I'm blinking, shaking, almost in tears. 'Don't you get it? They know we're here!'

None of them replies, and I watch as they drop their gaze from me and exchange glances with each other instead.

'Alec, the name the waiter said was Clayton,' Daniella tells me. 'Not Haiden.'

Mum nods. 'It was Clayton I heard too.'

My heart is pounding and I'm breathing fast. My whole body is soaking. My legs feel as if they're about to uncoil and spring into action without my say-so.

The psychologist warned me this could happen too.

'Alec, are you okay?' Daniella says.

'You all heard the Colbeck name?' I snap. 'You heard that.'

'So? I've got a friend called Liz Colbeck.' Mum puts a hand on mine. 'It's a common enough name, love.'

'Liz Colbeck? Since when?' My mind is racing: did Sindy choose a name that was associated with us? Did she already know? Which came first?

It's all I can do to stay in my seat. My knees are jiggling, trembling, waiting to push against the starters' gates. I can't keep still; I'm sitting here but every part of me is moving.

'Alexander, calm down,' Mum whispers, looking at me.

'Did you tell Sindy about that friend? That...Liz?' I say. 'Is that why she chose the Colbeck name? Did she get it from us in the first place?'

I don't know who I'm accusing of what, but I'm certain there's a link in all this. Everything's connected but I don't know how. We think we're acting freely but who knows what's going on beneath the surface;

what Sindy's mob are finding out about us, what information they're skimming.

'Maybe we should go,' Daniella says, looking at me. She's about to get to her feet.

People are watching us from other tables, seeing what these oddballs are up to. Even the guy on the coffee machine is standing with his jug mid-air. I've been much louder than I'd realised.

I swallow. Take in a deep breath, just as I've been taught. Make my way down those imaginary steps, one by one. Breathe, step, pause; breathe, step, pause. I close my eyes. Breathe in, blow out. Nice and slow. My heart rate starts to calm. My neck tingles as the sweat cools.

'Sorry,' I say. I pick up my beer and roll the bottle against my forehead. 'It's just...'

'The demons,' Dad says, gently.

When I look back at him, I can see he has them too.

I ease down in my chair, eat my food, listen to the chatter around me. Outwardly, I'm calm. But inside, I'm still wired and every time that fucking phone rings, I expect to hear of a Mr Black or a Mr Stobes or some other Godforsaken name I never want to hear again.

I get through it, though. I keep my head down, I fork food into my mouth, smile in the right places.

Finally, it's almost over.

Beside me, Dad studies the bill, his finger tracing down each item. 'Your waitress today was Gina,' it says, and that invisible hand around my throat squeezes tighter.

Mum and Daniella pick up their bags from the floor and I can't wait to leave.

I'm about to stand when I hear music outside: the doof-doof-doof of a car stereo, its bass up too high. The sound is distorted, and I can't pick out the tune.

It's a slow, languorous process, my mind filtering that particular mix of sounds. I mentally turn down the bass so I can focus on the treble;

then I find the riff. And it's that crazy-maniacal riff, the melody, the angry beat, that snarling voice. It sounds so foreign here, so out of place and I try to grasp why.

And then the song emerges fully formed and it's like I've spotted the shape of the devil in the clouds. 'Ace of Spades' – it pumps out, thick, toxic, polluting the air.

My gaze pins itself to the window like it's been stuck there with chewing gum.

Right outside, the car is waiting at the lights, its passenger window down despite the cold.

A girl in the front seat is looking straight ahead; her hair tucked into a black bandana. She's young, pretty; could be anyone.

But that profile.

Daniella and Mum turn in their seats to see what I'm staring at. 'It's just a car, Alec. Just a random girl in a car.'

And, yes of course, it is. I need to accept it: it's just a random girl.

But then, as the car peels away, the girl swivels towards us and her lips ease into a smile. She lifts a hand to her bandana, a big-ass watch oversized on her tiny, twig-like wrist.

Acknowledgements

It's a pretty magical experience, having the stories and characters you've dreamt up in your head made 'real' in book form. In my case it's a magic created by MidnightSun Publishing, and I owe them an enormous debt of gratitude. To Director, Anna Solding, thank you for all your wise counsel, for your encouragement, your level-headedness and for your vision. I'm truly thankful and humbled that my manuscripts were plucked from the pile by you.

My thanks also go to the whole team at MidnightSun Publishing, especially to Kim Lock for the awesome cover which I never tire of seeing, and to Zena Shapter, layout designer extraordinaire who, I've happily discovered, loves to talk chocolate as much as I do. Thanks to all of you for turning my words into something real and beautiful.

South Australia is brimming with creative talent, and I have been blown away by the welcome and support I've received from the wonderful 'book people' I've met along the way. I want to give a special shout-out to my lovely debut author buddies, Poppy Nwosu and Kristy Fairlamb, for their friendship and support. I'm so glad we found each other to share this strange and wonderful journey.

I probably wouldn't be a writer if I hadn't been an avid reader first, and for that I have my parents to thank. Being read to as a child, being taken to libraries, having books as gifts, and being given 'incentives' for learning and reciting poetry – all these things gave me a love of the written word. I wish my dad was here to see where those poetry-bribes eventually led, but hopefully in some distant place, he'll have his feet up with his very own copies of *Heaven Sent* and *Hide* and feel proud. And to my Mum, thanks for encouraging me to always look up the words I didn't understand and for surrounding my childhood (and adulthood!) with all those dictionaries.

To all my family and friends, near and far, who continue to cheer me on and celebrate my successes, a heartfelt thank you: your words of encouragement and your enthusiasm honestly spur me on. A spccial shout-out to my friend and 'tour manager', Julie Astley-Jones who has kept a book-flag flying for me ever since I first put pen to paper.

Thanks also to Laurinda Luffman and to Julia Stiles who read very early drafts of *Hide* and gave me valuable feedback which helped to shape the story. A massive thank you, too, to my other-side-of-the-world writing buddy and wonderful friend, Claire Whatley, who has probably read as many versions of *Hide* as I have. Claire, I hope you'll love the finished version and that you can bear to have 'one more wafer-thin read'!

Finally, to my Wil-a-gang, my home-crew – some of whom aren't even at home now (that's right, I'm looking at you, Phoebe). Home or away, they continue to encourage, motivate and inspire me. They make me laugh, send me GIFs, keep me grounded and make sure I never take myself too seriously. They are my most fervent and loyal band of cheerleaders. Words would be gobbledy-gook without them. And to Robbi – thank you for all the football-not-soccer advice and for reminding me there are no sparkling waters in Cardiff. Robbi is my personal superhero and, while I get to live my dream every day, he quietly goes about making it all possible. And he does it with generosity, enthusiasm, care and love. He is, and always will be, my dear one.

About the Author

S.J. Morgan grew up in the UK and arrived in Australia many years ago, via a twelve-month round-the-world air ticket. In her former life she was an Occupational Therapist, but she now writes full-time. She writes across several genres and has won prizes for short fiction as well as an ASA mentorship for her children's writing.

In 2018, her debut YA novel, *Heaven Sent* was published by MidnightSun Publishing. *Hide* is her first adult novel. She lives in the Adelaide Hills with her family and two very slovenly greyhounds.

You can find more information at www.sjmorgan.com.au

Michael Pu[illegible]on

Silhouettes

Dear Patrick,

Thank you for all of your support and being such a good mate!

Michael Purton is the editor of three newspapers in Gloucestershire – the Stroud News & Journal, Wilts & Glos Standard and Gazette series. He began his journalism career in London before moving to Tokyo and then Gloucestershire, and now lives in Stroud. Silhouettes is his first novel.

4

For Him

No way of knowing

What any man will do.

An ocean of violence

Between me and you.

You've got your reasons

And me, I've got mine…

Arcade Fire

1

The boy watches the pub from an alleyway, the rain slanting into his face as he stands beyond the reach of the hazy streetlight. An engine rumbles closer and a taxi turns into the empty square. Its headlamps sweep across the wet tarmac and judder on the railings as the left wheel clanks through a pothole. The cab stops outside the pub and two middle-aged men appear from inside, one squat and bald and the other tall with swept back greying hair. They pull on their overcoats and shake hands, and then the short man climbs inside and the taxi disappears around the corner. The tall man is a silhouette against the pub's amber window as he slides his umbrella open.

"Councillor Jordan?" the boy calls out, crossing the road.

He holds the umbrella aloft and squints at the hooded figure.

"I'm one of Dan's mates. He told me to come get you."

"Why?"

"Some lads have beaten him up."

"What? Where?"

"In Liquid."

"But he's at home."

"We went out. We were in Liquid and these lads started on him and then the bouncers chucked him out. He's outside now. He's pretty bad."

The councillor stares at the boy's cat-like eyes and the faint scar above his lip, and then he starts striding towards the town centre, his brogues clapping the pavement and umbrella trailing at his side. “Is he alright?”

“I think his nose is broken.”

“But he’s conscious? Able to stand?”

The boy nods, keeping pace as they head towards the end of the street.

“His mother will kill him.”

“It wasn’t his fault – they started on him for no reason.”

“How did you even get into the club?”

The boy shrugs.

“What did you say your name was?”

“Jon. No H.”

“Was it just the two of you?”

He nods.

“And the lads have gone?”

He shrugs. “The bouncers only chucked Dan out.”

His hand tightens around the umbrella and he breaks into a run. The boy keeps up, their shadows one single black shape beneath each lamppost. The road comes out on a narrow street lined with parked cars, the doors gleaming in the light of a bus approaching from the right. They stop between a Mini and a white van. The councillor’s hair and forehead are damp with sweat and rain. The boy’s hands are shaking inside his pockets. As the double-decker draws near the boy sidesteps behind the councillor and shoves him into the road, his body and the umbrella silhouetted and then swallowed as he bounces off the headlight and disappears. The tyres shriek as the bus skids to a halt and a rear wheel thuds over him, jerking the vehicle to the left and grinding into the parked cars.

Lights spring on in the houses. The boy sprints back the way they came, the 9mm swaying in his pocket and his whole body trembling as he runs through side streets and alleyways, away from CCTV cameras. As he passes below a flickering lamppost he doubles over and vomits in the gutter, the image of the councillor’s mangled body by the crushed umbrella flashing before him with each spurt of light, and he feels his mother’s presence in the black edges of his vision and pictures her watching and rejecting him, her expression part recalled and part imagined, her eyes hollow and haunted.

*

Outside in the darkness, Alex stares up at the bedroom where his parents used to sleep, picturing the green curtains that blocked out the moonlight 20 years ago, when he was a child and would feel his way along the edge of the bed until his fingers found the bottom of the covers and then crawl in between their sleeping bodies, their warmth enveloping him. They would always awake briefly, his father reaching out a palm to his back and his mother sighing “Oh Alex”. “I had a bad dream,” he'd whisper, and then he'd wriggle his hips and settle into a deep, dreamless sleep.

The TV is on in the lounge, glowing in the corner. He can see in between the half-closed curtains: a pale face on the screen and then a silhouette holding a gun. The light snaps on in his parents' old bedroom and a figure appears in the window, a teenage girl looking out at the street. She spots him at the end of the driveway and flinches back into the room, out of view. Alex paces away towards his car, his head bowed against the rain as he pictures his bare room in a shared house where nobody knows him.

In bed he studies Emma's Facebook page, his face half-lit by the phone screen. Her profile picture shows her with her new friends in her new city, her hair and lips glistening in the flash of the camera, her eyes dull and hollow like a dry well in torchlight. Her page is locked to him now. She deleted the album titled 'With Alex' months ago. He stares at the damp-stained ceiling, listening to the voices in the takeaway across the road as the light from its neon sign seeps in between the curtain, bathing the tiny room in a pink hue.

When he falls asleep he sees her. They are showering together. She grins as he soaps her and slides his hands down over her ribs. It is night outside – he can see the black sky through the frosted glass. They get dressed and climb into his Focus and drive out to a multi-storey car park, following the spiral up to the deserted rooftop. She jumps out of the car and paces to the edge, staring out at the yellow lights of the city, and then she looks back at him over her shoulder and says something he can't hear. He moves closer to listen and watches her lips as she forms the words but only silence comes out. When he tries to speak he can't move his own lips. His mouth hangs open, slack-jawed. She stares at him, her eyes tightening with disappointment and contempt, and then she turns her back and moves closer to the edge. He tries to lift his arms but they are limp, his hands dangling by his side. She keeps walking slowly to the verge of the roof and, without breaking stride, steps over the edge. As she falls her body blocks out the lit windows in the skyscraper opposite like a power cut shooting down through the building.

Halfway between sleep and consciousness, the sound of muffled sobbing slithers inside his head, dragging him awake. Parting the curtains, he looks down at the takeaway; the manager washes his hands behind the counter, his gut spilling over the sink. As he grabs a towel he pauses, head cocked, and then hurries off into the back of the shop. Alex opens the window and the crying sweeps in on the wind and spreads through the room, the sound of a woman, her sobs pouring out of an open window on the floor above the takeaway. The blinds are almost closed with nothing but a weak light between the slats. He angles his head to try to see through the gaps but the slits are too tight. Something blocks the light inside, blackening the window, and then a thick hand jabs through the blinds and yanks the window shut.

Two minutes later the manager reappears downstairs, his head bowed and jowl creased as he reads the newspaper. Alex stares at the window above until eventually a thin hairless arm slips through the blinds, turns the handle and pushes the frame open, before retracting inside. Holding his breath, he waits for voices or crying, but there is nothing more.

Lights on, he inspects himself in the wardrobe mirror as he dresses in a blue denim shirt and black jeans. There are three expensive colognes on the shelf in the wardrobe, each one half empty; he sniffs the caps before choosing Valentino Uomo and spraying his neck and shirt, and then he looks at his reflection with contempt, seeing himself as another desperate lad wearing too much aftershave, but the sensation doesn't last, the feeling evaporating into his lust.

The streets of Gloucester are deserted as his battered silver Focus rolls through the wet night, the hip hop on the stereo drowning out the noise in his head. In Cheltenham the illuminated bars streak past the window, the colours flowing together in the rain. Couples huddle in doorways and beneath umbrellas, their bodies locked together. He can hear the throbbing bass from the club as he draws near. A wave of body heat washes over the queue every time the bouncers open the door. A blonde girl turns around to say something to a friend. He meets her eye, a close-lipped smile forming on his lips, but she looks away.

Standing on the edge of the dance floor, his gaze lingers and leaps from face to flesh. A brunette nudges past and Emma's apple-tinged perfume envelops him like a hovering spirit of the past. He watches her push her way through the tangle of bodies to a circle of girls, her thick figure held in by a red dress. Her eyes are glassy as she glances over her shoulder and takes his hand, pushing his palm down to her hip and moving his fingers onto her exposed thigh as she grinds herself into him. She spins around and thrusts her lips against his, stabbing her tongue inside his mouth, the twisting bodies and punching synth closing in around him as he tastes the sweat and alcohol.

As she presses her palms against the alleyway wall a false nail falls off, revealing the bitten finger beneath. His adrenaline evaporates with the scent of her perfume in the stench of the rubbish as he watches her flesh ripple, summoning images of Emma, visions both beautiful and painful. Panting, they pull apart and lean on the damp bricks, throwing sideways glances, waiting for the other to smile or speak first. She straightens her skirt and runs her fingers through her hair, the cloud of alcohol gone from her eyes; he stares back, no words on his tongue. "Bye, then," she mutters, rolling her eyes. Her heels click against the concrete as she walks away. He looks down at the crimson nail on the wet tarmac.

"You can do better than this," he calls out.

She stops and peers back, waiting for him to say more.

The taste of sweat and alcohol is still on his tongue as he listens to music in bed, his iPhone set to shuffle, impatiently skipping from track to track. When he hears the opening chords of a playlist Emma made for him, he presses stop.

2

The boy taps on the door and waits with his hands balled inside his pockets. The distant sound of a siren echoes through the pitch black alleyway as the stench from the bin bags clings to him like a mask. After a few seconds he hears shuffling on the other side and he pulls his hood down and looks at the spyhole. Steel scrapes against steel as the locks are undone and then the heavy door opens a fraction and he slips inside.

"Alright?" Jo asks, studying his face, her wrinkles like valleys in the light from the bare bulb above. He nods. "You sure, love?" He nods again. "He's upstairs." As he climbs the creaking steps she hobbles back to the tiny taxi office, the dusty light falling on the broken hand radio and years-old ledgers and then her pink dressing gown as she eases herself down behind the desk.

Derek is sitting at the kitchen table, smoke rising from his ashtray and spreading to every corner of the cramped flat. The curtain between the kitchen and living room is pulled back and he's watching a black and white film, the flatscreen TV the only light. "Alright?"

The boy nods, standing at the top of the stairs.

"You sure?"

"Yeah."

"Jo," he yells, his voice cracking.

"I'm calling him now," she shouts from below.

Derek grips the edge of the table and pushes himself to his feet with a sigh, his elbows like knots in a piece of string. “He left something for you.” His beige trousers flap around his ankles as he slowly makes his way into the bedroom and comes back with an envelope.

The boy parts the flaps; there’s a wad of twenty pound notes inside. “Why?”

“Dunno. I don’t ask questions.” He groans as he lowers himself into his seat. “He wants to talk to you, in person.”

“Now?”

“Tomorrow. Here. One.”

The boy nods.

“You sure it’s done?” He glances sideways at him, his face ghostlike in the smoke and grey light from the TV.

“They put the blanket over his head.”

“You went back?”

“To check.”

He sighs and shakes his head, his white hair brushing against his ears. “What did you do with the gun?”

“Didn’t need it. Pushed him in front of a bus.”

“A bus?”

“No-one saw. We were behind a van and he’d been drinking. It’ll look like he stepped out without looking.”

“A bus.” He puffs out smoke, scratching his temple. “Give me the gun anyway – you don’t wanna be walking around with that on you.”

“It’s in the car,” he says, feeling the weight of the 9mm in his pocket.

Derek studies his face, his eyes narrowed, and then waves to the bathroom. “Your disguise is in there.”

Electric clippers and a packet of blond hair dye lie on the sink. He closes the door and strips off his jacket and jeans, careful not to let the gun smack on the lino floor. The sweat-soaked cotton of his T-shirt and boxers clings to his skin. He sits on the toilet lid and holds his right hand in front of his eyes, breathing slowly until his fingers stop trembling.

When he comes out of the bathroom there’s a sandwich and a can of coke on the kitchen table and a lamp is on in the corner, a column of dust rising from the bulb. The bedroom door is closed and he can hear Derek on the phone on the other side, his voice barely above a whisper, the words indistinct.

“That’s for you,” Jo says, poking her head around the side of the battered armchair and jutting her chin at the sandwich. The tortoise-shell cat is pressed to her shoulder, nuzzling the hair around her ear. “You look like Eminem.” She turns back to the TV; the black and white film – some kind of detective story – is still going; two men sip whisky in a dingy bar as they eye a curvy waitress. “Feel different?”

One of the men follows the waitress into the bathroom. "I don't know."

"You just remember that he deserved it." She waits for him to reply. The cat starts to suck her earlobe. "You did it for Tom. You've nothing to feel bad about."

"I know."

She leans on the armrest and looks back at him, her skeletal face backlit by the TV. "Are you gonna tell us where you've been, then? We tried calling, we went to the flat. We wanted to tell you properly."

"I saw it on the news."

"You weren't at the funeral. We don't hear from you for days and then you turn up without a word and go straight to Peter, outside court of all places..." She lights a cigarette and takes a long drag, all the while watching him as he stares down at the sandwich with his palms on the table. "I don't blame you. You must have been broken up." She taps the ash into a saucer, the cat still clinging to her. "What I'm trying to say, love, is you can always talk to me. I always thought of Tom as a son, you a grandson. I've watched you grow up."

He nods, eyes down.

"You shouldn't feel bad, love. He deserved worse than a quick death." She shifts in the chair, her collarbone catching the light. "I cried when I heard about Tom. You're just like him – the way you never say nothing."

He pushes the plate aside and stands up. "I'm not hungry, sorry."

"Hold on, love." She puts the cat down and struggles to her feet and hobbles towards him, dragging her bad leg. "Hold on. What's your hurry?" He flinches as she reaches out to take his face in her hands. "Honestly, it's like breaking in a horse," she sighs, and he lets her put her palms on his cheeks and tilt his head as she inspects his hair. "Not bad for a DIY job. What grade did you use?"

He shrugs and steps back to free himself.

"You've missed a few bits at the back, though."

"It's fine."

He can hear Derek saying "what's happened's happened," into the phone.

"Don't be daft," she chuckles, "it'll take two minutes."

She shuffles towards the bathroom. Derek says "he'll be fine," on the other side of the door.

"Ezra," she calls from the doorway. "Do you want people to laugh at you?"

He follows her in and lets her wrap a towel around his shoulders, her antiseptic smell closing around him. She points at the bathtub and he sits on the rim facing in as she plugs in the clipper and runs her finger over the blade. "I thought it was a number three. I used to do the boys' hair before they..." She trails off as she steps behind him. "I'm gonna do a two on the back and sides, make it even." He feels the razor vibrating on the back of his head. "You know you're always welcome here with me and Derek, don't you, love?" She pulls the clipper away, waiting for him to nod. "You were always welcome with Tom and you're still welcome now. Nothing's changed there. Has it?" She holds the clipper back again and, after a pause, he nods, barely moving his head. "What happened was… well, no-one could've known..." She rests the clipper on the sink and tips his head forward with her finger, her stale breath warm on his cheeks as she inspects the sides. "Perfect." She carefully removes the towel and as she shakes the dead hair into the bathtub he catches sight of himself in the mirror; he's washed out, his skin almost as pale as his eyes.

"Thanks," he says, pacing into the kitchen.

"You can stay here if you like, love."

"I'm ok."

"We can't have you out there on your own, love. Stay here. I'll make up the sofa."

"I'm ok," he says, moving towards the stairs.

"Are you still in the flat?"

He ignores the question as he jogs down the steps.

"Ezra, love," she calls.

He can hear her lopsided footsteps on the wooden floor as he quickly turns the locks and slips out into the alleyway. *I don't trust anyone,* Tom had said.

*

The moonlight bathes Alex in a ghostly pallor as he hunches over his laptop wearing his duvet like a shawl and types 'black hair +

pale skin' into the search bar. Dozens of results appear, each image a doorway to the video beyond. He scrolls down the list until he finds a girl who looks like Emma, clicks play and minimises the browser so the screen is split between the video and a photograph of her standing naked next to his bed, the smile on her face half confident and half self-conscious as she jokingly posed with her hands on her hips, her body – slight and pale with narrow hips and heavy breasts – outlined by the midday sun sweeping in through the window. He picks up his phone and scrolls to her name and presses call, half-listening to the familiar sound of the recorded voice saying the number has been disconnected.

The light comes on in the window above the takeaway. He can see in through the parted blinds: white walls and a black duvet with a silver floral pattern. The window frames the bottom-half of the double bed, a dressing table against the far wall and the doorway by its side. The fifty-something manager waddles into the room followed by a slim woman in her mid-thirties, her hair tied back in a ponytail. She is wearing light jeans and a fitted white blouse; he's in a navy button-down shirt and baggy black trousers. They are arguing. She shakes her head as she stands by the edge of the bed with her palms out. The man moves closer, towering over her. He takes her hands in his and steps forward, sitting her down on the bed, and kneels between her legs, one hand on her thigh and the other stroking the side of her face as he speaks, and eventually she nods her head and allows him to lean in and kiss her on the lips.

The manager slowly rises to his feet, pecks her on the forehead and leaves the room. She begins to unbutton her blouse, her wedding ring catching the light. He comes back with a portable stereo which he places on the edge of the dressing table before going out again. She peels off her blouse and jeans, her skin the ruddy colour of a sunbed user, the tone all the darker against her white underwear. She steps out of Alex's view, towards the top end of the bed. The manager emerges downstairs in the takeaway, standing by the door as the steel shutters lower over the window and the neon sign clicks off. The woman moves around the edge of the bed to the dressing table. She's wearing a red negligee, the skirt falling short of the crease where her thighs meet her buttocks as she walks towards the mirror and sits down in the chair with her back to Alex and begins dusting her cheeks with a brush. The manager appears in the doorway and watches her before reaching forward and clasping his hand around her breast. Alex can see his stubby fingers in the mirror, slipping under the silk.

Movement in the street below catches his eye. A bald man in a brown leather jacket stands before the shutters. He walks in front of a phone booth, his outline blurred by the glass box, and when he comes into view again he has a mobile to his ear as he looks up at the window. The manager lets go of the woman and takes his phone out of his pocket to answer the call. Alex strains to hear what the bald man is saying, catching only 'outside'. They push their phones inside their pockets at the same time and the bald man paces towards an alleyway ten metres down from the takeaway, his head reflecting the flickering light from a streetlamp as he passes below and disappears into the darkness. When he looks back to the bedroom the manager has gone. The woman stands up and inspects herself in the mirror. She removes a clip and her hair falls onto her shoulders, the chestnut curls bouncing on the red straps. She turns around and stares straight out of the window, right into his face as he peers out from between the curtains. For a moment he thinks she's seen him, but her expression is blank and unseeing.

She disappears behind the wall and re-emerges holding a pair of black stilettos. She perches on the edge of the bed as she slips her feet inside, before moving towards the door and switching off the ceiling light, leaving the room in the amber glow from a lamp somewhere in the corner. She steps over to the window and grabs the drawstring for the blinds and closes the slats as the manager appears in the doorway, the bald man standing behind him, both of them watching her as they all disappear between the shrinking rows of light.

Alex's heart is throbbing as he stares at the darkened window, the computer screen sleeping at his side. After a few minutes he sits down at the desk, opens a new webpage and types Barton Street plus brothel into Google, but the results are no use. He searches again with different variations – massage parlour, escort – but again they reveal nothing. Back behind the curtains, he watches the window. The street below is deserted, just parked cars and shuttered shops. The alleyway is between a laundrette and a newsagent – a black hole in the parade of shops. He needs to piss but he keeps watching, eyes fixed on the plastic blinds, minutes ticking away as he stands there transfixed. Eventually the pressure on his bladder is too great and he pulls on a T-shirt and shorts before quietly opening his bedroom door and tiptoeing out into the hallway, creeping silently past his housemates' rooms and into the bathroom. When he comes back the blinds are still closed and the street below still lifeless. Aware of the cold again, he picks up the duvet and pulls it around his shoulders.

After half an hour the bald man emerges from the passageway. He zips up his jacket and turns right, his outline merging into the darkness as he hurries away. The blinds are still closed, the same bleed of light at the fringes. Two minutes pass. The duvet slips down from his shoulders. The light behind the blinds vanishes. They slowly rise. She's there, her silhouette a darker shade of black than the unlit bedroom. A bulb springs on beyond the doorway, casting a dim glow behind her as she pulls the drawstring until the blinds are gathered at the top of the window. She is naked, the edge of her teardrop breast outlined by the amber light. She stares out, her face veiled by the darkness, and then opens the window before disappearing behind the wall. After a few seconds her bare feet slide into view as she shuffles down the bed, a pink dressing gown covering her thighs. She rolls onto her side, facing Alex as he stands behind the curtains, leaning towards her. She pulls her knees up to her chin and hugs her shins. He listens, trying to hear if she is crying, only catching the distant murmur of cars on the main road.

The light beyond the doorway goes out. The manager appears, his vast body filling the window as he pulls the handle shut and drops the blinds.

3

Shards of sunlight slashed across Alex's face as he walked alone beneath the trees on the promenade. Montpellier Gardens was crowded, the grass strewn with clusters of colour where groups and couples gathered, their laughter drowned out by the mournful song on his headphones. As he spread out his towel he noticed four girls sitting in a circle a few metres away. He watched them from behind his sunglasses: students, home for the summer or arrived early for the new term, a couple of years younger than him, their smooth legs and shoulders glowing in the sun. He took out his book and tried to focus on the page but his eyes kept rising to them, unable to resist, and eventually he turned away to lie on his other side and reached into his bag for a can of Dr Pepper.

After a few chapters he went over to the park shop, passing four lads with a football who were edging closer to the group of girls with every kick. As he walked back carrying an ice cream he noticed that a girl had appeared around five metres from his spot. She'd laid her purple blanket in the shade of a cedar and sat with her knees tucked beneath her chin as she read. He felt her glance up at him as he sat down. As he picked up his novel he stole a look: her jet-black hair was like a waterfall of oil on her pale shoulders and she leaned into her book as though the page was pulling her in. Half concentrating, he read a few pages as the afternoon sun dragged beads of sweat down his spine. A shriek from the playground pierced the murmur of voices.

A woman ran to a boy who had fallen off the climbing frame, his face frozen in shock and then melting into tears as she embraced him. As he turned back to the book he caught the girl looking at him. She held eye contact and, just as he was wondering whether she was unaware that he was watching her from behind his sunglasses, she smiled at him, a shy close-lipped smile, and said something which was lost in the air between them. He cupped his ear and said, 'Sorry?' and she rose to her feet, her black jeans tight, and walked towards him.

"I was just saying that I love that book," she said, pointing to his novel.

Flustered, he looked at the cover and read the title aloud as though the book belonged to someone else. "*The Girl at the Lion D'or.* Yeah. It's good. I'm almost finished."

"It's such a sad ending." She was standing a metre from his towel, gripping her own book. In the sharp sun her skin was luminous like a swan's feathers in winter. She wore a black vest with a grainy print of a police mugshot.

"Yeah, you can feel it coming all the way through. What are you reading?"

She showed him the cover. *A Sport and a Pastime.* "It's set in France too. Kind of a similar mood to yours."

"Cool, I'll have to read it."

"You like Dr Pepper."

He looked down at the empty can. "I do."

"I have a bottle in my bag. Want some?"

"Really? Er, yeah, ok, cool."

The sunlight outlined her narrow shoulders as she walked away. She scooped up her handbag and blanket, trailing the frayed edge on the grass as she made her way towards him with the four girls watching and exchanging knowing grins.

"So what's it about?" he asked, nodding to her book as she arranged the thick woollen blanket next to his towel so the edges overlapped.

"An American guy and a French girl that fall in love… kind of. He ends up feeling trapped."

"Do you know what happens in the end?"

She shook her head. "I can't see it being a happy ending, though."

"The best ones always end badly."

She unscrewed the Dr Pepper and held it out to him. Her heart-shaped face was dusted with freckles.

He nodded at her vest. "Who's that?"

"Steven Avery. He was wrongly jailed for murder in America."

"Oh."

"There's a documentary about it on Netflix, *Making a Murderer*."

"Oh, the one where the police set him up?"

"Yeah, it's awesome."

"I'll have to watch it."

She was sitting cross-legged, facing him as he leaned on his forearms. She looked down at her Converse and fiddled with the laces. “You really look like someone, by the way.”

“Yeah? Who?”

“You’re either going to take this as a compliment or an insult, or you won’t have heard of him.”

“I’ll brace myself.”

“The lead singer of A-ha, Morten Harket.”

“You were right, I have no idea who that is.”

“He sang *Take On Me?*”

He shook his head.

“It’s one of those really cheesy 80s pop songs.”

“Sing it for me?”

She smiled, shaking her head. “I’ll play it for you instead.” She reached into her bag for her phone; blue headphones were wrapped around the screen, the wires symmetrical on either side of the port. “Ok, you’re probably going to hate it.” She shuffled alongside him, their shoulders almost touching and her apple perfume enveloping him, and slid open the screen, revealing a background picture of herself hugging an elderly woman in a black dress.

“Your grandmother?”

She nodded as she scrolled down the list of artists to A-ha. “Yes, I really do have the song – it’s so bad it’s good.”

He smiled, meeting her eyes, the crystal blue of unpolluted seawater. She swept back her hair and pushed the headphone into her ear, revealing a thin hearing aid. As she handed him the other bud she leaned in closer, her shoulder touching the top of his arm. At the first chorus he recognised the track.

"I know it – it's not bad."

"It's Scandipop at its cheesy finest. And you do look like him, see." She pointed to the lead singer on the album cover.

"Compliment or insult?"

"I'll let you decide."

There was a yell behind them and they turned in time to see the girls ducking as a football went flying past their heads. "Sorry," called out one of the lads as they walked towards them, grinning.

"I love a well thought out chat up line," she said.

"Nothing says I want you like a ball in the face."

"I'm Emma, by the way."

"Alex."

Her hand was small and warm in his palm.

*

The boy was five and his mother and the people who hung around the flat called him Jon. He was lying in his cot with his legs dangling out the end where Big Jim had ripped off the bars, gazing at the summer sky at the edge of the frayed orange curtains, when a shadow rose up over the damp patch above the skirting board. He rolled over and saw the man standing in the doorway, a tall silhouette against the light in the hallway – dressed in black with a rucksack over his shoulders. The man walked silently over the floorboards and looked down at him, fixing on the cleft above his lip and then taking in the bruises and scratches peppered across his scrawny naked body. The boy hugged his ribs as he stared back, trying to remember if he'd seen this face before.

"What's your name?" His voice was a deep rumble.

"Jon," he whispered. "No H."

"Where're your clothes?"

He pointed to an unwashed tracksuit on the floor.

"Get dressed."

He climbed out of bed and pulled the tracksuit on. When he tried to do up the top the zip got stuck and the man leaned down and yanked the trapped material free before re-aligning the metal teeth and slowly drawing up the fastener. His hands were covered by see-through gloves.

"Where're your shoes?"

The boy shrugged.

The man shifted the rucksack around to his chest and kneeled with his back to the boy, who stared back in silence before tentatively climbing on. As they passed the living room he saw his mother and Big Jim side-by-side on the sofa with their heads tilted back and mouths hanging open.

The front door was ajar as usual and the man stopped and peered out before he toed it open and took him outside onto the landing above the courtyard. He scanned the windows of each flat as he strode to the central staircase, peeling off his gloves and stuffing them inside the rucksack as he moved. He clamped his arms tight around the boy's legs as he went down the steps, and as they neared the bottom they heard voices in the courtyard and the man reached into his bag with his arm tensed as they came out of the stairwell and saw two teenagers with a pitbull walking towards them. The boys stared at them as they approached and one of them said 'Ain't that Lisa's boy?' to the other, but they passed by and started climbing the stairs and he could hear them muttering and the dog breathing heavily as the man carried him towards the street. There were a few people outside the pub by the flats but nobody looked their way as they crossed the road and turned into a cul-de-sac.

"Where we going?" he said when the man put him down by a black Ford.

"On holiday." He held open the passenger door.

"Holiday?" he sounded out each syllable, the word new on his tongue.

"Yeah."

The boy glanced back to the main road and then stared up at him, searching for that fish-eyed callousness he saw in the other men that came to the flat, but finding something else, something he hadn't encountered before. "Name?"

"Tom."

He tilted his head and blinked, and then climbed inside the car.

*

The sun was setting as Alex and Emma walked along the High Street, weaving through the crowds pouring out from the closing shops. As a group of Japanese students came rushing towards them he took her hand and led her through the throng of backpacks and raincoats, and when they came out the other side their fingers stayed locked.

"So do you miss home?" he asked as they crossed the road.

"Sometimes. I prefer it here, though."

"And you've got your grandmother here, I suppose."

"I did. She died last year." She glanced up at him, a 'don't worry' look.

"Do your parents come back to England much?"

"Not really. They've only been once since they moved."

"So you go over there a lot?"

"I don't really like it. Too hot." She pointed ahead to a small café with an Italian flag in the window. "That's it. Are you sure you want Italian?"

"I am."

"Just because I'm learning Italian?"

"I'll be testing you."

"But you don't speak Italian."

"I'll consult the waiter."

“What do you recommend?” he asked as they looked at the menu, sitting at a corner table while a deep voice crooned from the speaker above them.

“Haven’t you had Italian before?”

“Yeah, but you’re virtually Italian.”

“Because of Rosetta Stone level one?”

“I’m going to call you Andrea Pirlo.”

“Who’s that?”

“A footballer.” He nodded at the speaker. “Do you know what he’s saying?”

She listened for a few seconds. “He’s begging a woman to come back to him.”

“I just use chloroform.”

“Is your best chat up line ‘Get in the van’?’

“Ball to the face.”

“That’s a bit forward.”

In a packed bar they perched on the edge of a table, the RnB music vibrating the floor beneath their feet.

“So are you reading the book for your course?” he said into her good ear as she held her hair back, her red nail polish gleaming in the spotlight.

“No, I just found it in Waterstones. It’s the holiday at the moment.”

He sipped his Jack Daniels and coke; it was the first time he had tried the drink, ordering it without thinking when the barman asked what he wanted with the sauvignon blanc.

"Ah yeah, of course. So is it all lazy days and Italian for you at the moment or do you have a job?"

"Lazy days, sitting around watching *This Morning*. No, my grandma left me enough money to get through uni but I have been looking for a summer job."

"Yeah, anything in particular or…?"

"Well, when I say looking I mean occasionally typing the word job into Google."

"Well, *This Morning* is pretty engrossing."

"And educational. Did you know that leggings are going to be the next big trend for guys?"

"I was hoping for the Jacobean ruff."

"You could team the Jacobean ruff with the leggings – that's a strong look."

"I'm not sure I have the legs."

"Really? My first thought when I saw you was 'Oh boy, he has the handsome legs of the antelope'."

"You're a fan of *The Mighty Boosh* too then?"

"Yeah, pretty much all my jokes are stolen."

"I pride myself on having no original ideas."

They smiled and sipped their drinks, the passing seconds counted by the throbbing bass.

"Anyway, my jeans aren't that tight are they?"

"No, but I can tell the shape of a guy's legs just from the look in his eye."

They stood to allow two couples to squeeze past them into a booth with a reserved sign.

"I do that too," he said, "go into a bookshop without knowing what I want and read the covers until I find something."

"I can spend hours browsing like that. I'm even worse in clothes shops."

"Me too. Don't tell anyone, though – I have a macho image to maintain."

She ran her eyes over his denim shirt, jeans and boots. "It's kind of a cross between biker and boyband."

"Again, compliment or insult?"

"Aren't you hot though?"

He shrugged and pointed to her jeans. "What about you?"

"I have incredibly pale legs, I didn't want to scare anyone in the park."

"I have the handsome legs of the antelope – I didn't want to show off."

The bar was starting to fill up, guys in tight T-shirts and girls in short dresses filtering onto the dance floor.

"Have you been here before?" he asked, the tip of his nose against her hair, breathing in her cherry shampoo.

"No, I'm not really a big clubber."

"Me neither."

"We can go back to mine, if you like? You really should start watching *Making a Murderer* before they ban you from Cheltenham."

"I live in Gloucester, actually."

"Ah, a boy from the wrong side of the tracks."

She lived alone in a small one-bed flat above a bicycle shop in Pittville, a cramped space made bigger by white paint and sparse furniture.

"It's hard to believe my grandma and I managed to both live here for three years."

"It's nicer than my place; I have a single room in a shared house in Barton."

In the living room a small two-seater sofa faced an old TV with a black coffee table in between.

"One of the few things she brought with her," she said, tapping the marble surface.

The picture from her phone was framed on the mantelpiece above the bricked up fireplace. "She was very elegant," he said.

"She wouldn't even go to the corner shop without make-up. She did some modelling and acting when she was younger."

"You can tell. You look a lot like her."

"I wish."

"Was she from Cheltenham?"

"No, she moved here in 1995. She met my step-grandfather, got married and moved here with him, but he died a few years later in a crash. She didn't have much luck with men. Her first husband – my grandfather – killed himself. I have one of those messed up families. My parents are either fighting, cheating or making up."

"My family is boring – they're all Christians and I can't think of a single scandal."

"Are you?"

"Boring?"

"I think we've already established that," she grinned. "A Christian?"

"Sorry, I'm just so used to being insulted. Er, well I've been going to church since I was little with my family, but I was more on and off at uni, and since I moved here I haven't really gone much, so… What about you?"

She shook her head. "It's just never been a concept in my family."

"Yeah, I suppose it depends on what you're raised with."

"Yeah, I guess so. You can sit down, if you like. Dr Pepper?"

"More? You're worse than me."

"Addictive personality," she smiled, standing in the kitchen doorway.

"I'm going to just say no. I usually limit myself to one can a day. I'm actually very boring, as we've established."

"Well, sure, some people would say collecting pencil sharpeners is boring but…"

"Pencil sharpeners?"

“You don’t collect them? You look like you do.”

“Oh yeah, yeah, I’ve got a huge collection.”

“How about some green tea? It’s detoxifying, it will clean away all the sugar and caffeine from the Dr Pepper.”

“Are you saying my insides are dirty?”

“Filthy.”

“Ok, clean me out.”

In the bathroom he wet his hands to restyle his hair and swilled a drop of mouthwash as he inspected a faint blemish where a squeezed spot was healing. There were dozens of beauty products; creams and hairsprays filling the shelves, face washes and shampoos lining the bathtub, all arranged in rows with the labels facing forward.

When he returned to the living room she was kneeling by the TV as steam rose from two mugs of green tea on coasters on the coffee table. She’d turned off the lights.

“I told you it was a bit OCD,” she said, looking up at him as he sat down.

“My pencil sharpeners are lined up the same way.”

She joined him on the sofa, a couple of inches between their thighs as she held the remote. “So did you know anyone when you first moved here?” she asked, scrolling to the episodes screen.

“Nope. I had the interview, got offered the job the next day and moved here a month later. It was all a bit of a blur.”

“Why Gloucester instead of Cheltenham?”

"Work. I'm a five minute walk from the office. I used to live in Cheltenham, though. Only for a couple of years, when I was four or five – I barely remember it."

"Which part?"

"Near the uni."

"So were you living with your parents before Gloucester?"

"Just while I was doing the journalism course."

"You must have made friends here, though?"

"Yeah, a few at work."

"What about your housemates?"

"They're nice, but they're hardly ever in and they've all got their own lives here already."

"How many are there?"

"Four including me."

"All guys?"

"Two girls and one guy."

"Your age?"

"A bit older."

"How much? A couple of years or…?"

"They're around thirty, I guess."

She nodded, uncrossing her legs.

"Yeah, I got the job so fast I pretty much took the first place I found that was clean and affordable. It could be worse."

"I don't know that many people either."

"What about at uni?"

“Not really.”

“What about the college you went to?”

She shook her head, her face tight, and then clicked play.

After a few minutes he reached out and held her hand in her lap and she turned to him. “Just so you know, I’m not into picking up guys and bringing them back here.”

“I know. Me neither.”

“I just saw your book and…”

“Dr Pepper.”

“And Dr Pepper.”

“I know, it was all a bit random.”

“Very random.”

She stared at him in the glow of the TV screen, searching for something in his eyes, and then she leaned in and kissed him. Her breath was laced with mints and cherry lip gloss and as he held her ribs the heat of her body radiated through him. She pressed herself into him, draping her leg across his thigh, and he pulled her closer until she was straddling him. She peeled off her top and as he unhooked her scarlet bra he saw the sweat glistening in the hollows of her collarbone and the freckles above her teardrop breasts like a constellation of stars.

As he kneeled before her in the half-light he couldn’t help but briefly remember that teenage vow he had made to wait until marriage, a promise he had broken so easily in his second week at university.

Afterwards they lay on the sofa, his head on her stomach and her fingers tracing his spine, silent, half-listening to the repeating chords of the menu music.

"You can stay over," she said, "if you like."

"Ok," he closed his eyes, "thanks."

In the middle of the night, between sleep and consciousness, he awoke disorientated by the warmth of her body next to him and the moonlight slanting in from the left, and then he felt her back pressed against his chest and her neck in the crook of his elbow, and he drifted off into a dreamless sleep.

In the grey dawn he was gently lulled from his slumber, finding himself on the edge of her, her profile outlined in the ashen light as she looked at him over her shoulder before pushing back and enveloping him.

*

When the boy awoke it was the middle of the night and they were in a service station car park. The driver's seat was empty and when he peered out the window he saw Tom in a phone box by the entrance of the glass building. He was watching the car while cradling the phone and when he saw him looking he waved and the boy took it to mean 'come here', so he unbuckled his seatbelt and heaved the door open and walked across the tarmac, treading carefully in his bare feet. Tom held his palm out to say stop, but when he saw the look on the boy's face he turned his hand around and beckoned him to keep coming.

"See you at eleven," he said into the phone as the boy reached him, and then he hung up and scanned the almost empty lot, the silence giving way to the sound of crickets chirping in the grass verges. "KFC?"

The boy nodded.

He looked down at the boy's feet and pointed to the car. "Wait here."

"Where mummy?" he asked as Tom was closing the passenger door on him.

"Do you like her?"

The boy shrugged.

"What about her friends?"

He shook his head.

"Chicken burger, fries and a coke?"

He stared back, unaccustomed to being asked what he wanted.

As Tom disappeared into the bright foyer the boy looked around the car, gripping the steering wheel and shaking the gear stick. The rucksack was on the floor in the back. He reached between the seats and pulled the heavy bag onto his lap. Inside there were rolled up socks and boxer shorts on top of a pair of jeans and a grey sweatshirt with something hard wrapped inside. He burrowed his hand in and pulled out a gun, staring in wonder at the glossy barrel and dimpled handle as his finger curled around the trigger. The small black pistol was heavy but he managed to raise it with two hands, pointing the barrel at the windscreen and mouthing a bang, aping the films he had seen on the TV in the tobacco-stained living room as his mother slumped unconscious on the sofa or argued with her friends. He carefully wrapped the gun inside the sweatshirt and stuffed it back inside the rucksack. In the side pockets he found a screwdriver and a short double-bladed knife.

Tom emerged through the automatic doors with a paper bag in his hand. Yanking the zips shut, the boy placed the rucksack back on the carpet with the straps facedown. As Tom approached he was plagued by the feeling the bag had been lying the other way, but it was too late, he was almost back, his cheekbones cut by the lamplight above as he loomed over the door. He slid inside and opened the paper bag on his lap, reaching in and handing him a burger. The boy wolfed the meal down with desperate bites.

"When was the last time you ate?" Tom asked as he took another burger out of the bag.

The boy shrugged and tore open the wrapper. As he swallowed the last bite Tom handed him a packet of fries and the boy tore through those just as quickly, stuffing handfuls into his mouth as Tom tried to laugh it off.

"You want mine too?"

He shook his head, but Tom reached into the bag and pulled out another packet of fries and held them out, and the boy met his eye and nodded and took them from him, this time eating more slowly, chewing with the same pace as the man. As Tom handed him a coke he glanced down at the rucksack and his expression changed. The boy avoided his eyes and sipped his drink, tensing himself for a smack as Tom grabbed the bag and reached inside and then checked the side pockets. The boy kept staring ahead with his lips tight around the straw as his heart juddered in his chest. Eventually Tom pushed the key into the ignition and started the car.

Half asleep, he felt himself being carried and recognised Tom's smell. Through his eyelashes he could see the stars like pinpricks in the cloudless sky. There was the distant hum of traffic and Tom breathing, and his arms under his back and knees in a warm grip, and he was vaguely aware of a glowing green sign as he drifted away.

The next time he awoke he was in a hotel bed with the unfamiliar scent of clean linen enveloping him. It was light outside and the bed next to his was empty with the duvet turned back. He sat up and found a T-shirt and jogging bottoms in his size laid on the end of his bed, and when he shuffled forward to reach them he saw a pair of trainers on the floor. He was inspecting his new outfit in the mirror when he heard the lock turning and Tom came in wearing the grey sweatshirt and jeans with the rucksack slung over his shoulder and a carrier bag in his hand.

"You like them?"

He nodded, holding the end of the T-shirt and avoiding eye contact. "Ta."

"You're welcome."

"You're welcome?" He glanced up at him and then down at his trainers.

"It means 'no problem' or 'it's ok'."

The boy nodded, twisting his fingers behind his back. In the daylight Tom was bigger – tall and triangle-shaped with stubble like black sandpaper.

They stared at each other in awkward silence, and then the boy asked, "How old are you?" unsure what else to say.

"How old am I?" Tom smiled, trying to sound upbeat. "Guess."

"Dunno," the boy shrugged, numbers over ten a mystery.

"Twenty-six."

The boy pursed his lips, pretending to understand.

"How old are you?"

He held up five fingers, recalling his mother's black-rimmed fingernails and the prick-scabs on her arm.

"That's old," Tom said, and then, after another prolonged silence, he held up the carrier bag and announced, "Breakfast," before taking out a selection pack of cereals and a bottle of milk. "What do you want?"

As he inspected the boxes Tom pointed at his lip and the boy instinctively raised his hand to cover the cleft.

"Sorry," he murmured, embarrassed. "Does it hurt?"

Still covering his mouth, the boy shook his head.

"We could fix it."

He tilted his head.

"Make it like mine?" He pointed at his own lip.

The boy stared up at him, blinking slowly and twisting his fingers behind his back as he tried to place this open-faced man on a map populated with people who slapped him and pissed on him and stubbed cigarettes out on him while hissing 'split-lip cunt' and 'mutant shit' as his mother watched in a glassy-eyed trance. She would return once the flat had gone quiet, cradling him with a blanket and whispering 'I'm sorry' in a tearful refrain as the rough wool rubbed against his burns and bruises.

4

The crowd surges against the police barrier as the prison van comes around the bend. Flushed faces bawl insults, shrieks of 'pervert' and ‘scum' piercing the din. A glass bottle arcs out of the crowd and smashes against the side of the van, the shattering glass sparkling in the flash of news cameras. Heads turn towards the alleyway leading to the courthouse car park as more officers march forward to form a blockade. They part to let the van enter and then link up again as the mob shoves forward. For a second the van stalls and a cheer goes up from the crowd, followed by a groan as the wheels starting moving again and the vehicle disappears behind the wall. Alex and Mike follow the press crowd around the back and watch as the van reverses towards the rear entrance. The photographers scurry around the side of the vehicle and wait poised as the back doors open, and then unleash their yellow wave of flashes as a tall police officer climbs down. Blinking, he turns to the van with his hand outstretched and waits for the prisoner to emerge. Silence descends on the pack of journalists, their breath spiking the cold morning air. Five seconds tick by without any movement from the van, and then a blanketed figure slowly steps down onto the tarmac, the woollen shawl revealing only a pair of scuffed black shoes. The officer grasps his shoulder through the blanket and directs him to the back door, and they disappear inside in a haze of clicks and flashes.

“More than enough for a spread,” Mike says, scrolling through the pictures on his camera.

Alex slides his notepad and pen inside his bag. “I better get in there.”

“Have you found a church yet?” his mother asked in their last conversation before he stopped answering her calls and began responding only by text.

“Not yet.” He was sitting on his bed with the curtains closed on the bright afternoon.

“What about that one you went to a couple of times when you first moved – St Mary's, was it? Was it no good?”

“Not really.”

“A bit too happy clappy, was it?”

“Yeah, a bit.”

“Oh well, I'm sure you'll find one that suits you.”

“Mm.”

“I was messing around on the web last night, actually, checking emails and all that, and I Googled some of the churches near you and there are a few that look quite good, actually. I can email you a list, if you like?”

“Yeah, ok.”

“Or I can just leave you to do it yourself; I'm sure you're looking yourself anyway?”

“Mm.”

She was silent for a second. “So are you still looking for a church, then, son?"

"Not really." He pictured her in their airy living room, sitting on the big blue sofa next to his father with the phone tilted so he could hear his answers too.

"Oh. Have you not had time, then?"

"I just don't…" He paused, swallowed the rest of the sentence and started again. "I'm just working so many Sundays now."

"Oh, I didn't realise you were doing Sundays."

"Yeah, weekend shifts."

"Most churches do midweek groups, you know."

"Yeah, I'm looking into that."

The groan of a steel door directs everyone's attention to the dock and they watch as Thomas Unsworth is led up into the dock, his hunched shoulders and greying hair placing him a lifetime beyond his 32 years of age. He stares down at the floor, his green eyes circled by dark bags.

The prosecutor exchanges a knowing glance with a woman among the reporters from the nationals who huddle at the back of the small courtroom. The clerk picks up her phone and whispers something and then the door to the chambers opens and everyone stands as the magistrates file into the courtroom; all three are over sixty, the chairman a soft-faced man with freshly dyed hair and rimless glasses. He glances at the crowd of reporters as he sits down and unbuttons his navy pinstriped suit, and then he stares at

Unsworth, studying his face, before turning to the folder on his bench.

The clerk fixes her gaze a couple of inches above Unsworth's head. “Would the defendant please state his name, full address and date of birth.”

Unsworth stares blankly at his barrister, who mouths “name” and motions for him to speak as though he is a puppet on her hand.

“Thomas David Unsworth.”

A couple of seconds pass as everyone waits for him to continue, but he remains silent, oblivious to the bemused faces. Some of the reporters nudge each other.

“And your address and date of birth?”

He speaks in a flat, distant manner.

“Thank you, please be seated.”

He remains standing, his hands motionless by his side.

“You can sit down now, Mr Unsworth,” the chairman barks, halting the prosecutor as he rises to his feet.

Unsworth sits down and rubs his eyes. The chairman sweeps his hand through his hair and turns to the prosecutor. “Please proceed, Mr Etherington.”

*

“He’s waiting for you in Costa,” Derek says, squinting at the daylight, the iron door concealing half of his face.

“Which one?”

"King's Walk."

"What did he say?"

"Nothing. I don't ask."

He peers down the alleyway. The black rubbish bags glisten in the sun, still slick from the rain.

The magistrate sits alone at a table by the window, reading a newspaper. Ezra zooms in with his camera phone and snaps a picture, capturing his head above a streak of sunlight on the glass. His mouth is bone dry as he walks across the paved square.

"Ezra." He rises to his feet and extends his hand. "Peter." His bones feel fragile in the boy's palm. "It's good to finally meet you." His voice has the same smooth enunciation as when he'd overheard him 12 years ago, while he was sitting in Tom's bedroom with a Dr Pepper and a plate of biscuits, his five-year-old mind trying to comprehend the hushed conversation next door.

Derek: "I know you feel responsible but, trust me son, this will change the rest of your life; you'll never be able to just go off for a weekend with a girl or even down the pub for a pint."

Jo: "The poor lad needs a home, we can't just chuck him out on the streets."

Peter: "This is a chance to change that boy's life forever, to give him stability."

Tom: "I'm not going to just abandon him."

"Tom told me so much about you," Peter says, his eyes watery blue behind his frameless glasses. “Take a seat. How do you take your coffee?”

“I’m ok, thanks.” Ezra perches on a wooden chair with his back to the window. The magistrate’s eyes follow something beyond the boy’s shoulder, out in the square, and then he fixes his gaze on his face, glancing at his scar before smiling with whitened teeth.

“Come on, have a drink,” he says, and he waves at a girl clearing a table. “Excuse me, could my friend here have a – “ He looks at Ezra and says “Americano?” and the boy nods, and then he turns back to the girl, who continues piling cups and plates onto a tray as she listens with impatience flickering in her eyes – “an Americano, please?”

“You order at the counter, sir.”

“I know,” he says, winking at Ezra, “but I’m an old man – every step I take is another one closer to a hip replacement. Won’t you save my hips, if only for another day?”

The girl chuckles and heads off behind the counter. Peter unbuttons his pinstriped suit jacket on a spotless white shirt and yellow tie as a sombre expression falls over his soft oval face. “I dashed here straight from court. Horrible case.” He spreads his fingers and pushes his palm up from the table, his hand like a poised spider. “I still can’t believe he’s gone,” he sighs. “How are you?”

The boy shrugs. “Ok.”

“Is there anything I can do? Anything you need?”

He shakes his head. “Thanks for the money.”

He nods, lips pursed. "You weren't at the funeral." He starts to say more, but raises his mug instead and takes a sip. The girl appears with the Americano. "Thank you, that's very kind of you," he says, taking his wallet from his overcoat, separating 10 pounds from a wad of notes and holding it out to her. "If your manager asks, tell her I gave you the exact amount." The girl pauses, confused, and then his meaning clicks and she smiles and whispers her thanks before hurrying away.

"I won't bore you with stories of how close Tom and I were," he says, raising his eyes expectantly as he adds, "I'm sure he told you all about me?" and the boy nods, murmuring, "Like a father," the words rippling the magistrate's pupils.

"The councillor – did he say anything?"

"No."

"A bus. Clever, if a bit loud."

"He'd been drinking. It'll –"

"– look like an accident. I know. But you were out in the open."

"There was nobody around. I kept away from the CCTV."

"The gun..."

An old woman approaches in a mobility scooter and the magistrate leans forward on his chair so she can squeeze past, smiling at her as she rolls away towards the counter. "If this was a film we'd be talking in a dark cemetery," he says to the boy, waving his hand over the crowded shop and trying to smile. "The gun – keep hold of it. For Gardner."

“You’ve found him?”

“You will. His neighbour spoke to the police. She knew the councillor’s daughter.”

Ezra nods. “It still doesn’t make sense – the councillor changing his mind and warning Gardner, after what he’d done to his daughter...”

He twists the wedding ring on his long piano-player finger as he stares into his half-empty coffee cup, and when he looks up at the boy there is a hardness in his eyes. “I know.”

“Who else knew?”

“Besides Tom and I? Derek and Jo. David.”

“You and David – you decide the targets?”

“And Tom. He could say no.”

“Did he ever say no?”

“No. He believed.” A sad smile passes over his lips. “You know that. This and you – it was his life.”

Two skinny teenage boys slink past in school blazers, eyeing Ezra’s bleached hair.

“What happened?” the boy asks. “Derek and Jo won’t tell me.”

“In the face,” he whispers, tapping his cheek below his right eye.

The image is like a gut punch.

“I still can’t believe we’re talking about him in the past tense,” Peter says.

They fall silent, the magistrate gazing out of the window and the boy staring into the crowd.

"So you're seventeen now."

"Last month."

"The age you realise that adults are just children too." He tries to smile but the sadness is too heavy on his face. "I was seventeen when my father left my mother for another man. What did Tom tell you about the people we target?"

"That they deserve it."

"Yes, but it's more than that. It's not just retribution, it's prevention. Gardner, for example: what we're really doing is preventing him from abusing other women. Because he will. He won't change. People don't change. If a dog bites, we put it down to stop it biting again…"

"Tom used to say that."

"Tom got it. He always got it. James Delaney – Big Jim – was his third. What he did to you, son... well, no-one could argue that he deserved mercy or another chance. He'd done it before, he'd have done it again, like a broken record." He sips his drink and clears his throat, his eyes trailing a father and daughter as they pass the window, the girl sitting on the man's shoulders. "I've got to get back," he says, glancing at his Rolex. He reaches into a pocket and lays an envelope on the table. "Tom was very proud of you, son."

As the magistrate glides away through the crowd Ezra checks the envelope under the table, finding a faded photograph of Tom. He's the age the boy is now, standing next to a new car and beaming as he holds up the key. It's the black Ford. A middle-aged couple stand either side of him, Tom's features reflected in their smiling faces. There are two handwritten notes on the back of the photo, both in black ink. The first says 'Thomas' 17th, 1987'; the second, in Tom's handwriting, reads 'My parents'.

5

Ezra stands before the intercom panel, staring at the columns of buttons. He scans the street before cupping his hands to the door and peering inside: pigeonholes by two lifts and a staircase, doors to the corridors either side, the whole lobby looking like it has just been scrubbed and polished. There is a letter with a police logo pinned to the noticeboard. A To Let sign has been tied to the railings at the bottom of the lawn, by the spot where the news reporters stood as they described the shooting, focusing more on the shockwaves the crime had sent through genteel Cirencester – the heart of the Cotswolds – than the man whose life had been taken. He pushes the buzzers for the ground floor flats; after a few seconds there is a crackle at the other end and then a tentative hello.

"Hello," he says into the speaker, "I'm here to look at a flat and the estate agent's not here and it's hammering down."

"Yes. Cats and dogs. Isn't it?" An old man, his voice slow, the words disconnected.

"Can you buzz me in? So I can wait for him inside?"

"Who?"

"The estate agent. I'm here to see flat nine."

"Oh. Yes. Empty for months, that one. There was a shooting upstairs last week. Or was it the week before...?"

"Can you buzz me in, please?"

"Ok."

"Thank you."

The line goes dead but nothing happens. He's about to push the button again when the buzzer sounds and the door clicks open. Inside, a CCTV camera surveys the lobby from above the pigeonholes; he pulls his hood down to his eyebrows as he walks past and sees two typed envelopes addressed to Kerry Jordan in box 22. The stairwell smells of fresh paint and each corridor is silent and immaculate like a hotel off-season. Flat 22 has a new door: white uPVC with shiny brass numbers. An image of Tom in the exact same position flashes through his mind; he closes his eyes, focusing on the ochre hue on the back of his lids, and then pushes the bell and presses his ear to the door, hearing what sounds like murmuring inside. There are two voices, a man and a woman, and then there is music, a jingle, and he realises that the sounds are coming from a TV. He knocks louder and looks in through the letterbox. A short hallway leads to a living room with a kitchen and bathroom off to the right, everything white and covered with the smell of fresh paint. The carpet has been removed in the hallway and there is a damp patch in the middle of the floorboards, the wood still drying from being scrubbed, and he has to close his eyes again to stop the image of Tom's prone body forming before him.

The sound of the TV is not coming from inside. At number 21 he can only hear his own breathing. At 23 he hears the TV. As he knocks he lowers his hood and unzips his coat on a white shirt and school tie. Footsteps approach on the other side and the spyhole darkens. “Hello?” A woman’s voice, cautious.

“Hello, sorry to bother you, I’m looking for Kerry.”

“I haven’t seen her for days. Since what happened.”

“Oh. What happened?”

“Haven’t you heard?” The door opens on the chain and a haggard middle-aged face appears at the slit. “Someone was killed in there. Shot. With a gun.”

“What? In Kerry’s?”

“A week ago.”

“Is she ok?”

“She wasn’t there at the time. It was her boyfriend.”

“Killed?”

“Who did it. I was here. I heard everything.”

“What happened?”

“I heard someone knocking on the door – I thought it was me so I came to the door – and then I heard the door opening and closing, and then they were talking in the hallway, her boyfriend and another man, just talking, not shouting, and then, from nowhere, a gunshot. I jumped out of my skin. It was so loud. It doesn’t sound like it does on the TV. I was running for the phone when I heard the door fly open and someone go flying down the stairs. When the police got here I went out and had a look. He was lying there in the hallway.”

“They were talking? Did you hear what they said?”

She shakes her head.

“And it was definitely her boyfriend? Frankie?”

"I know his voice."

"Did you see him?"

"No. They still haven't caught him. I'm not surprised he did it. He's a nasty piece of work. I used to hear him effing and blinding at her. I called the police a couple of times. Why she was with him…? Comes from a good family. Her dad's a councillor – he owns the flat."

"Her and Gardner – Frankie – how did they meet?"

"Through his sister, I think. She used to come over. They used to work at the same betting shop, I think." She nods towards the town centre. "Then he started coming with her, and then it was just him."

"What about the man? Had you seen him before?"

"I couldn't tell – he was a mess." She waves her hand in front of her face. "You alright, love?"

When he finally answers his voice is sapped of all tone and intonation. "I just can't believe it."

"You've gone white as a sheet, love. Do you want a gin?"

He shakes his head and murmurs his thanks.

"How do you know her?" she asks as he turns away.

"Cousins," he says, moving towards the stairwell.

"If you see her, tell her I said hello."

*

"Do you miss her?"

The boy looked up from the textbook and shrugged, the scar

above his lip thinner and fainter.

Tom scratched at his beard. “I can’t get used to it,” he smiled. He piled the books on top of each other and pushed them to the edge of the table, clearing the space in front of them. “My parents died when I was young. Not as young as you. 21. I was angry.” He looked down at his hands. “Are you happy here?”

He nodded.

“Really? You don’t want to go to school?”

He shook his head, the concept of school foreign to him; just a scene from TV shows, the crammed classrooms and hectic hallways giving him the impression of a hostile and overwhelming place. “What happened?”

“My parents? A man hit them with a car. Robert Nunn.”

“Did he go to jail?”

“Yeah. For six years.”

“What happened?”

“To him?”

He nodded, eyes wide, absorbing everything.

“He died when he got out of prison.”

He tilted his head. “Good.”

“Good?”

“Yes.”

“Why good?”

He tilted his head, thinking, and then shrugged.

Tom laid his hand on the boy’s shoulder. “You’re a miracle, you know?"

"What's a miracle?"

He nodded to the dictionary.

*

He recognises Sharon Gardner as soon as he sees her: the same chinless jawline as her brother's picture in the newspaper and the same narrow eyes, but much older, not quite middle-aged but heading there fast. She takes betting slips and cash from the customers, deflecting their attempts at banter with a weary nod. There is a small crowd beneath the bank of televisions, dishevelled men in tweed jackets that give off the scent of stale beer and tobacco, and he joins them and feigns interest in the race before slipping out into grey drizzle of Cirencester's Cricklade Street and crossing the road to Costa. He orders an Americano and a panini and sits in the window watching the betting shop, his stomach too tense to take the food.

*

"I'd follow him. He was living with his parents. He'd go to work, the pub, football. Just… normal. Living. Like nothing had happened." He picked a long blonde hair off the duvet and held it up. "Where did that come from? Have you been wearing a wig?"

The boy smiled, his scar now just a faint white line. "The

woman at the laundrette?"

"You're always so logical."

Ezra shifted his back against the pillow. "Go on."

Tom leaned forward on the chair. "I have no idea if I should be telling you this. Not exactly a normal bedtime story for an eleven-year-old."

"I want to know."

He nodded, running his hand over his shaved head. "I used to work for the local paper as a reporter and I heard that he'd been caught speeding. My boss didn't want me to cover it – he knew what had happened – but I said I'd take a day off if I had to. I sat at the back of the court. He didn't even know I was there. They banned him from driving. He didn't look bothered. Afterwards, one of the magistrates came up to me; Peter, the skinny man with the glasses, remember? Anyway, he told me he knew who I was and asked if he could buy me lunch, and we got talking about Nunn and he said it would only be a matter of time before he killed again and that the world would be a better place without him. And so…"

"What?"

"I said I'd like to kill him and he said I should. That he knew how." He paused, blinking at his palms in his lap. "It was just like that. Two men in a café talking about murder. It's never as complicated as in films."

"How?"

He sighed through his nose, his jaw tight.

“You promised.”

“That night. Me, Peter and another man, David – you don’t know him, but he’s a policeman – we followed Nunn home from a pub. He’d been out celebrating not going to prison, like he’d won. We grabbed him and put him in David’s car and drove him out to a quarry, that one near Crickley Hill, and...”

“How did you do it?”

“Stabbed him. About 20 times, more maybe. I lost control. When someone takes your...” he stopped himself before the sentence reached its inevitable conclusion, his eyes still fixed on his cupped hands as he leaned forward with his shoulders drawn in.

“Did you feel bad?”

“No.” He shook his head and looked straight into the boy’s eyes. “What are you thinking?”

“Dunno. He deserved it.”

“That’s what I tell myself.”

Ezra pulled the covers up around his chin and looked away, his silence pregnant. Tom waited for him to ask the unspoken question that loomed over them but the boy just stared into the pattern on the duvet, feigning tiredness as the murmur of the traffic outside was interrupted by the crackling approach and decline of a moped engine. As the sound faded, Tom cleared his throat and croaked his goodnight, flicking off the lamp as he stood up.

The boy watched his silhouette disappear as he pulled the door closed, leaving a slither of light.

6

Alex awakes soaked in sweat, the pillow sticking to the side of his face. The light from the takeaway sign slips through the gap between the curtains and the stripe of pink neon slides over him as he rises to his feet and steps towards the window. She's in her dressing gown, a slender silhouette against the unlit room behind her, the orange tip of a cigarette glowing against the black shape of her face. Her husband is downstairs in the takeaway, watching the TV behind the counter. Outside the street is empty.

As he checks the time the phone screen bathes him in pale light and when he looks back the angle of her head has changed, as though she is watching him. He clicks off the phone and steps backwards. She remains in the same position. He tries to make out her face but the flickering light of the faulty lamppost below doesn't quite reach her, the hazy rays fading away around her waist. Her husband is dozing now, the rolls of his neck compressed like an accordion. Alex walks to the door and switches on the light, and then pulls the curtains all the way back and pushes the window open, standing in the centre, half-naked, looking down at the street before gradually lifting his gaze to her. She doesn't move but he can feel her eyes on him. He slowly raises his hand into a wave. She does the same – her delicate arm bent at a right angle – and moves backwards into the gloom. There is a spring of light from the left side of the room, the glow of a lamp illuminating the bed covers and the dressing table. She steps into the window, facing him. Her hair is down and her fingers are playing with the hem of her dressing gown, kneading the pink cotton above her thighs. The belt is loosely tied, gathering the lapels in a V which reveals the inner curves of her breasts. She slowly unties her belt and the gown falls open, her tanned skin luminous in the amber light as she stares straight at him.

Her head jerks towards the doorway behind her and she wrenches the gown around her body. The takeaway is empty. When he looks back at the window the blinds are lowering, the slats already covering her face and dropping fast. They hit the bottom and then the light goes out inside. He watches the window, waiting for some sign of movement, but there is nothing.

He could see the light in Emma's window as he pulled up outside. In the doorway she looked at him with a close-lipped smile, shaking her head softly, and as she led him upstairs he could hear music oozing from her bedroom, a woman singing with grief – *'...and taught me to truly hate myself...'* His poem was on her computer screen. She turned to him, her eyes aglow. "That's the nicest thing anyone has ever done for me."

Afterwards, lying with his head on her chest and her finger tracing his spine, they listened to the rain pattering against the window, her flesh a radiator spreading warmth through his body.

"I can't imagine ever wanting to do that with anyone else now," she whispered.

"Neither can I."

The radiator is broken. He shivers as he sits up in bed, the TV screen emitting a black light as the credits roll on Making a Murderer. He has almost finished watching the series for the second time – he and Emma only made it halfway through. The blinds are still down in the window across the street with no light behind. On his phone he looks at Emma's Facebook account; everything but her profile picture is locked to him now. She is on the right of a row of four girls, wearing her red lace dress; at the other end of the line there's a slim guy with blond hair and blue eyes. The four girls have their arms around each other but he's standing slightly apart from the redhead to his right, smiling awkwardly like he doesn't really know them all, like he might be seeing one of them and has just met the others for the first time, and it's obviously not the redhead. He can't see his name – nobody has been tagged in the photo. On the computer, he types Emma's name plus Manchester into Google but there are no addresses or phone numbers returned by the search, just her locked Facebook profile and websites with details of other people.

The light goes on behind the blinds. He pushes open his window and listens, hearing only the occasional drone of a distant engine on the main road. A fat hand jabs through the slats and pulls the window shut and the room plunges into darkness. Alex watches with his head against the glass and his breath steaming the surface. Movement drags his gaze to the street and he sees them emerging from the alleyway.

Her husband strides ahead, a puffer jacket making him even bigger and a baseball cap on his head; she follows, treading carefully in skyscraper red heels with a black trench-coat falling just below her knees. They turn into a side street and approach a silver Volkswagen at the back of the row of parked cars; he gets in the driver's seat, closest to the curb, and by the time she reaches the passenger side he has already started the engine and turned on the headlights. As she holds the door she looks up at his window, her eyes lingering for a few seconds, and then she slides inside and they pull away.

He opened Emma's door with a freshly cut key and slipped inside, silently climbing the stairs to her bedroom and watching her through the crack in the door as she inspected her reflection, lifting her T-shirt and pinching the flesh of her waist and then smoothing down her hair, all the while softly singing along to the music on the stereo – the same song of grief.

"I'm watching you," he whispered.

She flinched and turned to him. "You scared me."

"Sorry." He stepped inside. "I just love watching you when you're in your own little world."

"Voyeur."

"I prefer the term 'pervert'," he grinned, pulling her towards him and cupping her breast.

"You just want me for sex," she smiled, but he could see that part of her was serious.

"Do you really think that?"

She shrugged.

"You know it's about more than that."

"Maybe."

"Where's this coming from?"

"Nowhere." Her gaze shifted to the mirror and then the overcast sky through the parted blinds.

"Do I really make you feel that way?"

"No. I just sometimes forget that you're not like the rest of them."

"The rest of them?" He stepped into her line of sight. "Who?"

"Do you really want to know?"

"Yeah."

"Really?"

"Yes."

"I was with this guy for a while who told me he loved me and wanted to be with me, and then I found out he was married."

She walked past him and perched on the edge of the bed.

"Did you love him?"

"I thought I did at the time, but it was just a stupid schoolgirl thing."

"How old were you?"

"Sixteen."

"And he was married? How old was he?"

"Late twenties."

“How long did it last?”

“A few months.”

“And you broke it off when you found out?”

She looked down at the carpet. “Eventually.”

“Even though he had a wife?”

“Not everyone was raised in black and white,” she said, staring back at him.

He opened his mouth to reply but paused, instead turning to the window and the weak glints of light where the sun was trapped behind the clouds. “Was he your first time?”

She didn’t answer. He looked back and saw she was nodding faintly. Her hair and skin was dull in the flat light. He walked over to the bed and sat down next to her, wrapping his arm around her shoulder. “I might have a wife from a drunken night I don’t remember.”

She smiled and leaned into him, and he kissed the top of her head and laid back so her cheek was on his chest.

“Is there anyone in your past?”

He shook his head against the mattress.

“There must have been someone.”

“Nothing that mattered.”

“What, just casual stuff at uni?”

“Mm, a couple of times.”

“So what am I?”

“The third. What am I to you?”

She hesitated briefly. “Fourth.”

He glanced down at her, a question on his tongue, but she spoke first. “Your heart beats really fast.” Her eyes were closed as she listened to the rhythm; he could see the tiny veins on the back of her eyelids and the pores on her nose.

He stared up at a hairline crack in the ceiling, feeling his pulse in his fingers as he held her ribs. “That’s the first time I’ve ever felt jealous.”

“Good,” she whispered.

“Good?”

She nodded, her eyes still shut.

His eyes on the crack in the ceiling, he calls her and listens to the recorded voice saying the number has been disconnected. The shadows disperse and reform as headlights pass below and he hears an engine idling and then cutting out. At the window he watches her emerge from the Volkswagen, barefoot and carrying the red stilettos. She glances up at his window as she walks around the car and joins her husband, one step behind him as they enter the alleyway.

Lying in the park on her purple blanket, they stared up at the cloudless sky. The sun was disappearing, dragging the light away and leaving a chill in the air. Emma pulled the edge of the blanket up over her shoulders and picked up the pendant from where it had slid into the crook of her neck.

"Where did you get it?" she asked, tilting the gold heart from side to side.

"I have my ways."

"Seriously, I want to get matching earrings if they have them."

"Well, you never know what might happen."

She turned her head to him. "I didn't mean it like that, I meant that I want to get them myself, to match, because I love it so much."

"I know."

"So…?"

"So…?"

"Are you going to tell me where you got it?"

"Nope."

"Why not?"

"Because I might want to surprise you again, at some point, if you're a good girl."

"And what does 'good' constitute in your warped mind?"

"Eating all your greens, finishing your homework, not talking to strangers."

"You were a stranger."

"A strange stranger."

"Fine, I'll just go round all the jewellery shops until I find it."

"I'll hide all the jewellery shops. I'll hide you."

"You're so annoying." She propped herself up on her elbows and looked around the empty park. "Everyone's gone."

He glanced at his watch. "It's almost ten."

She rolled onto him, her head on his chest. "Jacques and Suzanne?"

"Again?"

"Again."

He sighed exaggeratedly. "Go on then."

She kissed his neck.

"Ok, so there was this man called Jacques and a woman called Suzanne, and they both worked in the same building in the city, doing some boring office job, shuffling paper and staring at a computer all day, but on different floors, and sometimes they'd pass each other on the stairs and they'd smile at each other and feel butterflies in their stomach, but they were both shy so neither of them made the first move. At night they each went home to cramped basement flats in the centre of the city – they actually lived just a few streets away from each other – and they'd both think about their lonely lives and their dull jobs and the emptiness they felt inside and ask themselves 'Is this all there is to life?'

"Anyway, one lunchtime Jacques was going down the stairs and he looked over the banister, down the stairwell, and saw Suzanne sitting on a step a few flights down, and he could see that she was crying. He stopped on the stairs, thinking that maybe he should go back and not disturb her, but he decided to go down and when she heard him coming she turned around in surprise and started to stand up and wipe away her tears, all embarrassed, but Jacques just sat down next to her and put his arm around her shoulder and she leaned her head on him and then he gently kissed the tears on her cheeks and she titled her face up to him and he kissed her on the lips and she kissed him back.

"He asked her why she was sad and she said it was because she felt like she was wasting away her life, that she felt empty, and he told her that he felt exactly the same way, and then, without really thinking, he just said 'Let's run away together', and she said yes. So they left work and went to her place and grabbed her passport and some clothes and did the same at his place, and then went to the airport and booked a flight and flew away together to start a new life."

"Where did they go?" she whispered.

"Where do you want them to go?"

"Japan: it looks like such an amazing place."

"Ok, they flew away to Japan and started a new life in Tokyo."

"I love Jacques and Suzanne."

"I know you do – that's about the fifty-seventh time you've made me tell it."

"You can't laugh, you don't even know why you made them French."

He looked down at her head on his chest: her hair was tucked behind her hearing aid. Tilting his neck, he kissed the top of the flesh-coloured device.

"Don't." She batted his hand away.

"Why not?"

"I don't like it."

“I do. It’s part of you.”

“Yeah, yeah, yeah.”

He gripped her shoulders and rolled her onto her back, pinning her against the rug and staring down at her. “I’m serious. I prefer you with it.”

She sighed and stared up at him. “Alex, you really don’t have to. I know it’s ugly, you know it’s ugly, but I have to wear it, so let’s just leave it. It doesn’t have to be some big issue where you prove how much you like me by pretending you like it.”

“I’m not pretending. I think you’d look worse without it.”

“Really?” she said, sarcasm flattening the word. She tried to sit up but he kept her pinned to the ground. “Let go.”

“Not until you believe me. I’m not just saying it like some arrogant prick who thinks he can score some brownie points with a contrived compliment. I genuinely think you look better with it.”

“How can you possibly think that? It’s hideous.”

“But it makes you different…”

She grimaced at ‘different’.

“…from everyone else. I don’t know how to explain it. It makes you more than just another beautiful girl. It just… it makes you more.”

She rolled her eyes.

“And I don’t like you,” he said angrily, letting go of her shoulders. “I love you.” Red-faced, he quickly rose to his feet and began packing their empty cans and wrappers into a plastic bag before walking towards the gate. After a few paces he looked back over his shoulder; she was standing by the rug, watching him, the colours of her clothes and skin muted by the encroaching dusk.

"Come here." She spoke softly, her voice travelling uninhibited across the silent park.

He turned to face her.

"Alex."

"What?"

"Come here, please."

He slowly walked towards her and she stepped over the blanket and took his face in her hands, and then she turned her ear to him and rose onto her tiptoes so her hearing aid was level with his mouth. He leaned forward, breathing in the cherry scent of her hair, and as his lips touched the plastic she whispered, "I love you too."

That night he cried as he stared at himself in the mirror in his tiny room. It was too dark to see the tears in his reflection, but he could feel the heat of them on his cheeks and he had to muffle the sobs with his hand so as not to wake his housemates. He could not remember the last time he had cried, just that it had been a long time ago, when he was a boy.

Watching the dark window, he silently closes the door and crosses the road with the flickering streetlight batting his face. The alleyway is pitch black so he uses his phone as a torch, shining the white beam on the doors and wheelie-bins until he comes to number

27. There are two small windows above the door, both frosted and dark. He sifts through the recycling box, finding two halves of an envelope addressed to Craig and Tina Armstrong, the torn paper tossed among wine bottles and beer cans. He holds the ripped halves together and stares at the typed font, and then stuffs the envelope in his pocket and walks back towards the street.

"Do you really love me?" She studied his face as she straddled him, sliding back and forth.

"Of course I do, silly girl."

"Honestly?"

"Why don't you believe me?"

Her eyes were doll-like in the light beyond the window, part moon and part electric.

He held her thigh. "Why?"

She stopped moving, sitting all her weight down on his hips. "Why did you stop believing?"

"Believing?"

"God."

"I don't know."

"Did something happen?"

He shook his head, looking up at the ceiling beyond her shoulder.

"So, what, you just lost interest?"

"I don't know. I suppose I just got older, started asking

questions, doubting...”

“Do you think maybe it had something to do with sleeping with that girl at uni?”

“What do you mean?”

She slid off him so she was kneeling by his side with her knees digging into the mattress. “Well, you broke your promise. To Him. Maybe that makes you feel, I don’t know, unworthy or something.”

“I don’t know,” he shrugged. “Maybe.”

“And you’re quite a lustful person.”

“What?” He raised himself onto his elbows.

“Come on,” she sighed, trying to smile. “I see you checking out girls.” She stared at him, challenging him to disagree.

“When?”

“Come on, Alex, I’m not blind.”

“When?”

“All the time.” She pulled the duvet up, covering her chest.

“Emma...”

“I just think that maybe you can’t reconcile your lust with your faith; that believing makes you feel too guilty, so you just gave up.”

“I haven’t given up,” he said, surprised by the anger in his voice. “I just don’t go to church as much because I’m always with you.”

“So now it’s my fault?”

“I’m not saying that, I’m saying that...” He faded out, unable to articulate his tangled mind.

“I just worry that if you gave up your faith so easily, you could do the same with me."

"That's never going to happen." He reached out and held her neck. "I love you." He tried to pull her in but she refused, her body rigid. "Emma, I could never lose interest in you. I'm crazy about you, you know that. Emma..." She slowly softened against his hand, allowing him to draw her in so she was lying with her head on his chest as he stroked his fingers through the wispy hair at her neck, their bodies casting one shadow on the wall above the bed.

7

Sharon Gardner leans on the table with her head in her hands as tears drag mascara down her cheeks. The upstairs of the pub is all but deserted, a solitary old man and a group of teenagers the only other customers. The teenagers – two boys and two girls – watch Sharon from the sofa by the staircase, amused by the sobbing middle-aged woman, until her orange-skinned friend glares at them and they turn away, exchanging smirks. The old man peers into his pint glass, his shadow cast crookedly on the wall by the lopsided lamp behind him. Sharon's stocky boyfriend sits by her side with his tattooed arm around her shoulder.

Her friend hands her a tissue. "You're gonna get mascara all over your top."

"She only got it a couple of weeks ago."

"It's gorgeous, Shaz. Where d'ya get it?"

"Gorgeous?" She dabs her eyes. "It's Primark, Kel."

"Fine, it looks shit."

"I think it looks good."

"Shut up, Dave." She blows her nose on the tissue and drops it into her handbag on the floor, and in the same motion takes her phone out of a side pocket and checks the screen before sliding it back inside.

"Have you heard anything from him?" Kel asks.

"Nothing."

“I dunno what I’d do if it was our Lee.”

“Your Lee works in a phone shop – Frankie’s Frankie.” She downs the rest of her wine. “I need a fag. Coming?” She grabs her cigarettes from her bag as Kel finishes her drink. “Mind our bags,” she says to Dave, brushing her palm over his scalp. He nods and watches them go down the stairs and then takes his phone out and swipes at the screen as he sips his pint. Two girls in short dresses come up and walk past him towards the teenagers and he follows them with his eyes as he drains the glass, before tucking his phone in his pocket and striding towards the toilets, leaving the two handbags on the floor under the table.

Ezra slides out of a booth in the corner, holding a tray. He paces over to the table, glancing at the old man and the squawking teenagers. With his back to the stairs he loads the two wine glasses onto the tray and, with a gentle tap, knocks the empty pint onto the carpet. As he bends down to pick it up he plucks Sharon’s phone from her bag and slips it into his pocket. Straightening up, he settles the glass on the tray while scanning the room. The old man is staring straight at him. For a moment he thinks he’s noticed, but when he looks closer he sees that his eyes are rheumy and vacant. He leaves the tray and glasses in the middle of the table and strolls back over to the booth, sliding right into the corner, out of view. The toilet door swings open and Dave comes out, buckling his belt as he walks back to the table. He looks at the tray and around the room, before dropping onto his chair with a quick glance at the teenagers and returning to his phone.

There is no passcode on her Samsung. Scrolling through her messages, he finds one from a number without a name, sent just before midnight the previous day. 'Sis its me usin mates phone i'm gonna call in 5 min pick up ok.' Seven minutes after the message, a call came in from a Gloucester landline, lasting twenty seconds.

Sharon and Kel's voices rise up from below. He saves the text and landline number into his iPhone. As they emerge at the top of the stairs he tucks her Samsung inside his hand and walks to their table.

"Let me clear that away for you," he says, picking up the tray.

"Cheers," Dave mumbles.

He spills the tray on the floor by their handbags, the glasses thudding on the worn carpet. "It's ok, they're empty," he says as he kneels down, his back blocking their view of the bags as they move towards the table. As he picks up the glasses he slips the phone back inside. "Sorry about that," he mutters, looking down at the tray.

"No worries, love," Sharon smiles, "It's not the end of the world."

The rain lashes against the side of the phone booth as he dials the landline and peers out through the misted glass, watching a freight train rumble over the bridge. No answer. He hangs up and checks the number on his iPhone, seeing that it was correct, and then carefully dials again and listens as the rings go unanswered. Tom's Ford is parked under the bridge, gleaming in the moonlight. A fox darts out of the shadows and stops in the middle of the road, eyes glowing and something hanging limply from its mouth. He tries calling one more time, staring at the dial as he listens to the monotonous chime. After a few seconds the line comes alive.

"Hello?" It sounds like a young boy. He can hear the rain in the background at the other end.

"Yeah, I want to order a delivery, please."

"A delivery? Bruv, this is a phone box."

"A phone box? Where?"

"Barton."

"Which street?"

"Barton Street."

In the car he types a message to the mobile Gardner used. 'Bro its me usng mates phone need to spk got news ill call phone box in 1hr'. There is music somewhere, the bass thudding out and fading into the rain. Another train passes overhead, the vibrations shaking the car. His phone lights up. 'K'.

The shutters are down on the row of shops and the lights out in the windows above. Parked on the corner, he watches the phone booths through binoculars, the glass boxes cast in flickering light by a faulty lamppost. CCTV points down from above a launderette, the camera trained on the stretch of pavement to the right of the phones. A black hood and scarf cover everything but his eyes. His phone is on the passenger seat next to an open rucksack. With the window down he can hear the fat raindrops splashing in the puddles and the distant hum of cars on the main road.

A light goes on above the takeaway. He refocuses the binoculars and sees a woman pushing the window open. She draws on a cigarette and blows the smoke out as her free hand plays with the hem of her pink dressing gown. The boy zooms in on her face, trying to make out her expression through the downpour; there is a faint smile on her lips as she taps ash into the street and then loosens her belt, allowing her gown to hang open a few inches to reveal the inside of her breasts and thighs.

A change in the shadows on the pavement catches his eye. When he holds up the binoculars he finds himself staring into the face of Gardner as he steps out of the alleyway. His cap is low over his eyes and his hood pulled tight but the light catches the slope of his chinless jaw as he looks from side-to-side before pacing to the closest of the two phone boxes.

Leaning out the window, the woman watches Gardner as he stands by the booth, his head twitching like a bird's as he peers up and down the street. He waits for Gardner to look up and spot her but she ducks back inside before he turns her way. As Gardner pulls his phone from his pocket the light goes out in the window, drawing his attention. Ezra peers in: she's still there, an orange cigarette tip and narrow silhouette, out of sight but still watching. Gardner scans the street in either direction, pausing for a second on the house opposite the takeaway as though he's seen something in one of the windows.

The boy zooms in on his face, watching as he looks up at the woman's window again and then back down at the phone in his hand. With a shake of the head he starts towards the alleyway. Ezra grabs his phone and calls the box. The shrill ring stops Gardner mid-stride. He stares at the booth and then hurries over and opens the door.

"Sis?"

Ezra holds his phone out to the rain.

"Sis? You there? Can you hear me?"

The tinny words from the speaker are a split-second behind Gardner's lips as Ezra watches him through the glass wall.

"Sharon? Sharon?"

Ezra hangs up. The woman is still in the window, her silhouette a darker shade of black than the room behind her. Gardner fishes in his pocket and slots a coin into the phone. Ezra stares at his mobile, waiting for the silent flash of the incoming call. He answers immediately, speaking through the scarf. "Frankie?"

"Who's that?"

"Jon, Sharon's mate."

"Where is she?"

"Gone to call you."

"Where?"

"Payphone round the corner."

"She just called but I couldn't hear her. Tell her to try again, yeah?"

"Ok."

Gardner hangs up and shifts to his right with his head cocked in Ezra's direction. The boy slides down in the seat and holds his breath until Gardner turns back to the phone. The orange dot has gone from the window. Gardner's breath is starting to mist over the glass wall; he watches the vapour spread until he can only see the top of his hood and his legs. The rain intensifies, drumming on the tarmac. Ezra calls the payphone again. It rings once before Gardner picks up and he can hear his voice growing louder as he leaves the mobile on the seat, grabs the 9mm from the bag and slips out of the car.

Gardner is still calling out his sister's name as Ezra moves diagonally across the road, outside of the CCTV camera's range. He creeps towards the back of the second payphone and presses himself against the wet steel. The rain pounds on the booths, almost drowning out Gardner as he slams the phone down and hisses, "For fuck's sake." His hand trembles around the gun. He looks at the car and sees the phone light rising from the passenger seat. "Come on, for fuck's sake," Gardner yells, his voice cutting through the walls between them. "Pick up the fucking phone." He hears the receiver being slammed down and the door hinges whining. Craning his neck, he watches Gardner stride away as he holds the gun by his thigh, the latex glove sticking to his sweaty palm. Gardner is a dark blur as he disappears into the mouth of the alleyway. Ezra follows, his footsteps muffled by the rain. He slips a torch out of his pocket and clicks the switch, illuminating Gardner in a shock of light. He spins around, palm raised and squinting. A hiss of breath escapes him as he sees the levelled 9mm.

"I did what you said."

"What?"

"I did what you said."

"What who said?"

"You. You."

"What do you mean?" His hand trembles as he holds the torch, vibrating Gardner's shadow on the cobbles.

"You told me to kill him. You told me to."

"Who did?"

"You did," he squeals. "I did what you said."

"What are you on about? We know what happened. The councillor – Jordan – he warned you..."

"Kerry's dad?"

"Yes.

"What? I don't…" He starts slowly moving his hand to his eyes, blocking the light.

"Don't," Ezra snaps. "Who do you think I am?"

"Fuck. Fuck." He starts to hyperventilate, his whole body bobbing as he sucks in air. "I thought you were one of them."

"Who's them?"

"They made me do it. I didn't want to, I swear. On my mum's grave. Swear down."

"Quiet," he barks, his voice cracking. "Who made you do it?"

Gardner wheezes, trying to control his breathing. "They came up to me in the street, two of them, and said he was coming for me."

"Tom?"

"Yeah, but I'd never seen him before. I only know now 'cause of the news. They showed me a photo."

"Why?"

"They said he was fucking Kerry."

"Tom?"

"Yeah. They said he was coming to kill me and take her away and they gave me a gun."

"And you believed them? What did Kerry say?"

"Nothing. She told me to come over then she wouldn't answer her phone."

"So you just believed them?"

"He came, didn't he?"

"But he tried to talk to you."

"And then pulled a gun out, just like they said he would."

"So you shot him."

"What else could I do? Stand there and take it?"

Ezra is silent, his mind a dense blur.

"Who are you?"

When the boy speaks his voice is slow and quiet. "He was there to kill you because of the way you treated Kerry."

"What? The way I treated her?"

"You hit her."

"What? Who said that? I've never touched her. I swear down, on my mum's grave. I love her. Ask her."

The boy is silent, his eyes fixed.

"Ask her, go and ask her, I swear down. I'd never touch her. I love her. I'm crazy about her. I swear I'm telling you the truth. I swear."

"What they said about her and Tom..."

"Fucking lies. She'd never do that. She's mine."

"Have you asked her?"

"She won't answer her phone."

The boy studies him in silence. Gardner's stench – beer, tobacco, sweat, piss – permeates the distance between them.

"The two men? Have you seen them since?"

He shakes his head. "I've been here, at my mate's. I'm gonna go away. I'm just waiting for her. We'll go abroad. You won't ever see me again, swear down."

"Don't move," he says after a few seconds, and then slowly lays the torch on the ground, the beam on Gardner's dirty Nikes. He takes his phone out of his pocket and opens the picture of Peter in the coffee shop. "Is this one of them?"

Gardner edges forward until he's a metre away, watching the boy's finger on the trigger. His eyes reveal nothing when he sees the photo, but there is a reaction when he peers at Ezra's eyes between the hood and scarf, his jaw tightening as he sees how young he is.

"So?"

"They were younger." His voice is looser. "I know him, though.

He's a magistrate. I've been in his court. I can take you to him."

"What did they look like?"

"Dunno. They were covered up like you. Looked like one had a beard; the other was black or mixed."

"How old?"

"Dunno. Thirties maybe."

"Back," he nods to where he'd been standing and Gardner slowly steps backwards, his face disappearing into the darkness, only his feet lit.

The boy pushes the phone into his pocket. As he crouches to pick up the torch Gardner jolts forward, his Nikes scything through the beam. The boy fires but he keeps coming, tackling him as he rises, their bodies crashing back onto the cobbles, out of the light, Gardner on top of him, his weight on his chest, his breath on his face, one hand grasping for his throat, the other reaching for the gun in his hand. Ezra cranes his wrist and squeezes the trigger, hearing the crack of the shot and its echo bouncing away and fading out. Gardner collapses onto him, a dead weight against his forehead. The boy wriggles out from under him, his fist tight around the gun, still aiming. He pushes himself to his feet and snatches up the torch. The left side of Gardner's head is gone, just a pulp of blood and flesh. There is a hole in his jeans where the first bullet hit, the ragged denim soaked crimson.

A window lights up on the other side of the wall. He snaps off the torch and runs, sprinting out of the alleyway and across the road, sensing movement in the dark window opposite the takeaway. He wrenches the car door open and slides inside, fumbling with the key in the ignition. Grabbing the torch, he leans down and shines the beam on the hole and guides the key into the lock. Headlights off, he starts to pull out but stalls the car. He restarts the engine and lurches towards the junction as sirens wail in the distance.

8

A forensic officer emerges from the alleyway, her white boiler suit reflecting the blinking streetlight. She walks over to another officer – a man laying out numbered yellow triangles by the phone boxes – and says something in his ear and he nods. A cruiser is parked in front of the laundrette, its blue lights silently twirling across Tina as she speaks to a plainclothes detective. The squat officer holds a huge umbrella over her and she stands with one arm supporting the other as she smokes.

"So he ran across the street?"

"Yeah," Alex says, dragging his gaze back to the constable.

"Did you hear a car engine?" She holds the pen poised over the notepad, her coat dripping rainwater on the doormat.

"I think so. It was hard to tell with the rain so loud."

She nods as she writes. "Ok, Alex, let's go through this, make sure we've got everything. So you're looking out your window and you see the deceased outside the phone box. He goes in and makes a call. He leaves the box and walks towards the alleyway. Then a man appears – you didn't see where from – and follows him into the alleyway. A few minutes later, the same man runs out of the alleyway, across the road and, you think, gets into a car."

"Yeah. That's all I saw."

She glances up. "And the man was wearing a black jacket, hood up, about six foot."

He nods and points over her shoulder at the camera above the laundrette. “The CCTV must have got him.”

“We’re checking. Anything else?”

“Maybe. I think I might have heard another car pulling away, a second car. There was the first one, then as I was speaking to the woman in the control room, another, I think.”

Tina is lighting another cigarette as he closes the door on the constable, the tip of her nose orange in the flame, the rest of her face shrouded in the shadow of the detective’s umbrella.

*

Ezra stops the Ford halfway down the track and shuts off the lights and the woodland vanishes into the pitch black. He gets out and stands by the side of the car, listening: the only sound is the rain hitting the leaves. He grabs the torch from the inside of the door and clicks the light to the lowest setting, pointing the beam at the muddy path as he walks to the back of the car. The boot wheezes as he lifts it open. As he looks inside at the contents – a bin liner, holdall, shovel, small oil drum, two litre bottles of water and a plastic toolbox – he recalls Tom’s voice: “You create compartments in your mind and put the bad stuff inside and lock the door. It works, trust me. It’s like it never happened. Peter taught me.”

He takes out a screwdriver and uses it to remove the rear licence plate, and then he goes round to the front and does the same. When he's finished he puts them in the boot and then digs into the holdall and pulls out two matching licence plates tied together by a rubber band. Halfway through fixing on the back plate he hears a rustling in the bushes, something moving by his elbow. He jerks the torch towards the sound but the only movement is the leaves trembling as the raindrops hit.

He paces to the front of the car and takes the gun from the bag. After fixing in the last screw, he grabs the liner and holdall and tosses them on the backseat and climbs inside. Resting the flashlight on the back shelf, he strips off the cheap trainers and grey tracksuit and stuffs them into the liner, on top of the blood-specked outfit he was wearing earlier. Reaching into the holdall, he unties a shopping bag and pulls out a blue sweater and jeans, both still tagged. Leaning against the backrest, he stretches his legs between the front seats and hauls on the jeans and sweater before climbing forward and sliding into the driver's seat. He starts the engine and crawls further along the track, following the potholed tarmac for half a mile as it winds and narrows and eventually disintegrates into gravel and scrubland.

Sitting in the passenger seat with the door open, he pulls on a raincoat and wellies and leaves the headlights on as he follows the beams through the grass and weeds, the barrel of the gun cold against his spine. As he nears the end of the headlight's reach he clicks on the torch and keeps walking, squelching through the mud and reeds until he can see the glimmer of water and hear the rain on the marsh. He pushes the handle of the torch into the mud so that the beam is shooting upwards and walks back towards the headlights.

As he reaches the car he hears a sound like a cough somewhere to his left. He grabs at the 9mm but the handle slips in his wet glove and the gun falls onto the grass with a thud. He drops to the ground, scoops up the weapon and points it into the darkness where the noise came from. As he lies in the wet grass, listening to the silence, all he can see is his own breath spraying out in short, sharp bursts.

After a minute he slowly rises to his feet and, listening to every rustle with the gun poised, slowly walks to the back of the car and grabs the oil drum from the boot. The bottle of lighter fluid and box of matches rattle inside the iron barrel as he makes his way through the mud towards the column of light. He wedges the drum into the earth and returns to the car for the holdall and licence plates. Lit by the torch, he empties the bag into the drum and then tosses it in too, before squirting the lighter fluid on top, striking a match and dropping it inside. Nothing happens. He sparks another match and holds the flame to the scarf and the frayed edge catches light and then the fire spreads, filling the drum and licking up at the rim, the orange glow like the sun on Tom's anxious face as they waited in the hospital room before the surgery and then again before the plaster came off to reveal the thick purple scar above his lip, and both times he felt safe because Tom was there, the sensation surreal because it was so new, because with Tom there was no underlying fear that he could turn abuser at any moment – there was only warmth.

“I want to tell you what happened. You deserve to know. From me. I know you think about it, you must remember bits.” Tom’s face was cut with shadow as he spoke, sitting awkwardly on the windowsill in the boy’s bedroom.

Ezra watched from his bed, still half asleep, the pallid dawn a grey rim around the curtain.

“We were hired by the mother of a boy called Daniel Benjamin. There wasn’t enough evidence against Jim but David knew he’d done it. We found out where he was staying.” He stared into his cupped hands as he spoke. “I pretended to be a dealer, told him I had strong heroin. It was stuff David had seized and mixed. When I went back she was there. She said she wanted some too but he wouldn’t share – said he’d made the money so it was his. She offered herself to me. Then she said she had a kid next door and I could do whatever I wanted. I thought she was joking at first but it was in her eyes. I looked in next door and there you were, covered in bruises and shivering. So I went back in and gave them both what they asked for. Then I took you with me.”

When he finished he looked up at the boy, his eyes dry and red. Ezra felt as though his mind was flooding, words and sentences swept away as his thoughts drowned. Eventually he croaked out an “Ok,” and Tom must have taken from his expression that he wanted to be alone because he quietly padded away, stopping in the doorway and looking back briefly before he disappeared into the hallway.

He kept thinking of the times he had awoken to the sound of

Tom quietly sobbing in his bedroom next door, and the moments when he had suddenly realised he wasn't around and gone into the hallway and heard water running in the bathroom and pressed his ear to the door and found Tom crying, his deep voice coming out in muffled howls.

Two hours later, the boy appeared in the living room doorway, finding Tom slumped on the sofa in a daze. He sat upright and they stared at each other in blank-faced silence, their eyes locked, and then he said, "Would you like some breakfast?" and the boy nodded.

Once his clothes are just pulp beneath the flames, he takes the sim card out of his mobile and cuts it in four with a pair of scissors and tosses the pieces and the handset into the barrel. As the plastic melts he shines the torch on the marsh and hurls the licence plates in, watching them hit the water at the edge of the pool of light and stay under. Gripping the gun by his side, he goes back to the car for the bottles of water and returns to the drum and puts out the fire. He sifts through the lumps of gluey ash, making sure the clothes are indistinguishable, and then he tips the drum onto its side and rolls it in the cold mud with his foot. When the sides are cool enough he picks up the barrel and heaves it into the marsh. It bobs on the surface for a few seconds, the rusted iron dully reflecting the torchlight before slowly sinking. Back in the car, he crawls through the woodland with the headlights dipped until he is around a mile from the marsh and then climbs out and takes the shovel from the boot and tucks the 9mm into his waistband and points the torch ahead. The branches are like withered arms reaching for the light as he walks towards a yard of earth between two gnarled trunks. In the yellow haze from the embedded torch he digs a hole two feet deep and then wipes down the 9mm with his sleeve before carefully laying the gun inside. Gardner's words echo through his mind as he buries the weapon in the deathly silence of untouched nature.

*

She stands in the window, a black outline behind a glowing cigarette. He sits at the computer, webbing his grainy photos of the crime scene. As he texts the news editor to say the story is live, the light springs on in her window and she moves into view, looking straight at him and waving with the gown tied loosely at her waist. He parts the curtains and she gestures for him to come over, pointing down at the street, and he sees that their car is no longer in the side road.

"In here," she whispers from the doorway as he walks around the cordon with the eyes of a PC fixed on his face.

"I can't believe it." She wedges the door open, standing on the threshold with the light at her back. "I mean…" she shakes her head, "I know it's Barton but, still, fucking hell..."

"I know. What did the police say?"

"Nothing. They just asked me what I seen. You?" She folds her arms across her chest, the thin gown pulled tight over her breasts.

"Same. I couldn't see much because of the rain."

"Me neither. The one what got shot, he was waiting for a call in the phone box so… a set up or something?"

"Did you see where he went?"

"He got in a car and drove off."

"Was there another car? That left a bit after him?"

"I dunno, I went to get my phone."

"I thought I heard another car."

She shrugs and looks him up and down. "Where are you from then?"

"York."

"I thought you sounded weird."

He smiles and looks down at the ground with his hands in his pockets.

"D'ya smoke?"

"No."

"Well I need one." She turns into the hallway. "Come up while I have one." He glances at the PC and follows her up the stairs. The landing is whitewashed with no pictures on the walls and the smell of greasy food lingering. They pass the living room/kitchen and again there are no photographs, just white walls and black furniture. "So why did you move here then?" she asks as she leads him into the bedroom, glancing back over her shoulder. The room seems smaller from the inside; the end he can't see from his window extends far less than he pictured.

"Work."

As she walks to the window he looks past her to his own room where the glow from the computer screen outlines the desk and chair.

"Where do you work?"

"The local paper."

"The Citizen?" She lights up and perches on the sill, facing him, the gown just above her thighs. He stands by the end of the bed, his shadow a formless stain on the wall. "You gonna do a story on this then?"

"I just have."

As she blows smoke out of the window she stares down at the street, watching the forensic officers. "You're better off up north." She shakes her head and turns to him. "How old are you then?"

"Twenty-two."

"Fuck," she snorts, "that's young." She takes another drag and slides back on the sill, her legs slightly parted, a flash of skin among the shadows between her thighs. "How old d'ya think I am?"

He pretends to consider the question. Up close her eyes look heavier and her jawline softer. "Thirties?"

She laughs, puffing smoke above her head. "You are a charmer, ain't ya?"

He smiles, his mouth dry.

"D'ya like watching me then?"

He nods.

"Why?"

Shrugging, he murmurs, "You're hot."

As she leans across to stub out the cigarette her gown slips open. She pushes the ashtray aside and sits back against the window with a smile playing on her lips.

"Where's your husband?"

They lay side-by-side on the bed, his jeans rucked around his ankles and the taste of her cigarettes on his tongue. When she speaks her voice is rough with sarcasm. "At a business meeting. He'll be back soon."

"Why are you with him?" He tilts his head to look at her.

She rolls onto her side and lays her palm on his chest. "There's something very, I dunno... warm about you."

"Warm?"

"Your face, voice… you seem innocent. Sweet."

"I don't know about that."

"D'ya think I can do better?"

"Than him? Of course."

"Maybe. I didn't do better before him."

"The bald guy last night. Earlier tonight. Is that…?"

She chuckles, a rotten base to her breath. "You're not that innocent."

Her phone lights up on the bedside cabinet. She rolls over and checks the screen. "You better go."

“Will he even care?”

“Yes. A lot.”

She stands at the window with her arms folded, watching for the car, as he dresses in silence. “Ready?” He nods and she strides ahead. Her hair is tied back and he can see white marks behind her ears where the sunbed can’t reach.

“Tomorrow?” He says, stepping into the alleyway and turning to face her.

She nods as she closes the door, her eyes suddenly hard.

As he crosses the road headlights glide along the parked cars and he sees the silver Volkswagen approaching. Head down, he jogs past the PC and jabs his key into the lock, feeling the officer’s eyes on his back. In the hallway he holds the door open a crack and watches her husband pull into the space. She’s standing in the window, watching him too. She drops the blinds.

*

Jo answers the door in a dressing gown and fluffy panda slippers. “What’s wrong?”

“I need to talk to him.”

She holds the door open but he shakes his head, gripping the gun in his pocket. Light spills into the alleyway as a car goes past in the street. The rubbish bags have gone but the stench lingers.

“What is it, love?”

"Can you call him?"

"Come in." She studies his face: his eyes are feverish. "Derek will call him."

He stares at her like he's inspecting a painting for the hidden meaning. "Tom – did he say anything to you about Gardner?"

"Like what?"

He shrugs and turns away, looking at the slithers of light as another car passes.

"Well are you coming in, then? It's bloody freezing."

"What's wrong?" Derek asks, peering around the edge of the armchair as the boy comes into the kitchen with Jo struggling up the stairs behind him.

"He said something. He..."

"He's dead, though?" Derek snaps. "You did it?"

The boy nods.

Derek points the remote at the TV, plunging the room into moon-tinged darkness. Jo hobbles over to the corner and turns on a lamp. "Well?" he grunts.

"He said two men told him Tom was coming and gave him a gun."

"What? When?" Jo asks, taking the boy's elbow and steering him to the sofa by the window.

"He didn't say. That day, I think."

"Where were you?"

"Barton, in that alleyway behind the launderette."

"And you had a gun on him?" Derek asks, the moonlight giving his liver-spotted head a silver-blue tint.

Ezra nods. Jo is still holding his arm, her shoulder pressed to his as they sit on the two-seater sofa.

"Well, you can't really believe him then, can you? He'd have said anything."

"What else did he say?" Jo asks, giving Derek a scalding glance as she turns to the boy.

"That Tom had been seeing his girlfriend, Kerry."

As the words leave his mouth Jo turns to Derek, their eyes narrowed in unison.

"Was he?"

"No," Derek grunts at the boy.

"Did he describe them?" Jo says, breaking the silence. "The two men?"

"He said they were covered up, but one had a beard and one was black or mixed, and they were both in their 30s."

Again their eyes meet.

"You know them?"

"Come on, son, how many people are there with beards and dark skin? It could be anyone. Sounds made up to me, like he's been playing Guess Who – does he have a beard? Is he black? We know what happened: the councillor changed his mind and warned Gardner. That's it. Done."

"If he changed his mind why didn't he just call it off? Why tell

Gardner? Why not just call Peter or David? He must have known we'd come after him for Tom."

"I don't know, maybe it was too late? Maybe he changed his mind last minute?" He shakes his head. "Don't go trying to work people out, son. Most people don't know why they do anything, they just do it."

Confusion glints in Jo's eyes as she stares at her husband. "We have to tell him."

"Jo..." Derek turns away, unable to bear her gaze.

"Derek," she barks. "Call him."

The old man sighs and struggles to his feet before shuffling into the bedroom and closing the door.

"You're staying here tonight," Jo says to Ezra, squeezing his arm, her antiseptic smell closing in around him.

"I'm ok at home."

"You're in shock, love. What you've just done, and the councillor; it will haunt you – don't lie to yourself. What did Tom tell you? That you can put it in a cupboard at the back of your mind and lock the door?"

The boy nods faintly.

"You can't, love. I saw it with our Tony, before he… well, you know what he did, I expect. Coward's way out – that's what Derek calls it. But we don't know what was going on in his head; you never know, like he just said himself." She grips his elbow tighter, her eyes damp in the lamplight. "Stay, love."

"Ok."

She smiles, her eyes creasing to a slit of blue. "We can get to know you properly. Tom never wanted to bring you over, he wanted to keep you out of all this; I don't blame him. How are you feeling, love?"

He shrugs, an exhausted numbness spreading through him.

"Grief makes people – well, it's a form of madness; you're not yourself. When we heard about Tony, our Steve went straight round to Blacklock's house… Did Tom tell you about all that?"

He shakes his head.

"We never talk about it – Derek can't. Blacklock was a dealer; he got Tony hooked – he always was a weak boy – and said Tony owed him loads of money and, with Tony's problems, it just all added up on him and…" She blinks twice "… he hung himself and so Steve went round to Blacklock's and smashed the windows and when he came out he smashed his head in. All with the same tyre iron. One son dead and another in prison like that –" She snaps her fingers in a sudden fury-filled motion. "We spent all our savings on his legal fees. Had to sell the taxis too. Got him manslaughter instead of murder, 14 years instead of life." She coughs, a dry hacking sound, and tries to smile. "I'm always sick. Anyway, that's how we met Peter and David. They could see that our Steve was just as much a victim as Tony, that Blacklock was the real bad guy. They offered to protect him in prison, and we started being their messengers and met Tom. We get paid – we had to, Steve's fees left us skint – but that's not why we do it. We do it for the same reason Tom did, for the reason you do it now: to get rid of scum like Blacklock. To stop the Gardners and Big Jim's of the world hurting more people. I don't feel guilty. It haunts you, it does – I see their faces at night, in dreams – but I don't regret it."

As the final sentence leaves her lips she realises that her voice has risen to almost a shout and she smiles faintly and shakes her head. "That's the first time I've said all that out loud. Moaning old woman, eh? Why does it always feel better to say it out loud? If you want to, love, I'm always here to listen." She pats his hand, her knotty fingers tapping the broad knuckles of his clenched fist, and then she turns to the bedroom door. "What's taking him so long?" She lifts her hand away and struggles to her feet.

There are two sharp knocks on the door downstairs and then Derek emerges from the bedroom. "That's him," he says to Ezra. "He wants to talk to you alone."

"It's three in the morning," Jo says, sitting back down and holding the boy's wrist. "Where's he taking him?"

"When did we start asking questions?" Derek grunts, and then he turns to the boy. "Go on then, he's waiting."

Jo slowly releases her grip as Ezra rises to his feet, and she hobbles after him as he goes for the stairs.

The hallway light spills across Peter's face, drawing him from the shadows of the alleyway. His eyes are bright behind his glasses as he stands with his hands buried deep in the pockets of a camelhair overcoat. "You did the right thing, insisting on seeing me." He turns away into the darkness. “I want to show you something. You can tell me what Gardner said on the way.”

As Ezra pulls the door shut he sees Jo halfway down the stairs, her face twisted in fear.

9

"We could take up to 25 women and their children too, if necessary," the magistrate says, gazing at the unfinished roof beyond the hoardings. "Counselling rooms, communal lounges, a gym – it'll have everything."

The building is a four-storey windowless shell hidden from the road by a screen of freshly-planted trees. They sit in his palatial Jaguar, the polished bonnet an inch from the locked entrance gate. "There's nothing else like it here. I'm surprised Tom didn't mention it. Did he talk about me much?"

"A bit," the boy says, glancing in the wing-mirror: the narrow access road is pitch black with the tall fences blocking out the moonlight, and the light of the city centre is just an ochre pinprick in the glass. There are muddy tyre prints on the wet tarmac but no so sign of any vehicles in the construction site beyond the gate, just a dormant crane looming over the building.

"Hope House. Hope was Helen's maiden name, and the women who come here will see that there is hope beyond abuse and violence." His eyes burn as he speaks, the whites iridescent through the jail-bar shadows that fall from the iron gate. "If people knew what we were doing – can you imagine the headlines? 'Murder-for-hire gang', 'Hitmen killed dozens'." He shakes his head, smiling to himself. "They would be suitably appalled and indignant in public but secretly part of them would understand, would admire, what we've done. We've stopped rapists, paedophiles, drug pushers – stopped people who caused damage wherever they went, and would only continue to do so. People who did not deserve the gift of life." He turns to the boy and Ezra briefly meets his gaze before looking back down at his hands in his lap. "As you get older, son, you'll learn that people say they want to make the world a better place but actually all they want is to make themselves feel better about their place in the world. They volunteer with charities, donate £10 a month to Oxfam, but it's all about their ego, and they risk nothing. We physically make our part of the world better by removing the things that make it worse, and we risk everything. But we choose to take that risk because we believe so passionately in making this place better. Tom lost his life, but if he could speak now I firmly believe he would say that he regretted nothing." He peers up at the pale crescent moon over the half-done roof. "Yes, we get paid – we have to eat and pay bills like everyone else – but it's never been about money. It's always been about making a difference, and this" – he points at the brick structure – "will make a difference. This is my legacy – our legacy."

Peter reaches inside his coat and the boy has to fight the impulse to flinch towards the door. He pulls out a monogrammed handkerchief, the PA sewn in royal blue on the white silk, and then he takes off his glasses and wipes the misted lenses. "It's so good to talk to you, son," he says, fixing the spectacles behind his ears and turning to the boy. "It feels like a long time since I talked to someone properly."

"What about Tom and David?"

He dismisses the question with a curt shake of his head. "Did Tom ever tell you how all this started?"

"Kind of." The words eek out, stifled by his dry throat.

"I always regretted that he didn't let me see you more. I understood why he wanted to keep you out of it but, well, look at you: this is who you are." He shrugs, his frail shoulders barely moving the sleeves of his thick coat. "Earlier I told you that I was 17 when my father left us for a man; I was actually 12. I don't know why I said 17. Can you imagine my teenage years at school after word of that spread?" Smiling weakly, he glances at the dashboard clock and then opens the door and climbs out. A warning sound beeps as he walks towards the gate and opens the padlock and wrenches the railings apart. When he turns back to the car his eyes are lost in the glare of the headlights on his glasses. He slides inside and pushes the gear into drive and as they roll forward the boy peers into the wing-mirror, looking for a silhouette to emerge into the light at the end of the dark road, but the yellow haze remains unchanged.

"So what are we doing here?" he asks, trying to control his voice.

"Waiting for someone."

"Who?"

"Someone who can shed some light on what Gardner told you."

They follow the dirt road around the back of the refuge and pull up by the hole in the bricks for the patio door, out of sight from the gate. "Did Tom tell you what happened to my wife?" He turns off the headlights, plunging the site into darkness. "It was David who broke the news. I didn't know him at the time. When the police knock on your door in the middle of the night, you know it's bad news." He gazes at his wedding ring as he grips the steering wheel; the band is loose on his finger. "She was walking home from the station. She always preferred to walk, even in the rain. She took the Honeybourne Line and he was waiting for her. He was waiting for any woman, it just happened to be her. Fate, if you believe in that – I don't. There was no-one around at that time of night. He had all the time he needed." He glances at the boy, who stares ahead into the darkness. "I'd see her name and picture in the paper, above 'raped' and 'murdered', and…"

Headlights slash through the barred gate. Peter looks back over his shoulder, his neck an inch from Ezra as he peers through the rear window, his leather and wood cologne shrouding the boy. His hands move in the dark between the seats and then there is a faint glimmer, something shining, and he is holding out a gun and looking straight into the boy's eyes. It takes Ezra a second to realise that he is holding the barrel to offer him the weapon. "The man coming," he says slowly, seeing the panic in the boy's eyes, "I think he's one of the men who warned Gardner."

"Who is he?"

"Saul Wiseman. A friend of David's."

"Why would he do it?"

There is a buzzing sound and Peter looks down at his pocket. “That’s him.” He raises the gun, the handle pointed at the boy’s neck. “I need you to stay here with this, just in case. He’ll have one.”

Ezra looks at him as though trying to work out an equation.

“I know how you feel, of all people,” the magistrate says, his voice hoarse. “I never really had any answers with Helen other than that Flynn was evil. But why? What made him that way? Why her? Why not another woman, five minutes earlier or later?”

“He didn’t say?”

He shakes his head. “Wouldn’t talk.”

“You had him killed in prison.”

“Did Tom tell you that?”

“No.” He shrugs. “Seems obvious.”

His phone buzzes again, the screen light rising from his pocket. “I want answers for Tom. For you and me.”

Ezra holds out his hand and Peter lays the gun in his palm. “Only if he goes for me.” The boy nods and clenches his fist around the snub-nosed pistol. The magistrate squeezes his shoulder and then opens the door and slides out, instantly disappearing into the pitch black. A few seconds later his silhouette emerges in the yellow beams as he walks towards the gate, and then the headlights cut out, sucking him back into the grainy darkness. Ezra slips between the seats into the back and winds down the window to rest the short barrel on the frame. He peers towards the gate, looking for movement, but the moon is too weak to shape outlines.

Pressure builds in his chest and he realises that he is holding his breath. He feels his T-shirt sticking to his damp back and the sweat pooling around his eyes. He hears the groan of a metal hinge and iron hitting iron, and then the hum of an engine growing closer. Dimmed headlights thrust through the dark and cling to the edge of the building. The car, some kind of saloon, stops by the corner wall and he recognises Peter's figure as he steps into the ochre haze of the headlamps. Saul joins him in front of the bonnet, his frame swallowing far more of the faint light. They are 20 metres away, too far for Ezra to hear anything but the indistinct murmur of their voices.

Minutes tick by, their words lost in the rain. His arms grow numb from holding the gun as he lies chest-down with his elbows wedged into the seat and the seatbelt buckle digging into his hip. Sweat rolls down his temples and soaks the collar of his coat. There is a sudden blur of motion: the two silhouettes shift and Saul's arm juts out towards Peter, who flinches back into the fringe of the light. Ezra presses his wrists into the window frame to steady his hands and holds his breath, fleetingly recalling Tom's instructions in the abandoned warehouse as he fired at burnt mannequins: "Breathe out with the bullet". Saul lurches towards Peter. The boy shoots. There is a dull thud as the bullet slams into the bonnet. Saul jerks towards him. He fires again and the windscreen shatters. Peter has vanished into the darkness. Saul dives towards the driver's side and Ezra squeezes the trigger again. His shadow seizes mid-flight and collapses as if sliding off his body. Peter's silhouette scythes through the light and merges with Saul's black mass before the headlamp. Their outline divides as the magistrate steps back with his arm pointed down.

"Ezra!" His yell slashes through the rain. "Ezra!"

The boy shoves the door open and sprints through the mud. Saul lies curled like a foetus, holding the side of his neck, the blood on his fingers like oil in the yellow beam. Peter aims a gun at his head, his eyes masked by the light slanting across his glasses.

"He told Gardner." His voice is a scorched growl.

"Why?"

"Ask him."

Ezra steps closer. Saul's face is ashen above his black beard. "Why?"

His lips twitch but no sound emerges.

He crouches over him. "Why did you do it?"

His eyes are frosting over. He tries to raise his head but his neck is limp.

Ezra looks up at Peter. "What did he say?"

"I told him what Gardner said, asked him if it was true, and he pulled out this." He nods to the 9mm in his hand.

"He didn't say why?"

"You started shooting."

"I thought he was going to kill you."

"He was."

Peter steps towards Saul, the gun trained on the side of his head. He bends down and feels his pulse, his hands covered by leather gloves he hadn't been wearing in the car. He looks at the boy and shakes his head, and then slips the gun into his pocket and straightens up and walks to the driver's side and leans in and turns off the lights.

"Help me move him," his voice is bodiless in the dark, and then he appears by the boy's side, one gloved hand on his shoulder and the other pointing to the trees at the back of the site, the branches ghost-like in the anaemic moon.

The boy pushes the pistol into his pocket and grabs Saul's ankles. They lift his heavy frame and struggle towards the trees. Peter leads the way, Saul's head resting on his hip, the hole in his blood-soaked neck exposed. "Here," he says, nodding at the strip of earth at the edge of the copse. They lower the body and Peter turns towards his car. "There's a shovel in the boot, I think."

As the boy watches the magistrate move away the reality of the situation floods through the numbness. He thinks about running, of disappearing into the trees and not looking back, but he pictures Tom's face – bathing him as a child, teaching him at their kitchen table school, standing between the posts as he practised free kicks – and the images entwine with those of Peter and Jo, their eyes desolate and forsaken, and he keeps watching as the magistrate fades into the dark and then re-emerges with a shovel in his hand.

The Jaguar's headlamps pull the tiny mariners' church from the darkness of the docks as Peter rolls the car over the deserted boulevard. The edge of the light falls across the canal and the sound of a dog whining reaches out to them from the moored barge boats. Peter stops before the shuttered convenience store on the corner, his eyes rising to an apartment on the fourth floor where the curtained window reflects the cloudless sky.

"Have you been back yet?"

Ezra shakes his head.

"Where have you been staying?"

"Hotels."

"You could have stayed with me. Tom did for a while, after his parents and Nunn. Did he tell you?"

The boy nods, glancing at the magistrate as he peers up at the smoky moonlight on the flat's window.

"We had Christmas together. Then he met Sarah and… did you know about Sarah?"

"No. Who was she?"

"I suppose she left almost straight after you came along."

"He never mentioned her."

"I thought he told you everything."

"He did." His fingers dig into his thighs. "What happened?"

"They were together for a few years. She lived with him in the flat in Westgate where you were at first. She didn't know about us, of course." He pauses, seeing the boy's expression. "Anyway, never mind about that. It's all history now."

"Tell me." He shifts in the seat. "I need to know."

"Well, when you came along he told her you were the son of a friend who'd died in a crash, but she didn't want to take you in. She said it would change their lives, make her your mother by default, that you'd be better with a family that wanted you. But Tom wouldn't change his mind."

"So she left?" His voice is weak. "He never said anything."

"He always put you first, son."

They sit in silence, staring up at the window. "What now?"

"We find the other man."

"You know who he is?"

"Possibly."

"Who?"

"He's called Micah."

Ezra starts to speak but Peter cuts him off. "I don't know where he is. He moves around. Just leave it with me for now, I'll find out." He glances at the dashboard clock: 04:18. "We both need some sleep. It's been a long night. I'll be in touch tomorrow."

"I threw my phone away."

He reaches across the boy to the glovebox and takes out an iPhone in a cellophane wrapper and hands it to him. "I'll call you in the morning." He glances up at the window. "Are you sure you want to stay here tonight? I have lots of spare rooms."

"I'll be ok."

"Tom would be proud of you, son." He lays his hand on his shoulder. "I'll be in touch."

Ezra watches the Jaguar round the corner and the afterglow fade into the night, and then he sets off towards the car park and strides through the empty spaces. He criss-crosses through the backstreets with his hood up until he reaches the old Ford in the road behind Derek and Jo's flat. Watching their window, he silently opens the door and slips inside and then starts the engine and pulls away, heading for Stroud.

All the windows are boarded up in the cottage. The gate hangs off the hinge and the short driveway is a tangle of weeds. As soon as his key goes into the door he hears the dog's claws on the floorboards. The mongrel scurries around his legs as he turns the lock, pawing at his ankles with his remaining front leg and panting and wheezing but not barking, never barking, his face – some kind of Jack Russell cross – always calm, and he hops after the boy as he strides into the kitchen. Leaving the light off, he peers out of the window at the tiny yard and then carefully picks up the newspaper the dog has used and stuffs it into a carrier bag and drops it inside a bin bag. He presses his ear to the frosted glass before opening the back door and tossing the liner into a pile in the yard. The dog licks his hand as he spoons food into his blue bowl and then wolfs down the chunks, oblivious to the boy as he changes the water in his red bowl and pours crunchies into the white one. Leaning on the fridge, he watches the dog eat: his tiny head is buried in the bowl as his stump of a tail wags ever so slightly. Ezra sets a loaf of bread and tub of margarine on the counter but then puts them back in the fridge, his stomach too restless to take food.

He climbs the creaking staircase to the bathroom and brushes his teeth and washes his face in the dark. As he dries off he hears the dog gnawing at the crunchies with his few remaining teeth. The main bedroom faces the narrow one-way street, the window boarded up. As he undresses he looks at the rectangle on the wallpaper where a picture once hung, and then lies on the mattress with the door ajar. The photograph of Tom with his parents and the car is propped against the skirting board by his pillow. The dog's claws tap the wooden steps. "Come on," he whispers, and he feels his front leg reaching up onto his thigh and then his weight on his chest and his breath on his chin. He strokes his soft fur, feeling the warmth of his body against his heart. A tear rolls down his temple and drops onto the pillow.

His odour of stale beer and unwashed clothes would drift into the boy's dreams and haul him awake. He'd be standing in the doorway, sometimes naked, sometimes in his red tracksuit top with the frayed white stripes on the sleeves. He was a small man, skinny and slump-shouldered with a round belly. His chest looked like a graffiti wall, the pale skin covered in crude pictures of naked women and scrawled clichés. The chocolate wrapper would always catch the moonlight slanting in over the sagging curtain. "I've got this for you," he'd say in his slack-jawed Dursley drawl, and then step forward from the doorway, his silhouette no bigger than the boy's mother, so that sometimes, between sleep and consciousness, he was unsure which of them was approaching. "Here you go," he'd say, holding out the chocolate bar, the ‘Big Jim’ inked on his arm like oil in the silver light. The boy didn’t want the chocolate but the hunger was so intense he couldn’t resist. Big Jim would watch him eating, the boy holding his hand over his cleft lip as those hollow eyes penetrated his scratched and bruised body. “You don’t mind, do you?” he’d say as he pushed himself inside the boy’s mouth, and he’d shake his head, staring at the slither of sky above the curtain; he could never see the moon, just the fog-like haze where its shine faded into the black sky.

Now, occasionally, he has a dream where he is Tom killing Big Jim but, instead of carefully injecting him, he holds the syringe like a knife and stabs the needle again and again into his pockmarked face and dead-body eyes, and when he awakes he is drenched in sweat and shaking and, like a broken tap, the memories of the abuse drip, drip, drip and he cannot stop them taking form before him as he stares up at the ceiling.

10

When Alex awakes he has the sense of emerging from an intense dream, the story forgotten but images lingering – Emma's face, her jaw set in disapproval; the dark moles on Tina's naked back as she lays face down with her husband's vast shadow looming over her.

In her bathroom, surrounded by the arranged bottles, he looked down at Emma as she slumped against the bathtub, hugging her knees.

"I don't understand," he said.

She shook her head.

"It doesn't make sense."

The speckled window split the bright sunlight into weak rays.

She tilted her face, searching his eyes. "What should we do?"

He looked down at the cold tiles, a numbness spreading through him like a shot of anaesthetic. "I don't know."

They stared through the TV, their eyes on a distant point beyond the screen. The room was as dark as the sky outside, the screen as pale as the moon. He laid his fingers on her wrist.

"The longer we leave it, the harder it's going to be." His voice sounded detached, like he was listening back to a recording of himself.

She nodded faintly.

"I can call in the morning."

"Ok." She held her hair between her fingers, gazing at the split ends. "I know we can't… I know I'm still at uni and you've just started… but maybe there's…" she looked up at him as she spoke, seeing something in his face that killed each sentence as she began.

Her heels clicked on the tarmac as they crossed the surgery car park. She was wearing a grey skirt-suit – the first time he had seen her dress formally – and her hand was cold inside his.

"How are you feeling?"

She shrugged as they turned into the broad avenue. The midday sun bounced off the passing cars. He took his sunglasses out of his pocket as they cut into a small park where a handful of students laid on blankets, their voices peppering the hum of the traffic with bursts of laughter.

"It's impossible," he murmured.

"Not impossible."

He glanced at her from behind his glasses. She stared straight ahead along the footpath.

Between sleep and consciousness he felt her warm body slip away, heard a door open and close, the shower running.

When he awoke she was already dressed in her grey suit, her hair and make-up perfect, her mouth a straight red line across her blank face.

"You slept well." She watched him in the mirror as she fixed an earring into place and adjusted her hearing aid.

He propped up on his elbows. "How are you feeling?"

She shrugged, focusing on the earring.

The taxi driver flicked his cigarette onto the ground and blew the smoke out of the window. "Hospital, right, mate?"

"Yeah," he said, pulling the door shut. "Outpatients."

She stared out at the passing streets, her fingers tight around her handbag. The town centre was deserted – just a street-sweeper and a bleary eyed woman carrying her shoes – with the pavements and shuttered shops bleached a pale yellow by the dawn sun. He lifted her hand away from the bag so their fingers were entwined on the baby-seat between them. She didn't react, her eyes still fixed on the window.

"Nothing serious, I hope," the driver said, looking in the mirror.

"Just visiting."

"Visiting outpatients?"

He met his eyes in the mirror and turned away, gazing out at the lifeless stores.

In the waiting room they sat in green armchairs facing a small TV with women's magazines piled on a coffee table before them. She stared at a page, her eyes glazed. Behind them a girl no more than 16 rested her head on her knees as she hugged her shins. In front a suited woman frantically tapped at her phone with painted nails. The TV was turned down low and he could hear his own breathing.

"How are you feeling?"

She blinked, her eyes still on the magazine. "Ok."

He could sense her trembling. He laid his hand on her thigh but she ignored him. "I'll be with you all the way."

She nodded, barely moving.

A young nurse appeared in the doorway. "Emma?"

The faint colour drained from her face.

"Would you like to come with me?"

Her fingers quivered in his palm as the nurse led them into a small room with a freshly-made single bed and pointed to a folded gown on top of the sheets. "Just slip that on and make yourself comfortable. I'll be back in a minute."

She picked up the white gown and went into the en suite. A jug of water, plastic cup and magazine sat on the bedside table. He took his phone out of his pocket and looked at the latest message – his mother asking when he'd be home for a weekend – and then scrolled through the chain with Emma, back to one of the first texts she'd sent: 'Looking forward to seeing you tonight, my sex giraffe. What time do you think you'll get here? I can make lasagne XX.' He'd read it at his desk; he'd been writing about a council meeting and laughing with the other reporters about an old councillor who was obsessed with building underground car parks. After they'd eaten she'd shown him one of her favourite films, Solaris, a mournful sci-fi, and he'd held her soft feet in his hands as they watched with the lights off. When the psychologist awoke to find his dead wife alive again, he glanced at her and saw she was weeping, and he held her face in his hands and kissed her cheeks, tasting her tears, and whispered, “I love you,” and she looked up at him, the purple planet on the screen reflected in her eyes, and said, “Really?” and he nodded, and she said, “I think I’ve loved you since that first day.”

The sound of steel scraping steel jarred him out of his reverie. The bathroom door slid open and she stepped out, the loose gown a shade paler than her face. She laid flat on the bed and he squeezed her little toe, not knowing what to say.

There was a knock on the door. “Are you decent?”

The nurse stood in the doorway with something concealed in her surgical glove.

“If you could just step out for a minute, please, Alex.”

He looked at Emma; she stared down at her hands in her lap.

“Please,” the nurse said, standing aside in the doorway.

In the corridor he pressed his ear against the door but their voices were drowned out by sobbing in the next room. In the waiting room the teenage girl was curled up on the sofa and the suited woman was talking manically on her phone. There was a pause in the sobbing and then a shriek echoed down the hallway. As he paced towards the sound the nurse blocked his path. “There’s a Costa just along the corridor,” she said before slipping into the girl's room, her hushed voice settling the cries into a fading whimper.

He opened the door to Emma's room and peered in through the

gap. She was lying on her back with her eyes and mouth closed. He stroked her hair, feeling the dampness at the roots.

"How are you feeling?"

"Ok," she whispered. "How are you?"

"Me? I'm fine. Do you want anything? Some water?"

Shaking her head, she shut her eyes again. "I think I'll try to sleep."

"Ok. I'll be here."

He watched her from the bedside. She looked like an apparition in a ghost film. He pressed his mouth against her ear. "This isn't going to change anything."

She barely nodded, eyes closed.

The blinds were drawn in the window. Around the edge he could see the courtyard below; there was an old man in a wheelchair with a drip and his children and grandchildren around him, laughing about something as they huddled near a fenced-off sapling.

She groaned, the faint sound barely escaping her lips, and then clutched her stomach and rolled onto her side.

"Emma?"

She didn't answer.

He opened the door and yelled into the corridor. The nurse's head craned out from a doorway. "There's something wrong with her."

She was breathing heavily, her face beaded with sweat. He put his hand on her back and her skin was icy through the gown. The nurse ushered him outside. From the corridor he heard her say, “It’s ok Emma, this is just what happens.”

The door opened and the nurse stepped aside, looking away from him before she headed down the hallway.

Emma held her stomach, her eyes clamped shut. He stroked her hair and kissed her forehead. She shifted her legs to the side – the motion pushing him away – and paced into the bathroom. He called out her name and pressed his ear to the door. She didn’t reply. The hinges groaned as he pushed inside. She was sitting on the toilet, staring at the foetus in her palm. The nascent arms were held up around the head in protection. She stared at him, her eyes burning. “Well?” He looked down at his feet, too weak to face her or their child.

Tina stands outside the takeaway, staring into the alleyway. She walks over to the phone booth and peers inside, and then fixes her sunglasses over her eyes and strides away, glancing up at his window as she passes. Her ponytail bounces as she clicks along the pavement in high heels. She wears a light dress with a mid-thigh hem, revealing her tanned legs and drawing glances. Alex hangs back and watches her go into Costa and then hurries past the window with his head down and turns into a second-hand entertainment store. He watches her from the window, pretending to inspect the games consoles: she sits in the corner with her sunglasses on top of her head; the man at the next table keeps glancing up from his newspaper but she doesn’t seem to notice; he folds the paper and lays it on the table, staring into his mug, and then leans towards her and says something, and she shakes her head and looks away.

His phone buzzes, a message from his mother. 'We're going to a garden centre – we're so hip! Have fun with your friends, don't do anything I wouldn't!'

He puts his headphones in and strolls into Costa with his eyes fixed on the menu board. He orders a latte and carries it to a table in the corner and sits side-on to the window. When he looks up she is watching him, her lips pressed together in a half-smile. She nods faintly and he does the same, and then she goes back to her phone. The tables start to fill up. The man with the newspaper leaves. A group of three guys and three girls, all around his age, sit at the table opposite him with their shopping bags by their feet, breaking into laughter every few seconds. She and he are the only ones sitting alone. She stares out of the window, watching the people who pass, her manicured fingers curled around the mug. He rises to his feet and heads towards the toilets. She doesn't react as he passes. Both bathrooms are occupied. She comes through the archway and stands next to him, her shoulder an inch from his as she gazes straight ahead with a smile at the corner of her mouth. She lays her palm on the front of his jeans. The lock turns on one of the doors. She pulls her hand away and nods at the elderly woman who comes out. Once the woman has gone, she grabs his forefinger and leads him into the toilet. In silence, she locks the door, perches on the lid and positions him in front of her, staring up at him as she unbuckles his belt.

"It's a nice night, do you want to go for a walk?" he asked, looking out of Emma's living room window. The sun was turning the sky purple as it faded behind the rooftops. A group of teenagers passed below, peering in at the bikes in the shop.

"Not really." He could barely hear her over the TV. She sat bolt upright on the sofa with the hospital bracelet still on her wrist.

"Do you want something to eat?"

She shook her heard. *Coronation Street* babbled from the TV.

"I thought you hated soaps." He tried to sound jokey but his voice fell flat.

She shrugged, staring at the screen. Two middle-aged women sat in a booth in a pub, gossiping about someone who was having an affair. A young couple walked in, the girl pushing a pram, and the boy scooped up the baby and passed him to one of the women – his grandmother – who cradled him and talked nonsense. He glanced at Emma; her face was blank and her eyes motionless. Wrapping his arm around her shoulder, he pulled her head into his chest and kissed her temple. "I love you," he said, and again his voice sounded weak.

She squeezed his hand weakly. "I'm tired, I think I'll go to bed." He watched her pad into the bedroom and close the door.

She was fast asleep when he crept into the bedroom, the duvet wrapped tight around her shoulders and her nose almost touching the wall. He slipped in beside her and as he stared up at the crack on the ceiling he remembered a phrase from a story he had written the summer before he went to university, when he had been full of ideas and energy: *The sight of my shadow forecast the dark vapour of a man I would become.*

When he awoke she was still in the same position, her hair draped across her face and matted on her lips. He carefully peeled back the cover and stepped down onto the floor but she stirred and rolled onto her back with her hand across her forehead to filter out the sunlight.

"I could call in sick and stay home with you?"

She shook her read and rolled back onto her side.

In the car he called the office and told the news editor he had the flu, and then drove out of the town centre – passing the rush hour traffic – and pulled into a cul-de-sac and parked across the road from a whitewashed semi-detached house. The driveway was empty and the curtains were open in all the windows. Leaning against the steering wheel, he stared up at the front bedroom; there was a rolled-up white shade where his parents' heavy green curtains used to be. The street was empty with vehicles in just a few driveways and the only sound was the distant hum of the traffic on the main road.

A bead of sweat rolled down his spine as he stepped out of the car and quietly closed the door. The sun was a golden disc in the cloudless sky above the houses on the bend of the cul-de-sac. Checking over his shoulder, he walked up the gravel driveway – it had been paved when he lived there – towards the uPVC door. As he passed the front window he looked inside: the living room was completely different, with a parquet floor where they'd had a navy carpet, a vast charcoal sofa where their television was and a bureau in the corner where they used to put the Christmas tree; but he wasn't sure whether he remembered the layout first-hand or from seeing photographs. He tried to make out the faces in the pictures on the mantelpiece but they were too distant and obscured by his own reflection in the glass. Most of his memories of the house were from the pictures his mother kept in glossy albums: him and his brother in the bath together as infants; opening wrestling figures on their last Christmas Day there; Charlie, the scruffy old Jack Russell that died when he was five. Of the few real memories he has, the strongest are of the times he would awake from nightmares and feel a presence in his room and rush to his parents, crawling in between them in their warm bed.

The nameplate on the postbox said Smith. There was a bell but he knocked on the door instead, barely making a sound. The glass panel had a frosted pattern and he could only make out a cream floor and staircase on the other side. A wooden gate and fence stood at the end of the driveway and through the slats he could see the back garden; the clothesline was still there and there was a family's washing hanging out – a young boy and a teenage girl along with the parents, judging by the clothes – but the timber den and small goal his father had helped him and his brother build were gone.

Back in the car he called his parents' house phone and listened to his mother's voicemail message, and then he rang her mobile.

"Hello son, is everything ok?" she asked, a note of panic in her voice.

"Yeah, I'm fine. Just thought I'd call to see how you are."

"Oh, that's a nice surprise. Are you not at work?"

"I've got the day off."

"Ah, lucky you. I'm about to set off, actually."

"Ah yeah, of course. I'll let you go then."

"Ok, I'll call you tonight, shall I?"

"Ok, cool."

"Are you sure everything's ok? Work going well?"

"Yeah, fine. It's really hot and sunny here."

"Yes, it's warm here." She fell silent, waiting for him to speak. "Ok, I'll call you tonight, then."

"Ok, speak to you later."

"Love you."

"You too."

"Bye, love."

"Bye."

He started the engine and pulled away, glancing up at the white shade on his way past. Following the signs, he headed for the motorway and a huge out-of-town shopping centre. The tarmac glistened in the sun, looking half melted, and the exhaust fumes curled up into a layer of fog. Stepping into the bright foyer, he spotted a Costa halfway down the eastern avenue of shops. There were only a few people around – retired couples, housewives, students – and the shop assistants were still setting up displays in some of the stores. He joined the short queue and ordered a latte and took a seat in the window, looking out at the gleaming parade of shops. In one of Topshop's windows a girl was putting a grey autumn dress on a mannequin, struggling to bend the plastic arms though the straps. She paused and leaned her shoulder on the window and caught him watching and smiled, sweeping her blonde hair behind her ear, and he nodded back at her, and then she turned back to the dummy and finished arranging the outfit before glancing back at him with a grin as she stepped down onto the shop floor.

Halfway through his coffee a couple in their thirties came in with a little girl. The father lifted her up to see the cakes in the display cabinet, her black hair bouncing as she nodded her head. When he put his headphones in and clicked shuffle, a song from the *Solaris* soundtrack leapt into his ears, a dreamlike wash of sound, and he almost knocked over his coffee as he jabbed the pause icon. He chose a hard hip hop track and hurried out into the plaza, leaving the unfinished drink behind. As he passed Topshop he looked in and saw the girl hooking the dresses on hangars; she smiled at him, running her fingers through her bleached hair, and he slowed his gait, almost stopping, but kept walking until he was out of sight and then turned into Boots and stood before the vast perfume section, drawn to the gleaming bottles, forgetting everything as he systematically sniffed the testers and inspected the packaging before buying two Jimmy

Choo fragrances – 'Man' for him and 'Illicit' for Emma – with fresh scents that conjured romance and glamour.

Emma wasn't home. It was the first time he'd been there without her. The drone of the traffic and voices in the road filled the empty rooms. He phoned her but there was no answer. "Where are you?" he texted, and then quickly sent another message. "Just got to yours. I've got a present for you…" He waited there for almost an hour, going from room to room inspecting her things – clothes, shoes, jewellery, CDs, DVDs – and picturing her holding them before she had met him, when her life was about hope instead of regret. There was an engulfing silence in the flat without her there, like a church after everyone has gone. He placed the perfume on top of her jewellery box with the logo facing forward. The sun was setting when he left.

A plane cut a straight white line through the sky, dividing blue diagonal halves. They laid side-by-side on her blanket silently staring upwards. She was wearing big opaque sunglasses she'd bought on the way to the park and she had grown sparer and sharper in the days since the hospital.

"I wonder what happened between those lads and girls in the end." He saw she hadn't caught his meaning. "The 'ball to the face' ones."

Her pale lips formed a brief smile.

"Probably in another park today, trying their genius chat up move on a different set of girls," he said, sitting up. The park was busy for a weekday morning, the grass dotted with clusters of students and parents with pushchairs. Their heads turned at the sound of an ice cream van coming through the main gate, the skewed melody of the faulty chime growing louder.

"We should go away somewhere," he said, watching people walk towards the van as it pulled up by the play area. "Somewhere with a beach. Cornwall maybe. There's a place we used to go every summer when I was a kid." He couldn't tell if her eyes were open or closed behind the glasses. "You'd like it." He lightly gripped her knee, poking his finger through the ripped denim to touch her skin. "What do you think?"

"I can't afford a holiday."

"I'll pay; it'll only be a couple of nights."

"Ok," she said passively, still facing the sky.

Two seagulls hovered over the shore with their wings outstretched. They swirled through the grey sky in circles, going in opposite directions but always returning to the same point. She followed their orbit as she chewed her haddock, her paper skin stretching over her cheekbones with each rotation of her jaw. The restaurant was halfway up the domelike hill at the centre of the island, looking down on the beach where families packed up their belongings while a handful of people remained in the sea, their heads bobbing on the water and the waves dully reflecting the fading light of the dusk.

“How is it?”

“Good,” she said, dragging her gaze away from the window. “How’s yours?”

“Good.”

They fell silent again. A car passed below the window, slowly following the winding road down to the pier. She refilled her glass of wine, draining the bottle.

“You can’t go to the seaside and not have fish and chips.”

“Exactly,” he said, surprised by the sudden energy in her voice. “Or lose lots of money in the arcade.”

“I was so close. I could have won, literally, more than seventy pence.”

“What would you have bought?”

“What wouldn’t I have bought,” she smiled, and he saw a light in her eyes like a bulb had been switched on behind her pupils.

She held his hand as they walked down the steep gravel path, the breeze blowing her hair back and pinning the red lace dress against her body. It was the first time he had seen her wear such a bright colour and her hair and skin gleamed in contrast. The path forked at the pier, the boardwalk on the right and the gravel on the left, continuing down to the shore where the tractor ferry went back to the mainland.

“Let’s have a go,” she said, looking at the glowing stalls on the pier.

“You’re addicted.”

They strolled past the rides to the ringtoss stand, where a wind-beaten woman was reading a book as she waited for customers. "You have to get the ring all the way over the square so it lies flat on the base," she said, standing up and laying her book on her chair. He gave her two pounds and she handed three rings to Emma. They were alone at the stall; the children and teenagers were playing the shooting games or queuing for the ghost train and the adults were sitting at the pop-up bars. She threw the first ring and the edge bounced off the closest corner of the square. She missed the next two shots too, the ring looping over the prize but catching on the box each time.

"Never mind, darling, he'll win one for you."

Emma turned to him, her eyes awash with the neon of the bumper cars behind him.

"Go on, show her you love her." She held out the rings and he took out his wallet and gave her a two pound coin.

"What shall I go for?"

"The iPhone."

"Haven't we both got one already?"

"We can sell it."

His palm was damp with sweat as he held out the first ring. A siren wailed from the speakers around the bumper cars; beyond them the sun had almost vanished, stretching a rusty hue over the clouds and water. People trickled past as the pier started to fill up, slowing down to see whether he'd make the shot. He looked at Emma and winked, his heart thundering in his chest, and tossed the ring and it arched over the cube and slipped down around the corners, lying flat on the platform.

"Yes!" she shouted. "You genius!"

On the tractor she leaned back against his chest, holding the iPhone box as they stood by the edge watching the water lapping around the huge tyres. An elderly couple were standing a metre along, the woman's hand resting on the man's as he gripped the railing. As they approached the shore the woman smiled at them, her raincoat and grey hair flapping in the wind. She looked like she was about to say something, but then she nodded and turned back to her husband, resting the side of her head on his arm.

"I think I'll keep it," she said as they walked between the caravans, past the lit windows and neat gardens.

"Yeah?"

"You won it for me. I can sell mine."

They dropped off the iPhone at the chalet and walked up the hill to the road, the caravan park a pattern of lights behind them.

In the taxi she gripped his arm and laid her head on his shoulder with her eyes half closed. "Are you alright?" he asked, and she nodded and smiled dreamily, staring out of the window as the dark country lanes turned into illuminated streets.

The walls of the tiny underground club were damp and the floor was sticky with spilled drinks. She downed her glass of wine and dragged him into the crowd, weaving through the ripped jeans and black T-shirts as guitars wailed from the speakers, the sound vibrating in the base of his spine. She danced in jerking motions, throwing out her arms and kicking her legs at random, and then shuffling backwards into the swarm before striding towards him with her eyes flitting between her own body and his face and her smile coy and seductive in the shadows which clung to her. She hooked her arms over his neck and swayed her hips as she stared up at him, and he held her waist and she stepped in closer so she was pressed against his chest and then he slipped his hands down so his fingertips were on her bare thighs and she parted her legs and he ran the side of his hand over the damp cotton. She looked over her shoulder, searching, and led him to the edge of the dancefloor and sat on a stool against the wall. She pulled him in by his T-shirt and spread her legs, kissing him hard as the people around them jostled against his back. She yanked open his buttons and pulled aside her thong and he pushed inside her with one hand on her back and the other steadying the stool. She gripped his waist, pulling him into her as she stared up at him in a way he'd never seen before. When he was about to come she pushed him away and he fired onto her thigh and the stool as cheers and murmurs swarmed around them.

Lying on his back with his head to the side, he stared at their reflection in the wardrobe mirror: his face above the covers, hers beneath and turned away. There was laughter outside the chalet, trailing past the window. Her dress and his jeans lay in a heap on the floor with a column of sunlit dust hanging above. He rolled onto his side and laid his palm on her back and pressed his lips to her ear.

“Morning,” he whispered, and she stirred slightly, her eyelashes fluttering. He kissed her shoulder and she hummed and then he traced his finger along her ribs and the groove beneath her breast, moving closer until his thighs were pressed against hers, and she bent her elbow and held his neck, half asleep. They lay that way in silence, the sound of the sea beyond the window, and then she suddenly shifted onto her back and he saw in her face that the night before had been just a mirage.

A door slammed in another caravan, the sound echoing through the bedroom. Muffled voices and soft moans filtered in through the window as they lay there, detached and staring at the ceiling.

They went to the cinema that evening. He chose a war film – she didn’t care what they saw – thinking it would have nothing about love or children. She didn’t react when the soldiers died, but near the end the main character, a bomb disarmer, visited his wife and baby back home in America and her eyes were moist in the light of the screen as she watched him talk to the infant in her cot, confessing himself to his tiny daughter, the child's face blank and without judgment.

Between sleep and consciousness he felt her hand on his back and her breath in his ear as she said his name.

“Don't you ever think about it?”

“I try not to.”

"It was a girl."

Nodding, he pictured the tiny body in her palm: her arms had been held up in defence as though she knew what was coming.

"Our daughter."

She began to cry, silently at first and then long deep sobs which rumbled through the bedroom. When he tried to hold her she pushed him away.

"Why didn't you ever ask me to keep her?"

"Did you want to?"

"You know I did. I tried to tell you so many times but you wouldn't listen, you just wanted to get rid of her, to wash your hands of the whole thing and carry on like nothing happened."

"I…"

"You're the one who is supposed to be a Christian," she shouted, sitting up, "but I'm the only one who seems to care that we killed our baby. Our baby. Sometimes I think you have no conscience, no soul. How can you say you love me but then want to kill our baby?"

He propped himself up on his elbows. "But it wasn't…"

She slapped him, her palm striking his cheek with the force of a punch.

He stood up and pulled on his clothes, his whole body shaking. She watched him in silence as he picked up his wallet and phone and left without looking at her.

The lights were out in all the caravans as he walked towards the beach. Standing by the shoreline he tried to make out where the sea met the sky but the two swathes of black seemed to seep into one another. He punched himself twice, stiff shots to the same side of the head she'd slapped. Dizzy, he sat down on the sand, digging his knuckles into the warm under-layer as he waited for the sun.

"I'm going to transfer to another university." Her voice was distant like she was at the other end of a bad line. "Manchester."

He watched the shadows on her ceiling, dark grey on grey, unchanging in tone or shape as no headlights passed by in the dead-end street.

On the train home the landmarks of the journey from her station to his were drained of their colour in the grey dawn. On his phone he searched for John 3:16, reading the words he had memorised during childhood, *For God so loved the world that he gave his one and only Son,* and he felt a presence on the empty seat next to him and an arm around his shoulder, and his lip started to tremble and he could feel the heat of the tears on his cheeks. The businessman across the carriage watched with cold curiosity. Alex turned back to the washed-out landscape – the homes, shops, parks and churches all so bereft of warmth in the emerging light.

"I'll go first," Tina says, checking herself in the mirror above the baby-changing table. "Wait a few minutes before you come out."

He nods as he buckles his belt – that arm around his shoulder long since dismissed as a fabrication of his desperate mind.

She opens the door a crack to check before slipping out. He turns the lock and inspects himself in the mirror; her make-up is smeared on his nose and lips.

When he walks back into the seating area she is with her husband, sitting with her back to the toilets as he talks at her. She doesn’t look at Alex on his way out.

Back in his room he sits on the bed and stares out of the window. His housemates are all out, with friends or away for the weekend. When he checks his phone there are no new messages and the only new emails are spam. The clouds have darkened. Rain taps the window. He rifles through the books and DVDs on his shelf and then the clothes and cologne bottles in his wardrobe, and then he puts his coat back on and walks out the door.

11

It is winter, late afternoon, the sky black and the streets empty. Ezra walks past the glowing windows, looking in at the families gathered around trees and twinkling lights, and he knows that his mother is waiting for him at home. Their house is at the end of the street. As he approaches he sees the golden light in the window. She is there, looking out for him. She smiles when she sees him. As he walks up the driveway he knows he is dreaming. There are no track marks on her arms, no bruises on her face. There is warmth in her eyes. The door is made of speckled glass. She is on the other side, a blurred outline. A dark figure floats in next to her, looming over her shoulder, and even though the pane is frosted he can see the tattoo on his forearm, the jagged lettering spelling Big Jim.

When he awakes his teeth are chattering. He has kicked off the quilt. The dog is watching him, head tilted, puzzled.

The sun is a pale line of smoke over the valley beyond the cottages as he locks the door, repeatedly glancing over his shoulder at the empty street. The dog stands patiently by his foot, wheezing clouds of breath into the cold dawn air. They walk towards the narrow cut-through, the dog sniffing walls and lampposts, and each time he cocks a hind leg to spray he looks like his front leg is about to collapse under his weight, but he always manages, panting with the effort.

They follow the steep footpath down to the main road and cross and descend the steps to the Waitrose. Music oozes out of an open window in the street above, the low bass the only sound in the vast car park where the shuttered supermarket blocks out the moonlight. There are only two vehicles, a white Transit van in the far corner on the canal side and a rusted green Micra by the steps up to the road. Ezra lets the dog off the lead and watches him hop around the car park, sniffing and pissing at the bushes and the spurts of weeds. Every few seconds he looks up at Ezra – who sits on the wall by the Micra – checking the boy is still there. The dog squats beneath a hedge and then kicks dirt, and as the boy bends down with a plastic bag he licks his wrist before running off towards the van.

When he turns around from the bin there is someone on the other side of the car park, at the top of the steps down to the canal. The dog is halfway between them, ears flattened and head bowed as he stares at the tall silhouette between the hedges. The man stands perfectly still with his hands by his sides as light angles across him from a lamppost, the rays absorbed by a black cap and rebounded by a leather jacket.

Ezra tightens his hold on the chain and calls Charlie, keeping his voice flat. The dog's ears prick up and he turns to the boy and hops towards him, glancing back at the man every few steps. When the dog is 20 yards away the man starts striding across the car park. Ezra hurries towards Charlie and scoops him up, tucking him under his arm as he turns around and paces towards the steps. As he reaches the main road he hears a door slamming and an engine starting. He sprints up the steep footpath, holding the dog to his chest and looking back as headlights arc across the car park and disappear. The engine hums somewhere below, growing fainter and then rising sharply, and then headlamps sweep over the damp tarmac at the bottom of the sloping path and the Micra appears between the walls and stops suddenly and kills the lights, plunging the street into blackness. Ezra peers through the grainy dark, feeling the dog's heart rattling against his chest. The car's window is down but it's too dark inside to make out the driver. After a few seconds the gears groan and the Micra speeds away with its lights off. The boy's breath is a jet in the icy air as he leans on the handrail with the dog shivering in his arms.

*

When he heard about Tom on the news he immediately packed a bag, grabbed the dog and the keys to the Ford and left. He drove without thinking, instinctively taking turns and joining motorways, and he was halfway to Bournemouth before he even registered that he was heading to the B&B where they'd stayed the previous summer. The couple who ran the place recognised him and gave him the same room looking out over the woods and the beach beyond, and said the dog was fine to stay. The walls smelled of fresh paint and the carpet was new, but the twin beds were the same and the painting of the old man and a boy working on a boat on the beach was still on the wall.

Tom had told him to meet him at the B&B if anything ever went wrong, if he ever didn't come home from a job. Nobody else knew about the place, he'd said, not even Peter or Derek and Jo.

"Why not?" he'd asked. "Don't you trust them?"

They were in the B&B, reading in bed. Tom had been holding his book up as they talked but he laid it flat on his lap when the boy asked that. "I don't trust anyone. Except you. Actually, that's not fair, I do trust Peter."

"Not Derek and Jo?"

"Maybe. Would you?"

The boy shrugged. "Have they done something?"

"No, it's just... When it comes to money, people do anything." He smiled wryly. "Even kill people."

"What about Peter?"

He paused a beat, the cogs turning behind his eyes. "Just come here."

Ezra stayed at the B&B for a week, only leaving his room to take the dog on long aimless walks through the woods and along the beachfront, winding up by the pier where he'd buy a Dr Pepper and watch the teenagers flitter between false hysterics and showy distaste as they galloped around the stalls. Throughout the week he half-expected Tom to arrive, thinking that maybe the news was wrong, and he ignored Jo's phone calls, refusing to hear his death spoken aloud. When the stories started to mention Gardner, he decided to go back.

It was a bright morning when he saw Derek and Jo climb into a taxi as he was sitting at the back of the café across the road, watching the front of the office across the half-empty tables. The cab pulled up and they came out dressed in black and he knew straight away where they were going.

They stood outside the crematorium, smoking, separate from the other mourners – a crowd who were gathered for someone else. He watched from the corner of the car park, sitting low down in the Ford with the hard sun bouncing off the paintwork. A royal blue Jaguar pulled into the driveway and Jo and Derek turned to the car as Peter stepped out in a black pin-striped suit. He strode towards them and nodded and they followed him inside the chapel. They came out less than 20 minutes later and walked between the headstones, following the footpath deep into the cemetery, towards the boundary wall. Ezra slipped out of the car and walked between the trees, careful not to be seen. They stopped in the corner by a black marble stone. The boy hid behind a cedar barely 10 metres away. Jo wept and Derek put his arm around her. Peter stood apart from them with his eyes fixed on the headstone. They exchanged brief sentences, their mouths barely moving and their voices too low for him to hear anything. Once they'd disappeared behind the chapel he walked over to the stone. Tom's facts were in straight gold lettering – name, date of birth and death – but the epitaph was slanted. *He shook the grass.* Peter had paid for the stone and chosen the wording, he knew.

He called Derek and Jo that night from a phone booth. She said they had the ashes and that he should take them somewhere Tom liked. He took the urn to the cemetery where Tom's parents' were buried and scattered him on their grave. It was another clear day, the sun coming through the leaves in daggers of light and catching the edges of tombstones to cast jagged shadows. Tom had taken him there a few times and pointed out that he'd named him after the author who wrote the poem engraved on their headstone.

And the days are not full enough
And the nights are not full enough
And life slips by like a field mouse
Not shaking the grass

It was his father's favourite poem, he'd told Ezra the first time they visited, when the headstones were lined with snow and the grass was a blanket of white dented with footprints. It was just before Christmas, their first together. They'd come straight from Toys R Us where Tom had led him around the store, telling him to remember what he wanted so he could write a list – for Tom, not Santa; he'd told him that Father Christmas was a lie, that it was his mother who hadn't given him presents, not a disappointed St Nicholas – and that he might get some as presents, that his first proper Christmas was going to be special. The boy's head was still swimming with the toys as they stood before the granite stone, staring at the etched poem together. "When I was eighteen my dad told me to make sure I shake the grass," he said. The boy nodded, the words lost on him, but he could tell from Tom's face that they meant something special. It was the first time he'd seen him sad and somehow it made him feel safer with him. "That's my line," he said, pointing to the italicised words below the poem, *They shook the grass.*

*

Voices seep out from under the closed doors as he climbs the steps to the fourth floor: television chatter, an argument, a rapper half crying and half slurring '*breaking on marble floors*' – the sounds merge and swirl around him in the glass-cased stairwell. When he reaches their door he pauses and stares at the pinprick of light through the spyhole with his fist clenched around the key in his pocket. He opens the door and slips into the dark hallway. There is a stale smell from the damp washing in the basket but the scent of Tom's cologne still lingers in the air. He walks into the kitchen, his eyes trailing over the dishes they used for the lasagne they made the night it happened. He lifts the dank clothes out of the basket and into the washing machine and places a tab on top and starts the cycle. Staring at the round window, he watches the water fill the drum and the clothes spinning, the whirring sound filling the silence that clings to the flat.

In Tom's room he takes in the neat order: duvet folded back, clothes hung precisely, cologne bottles in a straight line and facing forward. Three of them are the fresh scents that he always wore – Cool Water, Only the Brave, Guilty Black – but the fourth, the most recently bought, a month back, is a deep musk so different from the others that the boy felt a sense of alarm when he first smelt it on him. He picks up the heavy brown bottle, staring at the gold lettering – Intenso – and then places it back in its position on the cabinet, closest to his pillow, and grabs the Cool Water and sprays it on his neck and then goes around the flat dosing the air to vanquish the staleness and Intenso. As he steps into the lounge he can tell that someone else has been there. Little things are out of place: books in the wrong order on the shelves and papers ruffled in the bureau. He looks for a note from the police, thinking that maybe they would have left something if they'd searched the place, but there is nothing.

Back in Tom's room he pushes the bed aside and peels back the rug below. The floorboard is still in place. He grabs a screwdriver from the kitchen and removes the board to expose the dusty crawl space. Torch in hand, he lays flat on the floor and reaches into the hole and pushes away the carpet scraps and the wire mesh, revealing battered old suitcases and a dirty brown holdall. He unzips the bag and the torch beam bounces off the rusty door of an iron safe. Leaning down, barely able to reach, he dials in the code – the birth years of Tom, his parents, and himself, added together and then divided by four – and the lock clicks. The black plastic gleams in the flashlight. He fishes the bin liners out and lines them up on the floor, each one a tight brick. There are fifteen – five fewer than expected. He opens one and counts the cash – £1,000 in £10 and £20 notes – and then checks another to make sure it's also right. He places five of the bricks in his rucksack and stacks the rest back in the safe and locks the door, and then unclasps one of the suitcases and flips open the lid, revealing a rusty toolbox with a padlock around the handle. With the torch in his mouth, he turns the four dials to the date Tom's parents married and it clicks open. Inside there are four drawstring bags; he grips each cloth pouch, finding one empty. Sitting on the floor, he opens one of the bags and pulls out a 9mm Beretta and two cartons of bullets, feeling the weight of the gun in his hand the same way he had when Tom taught him to shoot, firing at mannequins in the abandoned industrial estate.

He closes the suitcase and seals up the floorboard and drags the bed back into place, keeping his eyes straight ahead to avoid the framed picture of him and Tom even though he knows the image by heart; they stand side-by-side on the beach in Bournemouth with the sea behind them, both in T-shirts and shorts, and even though they are not blood there is a resemblance between them: the same dead-straight dark hair and high forehead and an almost identical broad-shouldered and thick-limbed frame. “He's growing into you,” the grey-haired woman who took the photo said, her eyes reflecting the midday sun. “Unlucky,” Tom said, looking at the boy and smiling.

As he walks into the living room he pictures Tom sitting on the sofa the day before he died, trying to make conversation with the tension of the previous night still hanging above them. Then he sees his eyes a month back as he showed him the derelict cottage in Stroud, solemnly guiding him around the decaying building. There was a musty smell and the stairs groaned under his weight. He said they'd fix it up one day but for now it was a good place to have, just in case. "In case what?" Ezra asked as they stood in the dark master bedroom with the boarded-up window, but he didn't answer, just said he'd bought the place under a false name and to tell no-one.

Looking out of the window, the boy is semi-transparent, the docks and cathedral tower visible through his reflection. The double-glazing blocks out the murmur of the crowd in the Quays below and his footsteps are the only sound as he crisscrosses the room, putting everything back as it was – the books on the shelves and the pictures on the mantelpiece – and as he goes through the documents in the bureau he comes across a letter to Tom from The Gym, thanking him for joining, dated two weeks ago. He stares at the piece of paper, the smell of the Intenso slowly starting to seep out from below the Cool Water.

As he runs down the stairs his eyes sweeps across a man in a black cap and leather jacket on the stone benches parallel to the canal. He sits at an angle with his legs crossed and his head turned towards the door to the flats at the side of the convenience store. Ezra stops at the bottom of the stairwell and flips up his hood and then peers out through the glass panel: the man has shifted his position, the peak of his cap facing the tiny mariners' church between the flats and the other converted warehouses. As the boy steps out onto the boulevard the man turns to him and studies his face, and then he rises to his feet and starts towards him. Dressed all in black, he is like a silhouette, cutting the same shape against the misty rain as he did the hazy dawn in the Waitrose car park. He strides towards Ezra with his hands buried in his pockets, his pale face expressionless beneath the cap. The boy darts inside the convenience store, ignoring the suspicious glance from the girl behind the counter as he positions himself behind a newspaper stand so he is peering over the top at the automatic door. He fumbles open the rucksack and drawstring bag and grips the 9mm, turning to the door as the man walks past, his equine nose and pointed chin catching the faint light from the sign.

Ezra moves closer to the doorway and watches as the black cap glides away into the crowd outside the cafés and then fades into the swarm of heads streaming towards the shopping centre on the horizon. The boy slips the gun into his pocket and cuts across the square towards the towering glass block of The Gym, scanning the faces in the foggy rain and looking back over his shoulder with every step. As he passes the Wetherspoon's pub a bouncer glares at him over the heads of a group of teenagers who are trying to argue their way inside, expecting him to join the gang. He climbs the brick steps and crosses the road and paces alongside the gym, his eyes flicking at the long window of the bar opposite. As he rounds the corner the man rises towards him, ascending the stone staircase with long strides. The boy's hand pulses in his pocket, his finger curling around the trigger.

"Ezra," the man barks, raising his palms and flinching towards the railing. "I'm David, I knew Tom."

"The detective?"

He nods frantically. “We need to talk.”

The boy studies his face in wary silence as the rain sweeps across them from the canal; the detective looks exhausted, his pale eyes weighed down and his sagging jawline peppered with black and grey stubble. “Was that you in Stroud this morning?”

He nods. “I’ve been looking for you. I didn’t see you at the funeral.”

“How did you find me?”

“Tom’s car. You’ve changed the plates?”

“You were at the funeral?”

“Stayed in my car.”

They move towards the railings to make way for three teenage girls in gym gear who pass by with cautious glances.

“I was there. I stayed in the car park.” He glances at the detective, who gazes into the murky water with his thin lips pressed together. A barge boat glides by below and they watch as it fades away into the horizon of derelict mills and warehouses and the orange glow of the Sainsbury’s sign.

“Have you seen Peter?” David asks, looking sideways at the boy.

“Didn’t he tell you?”

“What?”

“About Gardner?”

“So that was you.” He turns to face the boy square on. “That’s why I’m here – to tell you that you should go away. Use the money he left you and…"

"Money?"

He shakes his head and sighs. "Peter."

"What money?"

"Ask Peter." He draws his hand from his pocket and grips the railing. "Tom wanted a different life for you, he never wanted you involved in this."

"Gardner was told to kill him," the boy says, pushing back from the railing and meeting the detective's gaze. "Two men told him Tom was coming, that he'd been seeing his girlfriend." He studies the detective's face as he registers the words but his weary expression doesn't change.

"Who told you that?"

"Gardner."

"Gardner himself or Gardner through Peter?"

"Gardner."

"I see." He glances at a seagull chick as it lands on the water and then turns back to the boy, his eyes hard. "And the two men?"

"One was Saul."

"Saul? He said that?"

"He told Peter."

He closes his eyes and shakes his head softly.

"What?"

"Has he shown you his refuge?"

"Yeah. Why?"

“Do you think there were enough Big Jims to meet that cost?”

Ezra stares at him, his face catching the glint of sunlight slicing through the clouds.

“Tom and I had stopped. Peter – it ended up just being about that refuge, about the money needed…”

“So what about Gardner?”

“I don’t know. I got out months back.”

“Tom and Kerry Jordan…”

“I don’t know, son.” He tries to smile but his bloodshot eyes show nothing but fatigue. “I don’t have any answers for you, just warnings: don’t trust Peter, and run. Forget all this and go.”

“Why haven’t you?”

“Gone? I wish I could, believe me. If Tom was still here he’d tell me to. He’d say the same to you – he’d drag you away.” Something catches his eye on the other side of the canal; Ezra follows his gaze to the broad back of a tall man in a navy duffel coat walking up the footpath to the highway. “But you’re a man now, right? You’ll do what you think best. Take care of yourself, son.” He moves away towards the stairs, striding quickly, but his gait slows as he reaches the top of the steps and he stops dead, looks back and calls out, “I’m telling you because I loved him,” before disappearing around the corner, his figure warped by the two glass walls between them.

The gym changing room is packed – teens, students, weightlifters, portly middle-aged and spindly elderly men – and almost all the lockers are padlocked. Standing in the entrance, he feels their eyes lingering on his scar and overhears two steroid-pumped men muttering about the gym being too busy on a Saturday. He slips off his rucksack and dangles the bag from his hand as he walks along the edge of the room, past the three-deep rows of lockers, almost all of them sealed by the Gym-branded combination padlocks from the vending machine in the lobby. In the corner he stands with his back to the room and his head casting a shadow on the lockers, and turns the four dials on a padlock to the same number Tom used for the safe under his bed, but the clasp remains in place. He tries the same code on the padlocks either side without success, and when he glances over his shoulder he catches an elderly Indian man watching him as he rolls his socks over his long yellow toenails. The boy shakes his head as though he can't remember which locker is his and then strides towards the door, glancing at the 24/7 poster on the wall.

Hood raised, he paces through the rain, alert to the faces around him. In Costa he orders an Americano and a panini but his churning stomach can only take the coffee and he leaves the sandwich untouched before heading out into the swarm and making for the shopping outlet, weaving between groups of children his age who swing bags and laugh and play music aloud from their iPhones. Inside he wanders past the glowing stores, his eyes gliding across the window displays but taking in nothing. As he passes the Fragrance Shop he pauses at the sight of the display stand for Intenso; a dark-haired man stares moodily over the top of the brown velvet-like bottle with the Dolce and Gabbana logo in gold. A young man who looks like he has stepped out of the advert stands before the display, holding the tester bottle. He sprays the inside of his wrist and shakes his arm before sniffing the skin.

"That's a lovely one," the shop assistant says, moving towards him.

"Yeah, it's a bit different."

She leans on the counter, her thick make-up powdery in the sharp light. "It's been really popular."

The boy watches from the bargain bin by the door, pretending to inspect the failed celebrity fragrances.

"Do you have Bleu de Chanel," the man asks, peering over her shoulder at the shelves behind the counter.

"That's another lovely one." She turns to the display and grabs two testers. "That one comes in an eau de parfum and eau de toilette." She carefully places them side-by-side on the counter and he walks towards her, his eyes burning as he takes in all the bottles and packaging behind her – Gucci, Prada, Diesel, Givenchy. "I'll do one on each strip. What's your name?"

"Alex."

"I love that name." She writes on the tester strips and then sprays each one. "That's the toilette." He takes the card and sniffs. "It's amazing, isn't it?"

"Mm."

She hands him the other strip. "The parfum is a bit stronger and lasts longer."

As he sniffs the card she notices the boy by the bargain bin. "One moment, please," she says to Alex, whose eyes are dancing over the bottles behind her. She walks towards Ezra, her smile failing to hide her irritation. "Can I help you?" she asks, her eyes flicking at his scar and bleached hair as the words leave her scarlet lips.

"I'm just looking," Ezra mutters, and as she turns back to Alex the boy slips out of the shop and goes across the aisle into the Nike store and stands by the window, watching. After a few minutes Alex comes out with a bag and sits on a bench, his face glowing in the white light as he carefully opens the Chanel packaging and inspects the dark blue bottle and then, with a surreptitious glance, sprays his neck twice. He takes out an iPhone and types away and then reads the screen. Ezra steps out of the Nike shop and walks behind the bench and peers down at the mobile in Alex's hand; an image of the Intenso bottle fills the top of the screen with reviews below. As the boy walks away he looks back and sees Alex rising from the bench and striding into the Fragrance Shop once again.

12

In the darkening afternoon Alex trawls through Tinder profiles, swiping yes almost every time and pasting in pre-written hello messages when he gets a match. He is back at Costa, a cloud of Bleu de Chanel hovering over him as *The Spy Who Came in From the Cold* lies open on the table. Acid rain lashes against the window and the clouds fill the sky so completely it feels like night. A teenage girl no more than 18 walks in, wearing a baggy pink jumper and black leggings so thin that he can see the outline of her underwear. As she walks past he looks up suddenly, as though he's waiting for someone to come through the door, and the abrupt movement grabs her attention, but when he shifts his gaze to her face she looks away and continues to a table in the corner where she sits down with her back to him, joined a moment later by a boy. A plumpish woman in her mid-thirties sits diagonally across from him, reading a fashion magazine. Her open raincoat reveals a blue sweater and he can make out the shape of her bra against the thin wool. She raises her eyes from the page and reaches for her mug; he stares down at his book, pretending to be engrossed, and then he looks up at her and she meets his gaze as she sips her drink, and he nods and smiles shyly, as though he didn't mean to catch her attention but is now glad he did, and she smiles back politely before returning to her magazine. He continues reading, glancing up at her every few seconds, but she is fixed on the page, and he quickly realises that she is not interested, that she just wants to be left alone to read and enjoy her coffee, not be bothered by desperate men.

In the high street a blanket of umbrellas shields the couples huddled together arm-in-arm. The downpour drenches him in seconds; streams run off the tips of his hair and down his face and neck. A homeless man sits outside Tesco with a dog and a flatcap containing a few copper coins. Alex goes into the shop and buys the sandwich with the most calories and a bottle of orange juice. From a distance the tramp looks to be in his 40s, but when he gets close he sees a man as young as himself behind the matted hair and overgrown beard. As he hands him the carrier bag he looks up with vacant eyes and then mutters, “Cheers mate,” failing to hide his disappointment that the gift is not money. “Listen,” Alex says, leaning in towards him, “things will get better for you, you know,” and he wants to say something else, something comforting and encouraging, but he can think of nothing and the man is looking into his eyes with alarm, as though he sees something terrifying in the black holes of his pupils, so he walks away, striding quickly with his head down as the rain whips against his face, and when he looks up to cross the road he sees a figure with hair like a waterfall of oil among the river of umbrellas ahead, and he hurries after the slim girl with the black hair, her name on his lips as he weaves through the crowd, but as he draws near, the light from a window display catches her engagement ring and he sees that her wrist is tanned and without freckles, so he continues past, glancing sideways and finding the face of a stranger.

*

"There's something wrong, I can feel it," Maggie says, standing in the living room doorway in her old paint-spattered jeans and shirt, clutching her gardening gloves.

"He's probably still getting over that girl," Alan says, looking up from the newspaper.

"It's more than that. I can just feel it. He never answers when we call. His texts are short."

"She was his first proper girlfriend. You know what it's like at that age."

"Have you seen his Facebook page? He hasn't put anything on there for weeks. I'm going to go and see him."

"Mags…" He lays the newspaper flat on his thighs. "Do you really think that's a good idea?"

"I have to." She steps into the room, squeezing the gloves. "He's not Alex. Something's wrong. I won't be able to relax until I know he's ok."

"Mags, I just think that…"

"I know I'm being silly, the hysterical mother, but I can just feel that something's wrong."

He sets the paper on the armrest and stands up and she walks into him and rests her forehead on his chest. "Do you want me to come with you?"

"There's no point in us both going. I'll get the train tomorrow."

"Are you going to let him know you're coming?"

"It'll be better if I just turn up."

"What will you say?"

"I'll think of something. I could say I have a conference."

"I'll drop you off at the station," he says, stroking her hair

She tilts her head to look up at him. "Do you think I'm being silly?"

"Yes, but that never stops you. You're right that he hasn't been himself, though. I just worry he'll think we're interfering."

"I know. I'll make something up – a lecture or a conference or something."

*

Alex stands behind a bench, the wooden slats too cold to sit on. The park is deserted and the thick hedgerows block out the light from the bordering streets so that the playground, trees and bushes all merge into one black mass. His eyes are fixed on the Park Road entrance, waiting for her to appear in the lamplight between the railings. 'I'm on a bench by the climbing frame,' he types, and as he's about to send the message a silhouette emerges in the amber haze of the gateway. She's wearing her trenchcoat. He sends the text and watches as she takes her phone from her pocket, the screen palely lighting her face. She follows the footpath with hurried steps, her feet silent on the tarmac. He calls out as she passes under the wilting branches by the playground entrance.

"Hiya." She stands in front of the bench, her expression lost in the dark. She's wearing jeans and flat-heeled boots. "I haven't got long – he thinks I'm getting tampons."

"Good excuse."

"You don't question that one."

They look at each other in silence, their faces masked by the shadows as they wait for the first move.

"I wanted to show you the climbing frame," he says.

"Did you now?"

"It's pretty impressive."

"Is this where you bring all the girls?"

"Just you."

"I'm honoured." She walks around the bench, her face fleetingly touched by the moonlight. "Come on then, let's see what all the fuss is about."

He leads her across the woodchip floor, past the swings and seesaw. "It's like being 14 again."

"I was 34 when you were 14." She turns to the climbing frame. "Look at the size of it, and all those tunnels and rope-ladders – I am impressed."

"Told you." He steps forward and kisses her, tasting the tobacco and lip gloss and that faint rotting scent as he presses her against a pillar and she clutches at the hair on the back of his head.

It happens quickly, the anticipation having swelled since she'd texted him in response to the reporter card he slid under the back door. She turns to the pillar and he pushes into her from behind. She grips the side of his neck and leans back against his chest as she whispers 'Do you want me? You want me, huh?' until he lets go inside her, and she holds onto him like that as their frantic breathing calms to a lull and the murmur of the traffic and wind in the trees rises to them again.

Her phone buzzes against his thigh. She breaks away from him and pulls up her jeans and fishes the mobile out of a pocket. "I have to go." She doesn't look at him as she straightens her sweater and ties her trenchcoat.

"How long have you been married?" He searches for a change in her expression – grief, regret, desperation – but her face is in the shadow of her hand as she smooths down her hair.

"Four years." Her voice gives nothing away.

"How did you meet?"

"Why?"

"I just can't work out how you ended up with him."

"Nothing's as simple as it seems when you're 22." Her phone vibrates in her hand. She swipes the screen and turns away from him. "I'm on my way back now, I bumped into Shelley. Five minutes." She hangs up and turns to Alex. "I have thought of leaving but…" She shrugs and forces a smile. "Do you want to see me again?"

"Of course."

"I'll text you."

"Can I ask you something else?"

"Depends what it is."

"The other night with the bald guy – is that a regular thing?"

"Not with him."

"But with other men?"

"Yeah." She folds her arms across her chest.

"Do you want to?"

"I'm not forced into it, if that's what you mean."

He nods, looking down at his boots. "So your husband…?"

"It's his idea."

"Do you like it?"

She reaches into her pocket for cigarettes and a lighter. "Suppose so," she says, fixing one in her mouth.

"Don't you feel used?"

The flame briefly illuminates her face. "Maybe that's why I like it. Do you watch porn?"

"Sometimes."

"Gangbangs?"

"Why?"

"It's the most popular. Men want to use women and women want to be used. Deep down, on a carnal level. It's the way we're made."

"Maybe," he murmurs, stepping closer to try to make out her eyes in the grainy darkness.

"Wait 10 years then see if you agree."

"Maybe you wouldn't feel that way if you were in love."

"Being in love makes you feel it even more. Jealousy makes it more intense. It's a carnal thing."

"If you love someone, don't you just want to protect them and keep them for yourself?"

She draws on the cigarette. "Only at first." The smoke hovers above her in a grey cloud. "It's messed up but it's the way we are."

"Have you ever been in love?"

She takes another drag and shrugs. "You?"

"I think so."

"What happened?"

"I messed it up." He takes two steps forward so he is a yard away and can see her eyes in the moonlight. "I think we're both messed up," he whispers, holding her wrist as she starts to raise the cigarette. "When I look at you I just see sadness. I think you'd run away if you could."

Her expression doesn't change. He is about to speak again when her phone buzzes.

"I really have to go now." She looks at his hand and he realises how tightly he is gripping her wrist.

He lets go and looks away, embarrassed. "Sorry."

"Don't apologise." She smiles faintly, shaking her head, and then walks away. Her silhouette disappears into the darkness. His eyes trail the point in the hazy black where he estimates her to be, but he's way off – she emerges in the yellow haze of the gateway as he's peering at the shadows around the base of a statue.

He sprints after her. When she hears his footsteps approaching she flinches, her eyes lit with fear.

"It's me."

She stops in the halo of light beneath a lamppost, scanning the windows of the terraced houses.

"Don't go back."

"I have to."

"We'll go to a hotel."

There is a willingness in her eyes.

"What do you have to go back to?"

She studies his face. When he speaks it is like he is underwater, his words muffled, drowned. "Do you really want to go home?"

"Which hotel?"

"New County."

She shakes her head. "Somewhere new."

They stride through the deserted city centre. A misty rain begins to fall. She pulls an umbrella from her handbag and opens the cover and he takes the handle and holds it at an angle to shield them both from the drizzle. The room is small and bare, with a musty smell and a trickle of grainy light from an arrow-slit window. They don't speak as they undress. She kisses him hesitantly at first, her body stiff in his hands, but then she softens as though submitting to a weight bearing down on her and she pulls him onto the mattress so he is on top of her and wraps her arms around his neck and her legs around his waist, pulling him inside her and clinging to him with all of her strength, and when she looks up at him there is something in her eyes beyond articulation – desperation is the word that comes to him but it is more than that – and she whispers ‘Slow, slow, tender’ with her lips pressed to his ear and her voice filling his head, and when he comes she doesn’t let go, holding him inside her and stroking his back, and there is music somewhere in the decaying hotel, the melancholy song seeping through the thin walls and enveloping them, and he can feel her tears on his skin as she buries her face in his neck and her body is like a furnace spreading warmth through him, and then she is pulling herself away, separating her limbs from his, and jerking her clothes on in the shadows with her face turned to the wall, and he sits up and starts to speak but she says ‘Don’t’ and hurries out the door without looking at him.

13

There is only one padlock left. The changing room is empty, the clock on the wall ticking towards midnight. Ezra rolls the dials to form Tom's date and the clasp clicks open. He impulsively holds his breath as he turns the handle and opens the door. An old phone and a flash drive lie inside; the mobile is a navy Nokia 8210 with a scuffed screen; the memory stick is short and black.

Outside in the light of the gym's window he tries to switch on the phone but the battery is dead. He scans the boulevard, peering at the figures that scurry through the rain-lashed darkness, and then cuts across the square towards the shuttered convenience store. The moored boats rock gently in the wind as the water laps at the dock. Glancing over his shoulder, he types in the door code and then pushes into the stairwell and climbs the steps in silence. He pauses outside their door and listens for movement inside, before slowly slotting the key into the lock and slipping into the black hallway.

The Intenso slithers around him as he goes into Tom's room and, with the light off, opens the bottom drawer of the bedside cabinet and takes out his laptop. As the computer loads he shines his phone into the drawer and rifles through the cables until he finds a charger that fits the Nokia. He plugs the mobile into the wall and, after a long pause, the battery icon appears on the scratched screen. He slots the flash drive into the laptop and a folder pops up. There are two files: a jpeg and a PDF. He double-clicks the jpeg and a photo leaps onto the screen: Tom and him, their heads pressed together, a Christmas tree behind them, Tom's left arm stretching beyond the frame to hold the camera and his right arm gripping the boy's neck. Their first Christmas. A smile stretches across Tom's face, his eyes gleaming in the flash. The boy's lips are pressed together in a self-conscious smile, the scar a thick purple line rising to his nostrils. The head of one of the wrestling figures, Chris Benoit, pokes into the bottom-left corner of the shot, and he remembers holding him up and the wrapping paper at his knees and the smell of the pine needles.

He clicks the PDF and a scan of a printed document appears. It is a text conversation between two phones. The numbers and messages are typed. By the numbers, in Tom's handwriting, are D and J.

<u>October 7, 00:23</u>

D: It's too late.

J: Why? Just tell him to stop.

D: I mean the deposit. Already done the prep work.

J: Fine. But it's off?

D: Yes. If you change your mind…

J: I won't.

<u>October 9, 14:08</u>

J: I've changed my mind.

D: I'll call you.

The boy grabs the Nokia and types in his own number and presses call; when his iPhone flashes the number on the screen matches J on the transcript. He opens the message folder on the Nokia; the texts match the transcript, but there are more, all outgoing to the number marked D on the PDF, sent on the night Tom was killed.

<u>October 9, 22.11</u>

I've been trying to call you. Call it off.

<u>22:14</u>

Is it off? Call me.

<u>October 10, 01:42</u>

What happened? Call me.

<u>01:44</u>

Did you get him? What's going on?

<u>04:22</u>

I didn't warn him, ok? I wanted it off. I didn't say anything to him. Where are you? Call me.

D is the only contact saved on the Nokia and the only calls are to him, outgoing and unanswered, between and after the text messages. Ezra calls D and holds the Nokia to his ear but it rings unanswered. He tries the number from his own phone, but again it just rings out. He calls Derek and Jo. Derek answers on the ninth ring, his voice hoarse.

“I need to speak to him.”

*

Dance music blasts from the radio, the bass shaking the speakers. The dual carriageway stretches ahead into a darkness penetrated every few seconds by the headlights of oncoming vehicles. The green arrow on his satnav points to the next right and Alex cuts across the highway into a narrow unlit road. The screen shows the chequered flag 20 metres ahead as a woodland flanks the window. He slows to a crawl, looking for a gap in the dark mass of trees and finding a strip of tarmac between the trunks.

The branches form a roof above the car as the tyres crunch over dead leaves. His headlights outline a cattle grid and the tyres clunk over the steel bars. The beams pick out the long blue body of a Mercedes. Beyond it there is another vehicle, and as he edges closer his lights drive away the shadows to reveal a red Seat. The cars are parked a dozen metres apart, their dipped headlights slanting across the overgrown grass verge and disappear into the clearing.

In the second row of spaces, on the other side of a picnic bench, there is a solitary black Chrysler, parked in the corner formed by the trees. A silver car sits in the final column of spaces, the same shape as their VW, but when he draws near his headlights capture the linked rings of the Audi logo.

He rolls down to the bottom of the car park and does a U-turn, his beams sliding over the dense woodland. He crawls over the cattle grid and pulls in on the left with his lights off. His phone flashes, the screen displaying a call from an unknown number. When he presses the speaker to his ear and says hello there is a pregnant silence, as though the caller is carefully forming their opening words or struck dumb by emotion, but then there is a click and a woman's recorded voice tells him to listen carefully to the following message about payment protection insurance. He hangs up and tosses the phone on the passenger seat, casting himself into darkness, but the gloom is instantly lifted by the lights of an approaching car, the wave of yellow sweeping over the avenue of branches and dazzling him. When the glare has gone he makes out the squat shape of a pink Mini bouncing over the cattle grid and the long hair of the driver inside.

There is the snarl of an engine and the Audi zooms past the other way. He watches its hind lights until they become red pinpricks and disappear, and when he closes his eyes the scarlet dots linger on the backs of his eyelids.

She was wearing her trenchcoat and red heels, following him out of the alleyway; she looked up at his window, her gaze lingering there as she climbed into the VW.

He peers in through the rear window of each car as he passes, the moonlight outlining only the heads of solitary drivers in the Mercedes and Seat. The black Chrysler is still in the corner spot, tinted windows concealing the inside. The Mini is down at the far end, parked right up against the trees and bushes, the shadows so thick that the car is only visible because the interior light is on. As he approaches he sees a teenage couple inside, glaring at his headlights. When his beams slide over the front of the Chrysler he sees a cloudy two-headed silhouette inside, and he turns in ten metres away from the black people-carrier. The trees are on a steep slope, their bare branches revealing the expanse of lights below: headlamps illuminating stretches of road and corners of buildings, the lit patches growing smaller and fainter towards the horizon where they merge into the moonless sky. He sits in the dark, the heater blowing hot air in his face as he peers at the Chrysler's passenger window. One of the cars further down reverses out and turns his way. As it draws near, the full beam of its headlights sweep across the side of his face and onto the passenger door of the people-carrier, revealing the hazy shadow of a single head inside. The Seat continues to the bottom of the car park and turns around and comes back, the light picking out the fuzzy silhouette of two heads this time – one leaning back against the backrest and the other bending towards the dashboard. The Seat pulls in to the left of Alex, two spaces away. A phone screen comes on inside, the dim white glow outlining the peak of a baseball cap in the driver's seat. There is a flash of blue – a lighter being sparked – and then the orange burning of a cigarette tip. The window rolls down and a cloud of smoke puffs out. He can feel the driver's eyes on his passenger window, squinting in.

Headlights slant over the cattle grid. A saloon rumbles closer, the passing stream of yellow picking out the shape of the capped head in the Seat before it rolls over Alex's face and onto the Chrysler, where just one blurry profile is visible beyond the glass. As the car curves around and the beam comes back he leans towards the people-carrier, once again only making out a solitary figure inside. The saloon keeps going all the way out of the car park. The temperature on the dashboard drops from 11C to 10. The Seat driver flicks the cigarette away – the orange glow arcing to the ground – and the window rises as the reverse lights blink on. The driver backs out slowly before the gears groan and he speeds towards the exit. The cattle grid clunks as the tyres bound over.

The car park is dark again. He looks at the motionless Chrysler, its black body almost invisible against the sky. He switches on the interior bulb and pretends to search for something in the glove compartment, and as he leans back he tilts his face, looking at the Chrysler through his own reflection in his side window before killing the light. His foot taps up and down on the dead accelerator pedal as he waits, listening to the wind swaying the stripped branches. The passenger window slowly rolls down. There is an amber glow inside. A face framed by long hair looks out.

The icy wind slithers inside his collar and curls around his ribs. The woman has her hand on the man in the driver's seat, slowly running her fingers up and down as she stares at Alex with a faint smile on her lips. She's wearing a tight black dress with a zip up the front, the metal teeth pulled apart at the top by her large breasts. Her legs are bare and as he steps closer she parts her thick thighs. She looks around 40, with a round face and bleached hair. The man nods at Alex, his glasses and bald head reflecting the light above. She grabs him through his jeans as he stands by the window.

A wave of light splashes over them, quickly followed by another, and he sees two cars crawling past. "Do you want to get in?" She squeezes between the headrests and slides the side door open. The seats in the middle are tilted forward and there's a blanket laid across the back row, the red and green floral pattern barely visible in the darkness. He stoops inside and sits down. The heater is on full blast in the front but it's still cold, and he shivers as she drops to her knees in front of him. From the front seat the man holds his mobile phone like a torch, casting a blue hue across her wide back and brittle hair as her head bobs up and down. She holds out her palm and he gives her a condom. As she rolls it down over him, Alex sees a face in the open passenger window – a man in his fifties with grey hair, craning his neck to look over the headrests; beyond his shoulder there is another man, also straining to get a view, his fat face topped by a black woollen hat. The man in the driver's seat nods at them and turns back to Alex and the woman who is carefully rising to her stilettoed feet. She rotates to face the men and then grips Alex with her hand and lowers onto him. As her weight falls on his thighs he looks at her left hand and sees her wedding and engagement ring, the smooth gold and solitaire flatly reflecting the blue beam from the phone; there is a ring on the hand holding the mobile too, the shadows painting the band a lighter shade of black than the finger.

She lifts herself off him and wrenches open the side door and the two men move into the rectangle of moonlight, ducking their heads inside. She raises a palm and they stop. She turns to Alex and leans back on the seat and spreads her legs. He rolls his jeans down to his ankles and kneels before her and she pulls him in, controlling his rhythm as her sweat fills his nostrils. She looks over his arm at the men in the doorway. He sees his own shadow on her chest and face, shifting shape and shade as he bangs his hips into hers, and she wrenches him closer, wrapping her arms and legs tight around his back in a deadlock as he fires into her. Arching back, he sees something beyond words in her eyes as she stares up at the roof.

"You're a lucky man," a cigarette-burned voice says, and he looks over his shoulder and realises the grey-haired man is talking to her husband. "Mm, she loves to put on a show for me." Alex untangles himself from her and she props herself up on her elbows and murmurs her thanks. "Cheers, mate," her husband says, his eyes hidden by his misted glasses as he holds out a packet of wet-wipes, and Alex takes one and uses it to slip the condom off as the woman pats herself down. The two men are still standing in the doorway, waiting uncomfortably; they move aside as Alex steps down from the vehicle and paces towards the car, the adrenaline draining away to leave only remorse and despair.

As he backs out he sees the woman sitting on the edge of the seat by the open door with the men looming over her. He drives along the winding path in silence, the headlights swaying through the trees with each bend and the droning engine the only sound. When he reaches the slip road he snaps the radio on, turning up the music until the bass is vibrating the steering wheel in his hand, his jaw clenched tight as he stares at the black road stretching ahead.

The light is on in her window, a glowing square in the dark expanse. He switches off the radio and rolls closer, stopping by their car and peering up, but nobody is there. When he steps into his room he sees her immediately. She leans against the windowsill, her naked back pressed against the glass. There is movement in the room beyond her. He moves closer to the window. Her husband is there, his gut hanging down over his thighs. There is another man next to him, lanky and pale, his ribs defined in the yellow light. Her hips are splayed and her elbow is bent as she jabs at herself. As the men move closer she glances over her shoulder, straight at him, her face blank and her forehead damp.

Alex bolts down the stairs, throws the door open and rushes into the misty rain. His feet slap the wet tarmac as he sprints across the road and hammers on the door, yelling her name. “Tina! Tina!” A window is cranked open next door, a shadowed face at the crack. “Tina! Tina! It’s Alex!” Light appears beneath the door.

“Who is it?” Her husband barks, angry and nervous.

“Alex.”

“Who?”

“I live across the road.”

“What do you want?”

“To speak to Tina.”

“She doesn’t want to speak to you.”

“She does, I know she does.”

“What? Fuck off, mate.”

“She does. You don’t know her.”

“What? She’s my fucking wife.”

“She hates you.”

“What?” The lock turns and the door opens a few inches with the chain on the latch, his vast body blocking out the light behind him. “What the fuck are you on about?”

“Last night. This morning. We…”

He slides off the chain and yanks the door back, his frame filling the doorway. “What the fuck are you on about?” His T-shirt is inside out and his baby-like legs naked.

Alex lunges at him, a wild swing carrying all his weight, his knuckle cracking off the bridge of his nose before he can get his arms up. As he staggers backwards Alex steps forward and kicks him between the legs. He wheezes as his hands jerk to his groin and he smacks against the wall, crumpling to the floor in a heap. Alex slips past him and bounds up the stairs, yelling Tina’s name in a savage roar. She is standing by the foot of the bed, the skeletal man beside her, both naked, limbs frozen, mouths gaping. She screams as he lurches forward and punches the man in the side of the head, sending him stumbling back against the bedpost in a tangle of brittle limbs.

"Alex! What are you doing?" Her voice is ragged, desperate. She backs away when he moves towards her. "I've come for you," he howls. "To take you away."

"What are you talking about?" There is terror in her eyes. It stops him cold, like chloroform on his adrenaline.

"To take you away," he murmurs, the energy fading from his voice. His middle knuckle is throbbing. The man has rolled onto the floor, waiting for a chance to escape. There are sirens outside, their screeches growing louder. Blue lights flash across the window. When he looks at Tina he sees relief.

14

"Ezra, you know where I live?" Peter says, standing in the doorway, his eyes bright behind his glasses despite the hour.

"I came with Tom once, a few years back," the boy says, the long driveway behind him. "I waited in the car."

"It must be important, son." His hands are buried in the pockets of a hastily-buttoned cardigan.

"I found something Tom left for me – in a gym locker."

The tension dissolves from the magistrate's face and shoulders.

Ezra speaks in frenzied bursts. "He got hold of Councillor Jordan's phone, printed out texts between him and someone saved as D. Jordan tried to call it off."

"Come in," Peter says, standing aside so the boy can slip past. He locks the door and strides ahead down the parquet corridor. His wife stares out from frames lining the long hallway; they are arranged chronologically, from a curly-topped infant gripping cot bars to a middle-aged woman clutching a glass of wine. "There's something you should see," he says, climbing the wide staircase where the pictures of Helen suddenly stop, replaced by framed certificates heralding his business achievements.

His study is encased with bookshelves filled with hardback anthologies. There is a Nokia 8210 on the desk, like the one in Tom's locker but less damaged. His laptop is on, the screen filled by a brochure with the title Perfect Dream in forward-slanting gold letters above a smiling elderly Japanese man. Peter sees Ezra looking and clicks the brochure away, and then holds out his hand for the flashdrive. As he reads the transcript he grows faint and has to lean on the desk.

"Are you ok?"

The magistrate nods and steadies himself, breathing sharply.

"There are more on the phone," Ezra says, holding out the councillor's Nokia.

Peter's face is ghost-white as he scrolls through the messages. He picks up the Nokia on his desk and detaches it from the charger, his cuff brushing over a framed picture of Tom and him; they stand either side of a towering Christmas tree, their less-lined faces beaming as they point at their decorating work. "This was Saul's," he says, handing the phone to Ezra. "I had it unlocked. Look at the messages."

There are four texts in total, all to and from an unsaved number.

<u>October 9, 17:02</u>

Done?

Done.

Will he?

That's what he said.

"Is it the same number?"

The boy nods.

"That's him checking that Saul warned Gardner." He sighs. "I should've seen this coming."

“What do you mean?”

He leans on the leather chair with his forearms digging into the backrest. “He was in love with Tom.”

“Who?”

“David.”

“David?”

“Who else?”

“I thought it might be Derek.”

“Derek? What made you think that?”

The boy shrugs. “David was in love with Tom? Isn’t he married with kids?”

“That means nothing to most people. I think he used the councillor and Gardner.”

“Why?”

“Why do people do anything? Maybe he told Tom how he felt and he laughed at him. I don’t know.” He rubs his eyes, pushing his glasses up onto his forehead. “It was David that told us the councillor had warned Gardner. We went on his word.”

Ezra is silent. He sees the councillor’s face in the sweeping headlights, his final thoughts of protecting his son.

“It’s the only explanation that makes sense. And it doesn’t make sense, really, does it? People don’t make sense.” He hangs his head, his eyes vanishing behind the lamplight on his glasses.

“What about the locker?”

“I think Tom knew something wasn’t right with Gardner so he

took the councillor's phone."

"And he went to Gardner's to warn him – that's why he knocked on the door and tried to talk to him."

"And why he put the phone in the locker. When he saw the texts with David he knew he couldn't trust him, so he left them for us to find, in case, and he was right – the texts the councillor sent afterwards prove that."

"Who was the other man with Saul?"

"It may have been Micah, as I said, but I can't be sure."

"Why would Saul do it?"

The magistrate raises his head, his eyes emerging from the light. "Money. Respect."

"Respect?"

"So he can say 'Look what I did'."

*

The boy squints in the headlights of an oncoming car, the tunnel of trees bleached white by the blinding rays. As the car shrinks in the mirror he sees the cattlegrid ahead and feels the vibration in his spine as the Ford's tyres bump over the bars. There are two cars at the far end, their roofs haloed by the hazy moon. The red Seat is wedged in the corner where the car park meets the woodland with a wind-blasted sapling hanging over the bonnet. He pulls in by the other car, a maroon Mitsubishi, and shuts off the engine. His hands tremble on the wheel as the hot air blasts him in the face. There are solitary silhouettes inside both cars. The Mitsubishi driver leans towards the dashboard, his head turned towards the boy, and then the engine groans and the taillights spring on, casting the tarmac and long grass in their scarlet glow as the car reverses slowly before speeding away into the grainy dark.

Ezra climbs out of the Ford and walks towards the woodland with his hood covering his face. As he passes the Seat he looks in, and after a second he hears the door opening and closing and glances back and sees David following him. He leads the way through the scrubland, the detective a few metres behind. A strip of light slashes through the trees as a lorry passes on the dual-carriageway and the boy turns away from the beam, burying his face in his shoulder. As the glare fades he picks his way through the brush, heading deeper into the forest with the detective crunching through the fallen leaves behind him. A car flies past, the headlights gliding over the crash barrier separating the woodland from the road. Ezra stops and watches as David strides closer. The branches block the moonlight from the boy's face as he draws the 9mm from his pocket.

"What the fuck?" David hisses, stopping dead.

He pulls his hood back.

"Ezra? What are you doing?"

"You killed Tom." His voice is flat.

"What?"

"You set him up."

"What are you talking about?"

"I saw the messages you sent the councillor and Saul."

"What messages?" He shuffles forward.

"Don't move," the boy barks, his voice almost breaking, and David freezes and raises his hands. "Tom took the councillor's phone. Peter took Saul's. We saw the messages."

"Peter," he sighs, looking up at the black sky and shaking his head.

The distant clunk of the cattle grid echoes towards them, followed by headlamps sweeping through the saplings on the edge of the woodland. As the light evaporates in the clearing David croaks, "How did you get the phones?"

"What does it matter?"

"Because he's lying to you, manipulating you – that's what he does. Where was Jordan's phone?"

"Tom left it in a gym locker."

"No, Peter did. What did the messages say? 'Kill Tom'? Do you think I'd be that stupid, to spell it out in a text message? I'm a detective. And I had nothing to do with it."

Ezra shakes his head, his voice wavering. "You know what the messages said."

"I don't, because I didn't send them. How did Peter get Saul's phone? How do you know the phone you found was Jordan's? He bought them and planted them to set me up."

"Why would he do that?"

“Because I quit and now it’s all falling apart. He wants to clean up – get rid of everyone who can tie him to this whole thing.”

“Why?”

“Why do you think? He’s worried he’ll be exposed, disgraced, and his precious refuge won’t happen. You know Peter, you know he’s not right – his wife, the refuge, his desperate need for respect.”

The boy stares at his shadow-veiled face.

“He’s so obsessed with that refuge, ‘his legacy’, his ‘look what I did’. What would happen if they found out how he got the money?”

“Tom printed the texts you sent the councillor.”

“No.”

“It was his handwriting.”

“No, it was Peter copying Tom. Ezra…” He exhales sharply, shaking his head. “He’s lying to you. He bought three phones and planned the messages, planned the whole thing.”

“Why would he want to kill Tom, they were like father and son.”

“That’s just it: were. Peter wanted Tom to idolise him, for him to have nobody else, the way he did…”

“Have nobody else?”

“Her.”

“Who?”

“You don’t know?”

“Know what?”

“Tom and the councillor’s daughter.”

“Kerry Jordan?”

“Yes.”

“When?”

“I don’t know – a few months. I thought you knew.”

The boy shakes his head.

“The night Tom was killed – I think he was there for her.”

A sharp beam slashes through the trees and across the detective. The boy reaches into his pocket and pulls out his phone. “If I call the number that sent those messages…”

“Go ahead. It’s not mine.”

He presses the phone to his ear and listens as the rings go unanswered.

“I told you: it wasn’t me.”

The boy peers through the branches at the car park and then looks at the detective. “Go.”

David pauses, squinting at the boy, and then starts walking back towards his car. Ezra follows a few yards behind, gripping the 9mm in his pocket. There are voices in the car park, an indistinct murmur. The detective looks back but the boy just keeps walking. When they near the edge of the woodland Ezra takes out his phone and calls the number again. There is a pause as the line connects, and then a faint light emerges within the Seat. David stops dead at the sight of the blueish glow rising from the passenger side. “No way,” he exhales. He turns to the boy and his eyes fix on the gun. “It’s not mine. He must’ve planted it there.”

Ezra clicks the safety off. “He trusted you.”

“It wasn’t me, son. I swear to you. I loved him.”

“But he didn’t love you back.” The boy steps closer so he can see his face in the moonlight. “So you killed him.”

“No. No. This is all Peter. He planned it all.”

He levels the barrel at the detective’s face. The sound of a woman cackling drifts towards them from the car park, followed by men chuckling.

When David speaks his voice is distant. “If it’s not you now it’ll be Micah tomorrow.”

“Micah?”

“His latest recruit. His new ‘son’. You kill me, Micah kills you, then someone else kills Micah, and round and round, and the only one left standing is Peter. I must be the only one who sees through his bullshit, and I’m fucking exhausted son, so just get it over with, eh?” He suddenly strides forward, his feet scything through the damp grass.

“Stop,” Ezra snaps, but the detective keeps coming until he’s an inch away and then slowly presses his forehead against the tip of the gun. “Do it,” he whispers. “I have nothing anyway.” His eyes burn through the darkness, his irises iridescent either side of the barrel. “Look at me. You get to a point where you’ve done so much that you can’t turn back.” He closes his eyes. “But it wasn’t me. I loved Tom.” The smell of his sweat and piss rises to the boy and clings to his face. “It haunts you, son, doesn’t it? The councillor, Saul, Gardner… It haunted Tom even though he believed they deserved it. Are you sure I deserve it, son? Are you certain? It's his word against mine. If you don't do this, if you walk away, he'll come after you, you'll see. Tell me you haven't looked in his eyes and seen the real him... I admit who I am and what I've done. He lies to himself. He's just an image." He sighs, his breath fading into the icy air. "That's all I've got. It's up to you."

Ezra stares at his gaunt face and heavy-lidded eyes and the sweat and saliva glistening in the moonlight. He pulls the gun away and steps back. David slowly opens his eyes. The boy nods towards the road and the detective starts walking, his footsteps uneven. Ezra follows two steps behind with the 9mm pointed at his back. When they reach the crash barrier a silver glow appears on the black horizon. "Over," he says, and David clambers over the steel beam onto the hard shoulder. "Turn around." He slowly faces the boy. The glow takes form as two white cones driven forward by a roaring engine. The detective glances at the lorry and looks back at the boy. "No," he grunts, suddenly furious. "You'll have to pull that trigger; it's you doing this." The headlights sweep across the side of his face as the lorry approaches.

"Go," Ezra shouts, but his voice is lost in the noise. He points down the sloping road to the hazy light of the roundabout. The lorry blasts them with a gust of air as it passes in a blur, and as the sound fades the detective starts to back away, his eyes wide and gleaming, and then he turns and sprints down the hill, only looking back once he’s a hundred metres away and then continuing on until his silhouette merges with the darkness.

15

It is murky dawn when Alex comes out of the police station, the thin sun held down by the charcoal clouds. There is a damp stillness in the air, a residue of the spent downpour, and he shivers as he stands outside the sliding doors looking down the deserted road.

Sitting in the back of a taxi, he peers up at her window. The light is out and the blinds are down. The takeaway shutters flicker between dull grey and gleaming silver in the faulty streetlight. As he steps out of the cab he looks up at his own window, taking in the void beyond. The taillights blink on him as he tries his phone but the battery is still dead. The red glow vanishes from his face as the taxi pulls away.

There is a cold darkness inside his room. The broken radiator clicks erratically and the sleeping computer hums relentlessly. He packs up his belongings, filling a small holdall with as much as he can fit inside. Leaning over the desk, he deletes his internet history and switches off the PC, and then he heaves the bag onto his shoulder and walks out without looking back. As he starts the car he notices movement in the bottom right window. His housemate Sian peers out, her eyes heavy with sleep. She waves at him and he nods back, and then she lowers the curtain. He plugs the satnav in and, as he waits for the screen to load, he unzips the CD case and slides out a disc marked For Alex in forward-slanting handwriting. As the soft, dreamy music starts, he types Manchester into the satnav.

*

His fist tight around a hammer, Peter bangs nails into the hull of the boat as the noon sun drops fast in the crystal sky behind him. The boy stands by his side, rubbing a sanding block against the wooden boards, the two of them working on the small sailing craft, the scene from the picture in the B&B. The sun keeps falling, a burning orb scything through the sky, plummeting behind the horizon and dragging the light into the sea. Peter jerks his head towards the water, squinting behind his glasses, and then he drops the hammer on the sand and strides out towards the shore. He is a silhouette a pitch darker than the black sky as he wades out until he is immersed waist high and plunges his hands into the water. The boy drops the sanding block and slowly walks towards the shore, the water lapping at his bare feet. Peter is struggling, the muscles tensed in his wiry arms as he holds something down under the surface. He turns to the boy and silently shouts for him to help. Ezra makes his way through the water, the rocky seabed cold and jagged on his soles. The moon ascends over the horizon, a sharp white disc, its pale light reflected in Peter's glasses as he bears all his weight down into the sea. As the boy reaches him he follows his eyes down into the water, seeing Tom's face beneath the rippling surface, his eyes closed and his body limp as the magistrate strangles him. Peter lets go and turns to the boy, nodding with satisfaction as Tom drifts away into the murky water until he is a vague shape on the seabed. The magistrate looks towards the shore. Ezra's mother is there, watching, her scrawny arms hanging loosely from the frayed sleeves of her white nightgown, her face pale and impassive.

He awakes drenched in sweat and face-down on the edge of the mattress with the duvet twisted around his ankle. The dog is gone. He sits up and scans the shadows, whispering his name, but there is no response. Grabbing the 9mm, he listens for movement downstairs. With the gun at his hip, he creeps down the steps and as he reaches the bottom he hears a scratching sound coming from the kitchen. He edges towards the ajar door, peering through the narrow gap into the grey-dark. The dog is facing the back door, his head and front paw concealed by the fridge. Ezra slips inside, the lino cold on his bare feet. The dog looks at him before turning back to the door and snarling in a low rumble. Hidden by the fridge, the boy raises the gun to shoulder height before pivoting out and pointing the barrel at the frosted glass.

There is nobody there, just the shadows in the yard warped by the patterned windowpane. He bends down and strokes the dog but he is oblivious to his touch as he continues to growl, crouching on his front leg with his stubby tail frozen upright. Ezra steps in front of him and listens by the glass but the only sound is the dripping from the cracked gutter. He gently turns the key in the lock and pulls the door open. Holding his breath, he strains to hear a reaction – footsteps on the concrete or hands on the fence – but there is nothing but the patter of the water. He sidesteps into the yard, his eyes whipping over the paved square with its pile of rubbish bags and bursts of weeds. Standing on his tiptoes, he peers into the gardens over the fence, but each one is as dark and lifeless as the houses. The dog scurries out and does a lap around the yard, sniffing every inch of the perimeter and around the bin bags before returning to the boy and licking his bare foot and staring up at him with his head cocked.

Ezra goes back in, locks the door and puts the key in his pocket. He scoops up the dog with his free hand and carries him up to the bedroom. In the bathroom he cranks the window open and looks down at the empty one-way street, his eye drawn to movement in the shadows across the road. A shaved head floats above the parked cars, slowly bobbing along and stopping every few paces. His face is turned to the pavement and when he moves into the gap between two cars the light bounces off a hi-vis vest and the boy sees that he is holding a sack and a grabber and picking litter out of the gutter.

He stares up at the ceiling with the gun by his pillow and Charlie on his chest. The dog breathes slowly as he drifts to sleep. Ezra closes his eyes but he is acutely aware of every noise the old cottage makes – creaking pipes, humming fridge – as he replays the conversations with Peter and David over and over in his head, scrutinising their every word and expression. He props himself up against the wall, carefully pulling up the cover so Charlie slides down onto his thighs without awaking. Holding the photo, he inspects Tom and his parents and then the two sets of handwriting on the back; his mother's letters are joined and forward-leaning while Tom's are separated and upright, the jagged characters hinting at those times when a darkness would fall behind his eyes and he would sound like an actor without a script casting around for words, and the boy would awake in the night and hear muffled sobbing next door. He flips open the laptop and compares the handwriting on the photograph with the PDF, finding variances small enough to be caused by both a different hand and the passage of time.

A car passes outside, the sound of the smooth engine rising and falling. When he types the councillor's name into Google he is confronted with a picture of him and his wife, son, and daughter, all smiling, abroad somewhere with dusty limestone buildings in the background. On Facebook he searches for Kerry Jordan. Her page is locked, only her profile picture visible: her hair is bright orange and her eyes like silver in the sharp sun; she is in a park and a man's arm curls around her neck, the rest of him cropped out.

The news report says the investigation into her father's death is ongoing, that it may have been an accident. He pictures the councillor as he stood on the kerb, the headlights illuminating the fear in his silver eyes as he thought only of his son. He sees Gardner in the torchlight with his face bleached like a photo negative. The Google results for 'Peter Armitage + magistrate' start with the rape and murder of his wife. There is a cropped picture of the two of them arm-in-arm among a huddle; they look like siblings – the same twinkly eyes and fine-boned features – but she is even more delicate, her cropped greying hair giving her an elfin quality. A month later there was a tribute article with comments from Peter; every line sounds hackneyed and impersonal, as though the grief had destroyed his eloquence: 'the light of his life', 'she always put other people first'. There is a picture of the two of them together in a restaurant, smiling up from a candlelit dinner, and a separate photo of Peter taken for the article in which he looks unbalanced, with one eye slightly narrower and redder than the other and the grey hairs more abundant around his right temple than left.

Another article, written 18 months later, details the sentencing of a 34-year-old man called James Flynn for the rape and murder. He is a scrawny, pock-marked man with fuzzy black hair, staring out from his police mugshot with feral eyes. There is no comment from Peter – he declined to give a statement – but the same photo of him is used with the article. Another story, a few months on, reports that Flynn was found hanged during his second month in prison. Again, Peter declined to comment, and again the same picture of him was used.

In later articles the magistrate is pictured attending launch events and charity fundraisers, his eyes bright again and his whitened teeth fixed in a smile. In a photo taken four years ago he is among a group outside the new police station, on the left of the huddle around the mayor as she cuts the ribbon with oversized scissors. Detective David Halliwell stands next to him, his face less drawn and the slug-like bags only just starting to form under his eyes.

The dog sighs and shifts his leg, his eyelids fluttering at a dream. A car starts up outside, the engine stuttering to life. The iPhone Peter gave him lights up with Jo's name above a message. "We need to talk."

*

The service station is almost empty, the food court tables glossy in the emerging sun through the floor-to-ceiling windows. Alex sits in the corner of the Costa, facing the car park with his phone plugged into the wall. He stares at Emma's Facebook page, his finger hovering over the empty message box. 'Hello' he types, and then he deletes the letters, his eyes on her face, recalling the warmth of her back on his chest and the small Italy-shaped birthmark at her nape with the northern edge running into her hairline. 'Hello Emma, I'm in Manchester today. Would you like to meet?' He reads the message over and over before finally clicking send.

*

Ezra strokes the dog and whispers goodbye before pulling the door shut. The sun has broken through the clouds, spreading watery light across the windshields, and the smell of acid rain lingers in the air as he steps out into the road. There is a loud screech as a Corsa whips around the corner and speeds straight at him. He leaps out of the way, bouncing off a wet bonnet and landing on the tarmac with his shoulder taking the impact. As he scrambles to his feet he hears a pop and something burning hot punches his ribs. A silhouette bolts from the car with a raised gun. The litter picker is two paces behind and pointing a 9mm. As they close in the empty Corsa starts rolling backwards. They both lunge forward, slipping on the slick tarmac, and the car glides behind them and smashes tail-first into the side of a parked taxi. Ezra jerks the 9mm out of his pocket and fires twice, hitting the litter picker in the stomach and the silhouette in the collar. As they hit the ground he grabs his rucksack and pushes himself to his feet, screaming at the jolt of pain in his ribs.

His left arm dangles by his side as he runs towards the spinning horizon. At the end of the street he stops and looks back, squinting in the dazzling slither of sun between the rooftops. Black smoke rises from the crumpled Corsa and taxi. The boy stumbles back with the gun still in his hand. The silhouette lies face-down with the hood covering the back of his head. When he rolls him over the face of a girl stares up at him from behind a black stocking. Her eyes are empty and there is a hole in her throat – a ragged cavity in her mahogany skin. Her blood has pooled like oil in the rainbow rainwater in the pothole above her head. Her gun lies by her crooked elbow. Her pockets are empty.

The litter picker is still alive. He holds the hole in his fluorescent vest, his 9mm a yard from his hip. His eyes focus on the boy as he crouches over him.

“Micah?”

His lips twitch. His skin has turned the colour of cigarette ash. An iPhone pokes out of a half-zipped pocket. Ezra takes the mobile as sirens shriek from the end of the street. He scurries towards the footpath, his legs numb and heavy. Blue lights whip across the crushed cars. At the bottom of the slope he crosses the empty car park towards the canal and takes the iPhone Peter gave him out of his pocket and, with his good arm, hurls the mobile into the murky water.

16

The boy limps across the road, trying to focus on the rundown hotel as the street slides around him. His left hand is tucked inside his pocket and every step is like an earthquake jarring his shoulder against the socket, the sharp bolts only momentarily distracting his pain sensors from the feeling of a lit cigar being twisted into his ribcage. As he catches his reflection in the window his mind snaps back to the hospital room and that same drowsiness before he went into surgery, that feeling of being between sleep and consciousness in a half-formed world as he looked in the mirror and saw himself with Tom in the background. He looks normal from afar as he approaches the grimy glass but when he goes inside and sees himself in colour in the mirror he is green and filmed with sweat.

The bar is empty, the weak sun illuminating columns of dust as it seeps in through the window. Sky Sports news rolls on the TV and stale beer clings to the floor. Footsteps sound on the other side of the swing-door and a scrawny woman appears.

"I need a room."

She looks him up and down. Micah's phone buzzes in his pocket. "How many nights?"

"One."

"It's thirty, up front."

He winces as he slides the rucksack off his back and reaches in for the money, separating the notes from the roll and laying them on the counter.

She tucks the cash into her back pocket. "Anything funny and we call the police."

He nods.

"We do food."

"I'm ok."

"Nine," she says, laying the key on the counter.

As he climbs the staircase he feels like he's about to pass out, but he makes it up into the corridor and manages to find the door and turn the key. The room is tiny, just a box with a bathroom and the faint smell of vomit. He lowers the bag onto the bed and slowly takes his clothes off, every motion inducing a stab of agony. The T-shirt sticks to his damp skin and he has to peel the cotton away and slip it down around his lifeless shoulder. There is blood and bits of material around the wound and the skin is a purple shockwave. He sits on the worn carpet and raises his knees to his chest and lifts his left arm with his right and hooks his fingers around his shins. Taking a deep breath, he leans backwards until his arms are extended, the pain excruciating as the muscles and nerves twist and stretch, but the shoulder won't pop into the socket. Panting, he leans forward, his arm limp on the floor. When he tries again he cannot stop himself from exhaling in a scream as he wrenches back, but still the shoulder won't crack into place.

As he hunches over, shivering, he feels the dog's cold nose on his back and he turns his head and starts to whisper his name but there is nothing there but stained carpet. He slides Micah's iPhone out of his jacket. There are five missed calls from a withheld number. He swipes the screen but it is locked by a passcode. He feels a presence in the corner as though someone has emerged from the yellowed wallpaper. When he looks over his shoulder he expects to see his mother but there is only empty space. Staggering into the bathroom, he flips on the light. His eyes are dilated and bloodshot in the scuffed mirror. As he stares at himself there is a sudden rush in his sternum and he doubles over and vomits into the toilet in a violent gush of acid. He crawls to the sink on one hand and reaches up and turns the rusted tap. Kneeling, he cranes his head and gulps down the icy water as his stomach spasms. After a few minutes he summons the strength to lean over the bathtub and twist the hot tap and then clamber inside, letting the scalding water gather under him and slowly rise up over his body as he watches himself in the mirror on the back of the door, staring through his reflection like he is one of those magic eye puzzles Tom showed him, where you have to peer through the picture to see the hidden image. There is a painting hanging above the bed: an old man and his son lean on the hull of a beached sailboat, looking in at the little boy inside. He lies back and stares at the picture, trying to make out their expressions, but the faces are obscured by the steam and distance of the reflection.

By the time he looks down at the bathwater it has turned pink and is almost neck deep. He shivers as he peers through the surface at the hole in his skin, watching the blood ooze out and fade into the water.

"Hey. Hey. Hey." His mother's voice. A hand on his shoulder. His eyes snap open. A girl's face looms over him, but no brown eyes, no stocking mask. Small emerald irises. Pale, translucent skin and a tangle of red curls. "Are you alright?" She flinches as he bolts upright, the water sloshing over the rim and onto the floor.

Her eyes fix on the wound and then his limp arm. His shoulder pulses as he instinctively tries to cover his groin and he has to push down from within to suppress a cry.

"What happened?"

He stares back mute, only halfway into consciousness.

"I heard you screaming. The door was unlocked." She has a faint Irish accent, her voice somehow unreal. "Are you alright?"

"I was in a crash," he mutters, his eyes casting around for the 9mm in the room beyond her.

"You need to go to hospital."

Still covering himself, he tries to rise and slips back and his shoulder thumps the rim of the tub and rips a howl from his lungs. An involuntary laugh escapes her, borne of tension and fear.

"Where's your towel?" She walks into the bedroom and he hears the drawers opening and then there is silence and he realises she has vanished. The ceiling light refracts on the back of his eyelids, twisting and multiplying like a kaleidoscope. When he opens his eyes she is standing over him with a towel like a paramedic with the death sheet. She slips her hand under his arm and helps him up, and all he can focus on is covering himself and then he is aware of how soft and warm the towel feels around his waist. The room swirls as he staggers towards the bed and lays back with her palm under his neck. When she speaks the sound is muffled and distant as though coming from a TV two floors up. Staring at the blurry figures in the painting, he feels her hands around his wrist and her toes wiggling into his armpit, and before he can register what she is doing she is yanking back on his arm and there is a cracking sound which echoes through his body as searing pain explodes from his shoulder, and when he tries to scream her palm is covering his mouth and her hair is brushing against his forehead, blocking the light above as the room shrinks in on itself like a black hole.

"If you only learn in an automatic – "

"What will I do if I suddenly have to drive a manual?"

"I know, I'm like a broken record," Tom said, smiling. They were sitting in the Ford in the deserted car park behind the derelict cinema at the Quays, the sinking sun hitting the old sign and the imprint left by the removed letters. "It's muscle reflex memory; eventually you don't even think about going from second to third, you just do it."

"Like shooting the 9mm?"

He shook his head. "You always have to think about that. Come on, let's go round again."

The boy started the engine and pressed the clutch and shifted into first.

“Find the biting point,” Tom said, looking down at his feet on the pedals, but he was too quick to lift the clutch and the car stalled. Ezra punched the wheel, growling with frustration.

“If you get everything right first time, life becomes boring,” Tom said, “and you end up being a twat.”

“I can’t even drive yet anyway.”

“Yes you can.”

“I’m not 17 yet.”

“What does that matter? Start the engine. And just relax – ”

“Saying that never helped anybody.”

“Ok, just don’t worry about fucking up. I’m the only one watching and I already think you’re a twat.”

On the ninth lap around the car park Tom said, “Do you think we should move away from Gloucester?” His voice was casual but his face showed it was not a spontaneous idea.

“Why?”

He shrugged. “A fresh start.”

Ezra rolled the car to a stop facing the canal. The water was streaked gold by the dying sunrays.

“You’ve just finished school. We’ve got enough money.”

“What about Peter and David?”

“They’d understand.”

“I thought you liked it.”

“Liked is the wrong word.”

"You know what I mean: you're doing something important."

There was something in Tom's eyes that held back his real answer. "I just feel ready for a change. Anyway, I thought you'd be happy. You're not exactly looking forward to college and you're always saying how boring Gloucester is."

"What about your job?"

"I can do that anywhere. I know you don't like change and nobody could ever – "

"Look," he interrupted, pointing to the canal. "What's that?" Tom pulled up his legs so Ezra could open the glovebox and grab the binoculars. When he focused on the footpath there was nothing there, just the dusty concrete and murky water beyond, but as he strafed further along he spotted something white behind a spurt of weeds. He jumped out of the car and strode across the tarmac and into the overgrown grass verge. Tom climbed out and stood by the door, his right hand instinctively in his pocket. "What is it?" he shouted.

The boy could hear shallow breathing coming from somewhere in the tangle of weeds. He followed the sound, moving slowly through the knee-high grass, and then suddenly saw it a yard ahead: a small dog lying on its side with its eyes gradually sliding shut. Its front right leg had been amputated and its ribs were visible through its patchy fur. The dog barely raised its head as Ezra knelt and carefully picked it up, cradling it against his chest as he strode back to the car. "He's alive," he called to Tom, his voice breaking and his eyes iridescent. Tom dashed to the driver's side and started the engine. He was looking up the nearest vet on his phone as the boy slid into the passenger seat.

As Tom turned out of the car park a smile spread across his face and he chuckled to himself.

"What?" the boy asked, his palm on the dog's slowly-beating heart.

"After everything, you're like this," he said, shaking his head.

"The door was open. You were screaming."

He can feel the mechanics of his body: heart clanking; pulse warbling; the dry slide of his eyelids.

"Can you hear me?"

He nods, his neck stiff.

"You almost drowned in the bath."

He's lying on the bed, propped up on the pillows. The duvet is turned back at his waist and the towel is folded under his shoulder. She stands by the door, clutching her phone by her side.

"What happened?"

His lips are crusted together. "Crash."

"You've been shot."

Even on the edge of consciousness he can sense the anxiety behind her cool stare and calm voice.

"Did you call an ambulance?"

She shakes her head, her orange-peel hair brushing her shoulders. "Do you want me to?"

"No." He shuffles up against the headboard. His shoulder throbs as he wriggles his fingers and slowly rotates his arm, recalling the feel of her foot in his armpit and the blast of agony. "Are you a nurse?"

She shakes her head and holds up her phone. "Google. I'm staying next door. You need a doctor."

His brain reconnects to his ribs and the fire inside the wound. "I'm ok."

She studies him, her jaw tight. "I can go to Boots and get something to help."

His eyes sweep over her broad-hipped figure beneath the girlish T-shirt and leggings, trying to work out how old she is.

"I won't tell anyone," she says. "You can't leave it in there – I looked it up."

He tries to place the strange twang in her voice but the sound is alien. When he tries to shift his legs to the side of the bed his feet feel weightless, as though the blood has been drained out. "Why?"

"Why?"

"Why help me?"

There is only a slither of natural light, sliding in over the top of the wall opposite the window, but it is enough to see her eyes narrow as she contemplates the question. "You need help and I'm here."

He nods faintly.

"I'll go to Boots." She looks down at her Nikes. "I don't have any money."

His eyes cast around the room for the rucksack, finding it

propped against the wall below the window. She follows his gaze and picks up the bag and lays it on the mattress by his hand before backing away to the door. The 9mm, Michah's iPhone and the rolls of money are still there. He separates two twenties and places them on the bedspread by his hip. She steps forward and slides the notes into her palm and tucks them into the waistband of her leggings, a silver navel ring catching the light.

"I'll be about half an hour."

"I'll wait here."

A smile flickers across her face. "Really?"

"No baths."

"Good. I don't know CPR."

"Just shoulders."

As she opens the door she glances back and says "I'm Holly, by the way," and then walks away before he can reply.

He can hear the traffic outside and a vacuum cleaner going somewhere in the building; the sounds melt into one rhythmic hum and he allows himself to close his eyes and let his mind float – the same sensation as after the anaesthetic all those years ago – and then he is wondering how he spoke to Holly when he is not a real person and can't interact with real people, contemplating the question from afar like a critic watching a drama or a ghost visiting his old home, but he doesn't believe in spirits or souls or anything, like Tom who said 'They're gone' when he asked him where he thought his parents were, but still he pictures the councillor and Gardner and Saul and the stocking-faced girl stretched out on the ceiling above, watching him with their faces contorted, and then Tom is between them, his eyes hard and his jaw tight, angry and disappointed and desolate.

A shiver quakes down his spine and he's suddenly aware of the rectangular crack on the ceiling where the plasterboard has come loose. He reaches into the bag for Micah's iPhone and slides his thumb across the screen and the passcode lock comes up.

There is a tap on the door. "It's me." She slips in with a bag dangling from her wrist. "I think I got everything." As she smiles at him, shy and close-lipped, he sees that she is no more than 15 and doesn't really know what she's doing. She reaches inside her jacket pocket and places his change on the bedside cabinet.

"How are you feeling?" She meets his eye for the first time, fighting the impulse to look away.

"Ok," he whispers.

"I got tweezers and anaesthetic. We should do it now."

He nods.

"It looks pretty simple."

"Google?"

She tries to smile but the anxiety overwhelms her. "It's gonna hurt. The gel should help but still…"

"Where?"

"In the bath is best."

He winces as he starts to rise.

"Can I ask you something? What's your name?"

He pauses, his jaw tight. She shifts the bag into her other hand. "It's just in case I need to shout at you."

"Ezra." He gathers the towel around his waist and slides out of the bed and pads into the bathroom. As the water fills the tub he inspects the wound, gently prodding the violet skin around the black hole. Turning to the mirror, he examines his face; the cuts on his temple have scabbed over but the slashes above his eyebrow are still raw and, with his bleached hair, he looks like a friend of his mother's, Jane, who'd bring him odd scraps she found on the way to the flat – tennis balls and broken dolls – and had a surreal wraithlike beauty, and stubbed a cigarette out on the back of his hand when he reached for one of her chips.

She taps on the door. "Alright?"

The bath is half full. Leaving his boxers on, he steps in and slides down in the steaming water. "Yeah."

When she opens the door her face is bleached with anxiety. "Ready?"

He nods.

"I've got anaesthetic gel." She holds up the tube and then folds the towel and lays it on the floor and kneels. "You need to be dry." She hands him a flannel from the bag and he dabs around the wound.

"Tell me something," she says as she gently pats the gel onto the torn skin.

"Like what?"

"About you."

“Why aren’t you at school?”

“Didn’t feel like it. And my mum’s at work.”

“Is she staying with you next door?”

She nods.

“How long have you been here?”

“Almost a week. She’s looking for a flat.” She touches the wound. “Can you feel that?”

“A bit.”

“So you’re not gonna tell me what happened?”

He takes in her face – the small lucid eyes and rosebud mouth – as she stares at his ribs. “Are you and your mum running away from something?”

She flicks her eyes at him. “Who’s Charlie?”

He stares back.

“You were saying his name. And Tom.”

“He’s my dog.”

“Charlie?”

He nods. She prods his rib.

“Numb.”

“It’ll still hurt, inside, but it’s right under the surface so…”

He looks up at her, the question in his eyes.

“I had a look when you were sleeping. You can kind of feel it.”

She takes a pair of tweezers out of the bag and leans her forearm on the edge of the tub, the fine hairs glistening in the steamy light. “Can you lift your arm?”

He slowly raises his arm and lays his wrist on the handle.

"You have to talk to me while I'm doing it, ok?"

He nods.

"How long have you had Charlie?"

"A few months."

She peels back the flaps of stressed skin. "Where did you get him?" Circling the top of the flesh with her finger, she feels for the bullet under the surface.

"I found him by the old cinema in Gloucester."

"Really?" She parts the flayed skin and edges the tweezers inside and he flinches and grits his teeth. "So he was a stray?"

Sweating and bone white, he speaks between breaths, gripping the handle with his good arm. "He was by the canal. Half dead. Tom was teaching me to drive."

She nods as he speaks, edging the tweezers further inside the wound. "So you rescued him."

He watches her eyes, narrowed in concentration and gleaming in the damp light. He gasps as the tips of the tweezers meet the bullet. She has to push to force the tongs into a grip. "Got it," she whispers, and she slowly draws the bullet out, the sensation sending a shiver through him. She holds it up to the light; the tip is flattened from the impact. "Your ribs must be wrecked."

He stares at the warped steel, blinking away the sweat gathered in his lashes.

She tips a bottle of antiseptic onto a cotton ball and swabs the wound. He clenches the handle, trying not to wince.

“Almost done,” she whispers, and she takes a packet of medical strips out of the bag. “Sit up.” She pinches the flesh together and stretches one across. “Does it hurt?”

“I don’t know anymore.”

She fixes another strip in place. “So who’s Tom?”

“My dad.”

“Where is he?”

“Dead.”

“Oh. Sorry.”

“It’s just me and him.” He nods at the doorway, expecting to see the dog.

“Ezra, stay awake. Where’s Charlie?”

“At home.”

“Near here?”

He nods.

“Shall I go and get him?”

He shakes his head and lays his hand on her arm, his fingers curled around her slim wrist. “How long are you staying?” he murmurs.

“Until we can leave.”

“Me too.”

She studies his cat-like eyes and the faint scar. “My name isn’t really Holly. I don’t know why I said it was. You lied about your name too.”

"I didn't lie."

"Really? Ezra?"

He nods. "Tom chose it. After a poet."

"I wish my name had a story. Sarah is so boring."

"It's good."

"Does the job." She presses down the final strip. "It says you can get them wet but I wouldn't." She kneels back, inspecting her work. "How's your arm?"

"Better than it was."

"Hungry?"

He shakes his head.

"You should eat something. KFC?"

He nods.

"I'll get salad."

"Yes, doctor."

"What do you want?"

"Whatever you have."

"Ok. I won't be long." She glides her hand through the water by his thigh before rising to her feet and walking away.

17

Alex stands by the railings, gazing at the halls of residence. The sun streaks the glass stairwell of the western tower where a handful of windows release music into the empty square below. Two Japanese girls come out with handbags under their arms and scarfs around their necks, chatting in their native tongue as they stroll across the courtyard. Alex moves towards the gate, pretending to make a call on his phone. The girls reach the other side and the one with a purple waterproof types a code into the keypad and the lock clicks. As they go through he steps forward and the shy girl at the back holds the gate open for him. Peeking inside the security hut, he finds an empty desk with a blank CCTV monitor and rows of locked postboxes on the wall behind. He checks Facebook on his phone: she has not replied.

A skinny guy with ginger hair emerges from the eastern block, his rucksack bouncing as he strides across the courtyard. “Excuse me, I’m supposed to meet my friend Emma,” Alex says, “but she’s not here and not answering her phone. I don’t suppose you know her? Long black hair?”

“No, sorry, mate.”

“Hold on.” He flicks through his phone and holds up her photo. “That’s her.”

“Sorry, mate.”

“Where’s the security guy?”

“There’s no-one there on Sundays.”

As the boy walks away Alex goes back into the hut and leans on the desk and switches on the monitor; the screen is divided into eight squares: outside the door to each block, the gate, the communal area in each building and a high-up view of the whole site. He inspects the students gathered in the communal areas – the cameras looking down from above the televisions – but she is not among them. Again he checks Facebook, finding no new messages. On her page he studies the profile picture of her in the bar with her friends and the blond guy, and then walks away into the biting wind.

*

"Do you want to know why we're here?"

"If you want to tell me."

She sweeps the wrappers off the duvet and into the box and perches on the end of the bed. "We're travellers. Pikeys." She picks a carton off the covers by his thigh and glances up to gauge his reaction, but there is no change in his eyes. "Do you feel any better?"

"Nobody feels good after KFC."

"We ran away. Well, she did."

"Why?"

"My dad." Her eyes are on the painting of the men and the boy in the boat as she speaks. "They've been together since she was 14."

"Is he looking for you?"

"They probably all are."

"Where do you live?"

"Near Dursley."

"You didn't run far."

"She wants him to find us. She's done it before. But I don't want to go back this time. I'm not going back."

"How old are you?"

"Fifteen. You?"

"Seventeen."

"I'm sixteen in two months. Seven weeks and five days. They want me to marry this boy. My mum doesn't want me to but…" She shrugs and glances at her phone. "She'll be back soon." The water pipes creak above. "I'll come back later, if you want?"

"I might not be here."

"Oh."

"I might have to go."

She glances at the taped up wound. "Our room faces the street: I'll keep watch." She backs towards the door. "See you later, then."

He nods, watching her slip away and then listening to the sound of her moving across the corridor and opening and closing her door and the bed creaking, and he pictures her slight hands tapping her phone and the pink skin of her nape as she ties up her hair.

Micah's phone rings again, vibrating inside his rucksack; another withheld number. He waits for the buzzing to stop and then slides his thumb across the screen and stares at the passcode prompt and tries 1234 and then Tom's four-digit code, knowing neither will work.

*

His eyes keep closing as he peers out of the wide doors into the crowd of umbrellas and grey faces, looking for oil-black hair.

"Alex. Alex." The clerk's voice breaks through to him and he turns to her. "Room nine." She nods at the key on the desk and smiles.

In the room he stands in the window with his forehead pressed to the glass. Jet streams rise in the square below, the bursts of water meeting the misty rain and blurring the lights of the shop signs and buses beyond. She still hasn't replied to his Facebook message. He picks up the phone by the bed and dials her number from memory and listens to the recorded voice saying the number has been disconnected, and then he draws the curtains and lies down and stares up at the ceiling. The shadows flicker as the light outside shifts and seeps inside, the same way the moon slithered into his room as a child, and he hears his mother sighing 'Oh Alex' and feels the warmth of their bodies surrounding him.

A vibration pulls him back: his phone in his pocket. 'Mum' flashes in white on the screen. He opens the bedside drawer. There is a bible inside. As he stares at the black cover and the gold lettering he feels his chest swelling and contracting as though his diaphragm has broken. He places the phone on the bible and shuts the drawer and lies back and closes his eyes as the buzzing fades out.

Between sleep and consciousness he feels Emma next to him, the warmth of her back on his ribs and her sole on his shin. When he rolls over his mother is watching him from the corner, her face veiled by the shadows as she grips the edge of the curtain. He slides out of bed and staggers into the bathroom and flips on the light. Tina sits on the toilet lid, naked, holding the unformed foetus in the palm of her hand. She stares up at him, her eyes cold.

*

Micah's iPhone vibrates against the floor, stirring him awake. Sarah is next to him, leaning against the headboard and reading her phone, her face half-lit by the screen in the grainy darkness. "Shall I answer?"

He shakes his head, still drowsy. As she sits back he glimpses her phone screen poking out from her hand: she has typed Ezra into Facebook. "I'm not on there," he whispers.

"Good." She blushes. "I don't want to see what you had for dinner."

He slowly pushes himself up, wincing and breathing hard.

"Where are you going?"

"I have to get Charlie."

"You need to rest."

"I can't leave him." He shuffles to the side of the bed and lowers his feet to the floor. She lays her hand on his shoulder, the warmth of her palm tingling down his spine. “I’ll go.”

He looks back at her and shakes his head.

She holds his gaze, her lips starting and discarding words. “I’ll come with you.”

He tries to argue but she is already on her feet and slipping on her trainers. “You won’t even make it to the door without me.”

She watches as he struggles to pull on his jeans one-handed, and when he tries to wrench his T-shirt on she steps forward and takes over, lowering the collar over his head and threading his bad arm through the sleeve and gently laying the cotton over his bandaged ribs, all in silence with her eyes fixed on her hands and her cheeks glowing and her fingers barely touching his skin.

*

The flashing lights reach across the cars and filter through the stripped branches. A police van blocks the road and striped tape stretches from lamppost to lamppost. Sarah studies Ezra’s face as they approach the street; he stares ahead, his eyes cast in the shade of his hood. They walk slowly, the boy wincing and holding his hurt arm against his ribs. As they pass the van they see the white tent and officers in boiler suits and neighbours gathered in doorways and speaking to reporters at the edge of the cordon, the scene pressed down by the charcoal sky and misty rain.

“We can get round that way,” he says, looking at an alleyway beyond a rundown garage with rotting wooden signs. In the passageway the paving stones start to spin before him and he has to stop and lean against the wall. She slips her hand into his armpit and holds him. After a few seconds he straightens up and walks on, his face filmed with sweat and his breathing ragged. She keeps hold of his arm. The alleyway opens onto a small residents' car park overlooked by a terrace. They cross the tarmac and turn into a footpath which stretches between the tall fences behind the rows of houses and he stops when they reach a black gate. "Would you wait for me?" She starts to protest but the look in his eyes silences her.

There is nothing different about the backyard: the boards on the windows are still in place and the bin bags are still piled up. Cupping the frosted glass, he looks for signs of movement in the kitchen and holds his breath, trying to hear the dog on the other side, but there is only silence. He takes the key out of his pocket and carefully slots it into the lock and turns, pausing when he's finished and straining to hear noise within, and then he slowly pulls down the handle and slips the door open, again stopping to listen before going inside. The kitchen is empty, the newspaper on the floor untouched.

Gripping the 9mm in his good hand, he slips off his shoes and creeps into the dim hallway in his socks, avoiding the squeaky floorboard and stopping before the dining room. The house is silent, not even the water pipes making a sound. He tiptoes towards the stairs and climbs the wooden steps, wincing at every barely audible creak. On the landing he pauses and raises the gun, the handle slippery in his damp palm, and then crosses the bedroom doorway. There is an empty space on the skirting board where the photograph of Tom and his parents had been. He steps inside and finds the picture poking out from beneath the mattress. Holding his breath, he listens for movement and then slides the photo in his pocket and goes into the hallway and calls the dog's name in a doubtful whisper. "Charlie," he refrains, his voice rising and breaking as he walks into each room with only the silence and void to meet him.

As he yells his name one last time there is a faint whimper and then a scuffle. He spins around and calls again, his voice a desperate scream. There is scratching, the sound coming from the bathroom. When he runs inside he finds the dog scrambling his way out of the gap between the bathtub and the wall. The boy lays the gun on the toilet lid and scoops the dog up with his good arm, pressing him tight against his chest as he licks his chin and pants hysterically, and then he feels the tears stinging his eyes and hot on his cheeks.

When he steps out into the yard she is standing by the rubbish bags with her phone in her hand. Her hair is the colour of fire in the rain and fading sunlight. Her face lights up when she sees the dog under his arm. She does not comment on the redness around the boy's pupils.

"What happened to his leg?" she asks as Charlie cautiously sniffs her knuckles.

"I don't know. He was like this when I found him."

*

Maggie rings the doorbell and steps back to inspect the windows. Heels click on the other side of the door and keys rattle in the lock, and a tall equine woman in a violet cardigan appears.

"Hi, I'm Alex's mum," she says, trying to sound cheerful.

"Oh, hello, it's nice to meet you. I don't think he's in, though."

"Oh." She forces a smile. "It was a bit of a surprise. Do you know where he is?"

"He left really early this morning. In his car."

"Oh. Did he say where he was going?"

"No. But he had an overnight bag."

"Oh, right. You must be Sian?"

"That's right."

"He said he was living with an Irish girl."

"That's me," she grins, impatience flickering in her dark eyes.

"Are you on your way out?"

"Church. Have you tried calling him?"

"He's not answering. Is everyone else out?"

"Yes, sorry." She looks at her watch. "I better get going."

"Can I just quickly check his room, see if he's forgotten his phone?"

"Ok," she says, hesitant. "It's the second on the left."

She can smell him as soon as she opens the door, the scent he has carried with him all his life, a freshness she would breathe in when he was a baby, but it is barely there, suppressed by the heavy colognes that hang in the air. His wardrobe door is open and two hangers are empty. She is shocked by the amount of clothes he has: shirts and jeans she has never seen before, some with the tags still on. The room is cold and there is a sense of vacancy, as though he has never been there. She switches on his computer and as she waits for it to load she steps closer to the window and glimpses movement across the road: a colossal man stands in the opposite window, peering in; if he has seen her he doesn't react, his round bulldog face pressed against the glass. She looks away, watching the loading wheel spin on the monitor, and when she glances back she can see his hulking back moving away.

The internet history has been deleted. She logs in to her own Facebook account and searches for Emma, recognising her from the photos that were on Alex's page. Her profile is locked but in the 'about' box her university is listed as Manchester.

"Are you alright up there?" Sian calls from below.

"Yes, thanks, just coming." She shuts down the computer and turns off the monitor, glancing at the empty window across the street.

"I thought it might have fallen on the floor," she says, coming down the stairs. "He must have it. Sorry to keep you."

"It's no bother," Sian says, smiling through her teeth as she stands aside in the doorway to usher her out. "He's probably just run out of battery."

"And he didn't say where he was going? Didn't mention

anything?"

She shakes her head. "Sorry."

"Do you see him much? I mean, do you spend much time together as a house?"

"A bit," she says, closing the door after them. "He's a nice guy."

"Oh, don't be taken in by his charm," she jokes, hearing the false tone in her voice as the panic billows inside her. As she says goodbye and walks away she tells herself that she is being ridiculous, but she can't shake the feeling, and she stops and paces back towards Sian as she's locking the door.

"I know it's a strange question, but have you noticed anything different about him lately? Has he seemed out of sorts?"

She hesitates before answering. "Listen, I didn't want to say anything because it's not my place to tell you, but I think he was arrested last night."

Maggie's hand jerks up to her mouth as the breath leaves her.

"I don't know what happened, but the police came and I saw them taking him out of across the road," she points to the door by the takeaway. "Our door was wide open."

"Oh god." She holds her throat.

"Sorry," Sian says. "It might have been a mistake or they might not have even been arresting him. It was dark so… They could have been asking him about the murder."

"Murder?" Her fingers tighten on her neck.

"He didn't tell you? Someone was shot in the alleyway." She

points to the dark gap between the shops. "Alex saw the killer running away."

"Oh god, why didn't he tell us?"

"It was only two nights ago." She looks past Maggie to the city centre at the end of the street. "I'm sorry, I've got to go."

"How did he look? This morning?"

"Ok. Fine. Like normal."

"Ok," her voice trails off as her eyes move to the door by the takeaway.

"Try calling him again. He was probably still driving earlier. I've got to go. Sorry." She walks away, leaving Maggie frozen on the pavement.

*

"Are you alright, mate?" the shopkeeper asks, watching him across the counter.

Ezra nods, his face a pale blur in the metal edge of the display cabinet. "Is it sorted?"

He lays Micah's iPhone on the counter. "It's easy, just expensive 'cos Apple have fixed prices."

Ezra swipes the screen.

"1234," the man says, taking in the boy's sunken eyes and scar.

He types in the code and scrolls through the calls: there are only the incomings from the withheld number. He opens the messages and instantly recognises Jo's number. 'Now'. It arrived just after she texted him to tell him to come over. There is an outgoing message, sent immediately afterwards to an Aimee. 'Now'.

"Everything ok?" the shopkeeper asks. "You look like death."

The boy nods and walks out into the high street. Sarah stands with the dog outside Costa, the light from the window spilling over them. "Could you take him back?"

"To the hotel?"

He scans the crowd of shoppers, searching for watching eyes. "I have to see someone quickly."

The dog stands by his foot, looking between the two of them as she studies his face. "Can't we just come with you and wait?"

"I won't be long."

"What is it?"

He looks away into the darkening town centre: people scurry from shop to shop, dodging the rain, their outlines like puppets in a shadow play.

"I'm not some stupid Facebook girl just looking for some drama to brag about, ok? You can actually talk to me. I keep secrets and I don't judge people. Everyone is messed up so…"

"Are you sure you're only 15?" he says, trying to smile.

"Ezra…"

"I know." He meets her stare. "I'll tell you when I get back, I promise."

*

Micah pulls up at a garage and climbs out of the Audi. The hard afternoon sun bounces off his glasses as he walks across the forecourt and shoulders open the toilet door. Inside, he rolls up his sweater and inspects the bruise on his sternum where the bullet hit the vest. He steps into a cubical and locks the door and leans his head against the wall. His shoulders tremble and his breath catches in his throat. He takes off the sunglasses and his bloodshot eyes glisten in the fluorescent light. He slides a packaged Nokia out of his inside pocket and removes the cellophane and dials his own mobile number. There is laboured breathing at the other end.

"I know you're there."

The boy doesn't answer.

"Look at the pictures on there. Her name was Aimee."

"His name was Tom." The line goes dead.

Micah adjusts his hat and puts his glasses back on and strides out into the forecourt. As he holds the diesel hose in the tank he slips the Nokia out to check that the boy hasn't called back. The pump clicks off and the trigger goes dead in his hand. He looks at the meter: just £19 in the tank. He waits a few seconds and then tries again but there is no response. When he looks towards the shop he sees the woman behind the counter watching him with her arms folded. He puts the pump back on the rack and wipes his hands on his jacket before striding into the shop, the cold air blasting his face as the automatic doors slide open.

"Is there something wrong with number three?" he asks.

"No."

"There's nothing coming out."

"That's because I stopped it." She is fortyish, her mousy hair scraped back and blemished skin untouched by make-up.

"Why?"

"Because you were on your phone."

"What do you mean?"

"You're not supposed to use your phone at the pumps."

"Why not?"

"Er, sparks? Petrol?"

"Sparks? It's a phone."

"Have you not seen that video on Youtube? I'd rather not die."

"Is this your rule or the garage's?"

"Every garage says no phones. There are signs."

He turns to the pillar by the pump; a scratched warning sign hangs at an angle. "Well can you turn it back on?"

"Are you going to use your phone again?"

He smiles, his eyes concealed by the sunglasses, and then scans the forecourt: a builder fills up a white Transit van while his mate reads the paper in the passenger seat; a teenage girl replaces the hose and closes the flap on her turquoise Beetle.

"No," he says, turning back to the woman.

She nods and turns away and he goes back out and crosses the forecourt and picks up the hose and fills the tank, his jaw clenched tight as he takes in the security cameras fixed to each pillar. Back inside he watches the woman as she serves the teenage girl and then the builder, and when he reaches the counter he pays in cash without a word and she takes the money and hands him his receipt with a clipped 'Thank you'. He stands there, staring at her from behind his glasses, their images reproduced in the monitor over her shoulder. She looks back at him with hard eyes but there is a glimmer of fear and he can see her knuckles tensed white on the edge of the counter, inches from the alarm button below.

He turns sharply and walks out and climbs into the Audi and pulls onto the main road before taking the next left into a cul-de-sac. Following the curve of the houses, he rolls down to the bottom and does a U-turn so he is parked by a footpath, facing the way he came in. The driveways are empty and the curtains drawn. The only sound is the rumble of the traffic at the end of the road. He opens the boot and takes off his jacket and hat and lays them inside. As he slips on a green duffel coat he feeds a crowbar down the sleeve so the tip rests in his palm, and then he fixes a baseball cap on his head with the rim pulled low before locking the car and setting off along the footpath into a woodland with an overgrown brook flanked by withered trees. As he strides along the backs of the gardens he hears a little boy laughing and a woman saying 'be careful' and then a crash followed by crying. The water curves to the right and the tarmac forks to the left, cutting between frosted bushes and saplings with the Esso sign looming above the stripped branches. The path ends at the back of the garage, halted by an iron railing.

There is only an empty blue Seat in the forecourt. Standing by the toilet block, he watches as a middle-aged man in a creased suit emerges from the shop and climbs in the car and drives away. He waits, listening for voices as his breath clouds the icy air, and then strides inside. As the woman looks up from the desk he relaxes his hand and the crowbar slips down into his grasp. She raises her arms and screams as he lunges forward and swings across the counter, the hook crushing her skull and the bar shattering her wristbone. She collapses against the cigarette rack, her arms limp and her legs dead as she smacks against the tiled floor. Micah looks down at her crumpled body, staring at the bloody dent above her temple, and then he walks out of the shop towards the woodland, breaking into a run when he sees a car pulling into the forecourt.

18

The locks scrape and the door opens a crack and, after a long pause, Derek shuffles out with a cigarette hanging from his mouth and a bin bag in his hand. Ezra steps forward, pointing the 9mm. The cigarette falls onto the cobbles and fizzles out. "Jo didn't know," he says. "I use her phone."

They stare at each other, their silence underscored by the humming traffic in the road. "Come in," he says, lowering the bag.

The old office is dark and thick with the smell of stale tobacco. "She's in bed sick." He lowers himself onto the stained orange sofa. "I didn't want to do it, son – not that it makes any difference." He looks the boy in the eye as he stands by the curtained window, gripping the gun by his side.

"Just tell me why."

"There is no 'why' for me."

"You sent them."

"He told me to."

The boy is trembling, his eyes feverish. "Peter?"

He nods. "Steve, our son – he keeps him alive in prison."

"Why does he want me dead?"

"Because you let David go."

"Did Peter kill Tom?"

"I don't know."

"You do."

The old man sighs. His eyes are dried out. "It sounds like you've already made up your mind. We weren't involved, though – you have to believe that, son."

"Was Tom seeing the councillor's daughter?"

He nods.

"Is that why Peter killed him?"

"I told you, I don't know anything."

The boy stares at him, waiting.

"People don't make sense, son – you learn that as you get older."

"And David – he was in love with Tom?"

"I don't know, son. I don't know. You won't get any answers that make sense. Why does anyone do anything?" He nods at the ceiling, the skin jangling around his neck. "When we were first together I used to cheat on her. Even when we were first falling for each other. I loved her and knew I wanted to be with her but I still cheated, and I don't know why. Do you understand?" He looks up at the boy, appealing for an answer. "I don't know myself and I don't think anyone does."

"How do you contact him?"

"Jo's phone."

The boy steps forward and a shaft of light slants in over his shoulder, capturing the floating dust. "Give it to me."

"It's upstairs."

He moves the gun to his weak arm, hiding the pain, and slips his hand into the pocket of Derek's cardigan and feels the phone inside, a battered Nokia. The old man smiles, the light already fading from his eyes. "I do what I have to, to keep my son alive."

Still pointing the gun, the boy opens the call list.

"It's the Cheltenham landline," Derek says. "It's a payphone. He's got it wired to a mobile."

The call was in the early hours of the morning. "It lasted 30 seconds. You didn't even ask why?"

He looks down at his liver-spotted hands. "I knew why."

"You've known me since I was five."

"I'm just the postman," he whispers. "He'd kill Steve." He sighs. "It was always going to end like this. It's murder for money, that's all. All that talk of 'deserved'; money kills them, it always has."

"Not for Tom."

The old man looks up and starts to shape a sentence but then pauses and swallows the words.

Sweat has pooled around the boy's eyes and his hand quivers around the gun. Derek nods at the barrel. "Not like that." The words stick in his throat, his voice almost gone. "I don't want her to know it was you, what I did." He takes a cushion from the sofa. "Here. Let her think it was peaceful, in my sleep, at least for a while." His exhausted eyes will him on as he holds out the frayed cushion. Ezra takes it in his weak hand, still holding the gun. "As if I could stop you," Derek wheezes, looking down at his skeletal arms, and the boy lays the 9mm on the floor, out of his reach, as the old man leans back on the sofa.

"When you're done, just go. Don't wake her up."

The boy holds the cushion out and edges forward until he is standing over him. "Go on," Derek whispers, closing his eyes. Ezra carefully lays the cushion over his mouth and nose and pushes down, staring at the freckles on his bald head and breathing in his nicotine smell. At first the old man doesn't move, sitting perfectly still like he's under anaesthetic, allowing himself to fade out, but then he jolts to life and struggles frantically, clawing at the cushion and scratching at the boy's hands, his whole body tensing and jerking and his jaw clicking as he tries to suck in air. Ezra is too strong, bearing down and holding him in place, his shoulder searing as he stares at the liver-spotted hands desperately grasping for life, and then he finds himself pulling the cushion away and stepping back and watching his wrinkled face gasping and frozen between shock and relief.

The boy lays the cushion on the floor and picks up the gun and then silently climbs the stairs to the kitchen, hearing Jo snoring on the other side of the bedroom door. She is beneath the duvet, curled in a foetal position and breathing in phlegm-soaked grunts. He shakes her shoulder and she stirs with a murmur and then her eyes spring open, red-rimmed and bewildered as she stares up at the boy in the murky daylight through the split curtain.

He holds out her Nokia. "Call Peter."

"What?" She sees the gun.

"Call him."

"Ezra, what are you doing?" Her face creases, the lines like dead-end roads on a faded map.

"Tell him to come here."

"Love…"

"Tell him," he hisses, pressing the Nokia into her hand.

"He won't come. He'll know something's wrong." Her eyes bolt to something over his shoulder and she screeches, "Derek, don't!" The boy follows her gaze: Derek stands in the doorway, shakily aiming an old revolver as he leans against the frame.

"I have to," he wheezes, pointing the rusted gun at the boy's back.

Ezra turns to him.

"Put it down."

The boy lays the 9mm on the bed.

"Derek," Jo says, sitting up. "What are you doing?"

"You're too soft for this," he says to the boy. "David, Micah, me – Tom would have done it like that –" He snaps his fingers. "That's the only way you survive."

"Love," Jo pleads. "We can work this out."

"No," Derek wheezes. "Nobody wins here." He clicks the hammer. "Sorry, son."

As Derek pulls the trigger something flies over the boy's shoulder and smashes on the top of the doorframe, spraying debris on the old man, whose arm jerks up and fires the bullet into the ceiling as Jo's scream of 'No' reverberates around them. Ezra snatches up the 9mm and shoots before she can say his name. Blood spatters the yellowed wallpaper. Derek slides down the doorframe, clutching at his throat. The boy stares at his fading eyes, frozen, and then jumps over him and sprints down the stairs as Jo struggles up from the bed. As he turns the handle he hears her collapsing in the bedroom doorway. Her cry is a breathless groan, as though she is gasping for air as her windpipe is crushed.

19

The sunset is washed out by the grey drizzle as Alex stands at the window watching the swarm of umbrellas, buses and taxis. There is still no reply on Facebook. He types Tina's name into the search bar and her profile picture shows her as a teenager in a school uniform; there is a look of defiance on her face as she poses hands-on-hips in the middle of a group of girls, all of them wearing their white shirts skin tight and their skirts barely below the groin. Her collar is open and her tie is yanked to the side to reveal a silver heart pendant, and she is the most developed of the group, her shape the same then, at 15 or 16, as when she undressed for him two nights back. At the bedside phone he pushes 9 for an outside line and dials her mobile. The line connects on the third ring but there is no answer.

"Tina?"

He hears breathing at the other end.

"Tina, it's Alex."

The line goes dead. He uses his mobile to call her but it goes straight to voicemail. After a second he tries again but is immediately greeted by her recorded voice, 'Hiya, it's Tina, leave a message.'

Gripping his wife's mobile, Craig listens to the sound of the shower running on the other side of the locked bathroom door. He takes out his own phone and types the Manchester landline into Google and the results show the name and address of the hotel. The water stops and he hears the curtain hooks scraping the rail. He saves

Alex's mobile number into his own contacts list and then slides Tina's phone back into the pocket of her dressing gown. In the living room he stands by the window, the fading light catching the bruise around his eye as he looks down at the rain rippling the puddles.

"Sharpy, how's it going, mate?" he says quietly, holding his phone to his cheek. "Remember that Micah fella you were telling me about?"

*

Shivering, the boy stares at the moon, the white crescent like a vapour cast off by the clouds. He has parked Tom's Ford among the warehouses of the abandoned chemical plant where he taught him to shoot. The 9mm lies on the passenger seat, concealed by the same shadow that halves his face.

Tom was staring at the TV, his face washed out in the white light from the screen, the boy's words still haunting the living room more than two hours after he'd spoken them. "You're not my father and you killed my mother, why would I want to stay here with you?" There had been a calmness in his voice as he pronounced each word, as though the sentence had been forming inside him for years, but it had been a spontaneous statement, erupting from somewhere deep within that was beyond his grasp. He paused in the hallway, watching Tom for a moment, before slipping out the door without a word, his rucksack filled with clothes and toiletries.

When he came out of the station he typed the address into the map on his phone and followed the arrow away from the shops and through the quiet residential streets. Nausea swirled inside him as the little man on the screen closed in on the destination flag. The house was two in from the end of the terrace, with a scratched wooden door and chipped paintwork around the windows. There was light behind every curtained window and he could see his own breath as he stood by the gate. He paused outside the door, listening for voices and hearing TV chatter. When he pushed the bell there was no chime so he tried again and waited but there was no response. He could feel his T-shirt sticking to his back as he gently knocked on the door, the sound followed by murmuring voices inside.

When the man opened the door he knew straight away that the address Tom had found all those years back was still correct, and he saw from his reaction that he too recognised his own image in the face before him. He stepped out onto the porch and quietly closed the door, glancing at the boy and then looking away into the starless sky. He was still in his work clothes, a white shirt hanging over navy trousers with Chelsea slippers on his feet. Ezra expected him to say something but he was silent, his Adam's apple bobbing in his slim throat as he stared at some fixed point above the rooftops across the street, blinking every few seconds, and then he looked at the boy, his gaze flickering over the scar and skipping over his eyes before resting on his forehead. He shook his head, a barely-there gesture, before turning his back and reaching for the handle and slipping back inside, carefully closing the door and turning the lock.

The boy stood in the driveway for a few seconds, staring at the locked door, and then there was movement in the window above and he looked up to find a little girl staring down at him from the edge of the curtain. He moved away, his eyes fixed towards the murky hue of the town centre as he passed each lit window. As he neared the end of the road he doubled over and vomited in the gutter and watched the pale sick trickle towards the drain as he gasped for air. Hands on his knees, he pushed himself upright and staggered towards the crossroads, regaining his balance as he moved until he was striding past the shuttered storefronts. He drifted east, following an aimless route which took him through housing estates and past glowing bars, and eventually he found himself outside a park, peering at the trees, the stripped branches like withered arms reaching into the dark sky. He found a bench between the hedgerows, away from the groups of teenagers lounging on the grass and in the play area. Across the road, beyond the railings, he could see people in the long windows of bars, their faces golden in the ochre light.

He was watching the flittering movement in the window when he heard footsteps and looked up and saw the silhouette of a man at the end of the path. He was about to run when he recognised Tom's gait and then a waft of his Cool Water. He sat on the edge of the bench, two yards away, and followed the boy's line of sight to the bars. A young couple emerged through a glass door, the girl leaning tipsily on the guy's arm as he hailed a cab and helped her inside. A minute later a group of teenagers approached along the pavement, heads bowed and hands in pockets as they tried to slip inside, but the doormen shook their heads and a pleading conversation ensued and eventually the boys and girls strutted away up the street towards more twinkling lights. Their voices had just faded away when a silver-haired man burst out of the bar and strode towards the road, followed by a woman in a short dress who slipped off her heels and carried them as she pursued him while asking, “Dave, what’s wrong?” again and again.

“At least I wore the right shoes,” Tom said, but Ezra just kept staring at the bar.

When a bus approached on their side of the road, he turned to the boy and studied his face in the sweeping light. “There is no-one else,” he said, his voice almost lost in the hum of the engine. “Come home.”

“Why didn’t he want me? My lip?”

“Because he’s weak and heartless. Like she was. It’s not you, it’s them. Them. You are a miracle because you came from them and look at you now. You have nothing to be ashamed of, you did nothing wrong.” As he spoke he closed the gap between them on the bench until their shoulders were almost touching. “Fuck them, Ezra. Fuck them. I’m glad they are the shits they are because otherwise I wouldn’t have you, and I chose you. Do you understand? I chose to be your dad or whatever you want to call our fucked up little scenario because –”

"You had to."

"Do you really think that? I could have left you in that house or dropped you at social services. Trust me, I could have walked away loads of times. To be honest, if you'd been a whiny little shit I probably would have, as bad as that sounds. But I didn't, I couldn't, because you are you: kind, thoughtful, brave, intelligent… a miracle. So fuck them, really. Fuck that abusive drug addict and fuck that fucking loser coward and move on. You're so much better than them."

He laid his bear-like hand on the back of the boy's neck. "You don't even really need me, anymore, do you?" He tried to sound jokey but Ezra could hear the hurt in his voice, and he briefly met his eye before shaking his head.

As he sits in the Ford, he counts the days backwards to that night and works out how many hours had passed between them arriving home and Tom disappearing off to Gardner, and he tries to remember what they said to each other in those 21 hours, but it was a time of silence and small mutterings, the mood still warped and fractured, and he can't recall anything of substance passing between them, nothing that would have provided reassurance for Tom.

He winds down the window and drops Micah's iPhone onto the gravel and then starts the engine and drives away.

*

The train flies past an abandoned industrial park, the pale moon slanting through the decaying factories and glassless windows. Maggie stands by the carriage door with a finger in one ear and her phone pressed to the other. "Tom, it's mum. Have you heard from Alex lately? Can you send him a Facebook message asking him to get in touch?" A train hurtles past on the parallel tracks and she sees her blurred reflection in the lit windows. "He's not answering. I think he might have lost it. It's probably nothing to worry about, just me panicking as usual. Ok, love, I'll speak to you later. Bye, love. Bye."

She makes her way back to her seat as the train pulls into a station. The carriage door slides open and a woman leads a little girl in by the hand and they take the seats across the aisle. As her mother wedges their suitcase into the overhead shelf, the girl, who is no more than four and wearing a bright red duffel coat, leans forward and peers at Maggie, who smiles back at her before turning to the window and watching the station fade into the dark horizon. At that age Alex asked questions non-stop, brimming with curiosity, seeking answers she didn't always have – Why does God let bad things happen? Why does God allow people to think he doesn't exist? Why doesn't He just tell everyone he's there? He would wake her up in the morning, a little face by the side of the bed, describing the day he had planned for them – swimming, the park, the cinema – a constant rush of energy, always driving forward to the next event, his mind so forceful that he couldn't switch off at night, his whirlwind of thoughts becoming a whirlpool of nightmares, graphic dreams of sudden paralysis and hideous mutation which he'd describe feverishly as he'd crawl into bed between them. That was when she felt her love for him at its most overpowering, when he was next to her in bed with his tiny warm hands on her back, needing her so absolutely. That vitality stayed with him throughout his school years – always inquisitive, devouring books and films, devoted to his faith, planning his future as an investigative journalist exposing corruption – and then, without explanation, it slowly evaporated while he was at university. Now, when she speaks to him, that 'Alex light' has gone from his eyes and his voice and, it seems, so has his faith. And she can't help but think there is something she has done wrong – something she failed to say or do, a missing ingredient needed for a happy, well-rounded adult. And, she tells herself, if she can just reach him again, just speak to him face-to-face, she can help him recapture that illumination, that glow she'd seen even when he was a newborn in her arms, when the midwife had handed her that messy, chubby bundle of flesh and his eyes had suddenly popped open, unpolluted blue, peering up at her, overwhelmingly alive.

*

David rolls onto his side and opens his eyes. As he stares at the framed picture in the grainy dark a figure takes shape by the wardrobe and the boy emerges from the corner with the 9mm gripped by his side.

"Haven't we done this already?"

"I need your help."

The detective rolls onto his back and leans against the headboard with his neck tilted at an awkward angle.

"I need to trace a mobile number." He holds up a scrap of paper.

"That won't work with him."

"Not Peter. Micah."

"He sent him after you, then."

"Like you said."

"If it's not Micah, it'll just be someone else."

"Not if I kill Peter."

He pulls the duvet up to his neck, his half-closed eyes sliding down over the boy. "Aren't you scared?"

"Of what?"

"Everything."

The boy shrugs, his face showing nothing. "Don't you want Peter dead?"

"I don't really care anymore." His eyes flick at the family picture on the wall, his wife and two sons – the only trace of them left in the house. "I've already ruined my life. He can take it."

"They know?"

He shakes his head. "I do."

The boy edges closer, his knees touching the edge of the bed. "Did you love Tom?"

"Yes."

"Did you tell him?"

"Why bother?"

"He wouldn't have been disgusted or angry."

"I know, but I was. When you come from where I have and turn out the way I did, you always feel that way about yourself."

"Do you know where Kerry is?"

"No. You want to know why Tom didn't tell you about her? You think he was going to go off with her and leave you behind? He wouldn't have done that."

The boy blinks. The seconds tick by on a clock in the hallway. "Micah – there was a girl with him."

"Aimee, his girlfriend."

"I killed her."

"She was trying to kill you."

The boy nods, his face like the cracking wall of a dam.

"I killed a man who raped his wife with a broken bottle. I still see his face: desperate, terrified – human."

They stare at each other, their eyes barely visible in the faint moonlight at the edge of the curtain. "The councillor…"

"I never spoke to him. I'd quit by then. He went through Peter."

"I killed him." His voice falters.

"What do you want me to say? That Peter tricked you? That you thought you were doing it for Tom? You still made the choice. This whole thing was borne out of grief and revenge but it never made it right. Look at us." He shakes his head. "Peter got me into this. I'm not saying I didn't make the choice, just… I don't know. Me and my wife were struggling and… he loved Helen so much, he was such a mess, just destroyed, when she… I was the one who told him, knocked on his door in the middle of the night, saw his face as my words sunk in… When we found out it was Flynn, that became his focus, our focus, but he wouldn't tell us why he did it; I don't think he knew himself. So we went to the prison, Peter and me – I knew a guard – and we hanged him with his bed sheet… He felt better for a while. I don't think I really did. Then there was the next one…" He sighs, staring down at his hands before meeting the boy's eyes. "Just walk away. You're the same age as my son." He glances at the picture on the wall. "You give up on being who you think you should be and resign yourself to being who you've become, and you never feel normal, at peace, again. Walk away while you can. Go to the other side of the world. Leave us to rot. Meet a girl, a boy, whatever makes you happy."

The clock ticks five times before Ezra answers, his eyes never leaving the detective's shadow-cut face. "Micah's phone."

*

It is gone midnight when Alex stands before the full-length mirror in the bathroom, spraying himself with Intenso. Moans filter in through the air vent, the sound of a couple in the room next door, their voices murmuring in Japanese. He plays music on his iPhone to drown them out. The dance song builds towards a vague climax as he buttons his shirt and inspects himself, his gaze falling everywhere but his own desperate eyes.

Outside a redbrick halls of residence he stares up at the lights behind the curtained windows. When three girls emerge from the gate in the railings he steps forward and shows them Emma’s picture, but they don’t recognise her, and they look back with suspicion as they walk away into the misty rain.

In a bar he dances with a drunk student in fishnets and a Ramones T-shirt. Her scarlet hair glows with each sweep of the strobe light and when she speaks her words are swallowed by the grinding guitars. They allow the crowd to jostle them towards a booth in the corner. Cold water drips onto his neck from a hanging pipe as he kisses her, leaning her back on the beer-stained upholstery. He forces his fingers through the fishnets and she limply grabs at his jeans. There is a hand on his shoulder. When he looks up a bouncer stares back at him, smiling with amusement and contempt.

In a club he stands at the edge of the raised bar, peering into the crowd for jet black hair. On the dancefloor he hovers near a raven-haired girl in a blood-red dress, trying to make eye contact as he swigs from a bottle of cider. When she sees him watching she turns to her friends and says something and then they all look at him with faces hardened by disdain.

In the toilet he locks himself in a cubical and leans his forehead on the door, his shoulders trembling as he silently weeps. His phone vibrates with another call from his mother. He strides back into the warehouse-like club and lingers near a plump woman with bleached hair and orange skin who seems lost as she gazes across the crowded dancefloor. As he's about to move in she raises her hand and he follows her eyes to a lanky man carefully carrying two glasses of wine through the tangle of bodies, and their faces light up at the sight of one another.

In an alleyway he texts Tina. 'I'm sorry about last night.' He leans against the wet bricks as he waits for her to reply. 'I'm staying in a hotel in Manchester,' he types, before deleting the sentence and opening Facebook to find that Emma still hasn't replied. Screams echo off the walls and figures rush through the cloud of light at the end of the passageway. A crowd gathers outside a taxi office, circled around something on the ground. As he moves closer he sees kicks jutting out from the huddle. The victim is lifeless on the tarmac, his limp torso jerking with the force of the blows to his chest and back. A middle-aged man stands in the doorway with a cigarette glowing in his hand as he passively calls out, 'Come on, he's had enough. Come on.' The light from the window spills across the attackers: three men and three women in their late twenties. Their victim's age is lost in their shadows and his own blood. When one of the men, a thin blond in a white shirt, begins stamping on his head, Alex bolts towards them.

"You're going to kill him," he cries as he bursts through and shoves the blond man back.

"I'll kill you if you don't get out of the fucking way," he hisses, squaring up to Alex.

“What’s he done?”

“Fucking pervert felt her up.” He jabs a finger at a red-haired woman in a green dress whose cheeks are stained with mascara.

Alex looks down at the motionless heap on the floor, seeing the face of a boy behind the blood and swelling.

“Mate, just walk away,” the blond says, almost nose-to-nose, his eyes bulging. The other men have gathered at his side, forming a triangle around Alex. There are specks of blood on their white trainers. “Just spark him, Ant,” one says.

“You’ll kill him.” His voice is strangled by fear.

“We’ll kill you if you don’t get out of the fucking way.”

“I don’t care,” he whispers.

“What?”

“Come on, lads,” the middle-aged man calls, sticking to the doorway. “Come on.”

“What did you say?” the blond asks Alex.

“I said I don’t care about myself anymore.”

The man on his right strikes first, hitting him in the jaw. Alex gets his hands up but they overwhelm him, raining down blows on the top of his head and neck. As he doubles over one of them knees him in the chin, sending him onto the ground by the boy, who looks strangely peaceful despite the black gashes and bruises. Sirens ring out. Everyone stops, their faces frozen as they stare towards the swelling sound before sprinting away. Blue lights whip across the cars at the end of the street. Alex pushes himself up and staggers into the alleyway, suddenly recalling that afternoon when he came home from college to an empty house and lay on the sofa and closed his eyes and pleaded for Him to come into his life, to finally reveal Himself as real after all those years of faith without proof, and felt nothing.

With the ceiling spinning and the shadows expanding and collapsing, he opens the bedside drawer and takes out the bible and flicks through the first few pages, looking for the 'Where to turn when feeling…' index, but the words are out of focus and in the end he just lies back with his eyes closed and the book clutched to his naked chest, saying 'Please God' again and again in a fading refrain.

20

The boy lurches forward at the sound of a tap at the door.

"Ezra," she whispers. "Ezra."

It takes all of his strength to shuffle out of bed and stagger to the door, the dog following at his heels.

"The police are outside."

"How many?"

"Just a car. They're just sitting there."

He glances at his rucksack in the corner and she grips his wrist. "Come to my room, we can watch from the window."

He breathes quickly, looking over her shoulder at the dark corridor.

"You can't run like that."

"What about your mum?"

"She hasn't come back. She does it all the time."

Sarah's side of the room is spotless; her clothes hang neatly in a wardrobe with missing doors and the sheets on her bed are tucked in so tightly that there is a visible indent where she was lying. Her mother's side is a mess, with dresses tangled on the bed and cosmetics scattered across the cabinet top. They stand side by side at the window, watching the motionless police cruiser parked ten metres down on the other side of the road, outside a shuttered convenience store. The dog sniffs at her ankles and goes on inspecting the room. She's still wearing the pink T-shirt and leggings, and in the dim streetlight she looks both child and adult. The boy has the quilt around his shoulders like a shawl; the frayed edge touches her arm and thigh. After a few minutes the car's lights spring on and it pulls away.

"You should stay in here. I'll watch the street."

He glances sideways at her. "Even after everything I've done?"

"I was thinking…" she murmurs, gazing into the space vacated by the cruiser. "What you said about doing so much that you can't turn back, can't start again: you're wrong. You can always say 'I'm not going to be like that anymore.' You can always start again."

Between sleep and consciousness he becomes aware of the shadows on the ceiling, the black shapes morphing and sliding as headlights pass, and then he feels warmth on his shoulder and when he looks he finds her asleep next to him, lying on her side with her forehead against the top of his arm and her hands linked around his elbow.

"Sarah," he whispers.

She hums, half asleep.

"Would you run away with me?"

She opens her eyes and leans back to study his face. "Ok."

*

Peter parks beneath the drooping branches of a willow tree, out of sight from the church and the road. His face is shielded from the moon by a flatcap and the high collar of his overcoat as he passes the church with a glance at the windows, his eyes trailing over the stained glass characters which are made colourless by the dark. He follows the path between the eroded tombstones, alert to every shifting shadow in the trees around the cemetery. Standing before her vast white marble headstone he can see the top of Tom's black grave in the far corner, but he doesn't look, just stares at the gold engraving:

Helen Armitage
Beloved wife
1952 – 2005

"I've made such a mess," he whispers, his hands balled into fists in his pockets. "Sometimes I wish I'd died with you. I know myself: I need respect, admiration… I want people to see the Jaguar and the Rolex, I can't help it. I'm weak. I know I'm weak. You knew I was weak but you loved me anyway, but without you…" He takes a deep breath to steady himself. "Tom and the others, I just… I need to finish the refuge. For you. If I build it and help all those women then everything I've done means something… Everything is so vague, so grey and meaningless – you're buried here and neither of us believe in God." He laughs, the sound more a sob than a chuckle. "I'm weighing all those women against Tom and the others, and all of them were capable of tearing down the refuge with just one wrong word. Do you see? I can't stop now. I can't." A rustling jerks his head towards the trees and his hand follows with the 9mm. The branches are silhouetted in the slanting moonlight like arms grasping at the sky. Eventually he slips the gun back into his pocket and turns to his wife's headstone again. "Am I a good man, my love? I hope you still think so."

His mobile vibrates in his pocket: someone is calling the phone booth.

*

"My face is all over the news, I have to go." Micah winces between words, his eyes feverish.

"The garage – what on earth were you thinking?"

"My girlfriend had just been shot dead in front of me; I wasn't thinking. They'd have been after me anyway, everyone knew we were together."

"She's dead, you know? The woman."

"I know."

"Well?"

"What do you want me to say?"

"It's so wanton, so pointless."

"Does it make a difference?"

"Of course it does."

"There are always reasons."

Peter studies Micah's face, preparing to say more, but he just shakes his head. "We can't leave the boy."

“I can’t go looking for him.”

“He’ll come after me. He knows where I live.”

“So leave too.”

“I’m a magistrate, if I disappear people will ask why, start digging.”

Headlights sweep through the alleyway, fleetingly illuminating their exhausted faces as they stand with their backs to the wall, facing each other across the narrow passage with their hands tensed in their pockets.

“I said three grand,” Micah says. “I take two and disappear, you take the rest and do whatever you want.”

“Two?”

“I’m the one doing it.”

“And you could tell the police about me.”

“I didn’t say that.”

“But it’s true.”

Micah shrugs. “I just need a passport.”

“Who is he?”

“Does it matter?”

“Just tell me.”

“He fucked the client’s wife then beat the shit out of him. He deserves it.”

“Really?”

“Does anyone?”

He narrows his eyes.

"Come on, your worship."

The magistrate stares at him in silence. Micah adjusts his hand in his pocket.

"Why tell me at all? He came to you. You could've got yourself a passport, taken the whole three thousand."

He shrugs. "I dunno… What you did for me after my brother… And that refuge you keep banging on about – call this my donation." His face breaks into a grim smile, but his jaw tightens when he sees the look in Peter's eyes.

*

Silhouetted against the moon-tinged sky, the refuge looks like just another unfinished building. Parked under the withered branches of a decaying tree, he watches the breezeblock shell from across the street, at a new angle, and the place looks so ascetic that he cannot imagine anyone living there in peace. The magistrate sits in his Jaguar, gazing like a ghost returned to the scene of his death, and he recalls the time, many years back, that he and Helen were in a gallery and he was standing close to a vast painting, focusing on the central figure – a man about to be executed by firing squad – and she told him to stand by her side, a few metres back, and when he did he saw the soldiers at the edge of the picture, coming to rescue the condemned man, and she said something and squeezed his hand, and he hates that he can't remember her words because they were so perfect, like her.

As soon as he saw Tom he knew he'd made up his mind. He was standing on the driveway in the dead of night, his face illuminated by the security light above the door.

"I'm sorry, Peter," he said. "I have to do this."

"Where will you go?"

"Bournemouth."

"Bournemouth?"

"Kerry likes the sea." His eyes flashed with her name.

"And Ezra?"

"There are good colleges there."

"Sounds like you've worked it all out." He held on to the handle as he stood in the doorway, afraid he'd collapse if he let go.

"I'm sorry. Everything you've done for me… But I have to do this, I have to try to live a normal life, give Ezra a normal life, I have to…"

"Move on." His voice was barely above a whisper.

"Yes. Isn't it time we all moved on?"

His half-buttoned cardigan drooped from his shoulders as he nodded. "Ok, Tom."

"I'm not saying it was wrong, just that… the last few, I feel like maybe, you know, maybe they didn't deserve it as much as when we started, that maybe David was right, that the refuge has, you know, made us… has influenced us…" He trailed off, seeing that his words were like gut punches to the magistrate.

“Ok, Tom,” he said weakly.

“So you understand?”

He nodded, his face ashen and his eyes dried out.

“Are you sure? I know it’s bad timing with the refuge not finished but if I don’t do this now, I never will. I wasn’t expecting to meet Kerry.”

“I know, Tom. It’s ok.”

They stared at each other in silence, Tom lit by the yellow bulb and Peter silhouetted in the doorway.

“Thank you, Peter,” he said eventually, holding out his hand.

“Goodbye, Tom.” His frail hand was limp in Tom’s clasp.

“We’ll see each other again,” he said, alarmed by the look in the magistrate’s eyes. “You can visit us in Bournemouth.”

“Of course.”

He watched Tom walk away up the driveway, his outline fading into the shadows in the street, and then he closed the door and paced down the long corridor, feeling his wife’s frozen eyes on his face.

“Kerry?”

“Who is it?”

“Peter. I’m a friend of Tom’s. He sent me to get you.”

She opened the door on the chain and peered out through the gap, her face softening when she saw the elderly magistrate. “I thought he was coming later."

"He thought it might be best if I came instead, in case your ex is waiting outside."

"Is he out there?"

"Gardner? No."

"Tom?"

"Yes, in the car, round the corner."

His eyes followed her finger as she typed in her passcode on her phone.

"His phone's playing up," he said as she held the mobile to her ear. His hands were deep in his overcoat as he stood in the corridor with his eyes flicking at the empty hallway behind her. "Something's wrong with the battery. He said to give you this." He produced a Dr Pepper from his left pocket.

A smile spread across her face as she took the bottle, and then she shut the door and slid off the chain. "I'll just get my things," she said, standing in the doorway in jeans and a sweater with her ginger hair tied up in a knot. She turned her back on the magistrate and paced down the hallway. The bullet hit her in the back of the neck, piercing the pink expanse of skin between her hairline and collar. The phone and bottle hit the carpet a split-second before she did. He locked the door and stepped over her. His hands trembled as he scrolled through her phone, studying the messages with Tom and Gardner.

"Come over tonight and we'll talk," he typed to Gardner. "8pm."

"I'm running late – so much to pack!" he texted Tom. "Can we make it 8.30pm?"

She was facedown, her cheek resting on the carpet and her eyes doll-like. He crouched over her and pulled down her eyelids with his gloved finger. Her blood was spattered on the navy carpet by her forehead.

Her phone lit up in his hand. "K. Really wanna work it out," Gardner wrote.

He grabbed her wrists and dragged her onto the floorboards in the living room.

"That's fine," Tom's message said. "I still need to talk to Ezra anyway. Love you missus!" The phone screen bathed the side of her face in pale light as Peter crouched over her, his eyes like the painted-on pupils of a mannequin.

Staring at the refuge, he hears a fox shrieking, the otherworldly sound coming from somewhere on the building site. The pale moonlight slants across his face as the ashen crescent emerges from the clouds. He takes out his mobile and types Micah's iPhone number into an app, and then he starts the engine and drives away.

21

She still hasn't replied to his message. Alex stares at her Facebook picture as he stands in the window, the laughter next door filtering in and surrounding him. As he takes a last look at the hotel room he notices the bible poking out from the twisted bed sheets. He puts the book inside the drawer without looking at the cover and then straightens the duvet and slings his bag over his shoulder and walks out, ignoring the buzzing call from his mother.

Approaching the halls, the clouds start to sputter fat drops of rain. They fall sporadically, bouncing off the pavement, a window, the tip of his nose. He ducks under the archway as the sheets of water start to lash down, his eyes darting from window to window on the five-storey redbrick apartments. Voices rise to him over the rain and two girls emerge from the glass doors. When they reach the archway he steps forward and asks if they know Emma and shows them her photo.

"I think she lives in that one," one says, pointing to the north side.

As they walk away he scans the curtained windows again, rehearsing what he'll say to her, his whole body tingling, recreating that anticipation he'd feel as he drove home to her after a late shift knowing she'd be half-asleep between the sheets, warm and waiting for him. He moves towards the gate, catching a flash of movement in the ground floor flat on the corner. A blonde couple cuddle on a sofa, the girl's pale legs poking out of a red dressing gown. Her. She has dyed her hair. The guy from the photo has his head on her chest. Her hand is down the back of his T-shirt, stroking his shoulders. She is smiling, looking between the TV and his face, her eyes alight.

Alex wheels away, squinting against the rain, the cold drops streaming down his open collar. A student steps out from the archway, his red hood gliding through the downpour. Alex moves aside from the gate, the rain stinging his eyes. Blinking, he peers at the student and as his figure takes shape in the murky shower he sees the sunglasses and the outstretched arm, and then a blue snap of light and a hiss, the muzzle flash repeating on the leaden clouds as they close like a mouth. In that final moment, as the light collapses in on itself, the image before his eyes is Emma in the window, and her face is like a rainbow on the dark sky, the colours translucent and bleeding into the black void.

*

Micah nods at the sleepy-eyed receptionist as he strides through the hotel lobby. In his room he drops the rucksack on the bed and goes into the bathroom and texts 'Ok' to an unsaved number, and then lays the phone on the sink and splashes cold water on his face. When he walks into the doorway Ezra is standing over the end of the bed. The rucksack is open, the red hoodie spilling out onto the white duvet. The boy pulls the gun from the bag and turns to Micah, his face bone white and his eyes feverish. Micah opens his mouth to speak but the bullet hits his throat before he can make a sound. He turns to the bathroom, his bulging eyes searching for some kind of weapon, and catches his reflection in the mirror: there is no blood, just a black void beneath his chin, but when he clutches the hole his hand is stained scarlet. Ezra steps into the doorway and shoots him in the base of the skull. The blood is like red mist spraying the glass and white tiles. His forehead cracks the edge of the sink and he crumples into a foetal position. His phone, spun sideways by the blow, flashes with an incoming message from the unsaved number: 'Ok'.

Ezra picks up the mobile and calls the unsaved number. The line clicks alive on the third ring but there is silence at the other end.

"Peter?"

"Ezra." Traffic rumbles in the background. "We need to talk."

The boy is silent. Voices echo in from the corridor, trailing past the door.

"I didn't kill Tom, son. You must know I could never do that."

There is a gentle knock on the hotel door. "Hello? Sir?"

"Ezra? We need to talk about this calmly."

"Sir? Sir? Is everything ok in there?"

"Ok then, son, if that's the way you want it. What happened to your dog's leg?" The line goes dead.

*

“Sarah, please answer. Just let me know you’re ok. I called the police. They should be there. Call me back, please.” He hangs up and drops the phone on the passenger seat. Traffic is gridlocked, the cars nose to bumper along Oxford Road and students with shopping bags and umbrellas weaving between them. A double-decker two cars ahead blocks his view of the cause of the tailbacks, but he can see a flicker of blue light on the horizon where the vehicles and buildings merge into a greyish haze. The bus opens its doors 10 metres from the next stop and a middle-aged woman jumps down into the road and shoots into the crowd on the pavement. Ezra watches her bouncing highlights until she disappears into the swarm of heads beyond the bus shelter. The double-decker shuffles forward, its exhaust fumes swirling up into the charcoal sky. The blue light ahead takes shape as the flashing beacon of a police van, parked on the right side of the road, the surrounding scene masked by the traffic and swarms of people. He sees the woman crossing the road fifty metres ahead, dodging between two cars. As he crawls forward he makes out a police cruiser parked just inside the van and onlookers around cordon tape, the scene concentrated around a tall redbrick building with officers in uniform and lab suits flowing back and forth through an archway.

She is sprinting now. People watch as she flies past with her brown coat flapping around her knees. She pushes her way through the crowd towards a PC standing guard. Her hand cups her throat as she speaks. The officer, a tall young man, glances at her and turns to the mass of watchers lining the cordon. She taps her phone and turns the screen to the constable and his posture slowly deflates as he inspects the photograph. He looks over his shoulder through the archway where officers swarm around a white tent, and then turns to her and lifts the tape and leads her through to the other side and they merge into the tangle of beacon-slashed bodies.

By the time the boy draws parallel the crowd is so dense he can barely make out anything on the other side of the cordon. Peering through the massed heads, he sees a blonde girl in a red duffel coat follow an officer from one side of the archway to the other, her arms wrapped tight around her ribs as she walks in a daze. He looks for the middle-aged woman but there is no sign of her.

*

Sarah's caravan is the only one lit in the whole park. A silhouette passes before the window, sliding through the yellow light. Ezra jumps over the gate and sprints through the mud, the rain lashing his face. At the door he knocks gently and calls her name but there is no reply. He tries the handle and the door opens. She sits on the edge of the sofa-bed, her back dead straight and her neck twisted as she looks at him blank-faced.

"Are you ok?" he says, stepping to her, searching for signs of injury. "Did you get my messages? I tried calling and –"

"I turned it off. I was hiding."

"Peter?"

"The police."

"Are you ok?" He lays his hand on her shoulder. Her skin is icy through her T-shirt. "Was he here?"

"I was walking Charlie in the woods and he was there suddenly," she whispers, her voice faltering. "Watching us. He said to tell you he was going away. Disappearing. He said he didn't kill Tom. He said I reminded him of his wife and that I would make you happy and we should run away together." Tears swell in her eyes. "He looked like such a sweet old man. Charlie ran over to him. He was stroking him as he was talking. He said that when you lose someone you love, you do whatever it takes to make sure their life meant something, and…" The tears start to stream down her ashen cheeks. He looks around for the dog. "He was just talking and talking, and then he picked Charlie up by the neck and started strangling him, still talking, calm, looking at me as he did it, saying I was like his wife, and… his eyes… his eyes…"

Ezra runs into the bedroom. The dog is on the bed, placed on his side with his eyes and mouth closed and his patchy fur faintly reflecting the moonlight. His body is cold against his palm.

22

Tina stands in the window watching the empty room across the street: through the fog she can barely make out the half-closed curtains and the dark space beyond. A reflection flickers on the glass and she turns to see her husband in the doorway, eyeing her in silence. He walks away and she hears the bathroom door closing and then the shower running. She tiptoes along the hallway, her bare feet soundless on the carpet and her eyes fixed on the door. Crouching over his discarded clothes, she slips his phone out of his pocket and scrolls through the recent calls, back to the night of the arrest – the night before Alex was killed. There is nothing strange, just the usual names. Listening to the water, she scans through his contacts list, pausing at the listings titled M and A2B Taxis and copying the numbers into her own phone. When she opens the messages her face turns white. The shower stops and she hears the curtain hooks scraping the rail. She stuffs the phone back in his pocket and darts away towards the bedroom, climbing into bed and turning the lamp off and lying on her side facing the window. After a few minutes he comes in swaddled in a dressing gown and closes the blinds. She shuts her eyes until she hears the floorboards creaking by the living room door and then the TV in the lounge, the sound muffled by the walls.

*

Ezra parks the Ford under the drooping branches of a willow tree, the headlights barely penetrating the dense fog which clings to the broad avenue. He takes out the binoculars and adjusts the focus until the iron lion on the gate takes shape in the grey haze, and then he scans the dark windows and the Jaguar on the driveway and the CCTV camera above the door. There are slithers of light in the surrounding houses where lamps burn against the murky dawn. He starts the engine and turns left into a narrow street of bungalows which arcs behind the villas and parks behind a pick-up truck at the inlet to a lake. Across the water he can see a boy on the shore holding the controls for a model boat which bobs on the rain-beaten surface. His mother sits on the bench behind him, holding an umbrella as she reads a magazine.

He flips up his hood and climbs out of the car and fixes the rucksack over his shoulders. Head down, he strides across the road and up the driveway of a bungalow and pushes open the gate and runs across the lawn to the tall hedge at the end of the garden. He takes out a pair of bolt cutters and forces his way through the hedge, the branches scratching at his scarfed face and gloved hands as he clips his way through to a chainlink fence and peers through the mesh at the magistrate's vast Georgian villa before hacking through the steel to cut a doorway. Hidden by the saplings and bushes, he sprints along the fence line and climbs the steps to the decking and slowly approaches wide French doors and peers in through the slits between the closed blinds. There is no sign of life in the wood-panelled conservatory and the hallway beyond is just as dark and empty, the sense of abandonment clinging to the cream walls and parquet floor.

He pulls a hammer from the rucksack and swings at the door. As the glass scatters across the floor an alarm sounds, a wail loud enough to be heard from streets away. Peter's wife stares at him from every angle as he runs through the conservatory and hallway, and he sees the coldness in her eyes in the later pictures as he approaches the staircase.

On the landing he can see neighbours standing in their doorways, peering at the house as the blue alarm beacon rotates across the Jaguar's bonnet. The framed photo of Peter and Tom is no longer in the study. Ezra turns on the PC and as the screen comes to life he scans the garden beyond the window, searching for movement in the bushes or beyond the fence. The internet history and folders have all been wiped. When he opens the recycling bin only one file remains: a PDF brochure for Perfect Dream. The smiling face of an elderly Japanese man and his younger self glisten on the cover. There is a Tokyo address in small font on the last page. The sound of distant sirens emerges into the patter of the rain on the window. When he looks outside there are three neighbours standing by the railing gate, their heads turned to the end of the road.

In the bedroom he takes lighter fluid from his rucksack and squirts the entire bottle on the bed and carpet and then pulls out a box of matches and strikes one and holds the flame to the duvet until the fire catches. He watches the flames spread to the four posters and pillows and lick at the emptied bedside cabinet, and then he grabs a framed picture of Peter and Helen from the dressing table, where her perfumes and lotions are still immaculately arranged.

Sprinting along the corridor, he hears the sirens screaming outside. He jumps down the stairs before hurtling through the conservatory and out into the garden. As he approaches the fence he sees a face through the hedge, an old woman staring at him from her garden. He glares at her, willing her to back away, but she is frozen in the middle of the lawn, a cordless phone in her dangling hand. The boy slowly makes his way towards her as the sirens swell behind him. She drops the phone and the handset bounces off the damp grass, and he arcs around her with his palms raised before sprinting towards the road.

*

Standing in a phone box, Tina looks out at a billboard for a florist, her eyes rising from the red roses to the leaden clouds above. She watches a delivery truck trundle past on the way to the town centre and then dials the number marked 'M'. Shivering, she listens as the call jumps straight to the default voicemail message. The square is deserted, the only sign of life the seagulls which squawk from their perch on the lampposts and chimneys. She calls the number again but there is no change.

When she slips back into the bedroom her husband is still

asleep. She stands at the end of the bed watching him as he snores through his nose and then she goes into the living room and curls up on the sofa, hugging her knees as she closes her eyes against the cold dawn light.

*

"I know where he is."

"Oh." Her face drops. "Where?"

"Tokyo. In some kind of retirement home."

She turns to the windscreen, her profile silhouetted by the slits of sunrise through the treeline at the edge of the caravan park. "How do you know?"

"I went to his house. There was a leaflet on his computer."

She nods faintly, still staring ahead.

"It was the only thing left on the computer, like he'd looked at it last before he left."

"What are you going to do?" She glances sideways at him, her face reacting to his inevitable answer before he even speaks.

"Find him."

"Why?"

"I have to know."

"You already know."

"I have to hear him say it."

"And then what?" She turns to him. "What about

Bournemouth?"

"We'll go when I get back."

"You won't come back."

"I will."

"You'll get arrested or killed."

"I won't."

She looks away, shaking her head. "I thought you wanted to start again."

"I have to do this first."

"What difference is there if he's dead or on the other side of the world rotting in a retirement home? He's still finished."

"But getting away with it. Getting away with what he did to Tom, to Charlie and all the others."

"Getting away with it? He's an old man with nobody. If you'd seen him there," she nods to the woodland, "you'd know that he hasn't got away with anything. He looked like a ghost."

"I can't let it go like this," he murmurs.

"So you're choosing him over me?"

He shakes his head. "We'll go when I come back."

"Ok, Ezra." She opens the door.

"Sarah."

"See you around." She steps out and closes the door and looks in at him through the window. "Goodbye."

He watches her make her way along the path between the caravans, her outline slowly fading into the grey haze. After a few minutes he gets out and follows, moving along the edge of the site in the shadows beneath the trees. He climbs over the fence and crouches below the window at the back of her home and peers in at the edge of the curtain: she is standing over her mother as she sits on a single bed with her knees pulled up to her chest, the woman an eroded version of her daughter. The boy edges to the other end of the caravan and squats below the bay window. Crouching there with the light spilling out above his head, he waits for some sound of violence – a shout or a bang – but there are just the recorded voices on the TV. Eventually, after five minutes of poised listening, he cautiously peeps inside; her father is dozing on the sofa in shorts and vest with an ashtray on his lap and a beer can by his foot. He looks nothing like the girl: balding and double-chinned with pudgy limbs, he resembles an overgrown baby; but there is a callousness in his thin lips and bagged eyes, the same pitiless expression he saw in Big Jim as he bore down on him in his cot, and he feels his pulse pounding and the weight of the 9mm in his pocket.

*

"Mm, tell me more," Craig grunts.

"You want me to tell you about Alex?"

His hand freezes inside her. She opens her eyes. The colour has drained from his face. He withdraws his fingers and leans back.

"What?" Tina asks. "Don't you want me to tell you how he did me?"

He stares at her, breathing slowly through his nose, and then he stands and buckles his belt.

"What's wrong?" She sits up on the bed and gathers the gown around her shoulders. "Doesn't that turn you on?"

They stare at each other, the silence pregnant, and then he turns sharply and paces away. She hears him clattering around downstairs in the shop as she leans against the window, gazing at the empty room across the street.

*

In the dead of night the boy stands at the edge of the driveway with his eyes fixed on the pale glow in the living room window. All the other windows are dark – the whole cul-de-sac is dark – and his feet crunch against the silence of the suburb as he crosses the gravel and peers in through the slit between the curtains. There are bouquets on every surface, the flowers bleached of their colour by the light spilling through the archway. Nobody is there and whoever is through the archway is out of sight. A framed picture consumes the wall above the mantelpiece and, in the shadows and the distance, the councillor looks like Tom – the same towering frame and greying black hair – as he poses with his arms around his wife and children and his face stretched by an unforced smile. The illusion drives the breath from the boy. His gaze jerks to Kerry – who looks no more than 16 and leans in towards her father – as he reels away.

At the front door he parts the envelope and checks the picture of Peter is still taped to the stack of money, and then he crouches on the mat and carefully opens the letterbox and pushes the parcel inside. As he does so he glimpses a silhouette, at the end of the corridor and through two doorways: half of a woman sitting at a table, her left side obscured by the doorframe. She sits bolt upright and motionless with her back to the boy. Her hair falls on the sagging collar of a dressing gown. She stares straight ahead, her head tilted towards a vast round clock on the wall, and he can't tell whether he is looking at Kerry or her mother.

23

As the boy paces across the hotel car park he feels a presence behind him. When he turns around Sarah is emerging from the driveway, her face halved diagonally by the shadows and the security light. She carries a duffel bag and there is a vulnerability in her eyes as she crosses the empty spaces in the small walled-off lot.

"When are you going?" she asks.

"Tomorrow morning."

"I've never been on a plane." Her eyes are fixed on the Ford's windscreen behind him as she speaks. "Never been abroad. What name's on your passport?" She glances up at him. "In case it's in the news."

"My name. Ezra Brazier."

"I thought maybe you'd have some fake name." She smiles but there is only sadness in her eyes.

A thick drop of water splats on the ground by her foot; another hits his shoulder and then the sky opens, the rain bouncing off the tarmac. They run to the fire door and he shoves it open on the stairwell. The smell of the acid rain wraps around them as they climb the stairs to his room in silence.

"Nice place," she says, scanning the cramped room with the single bed and yellowed wallpaper.

"Almost as classy as the last one."

"At least you had my hair to brighten it up." She nods at the mattress. “I keep expecting to see him there.”

“I keep looking for him, starting to call him.” He nods at her bag. “You’ve left for good, then.”

She perches on the edge of the bed. “They’re going away. Cornwall – a romantic holiday or something.” She pokes her finger through a tear in her jeans. “Home alone, like that old film. Have you seen it?”

He nods.

“It’s my favourite. Don’t laugh.”

“Why?”

“Dunno. Makes me feel Christmassy.”

“And his family want him.”

She looks down at her Nikes. “I must seem so desperate.”

“Everyone is.”

“Thanks!”

A fleeting smile passes between them. The rain taps at the skylight, casting water shadows that stream down the wall.

“I could stay here,” she says, looking away, “watch your empire.”

“Yeah, if you want to.”

“It’s better than home. Daniel keeps coming over and acting like we’re getting married.”

“I could kill him.”

“I never know whether you’re joking.”

“Neither do I.” He smiles faintly. “How long are they away?”

“A week.”

“I’ll be back by then.”

“Promise?”

He hesitates.

“Just promise. Sometimes it’s just about what you say.”

“I promise.”

She picks up the remote and switches on the TV and lies back against the pillows, the rain shadows like black tears falling on her head. He takes off his trainers and coat and slides alongside her as she flicks through the channels, stopping on a half-finished romantic comedy. She turns onto her side and leans her head on his chest and he tucks the loose strands of her hair behind her small seashell-like ear.

Between sleep and consciousness he feels the heat of her tears on his back, slowly rolling across his shoulder blade, and then her cheek on his spine and her arm tight around his ribs. “Don’t go,” she whispers.

The moonlight trickles in through the dusty window. “Don’t go.” Her voice is a trembling whisper. He cannot tell whether she knows he can hear her. “Ezra...”

He closes his eyes, the quiver in her voice spreading through him and seizing his lungs.

*

As Alan turns into the cul-de-sac he sees the orange halo around their house and the black smoke billowing into the sky. He pulls into the driveway, leaving the shopping bag on the passenger seat as he fumbles for his keys. As he closes the front door he sees a neighbour peering out from a window across the road. The kitchen glows in the light of the flames. Maggie stands in the garden, a silhouette against the fire, something in her hand.

"Mags?" he says, stepping out onto the patio.

She glances over her shoulder. "Hi." Her voice is lifeless. There is a book in her hand. She turns back to the fire and tosses the hardback into the flames.

"What are you doing?"

She doesn't answer. He stands alongside her. The book is *What's So Amazing About Grace?* The cover curls and disintegrates. He sees his bible through the flames, the gold lettering melting away. Her face is blank. The fire is spreading through the grass. She is motionless as he strides to the hose and turns on the tap and points the spray at the blaze. As the flames start to die she walks away, going into the house without a word.

*

The detective steers his Volvo into a lane behind a parade of shops and rolls to a stop. Sweat pools at the base of his spine as he waits, his eyes fixed on the mirror. After a few minutes she appears in the grey dawn at the end of the alleyway. She wears a trenchcoat and pulls a wheeled suitcase. He lowers the passenger window and she leans in with a phone clutched in her hand. "David?"

"Tina? Do you want to get in?"

She shakes her head.

"This is his. There's a photo of Alex, afterwards." Her face is drawn and her eyes are hard in the half-light. "The number that sent it, he'd saved it as 'M'; there's no answer, though."

She uncurls her fingers and he takes the phone from her palm. The rubber case is warm and damp.

"The passcode is 4975. Try it."

She watches as he keys in the number and the screen unlocks.

"It's my birthday," she says, her voice flat.

"Today?"

"The code."

"Oh."

"That's everything." She grips the door pillar as she withdraws and he sees that her ring finger is bare.

"Thank you," he says, leaning towards her. "You're doing the right thing."

She nods and turns towards the end of the alleyway.

"Where are you going? Can I give you a lift?"

She shrugs, barely moving her shoulders. "Dunno. My whole life has been about men… pleasing them, performing for them... I was always someone's woman, never just me. So I'm gonna go be on my own for a bit – start again or something." She smiles limply. "Mess up again in a new city."

"Don't be too hard on yourself. When you get older almost everything you did when you were younger seems stupid."

"I'm 42."

"Shit," he smiles, "you've got no excuse then."

"None. Will you arrest him tonight?"

"Probably. Is he at home?"

"Snoring. Do you know who M is?"

"I think so. He's dead. But there's someone else..."

"Who?"

"Someone who's been getting away with this for too long."

"Oh." She pauses. "I hope you get him."

"I will."

"Craig, he'll know it was me that gave you his phone?"

"Yes."

“Good. I’ll keep an eye on the news, wherever I end up.”

“Well, good luck.”

“I don’t believe in that anymore – luck or fate or whatever. Alex’s parents are Christians; do you think they still believe everything is part of some plan? If there is a God he’s a…” She shakes her head, looking to the black starless sky. “Anyway, goodbye.”

He watches her disappear around the corner and then opens the phone and clicks the photo icon and the screen jumps to ‘Albums’, with ‘Camera Roll’ and ‘My Photo Stream’ at the top of the white space. There is the same thumbnail image by both titles and it takes him a second to realise that he is looking at a shrunken image of Alex lying on the wet ground, his leather jacket reflecting the camera flash. His eyes are closed and there is a black-red hole above his left eyebrow. He zips the phone inside his pocket before starting the engine and reversing, the mirror glinting with the first vapours of sunlight emerging over the city.

*

The boy stares at the ceiling, listening as she breathes deeply and feeling the warmth of her arm across his chest. A cone of green light rises from his phone and he grabs it before the alarm can vibrate on the cabinet. He slips out from under her, shivering as he tiptoes to the bathroom in the dark and closes the door. As he showers he recalls fractured images of a dream: he was sitting at a round table with Peter, Tom and Sarah, eating lunch in a gallery cafe, and he could see the paintings through an archway, murky pictures of the crucifixion with faces twisted in agony and grief, and when he tried to point them out to the three of them his lips would not form the words and they just stared at him, expectant and disappointed, and when he turned back to the paintings his mother was standing in the archway, her expression bleached out by the glare of the spotlight cutting across her face.

She stands by the wardrobe in her pink pyjamas, her arms folded across her chest. “Morning.”

“Morning.”

“Want me to get some breakfast across the road?”

“I’ll get something at the airport.”

She takes his clothes from the wardrobe and folds them neatly and lays them inside the holdall. He dresses in the corner with his back turned.

“Ready?” she says. She stands by the door holding out the bag, her eyes turned down to the stained carpet.

He takes the rucksack and slips the straps over his shoulders. When he glances at her face there are tears welling in her eyes. She wipes her cheeks with the back of her hand and smiles self-consciously, shaking her head, and they stare at each other in pregnant silence, both partially obscured by the darkness.

"I better go."

"Call me when you get there."

"I will."

"Have you got everything?"

"I think so."

She nods, sniffing and wiping her eyes, and then opens the door and stands aside, the amber light in the hallway slanting across her.

As he walks past her into the corridor she raises her hand to his cheek and her voice tremors as she says, "Just come back."

"I will."

He can still feel the warmth of her palm on his face as he walks towards the rain-lashed window at the end of the corridor.

24

Kabukicho is a sea of neon, the signs cascading from the towering buildings, their colours reflected in the drenched pavements. Ezra veers away from the crowd flowing along the boulevard and turns into a dank stairwell with dripping cracks in the ceiling. A panel by the lift lists the businesses, with Bubble Massage on the ground floor and Perfect Dream on 7F. He pushes the button and waits as the elevator slowly descends in a barrage of clunks and whirrs, and then changes his mind and takes the steps instead. The narrow purple-lit stairwell coils up, with meshed windows onto the street and a closed steel door on each floor. When he reaches 7F the plaque says Forever Memory. He pauses by the door and listens for sound on the other side and then pushes the buzzer and, after a few seconds, the grill slides back and a pair of false-lashed eyes appear on the other side.

"Perfect Dream?"

"Please wait."

Bolts scrape and a small middle-aged Japanese woman in a business suit opens the door. "Welcome. You speak English?"

He nods.

"American?"

"English."

She smiles and leads him into a small but immaculate reception room with white walls and a navy carpet. A plug-in air freshener hisses as he passes, puffing out a pine scent. She motions to a leather armchair in front of a mahogany desk and then positions herself in the swivel-chair on the other side, smiling at him as she shakes the mouse to wake the large screen.

"Your name, please?" Her fingers hover over the keyboard.

"I don't have an appointment."

A look of concern sweeps over her face but she shakes it off and smiles. "Ok."

An awkward silence settles in as he waits for her to continue but she just keeps grinning, her whitened teeth glowing in the amber light.

"I've come to visit my grandfather. Peter Armitage."

"Visit?" She glances at the oak door at the end of the corridor.

"Yes. He's expecting me."

"Oh." She looks flustered as she clicks the mouse.

"Peter Armitage," he repeats, and he slides the photo of the magistrate and his wife out of his pocket and holds it up. She peers at the picture and then the boy, her eyes flicking at his scar, before turning to the screen and typing.

"Oh, so sorry, no Peter Armitage," she says, leaning back and folding her arms.

"No?"

She turns the monitor towards him and points at the screen, her long violet nail tapping a column of Japanese characters. "Not here, so sorry."

"What do you do here?"

"Do?" she subtly wheels back a few inches, out of his reach.

"What is Perfect Dream?"

"Retirement home."

"Where?" he turns to the oak door.

"This is office. Home not here."

"Where is the home?"

"Not here. This is office."

"Yes." He speaks slowly, emphasising each word. "But where is the home?"

She smiles, clenching her teeth.

Ezra rises to his feet and walks down the corridor towards the oak door.

"Stop," she shrieks, jumping up. "You stop now." She grabs the phone and dials frantically before speaking in a torrent of Japanese.

He turns the handle but the door is locked. He raps on the oak and listens but there is no reaction on the other side. As he calls out

Peter's name the sound is swallowed by the clank of steel scraping steel and when he turns around there are three tattooed men rushing through the open door and shouting at him in Japanese. They spread out to fill the hallway as they march towards him. The man at the front is short and broad with green and purple dragons and tigers on his neck and arms, and he looks bored as he grips Ezra' shoulders and quietly says "out". They escort him down the steps, their shaved heads reflecting the neon slanting in through the stairwell windows. At the bottom they steer him into the street and point towards the Kabukicho sign. "Go," the short man grunts, and they watch as he walks away, followed by the curious stares of the crowd. When he reaches the sign he looks back and finds that the men have vanished.

*

Sitting in the corner of an underground bar, the boy listens to the conversation of a group of teachers at the next table. There are seven of them, all mid-twenties and British, and they cheer as a waitress sets down two huge Sapporo beer pitchers and then call out 'Arigato' as she weaves through the bustling crowd, back to the Union Jack-adorned bar. Ezra sips his coke and watches the Premier League match on the big screen as the teachers – four men and three women – once again pick up the topic of irritating students. One of the men, the oldest of the group, barely speaks, his dark sunken eyes constantly roving between the football and the Japanese girls at the surrounding tables. There is a sense of restless anticipation in the way he shifts on his stool and scans the crowd, and when he rises and pushes his way towards the toilets, the boy follows.

He watches him go into the gents and joins the queue at the bar, nodding at the tiny girl who smiles shyly at him as he moves alongside her. He orders a pint of Sapporo and lingers at the edge of the queue, pretending to check his phone. When the teacher emerges, he steps forward into his path so that his shoulder brushes the glass, spilling the beer over the boy's trainers.

"Shit, sorry, mate," the man says, his voice almost lost in the din of chatter.

Ezra lays the half empty glass on a table as the teacher grabs a wad of napkins from the bar.

"Let me get you another pint," he says in a Geordie brogue.

"Don't worry about it, it's rammed in here."

"I insist, mate. What was it?"

"Sapporo. Cheers."

His gelled hair gleams under the spotlights as he manoeuvres his way through the queue, cutting a path for the boy to follow.

"I'm Danny," he says as he tries to catch the barman's eye.

"Jon."

"What are you doing over here?"

"Travelling. Gap year. You?"

"Teaching. English."

"How long you been here?"

"Two months. You?"

"Got here today."

"Alone?"

"My granddad is out here."

"What, working or...?"

"Long story," he shrugs. "I won't bore you."

"Cool, cool. I'm with that lot over there." He points across the crowd to the table of teachers. "Come and have a drink with us."

"It was just, like, what else do you do, you know?"

The boy nods.

"Playing in front of hardly any people, getting up at five in the morning to shove letters through people's doors... fuck that, you know?"

They sit at the end of the table, removed from the conversation of the others.

"When you've run out in front of thousands at St James's – I know it was just the League Cup, but..." His eyes are glazed, the nostalgia and alcohol glistening in his pupils. "You just can't make yourself give a shit about playing for Carlisle or York... it's not the same, you know... every season a new club in a lower down league." He leans towards Ezra, his gaze fixed somewhere between the boy's eyes and the cloud of smoke lingering above. "At school I was the best player by a mile, in the whole district – I broke loads of scoring records... All the girls..." He falls silent and swigs his beer, a cloud descending over his face.

"Are you teaching tomorrow?"

He shakes his head, a suppressed burp puffing out his ruddy cheeks. "Day off."

"Which area do you live in?"

"Shin-Nakano." He points his thumb over his shoulder. "Thirty minute walk. Where you staying?"

"In a hotel for now. Just round the corner. What are you doing with your day off?"

"Dunno. Sleeping this off," he smiles, his eyes half closed. "You?"

"I want to visit my granddad but I don't know where he is."

"What d'ya mean?"

"He's in some kind of retirement home out here but when I went to the office today they said they'd never heard of him."

"That's weird."

"I know. I know he's in one of their homes so..."

"Why would they lie?"

"I think it's like a secret home or something – where you go to cut yourself off, a cult or something."

"Didn't he say anything before he went?"

"He didn't tell us he was going. He just got on a plane one day."

"Shit. Sounds well dodgy."

"I know. I just want to see him, you know? Ask him why."

"Could I do anything?" His eyes are glassy and unsteady as he tries to focus on the boy's face.

"Not sure there's anything you could do."

"I could make an appointment or something. Pretend I want to send my granddad there or join myself."

"Really?"

"Yeah, fuck it, he's your granddad and it sounds weird as fuck."

"Really? You'd do that?"

"Yeah, why not? It's my day off." He grins, slack-jawed. "And I spilled your pint."

*

POLICE have arrested a 48-year-old man in connection with the murder of journalist Alex Castle.

A spokesman for Gloucestershire police said the man had been arrested at an address in Barton this morning and was being questioned at Waterwells station.

Alex, 22, was shot dead outside a Manchester University halls of residence, Oxford House, on October 1. His killer was captured on CCTV fleeing the scene.

Alex, originally from York, was a reporter for the Citizen and had lived in Gloucester since he joined the newspaper in June.

The police spokesman said: "Officers arrested a 48-year-old man at an address in Barton shortly before 10am today. He is being questioned by detectives from the Constabulary and Greater

Manchester Police at Waterwells."

The boy reads the story on an old pay-as-you-go computer in the hotel's lobby. Neon slants in through the oval windows, casting hazy circles of colour on the flaking wallpaper and stained carpet. The clerk sits behind a hatch, peering at a Manga book through thick glasses. In his room he stands in the square metre of floor space between the shelf-bed and mounted TV, listening for noise through the paper walls. He unzips his rucksack and takes out his toothbrush and paste and goes out into the narrow hallway, locking his door before he walks to the men's bathroom. Inside he turns the latch on the sagging door and steps into the shower cubical and cranks the small window open and peers across the street to the Bubble Massage sign and then traces the building down to the shuttered windows on the seventh floor and the dark doorway in the porch. Scanning the crowd, he cannot find the three tattooed men but there are others like them, posted beneath the flashing Pachinko Slot banners and cartoon nurses and maids. Nobody goes in or out of the doorway and the shadows in the stairwell windows remain unchanged.

The door rattles as someone tries the handle. Instinctively, the boy reaches for the flick-knife in his pocket, gripping the handle as he turns the lock and edges the door open an inch. A sunburnt face stares back. "Sorry, mate," the man says, his skin iridescent in the white light. Ezra slides the door open and steps aside and the man – ginger and fleshy – stumbles past him inside. As the boy paces back to his room, past the flashing condom vending machine, he glances in through an ajar door and sees a delicate Japanese girl standing by the TV in knee-high socks and a denim jacket, restlessly flicking through the channels.

In bed he stares up at the ceiling a yard from his nose. The sound of the ginger man and Japanese girl reverberates off the walls – fake giggles, fake moans – and when he does drift off he dreams of Sarah standing knee-high in the sea as Peter wades towards her, his moonlit silhouette shrinking against the leaden horizon as he closes in on her. He tries to run towards them but his legs are motionless, and when he looks down at where his feet should be there is nothing but smooth sand. As he turns back to the ocean he sees Peter's black outline blocking out the girl. There are bodies in the water – Tom, Gardner, the councillor – floating upright with their eyes closed. He feels a presence by his side. His mother is standing next to him, holding hands with Big Jim. They smile faintly as they watch the sea.

25

The sound of the bells and jingles and steel hitting steel is deafening inside the Pachinko Slot. Ezra sits at the front of the arcade, looking out at the rain-drenched street through the gap between the huge cartoons which adorn the window – samurais, ninjas, rollerskating schoolgirls with enormous eyes and no nose – and even at 2pm the gambling den is packed with customers of all ages feeding metal balls into the machines as they stare somnambulantly at the flashing screens. He plugs Yen into a retro Mortal Kombat game as he watches the porch below the Bubble Massage sign. There are no clocks inside the arcade, time lost in the endless cycle of coins and balls in the rows of clashing-coloured machines. When he checks his phone he sees that almost 30 minutes have passed since Danny took the lift up to 7F. His last message said only 'Inside now'.

Grasping the joystick, he has a flashback to the wrestling games he and Tom would play on the PS3 in the living room, leaning forward on the sofa as they bashed the controllers to direct their characters to smash each other with clotheslines and steel chairs. The boy would always win, and Tom always wanted to play tag-team mode so they could fight the computer-controlled characters together. As he glances over his shoulder at the maze of machines, he realises that he is the only white face in the place and that a security guard is watching him from the change counter, leaning his tattooed forearms on the desk as he pretends to flick through a Manga novel.

Eventually, a middle-aged Japanese man in a black suit and white shirt emerges, closely followed by Danny. They stand facing the Kabukicho sign as the man talks and points, his gold watch catching the light. Hands clasped, he bows and shuffles backwards as Danny walks away towards the flashing red banner. Ezra waits until he is halfway down the street and then follows, scanning the crowd for tattoos. As Danny reaches the end of the street a black Honda pulls up on the zebra crossing and a young woman in a silver suit and stilettos emerges from the back. Her dead-straight hair bounces on her narrow shoulders as she bows and motions to the car. Danny climbs inside and she shuts the door and gets in the other side. He glances back at the boy as the car edges into the traffic before gliding away, the gleaming paintwork reflecting the shifting neon colours. Ezra's phone vibrates in his hand. 'Fuchinobe'

The home looks like a government building. Four storeys and whitewashed with tinted windows, it is protected by railings which stretch between two clinic-like buildings in the concrete parade of shops. There is a sense of quiet to the vast building; nobody comes or goes and no noise filters out, and there is no buzzer or intercom at the iron gate, just two CCTV cameras perched on the pillar, one facing the street and one trained on the long driveway. Ezra stands inside the convenience store across the road, holding a manga book as he gazes up at the dark windows on the top floor. The clerk, a teenage girl, keeps looking at him from behind the counter so he puts the book back in the rack and pretends to browse the other titles before strolling to the drinks cabinet and grabbing a can of Dr Pepper. As he pays he notices how striking the girl is – skin like tanned silk and amber hair tucked behind small protruding ears – and he feels her eyes darting over the fading cuts around his eyebrow and the scar above his lip, imprinting his wounded face in her memory. He tries to appear casual as he cracks open the drink and walks outside and crosses the road. As he passes the railings he peers at the glass porch at the end of the driveway; the only movement is his own reflection on the windows, distant and formless.

The boy is outside a laundrette on the corner when the railings slide open and Danny emerges with the young woman, who bows repeatedly before heading back down the driveway. He is holding a brochure and as he turns towards the street there is a dazed and pained look on his face, as though he has just awoken from a blissful dream and remembered his brutal reality. As he sees Ezra approaching he shakes his head, breathless, and says, “You won’t believe it.”

“It is a retirement home. When you first walk in that’s what you think, but...” They stand in an alleyway at the side of the laundrette, the sunlight trapped by the walls. “The top floor, it’s like a computer game studio or something; I don't know how else to describe it. Mayuko said you can tell them your happiest memory and they can recreate it and loop it in your mind so you're living it again and again and..."

"Loop it? What do you mean?"

"I know, right? She said they put you to sleep and show you the memory on a loop so it, like, embeds itself, just going round and round on a loop. I know, it's proper sci-fi shit. Mental. She showed me them through a window, though, and the screens with the memories..."

"Was he there?"

"I didn't see him."

"How many were there?"

He shrugs. "Nine, I think. It was so weird. They were asleep, hooked up to these big screens on the wall, and you could see the memories."

"What do you mean?"

"On the screens. You give them photos and videos and they build the memory, like virtual reality or something. It's mental."

"But he wasn't there?"

"I didn't see him. It was dark though and their faces were covered with these machines."

“What about in the retirement part? Downstairs?”

“Didn’t see him. But we walked through quickly.”

“How many people were there on each floor?”

“Ten or so maybe.”

Ezra peers up at the black windows on the top floor. “How did you leave it? Are they expecting you back?”

“I said I’d have to think about it. They asked me to give them pictures and a video from the match.”

“The match?”

“I told them it would be that League Cup match where I scored – if I was going to do it. I have it on DVD. It was on Sky.”

“How long does it last, the loop?”

“As long as you want.”

“What, hours? Days?”

“Months or years, if you want.” He points to the brochure in the boy’s hand. “It’s all in there.”

“Is it even legal?”

“She said it was a trial at the moment so...”

“How much is it?”

“Depends on the memory and how long you want.” He points to the brochure again. “You should read it, it’s amazing.” He smiles faintly. “I still can’t believe it’s real.”

“Could you take me with you when you go back? Say I’m your brother and you want me there?”

“Yeah,” he answers immediately. “My first class isn’t ‘til one tomorrow so...”

“What about this afternoon?”

He hesitates. “Ok.”

“You don’t mind?”

“Honestly? Don’t take this the wrong way – I know it sounds really insensitive – but I’m actually enjoying this. I was bored as fuck before. Teaching becomes very monotonous very fast, and the other teachers are a bit weird – out here because they couldn’t make it back home. So doing this...”

They pause and turn to the street at a sound like a gunshot. A moped chunters past in a cloud of black smoke.

*

“It’s me.”

“Are you alright?”

"Fine." He peers out of the phone booth, his eyes on the white building towering above the streetscape. "You?"

"I'm alright. Have you found him?"

"I think so."

"Oh." She sniffs.

"Have you got a cold?"

"No. You're saying goodbye."

"I'm not."

"You think you're gonna walk in there and do what you're gonna do and then just walk out and come home?"

"I have to."

"You already know it was him."

"I have to hear him say it."

"But he won't say it. You already said he lies to himself, compartmentalises or whatever he calls it."

"I'll see it in his eyes."

She sighs, her breath rustling the line. "And then what?"

"I don't know."

"You do."

He pictures her on the hotel bed in her pyjamas and an overwhelming sense of longing floods through him.

"You sound so close," she murmurs.

He hears the sound of traffic in the background at the end of the line. "Where are you?"

"In town. I was going mad in that tiny room."

"When are your parents back?"

"Dunno. Never, I hope." She falls silent. He can hear her choosing her words. "Ezra, if he's just a pathetic old man in a home waiting to die, can't you just leave him?"

He doesn't answer.

"Are you listening?"

"Yes."

"So?"

"I'll come back."

"How do you know?"

"I know."

There is a pause, each of them waiting for the other to speak.

"I don't know what else to say," she whispers.

"You'll see me soon."

Her voice breaks as she murmurs goodbye.

As he hangs up he realises that the clouds have opened. He walks back towards the Family Mart with his head bowed as the rain lashes his face, his whole body shaking with tremors which ripple out from his core.

*

The Honda glides into the driveway and stops before the gate and Danny pushes the rear door open and calls across the street. As Ezra walks to the car he keeps his face turned down, away from the CCTV camera. Danny holds a photo envelope and CD case in his lap.

"Jon?" the woman in the suit says, peering between the front seats. "I'm Mayuko. Pleased to meet you."

She extends her delicate hand and they shake.

"It's very kind of you to accompany your brother." Her eyes, dark and false-lashed, skirt over his scar as she takes in his face.

"It's a big decision."

"Yes, but the right decision. Your brother needs catharsis before he can move on." She looks at Danny and smiles, her face smooth with empathy. "Reliving the match for a day will provide this." She nods at the driver, a thickset man with shaved greying hair and tattoos poking out from his sleeves.

"Are you really going to do this?" he whispers as the gate slides open.

Danny shrugs. "It'll give you time."

The driver pulls up by the porch and Mayuko climbs out and holds the door open for them. As she approaches the glass doors a buzzer sounds and they slide open, revealing a tiled foyer with white walls and a domed ceiling. A security guard in a powder blue uniform watches a bank of monitors behind a desk, his alertness concealed by the same sleepy-eyed coldness as the tattooed men in Kabukicho. Mayuko nods at him and mahogany double-doors swing open as she approaches with her heels clicking on the tiles. "Would you like to see where our residents live?" she asks, looking over her shoulder at Ezra as she paces down the corrdior. She holds her ID card in front of a small panel on the wall and an oak door slides open on a square lobby leading to a communal room with armchairs, wall-mounted TVs, stocked bookcases and patio doors looking out on a courtyard. The men and women, all Japanese and elderly, turn to them expectantly before their expressions shift to a mix of curiosity and disappointment at the sight of the young gaijin. Mayuko leads them up the stairs past paintings of barren landscapes and frenzied cities, showing them the tranquil lounges on each floor where the residents dose in armchairs. When they reach the top floor they are confronted with a locked door.

She holds up her ID card and types a code into the panel and the door clicks and she pushes it open. Inside there is a reception room with a leather armchair facing a desk with a computer and seat. She holds the door open for them and then closes it firmly. Glancing at the single armchair, she smiles at Danny and Ezra and hurries into a store cupboard and comes out with a folding stool.

"Usually people come alone," she says as she walks behind the desk and sits down.

Ezra perches on the stool, the cold handle of the flick-knife digging into the base of his spine. "How many people have you had?"

"Nine," Danny answers. "I'd be the tenth."

"Have you had many foreign people?"

"No," she says. "But we're still in the trial stage."

"How does it work?"

"It is very simple and very safe. You show us your happiest memory or perhaps an incident which you wish to overcome and we recreate that memory with CGI. For Danny, this is the football match." She looks at Danny with an understanding smile. "We then show you the memory again and again on a loop, for as long as you wish, so you can relive the happiness or perhaps reach catharsis."

"What do you mean by 'show' the memory?"

“They use the photos or videos,” Danny says, “to recreate it, like a film or virtual reality.” He glances at Mayuko and turns to Ezra. “You’re put in a really deep sleep...”

“A coma?”

“Kind of, yeah. But your eyes are open and you’re watching your memory on a loop. Your brain takes it all in; subconsciously you’re reliving it, dealing with it.”

“It happens gradually,” Mayuko adds. “At first it is five minutes and then we wake you up to check whether everything is ok. Then it is thirty minutes, then one hour, and so forth for the time you booked.”

“What’s the longest someone has booked?”

“Six months. They are on a drip. We do physiotherapy while they are asleep, to maintain muscle strength, but –”

“Not everyone wants to wake up?”

She smiles calmly. “That has not happened.”

“Has anyone woken up and said they don’t want to go on with it?”

“Not yet,” Danny says.

“Can we see the rooms?”

“Of course.” She leans down behind the desk and holds her card against a panel above the skirting board and keys in a code, and a door opposite slides open to reveal a corridor. They follow the hallway into a tiled lobby lined with glass-panelled doors through which there are small rooms like hospital suites. In the first there is a frail Japanese man strapped to a reclining chair with a machine like a huge pair of binoculars fixed to his eyes. There is a screen on the wall above him on which a film plays on a loop: a younger version of him strolls through a bustling university campus in a severe uniform; he goes into a bathhouse and undresses in the empty changing room before walking into the onsen and stepping into the steaming water and wading to the far wall and sitting on the step beneath the surface; there is a small hole in the wall and when he presses his eye to it the picture cuts to a girl standing thigh deep on the other side, ladling water over her neck as her small breasts and pubic hair glisten in the steamy light; she looks straight at him, her alarm softening into a coy smile as she goes on washing herself, glancing sideways at him every few seconds; she makes her way towards the changing room and the picture pulls back to show the man ploughing through the water and grabbing a towel from a shelf and wrapping it around his waist before he peers out into the hallway, where he catches the girl, also in a towel, doing the same.

"Some people choose to enhance the memory," Mayuko says, appearing at his side. Danny is standing at the next door, watching the middle-aged woman inside. Ezra walks across the lobby, looking in through each window. When he reaches the door at the far end he sees Peter's wife inside.

Her face fills the screen. She looks as she did in the newspaper stories and photos in his study, but illuminated with the glow of fiction. The picture is from Peter's view; her delicate face and neck are outlined by the grey sky beyond the rain-lashed window, and when she smiles at him her pupils shine. They are playing Scrabble. She lays out her tiles and the reason for her childlike grin is revealed in the word she spells: filthy.

The bed below the screen is empty.

"What's up?" Danny asks, suddenly beside him.

Mayuko's heels click on the tiles and her perfume envelops him as she appears at his shoulder. "We are still preparing this room."

"When does he arrive?"

"Tonight."

"How long does he have?"

"Six months."

"Of the same memory?"

"That was his wish."

"What did he say?"

"That is confidential, sorry."

"Where is he now?"

She shakes her head softly, the white light reflected in her narrowed eyes.

26

A REFUGE for abused women has been destroyed in a shocking vandalism attack just months before it was due to open.

Hope House, in the city centre, has been left in ruins after a JCB digger was crashed through the front wall in the early hours of the morning, leaving a gaping hole in the four-storey building.

The refuge had been due to open in spring and was the brainchild of Cheltenham magistrate Peter Armitage, who had funded the project himself.

Mr Armitage, 65, whose wife Helen was raped and murdered…

The magistrate's eyes fall to the embedded video. The clip is just 30 seconds long and filmed from the police cordon; the building has collapsed in on itself around the digger, and with the exposed concrete and empty windows the structure looks old and ruined by time, not built for the future. By the video there is a link to an article titled 'Fire ravages Cheltenham magistrate's house in suspected arson attack'.

A violent gush of acid rises from his core and erupts before he can reach the bathroom, spraying across the joint where the white tiles meet the cream carpet. On his knees he stares at the vomit, his whole body trembling, and then he pushes himself up and staggers into the bathroom and grabs a toilet roll and begins sponging the sick, before wetting a towel and frantically rubbing at the carpet, and then mixing in soap and shampoo, but everything he tries fails to remove the stain. Giving up, he collapses onto his side and lies in a foetal position with his head by the damp blemishes and his glasses digging into his temple.

He lies that way for a long time, looking through his sunken reflection in the wardrobe mirror in the silence of the double-glazed suite. Eventually he pulls himself up on the bed and moves to the window and gazes down at the neon maze of Shinjuku. The word Love is spelled out in giant red letters on the pavement below and couples gather around the artwork taking selfies as traffic hurtles past in a blaze of yellow light. They are so distant as he leans on the glass – just coloured stick figures against the encroaching dusk.

At the bedside phone he dials David's mobile from memory. As the voicemail message plays he catches his reflection in the window: he looks so old in the giant bathrobe, his frail neck and arms outlined by the purple clouds. He hangs up and dials again and waits for David's voice to stop and then the tone.

"David, it's me." His voice sounds trapped in his dry throat. Seconds tick by as he decides what to say. "I know you think I've been telling myself the same lie for so long that it's become true. But I didn't kill Tom. I didn't. Everything I did was to make the world better. I want you to remember that, now that I'm gone."

After hanging up he looks at himself in the glass, just a fleeting inspection, and then he moves towards the wardrobe and opens the door. His pinstripe suit hangs symmetrically inside, the fine lines an immaculate white.

*

As the Honda rolls into the deserted suburb its black body is almost lost in the darkness of the unlit shopfronts and the home is just a vague outline against the starless sky. The car stops at the driveway but the gate doesn't move. The railings judder and screech as something holds them back. The driver climbs out and bends down, disappearing behind the bonnet, and when he re-emerges he is holding a brick aloft and shrugging towards the passenger seat with his face bleached by the headlights. As the gates slide open with a soft hum there is a tap at his window and Peter pushes the button before Mayuko can call out from the front. The glass descends and Ezra lunges inside and clutches the magistrate by the hair and points a knife at his throat, the boy's face lit faintly by the amber glow from the backseat.

"Get out," he barks, yanking Peter towards the window as Mayuko screams and the driver watches from the gate.

Peter looks sideways at Ezra. His throat grazes the blade as he speaks. "You're making a mistake, son." He slowly reaches for the handle and pushes the door open and awkwardly climbs out with the boy still gripping his hair through the window. Ezra releases him so he can stand up straight and then grabs him again with the knife poised. The magistrate's eyes are lost in the darkness. As he opens his mouth to speak there is a hiss and his throat explodes across the boy's face.

There is someone on the other side of the car. "Ezra," David shouts. "Run." His head and shoulders take form in the shadows.

“Go.”

The boy steps back and Peter crumples to the ground, his glasses shattering on the tarmac.

“Ezra,” David screams, his voice bodiless across the roof of the car. “Last chance.”

The boy sprints towards the alleyway, his silhouette fading into the black haze as he moves away from the light.

27

"I didn't know he was coming," Emma says. "I'm not sure there's much I can tell you."

"I'm just trying to understand what was going on in his head."

They sit in the corner of a dusty coffee shop, facing each other across a small round table with the window at Maggie's back. In the courtyard behind her the chairs are stacked upside down and the umbrellas folded shut.

"Do you prefer Manchester to Cheltenham?"

"I suppose so. It's different." The sun outlines the steeple looming over the streetscape and slants in through the window, revealing the ginger roots beneath her bleached hair as she bows her head to sip her Americano.

"I know why you broke up."

"Oh." She pauses with the cup aloft, the muscles tensed in her thin arm.

"Don't worry, I'm not one of those Christians." She tries to smile but her face shapes a grimace.

"He told you?"

"In a way."

"What do you mean?"

"He'd started writing something. I found it on his computer."

"Oh." She tucks her hair behind one ear while smoothing the strands down over the other. "Can I see it?"

Maggie opens her handbag and takes out neatly folded sheets of A4 and lays them on the table. As Emma reads the colour drains from her face. “That last line after the gap,” she whispers, her voice breaking. “*She was trapped* – that’s not me.”

“Tina Armstrong?”

She shrugs.

“Did they tell you he was arrested?”

She nods.

“And the murder in the alleyway?”

“Yes.”

“Did he ever mention her to you?”

She shakes her head. “He must’ve met her after me.”

“I think her husband, the man they’ve arrested, had him killed because he’d become friends with his wife.” She pauses to study Emma’s reaction, but she just looks down at her half-empty mug. “*She was trapped.* I think he was trying to save her from him.” Her eyes are burning behind her glasses. “What do you think happened?”

“I don’t know. I try not to think about it.”

They turn to the window at the sound of a siren. Blue light haloes the courtyard wall as a police car speeds past on the other side. When Maggie looks at Emma she sees that she is rebutting a memory, her eyes freezing and thawing in a split-second.

“I’m sorry,” Maggie says, fighting the impulse to lay her palm on the girl’s freckled hand, “for dragging you through all this again. I just... I need to know what happened to him, what made him change.”

"I want to help, it's just... we'd cut off from each other so completely. I guess it was just... I don't know... it's like our time together was a film – while you're watching it it's all you think about, but then when it's over you remember that there's a world outside."

"Were you in love?"

"I think so. Yes."

She nods, poised to speak, but then picks up her drink and takes a sip and the collar of her cardigan slips forward to reveal a rash at the base of her neck. "Did he ever talk about his faith?"

"Sometimes."

"What did he say?"

"That he used to believe."

"Used to?"

"He said the older he got, the less likely it all seemed. He once said I was his god." A smile forms and vanishes on her lips. "He was joking," she adds, seeing the look on Maggie's face.

"Did he ever say why he stopped believing?"

She shakes her head. "Just that he got older."

"Nothing specific? A moment?"

"No. Sorry."

"He was supposed to be someone else," she murmurs, leaning forward as though she is collapsing in on herself.

*

The dawn is like smoke at the base of the trees as Ezra sits in the Ford on the edge of the woodland, watching her caravan. There is light in her window, a dim glow from a lamp somewhere inside. The dashboard clock clicks to 06:04. As the rain dies he can hear the sound of the wind and the birds and beyond that the traffic on the main road. He climbs out and paces into the woodland, crunching through the dead leaves and passing the thick oak where they carved Charlie's name after burying him below. When he reaches her caravan he climbs over the fence and crouches below the bedroom window and peers in through the gap between the curtains. She is perched on the edge of the bed next to her mother. They are holding hands on the quilt. When the woman turns towards the hallway the bruise around her eye catches the light in a purple shine. He creeps towards the front window, finding the cramped lounge empty. Sarah walks in and fills a glass of water at the sink, her face gaunt and her eyes red-rimmed. As he raises his hand to tap on the window her mother appears at the bedroom doorway. She hugs her ribs as she silently studies her daughter, and there is an expression on the woman's face that he cannot decipher. When Sarah turns to her she uncoils her arms and smiles weakly and then goes back into the bedroom with her daughter following with the glass. Ezra watches her disappear through the doorway, his eyes remaining on the amber-lit gap once she's gone, and then he turns away and slips back into the dark woodland.

The rain starts again as he reaches the oak, piercing the stripped branches and hitting the fallen leaves and sweeping into his face.

Back in the Ford he watches the window again, his heart sinking as the drops stream down the windscreen, but he keeps sitting there as the minutes pass and the pale sun slowly climbs over the trees, his mind clouded in the scent of her apple perfume rising from the passenger seat and the Cool Water he sprayed throughout the car, and the road ahead just a dark and barren cavity without her.

As the clock strikes 07:08 he sees the caravan door open and her silhouette emerge in the threshold.